Red Moon Rising

J.T. Brannan

GREY ARROW PUBLISHING

First published in 2017 by Grey Arrow Publishing

ISBN: 978-1520532219

For Justyna, Jakub and Mia;
and my parents, for their help and support

AUTHOR'S NOTE

Writing this novel has been immensely rewarding, exciting and fulfilling work. At times, it has also been damned scary. Some nights, I couldn't sleep. It has even altered the way I see the world, to a certain extent.

Serial killing is a major theme of this book and, to make sure I presented it as accurately as possible, I threw myself into researching this intriguing area. I devoured textbooks on the subject, true-life crime novels, fictionalized accounts, movies, documentaries, interviews with serial killers and other violent offenders, I was completely immersed. And, as a result, became increasingly disturbed.

In fact, this novel has taken three years to write – mainly because I stopped writing after completing half of the manuscript, because I wanted to forget everything I'd ever learned about the subject. But the story kept on pulling me back, until I decided – eventually – that I had to finish it.

Some of the scenes in this novel maybe be disturbing to the reader, so please take this as fair warning. Although this novel is pure fiction, many of the activities, behaviors and methodologies that I describe are based on real life case-histories.

That being said, I truly hope that you enjoy Red Moon Rising. It has been a labor of love, and of terror, in equal measure.

J.T. Brannan

"In Einstein's equation, time is a river. It speeds up, meanders, and slows down. The new wrinkle is that it can have whirlpools and fork into two rivers. So, if the river of time can be bent into a pretzel, create whirlpools and fork into two rivers, then time travel cannot be ruled out."
– Michio Kaku

"You feel the last bit of breath leaving their body. You're looking into their eyes. A person in that situation is God!"
– Ted Bundy

PROLOGUE

1

The bullet hits me in the head at fourteen hundred feet per second.

Blood, bone and tissue spray across the grand steps of the New York County Courthouse.

And I am dead.

At least that's what I remember, what I cannot fail to remember, the final part of that day in New York, all those months ago. It was the same story that Detective Jake Franks told me, when I'd woken up in Mount Sinai half a year later. The shot to the head – along with another to the clavicle, and one more to the hip – had put me into a deep coma; I *had* actually been considered clinically dead, at first.

But I *didn't* die.

Some miracle saved me, and I still don't know why.

My life had fallen apart around me back in New York, and all I had left when I was released from Mount Sinai was the fear. Fear of another attack, fear of what the bullet might have done to my brain, fear of what I was going to do for the rest of my life.

Before the attack, I'd been Jessica Hudson,

Harvard alumni and hard-charging Assistant DA of New York County, with a place on the Upper West Side and a fiancée who was the partner of one of New York's most prestigious law firms. I'd had it all.

And now?

All I have now is the fear.

I feel it now, as I stand in the field with one of my horses, my ranch situated right in the middle of the empty farmland of Alaska's Mat-Su valley – an icy dread, a deep sense of foreboding I just don't seem able to shake. I can feel the breeze even through my jacket as I brush Hero's silken flank. It's nearing winter now, and night-time temperatures are starting to drop rapidly.

I try and tell myself that this is where the icy feeling in my veins comes from – it's not the fear, it's not, it's *not* – but I know I am only lying to myself. It was this fear that drove me from my home in Manhattan to the wilds of Alaska in the first place.

The fear that refuses to go away, no matter what I do.

I try not to remember, try to keep my thoughts on the present, live in the moment, but it's too hard . . . too hard . . .

And eventually, my mind slips back to New York.

New York . . .

Where it all began.

2

ELEVEN MONTHS EARLIER

Goran Zebunac is a cruel, cold-hearted son of a bitch. He raped, tortured and killed his way across the Balkans as part of Arkan's Tigers – a ruthless paramilitary force active during the Yugoslav wars – before turning his hand to organized crime, first in his home country of Serbia, and then right here in America.

But today is the start of the end for Goran, and I'm going to make sure he never makes it back onto the streets.

My father – head of one of Boston's largest law firms, a man who made his name defending the city's Irish-American gangs, and a thoroughbred bastard – has already warned me off the case, several weeks ago. But I am treating that as I treat all other warnings.

I am ignoring it completely.

The DA's office is taking things slightly more seriously however, and there are two armed NYPD undercover officers waiting outside my apartment to escort me to the courthouse. Just a precaution, they tell me.

I look in the bathroom mirror, checking my appearance closely for this first crucial day in court. Not too much make-up, just enough to smooth the edges. It's a balancing act, to be both professional to the judge and yet appealing to the jury.

I look at my watch and decide to make a move; I'll check myself again in the washrooms at the courthouse. I don't consider myself a vain woman – who does? – but I long ago realized the necessity of looking the part. The battle is to secure a conviction, and appearance is but another weapon I use to win that battle.

I pass the bouquet of flowers on the kitchen table and smile; a good-luck present from Paul. He's on the other side of the business, a defense lawyer like my father, and a damned good one too. Ever the early-bird, he's already left for the day. Paul keeps trying to convince me to go into private practice, but I think he's finally starting to understand that it's not going to happen. Maybe the flowers are part of that understanding.

I let my nose drift close as I go past, the sweet scent of gardenias and roses following me as I leave the apartment.

3

"Good morning Ms. Hudson," says the policeman outside my door.

"Morning, James," I reply cheerily. Sergeant James Traynor is a big man, six feet four and well over two hundred pounds. I don't know how he gets on with undercover work, but as a bodyguard, he's a terrific visual deterrent. His partner, Tom Brooks, must be waiting in the car. I know he will be watching the street, engine running. Transitions to and from the car are always the most vulnerable times, both men keep telling me.

"How you feeling today?" James asks as we wait for the elevator.

"Good thanks. Confident."

He nods his head. "Good," he says as we move forward through the open elevator door. "He needs to be put away for a long time."

"You're not wrong there. And trust me, I'll do my best."

We travel the rest of the way down in silence, James alert as we move from the elevator, through the foyer, his eyes scanning the street as he ushers me towards the Ford Mercury sedan parked outside the building. One hand on the gun under his jacket, the other reaching for the door handle, opening it and sweeping me inside in one practiced movement. Seconds later, James is in the passenger seat and we're in motion, Tom pulling the car out into the heavy morning traffic. Siren on, and we're turning onto Broadway in record time, heading south from the Upper West Side.

My apartment's in an upscale neighborhood, but it wasn't always the case; I lived in a small one-bedroom unit in Brooklyn for five of my six years in New York. Law school didn't come cheap, and a large part of my monthly paycheck went on loan repayments until only just recently.

Although Paul lives with me now, he still has his own place on Amsterdam Avenue, which I see as we glide past, still overtaking the Broadway traffic. He sublets the place now, always looking to make the quick buck.

I stare out of the windows as we cruise past the Lincoln Centre, Macy's, the Flatiron Building. I see it all, and yet none of it, my mind gearing up for the battle ahead. Past Greenwich Village now, Soho and Little Italy, the sights filtering through my eyes without processing any of it. Focused. The boys in front know better than to talk to me; they don't even talk to each other.

Chinatown on the left now, the turn-off to the imposing Babylonian temple of the Criminal Courts Building swept away behind us, the case too important to be dealt with there. It is the New York County Courthouse for us today, seat of the Supreme Court; my first time as lead prosecutor within those hallowed halls. I shake the thought away, not wanting nerves to get the better of me.

And then we're there, and I see the huge pyramid-topped tower of the United States Courthouse opposite before the neo-classical grace of the County Courthouse, its fluted Corinthian portico giving shelter for the gathered news crews who crowd the wide steps beneath.

"Okay Ms. Hudson," James says from the front seat. "There's a place for us by the steps, I'll get out and open the door, and courthouse security will escort you inside."

"Thank you, James," I say, steadying my breathing, wanting to be poised for the first shots of the cameras, the first shouted questions of the reporters.

The big Ford rolls to a stop just as James says, right on the steps of the courthouse. He jumps out, running around to open my door, and I step out into the bright morning sunlight, hand going up reflexively to shade my eyes.

I see James's head turn then, even as I hear the noise. An engine, revving hard, loud rumble getting closer. Faster.

I turn to follow James's gaze, see the black SUV

heading straight towards us across the traffic; so close now, so terrifyingly close. I hear James shout something at me, pushing me down, his hand flapping at his coat, flash bulbs going off behind me from unseen cameras; and then the massive front end of the SUV smashes into the Mercury like a medieval battering ram, smashing the vehicle over onto its side.

The violence of the impact sends me reeling across the steps; I see the terror in Tom's eyes as the car rolls, see James's body trapped, crushed, by the tons of moving metal.

A cacophony of noises, indistinct and yet curiously identifiable; camera shutters opening and closing, screech of metal on concrete; men and women screaming, shouting, car doors opening; gunshots popping.

I look up, look across the wrecked Mercury, see a second SUV rolling to a stop in the street, two men jumping out, masks on, sticks in their hands.

Flames shoot from the sticks, I see red mist flying across me; the men move closer, the flames brighter. The sticks are pointed at me.

I feel a curious sensation in my chest, my hip; like a bee sting, but the force knocks me back onto the steps. I see the red mist again.

I look up, see a man standing over me, his face black, woolen, indistinct, green eyes the only thing visible. The stick rising before me, a hole in the end.

I see the flame, hear a rough bark; feel the bee sting in my head.

And then nothing.

Lights, flashing above me, around me.

Voices, urgent, strident; other voices, calm, warm. I hear no words. I see nothing, only shadows, sinister shadow-shapes etched against the flashing lights.

Everything is confusion. My brain cannot sift the information.

I cannot feel anything.

I lie flat, looking up. Faces above me, leaning in close then pulling back. I recognize no-one, again the mysterious shadow-people, marionettes in a black-and-white puppet show.

I can hear nothing, nothing at all.

A curtain of red streams across my vision, fluid, viscous; a storm-cloud come to take me away.

The red fades to black, and everything is still now, so still, I can sense nothing around me except the cold.

It is so cold.

I feel my body giving in, releasing itself to the promise of sleep. A wonderful, deep, comforting sleep.

The feeling is wondrous, and I know in an instant that I will never wake up.

DAY ONE

1

I stroke Hero's smooth chestnut flank with a body brush. He's perfectly clean now, this is just to relax him; soothe him. Like me, he's been through a lot.

It wasn't long after I arrived in Alaska to take possession of my farm, that I stumbled upon Alaska Equine Rescue in Eagle Creek, down the Mat-Su valley between Palmer and Anchorage.

They were looking for suitable foster homes in which to re-house neglected and abused horses, and I immediately offered to help. One of the reasons I'd gone for Little Creek Ranch in the first place was the forty acres of grazing land that came with the property, immediately seeing horses frolicking across the fields. My dream; since becoming obsessed with riding at the age of four, always my dream. I hadn't always wanted to be an attorney; I was going to be an eventer, mixing the style of dressage with the thrill of cross-country racing. I was going to be the best, and for a time it looked as if I might even make it. Until my father – for a reason still

15

completely unknown to me – suddenly decided to ban me from taking part in the sport when I was thirteen.

No more Boston Equestrian Centre, no more trips to the family ranch in Westford with its dozen horses, my beloved Beauty the best of the bunch; no more horses at all. And later, no more ranch either, sold off just three months later. It was as if my father wanted to expel the countryside from me altogether. There was just the enormous townhouse on Commonwealth Avenue, perhaps a weekly game of tennis at the Saxon courts over the bridge across the Charles River.

But after the attack, needing a change, I drifted back to those old memories; the smell of grass and hay and horses, the sun warming my body as I ride across a field, golden-green in the heat of an Indian summer.

Yes, I'd thought, that's what I want.

And with the multi-million-dollar pay-out – the damage to my brain was declared to be so severe that I would never be able to work again, certainly not in public office – I had gone ahead and bought this ranch outside Palmer. Little Creek Ranch. A childhood dream. All I'd needed were the horses.

When I moved in, I commissioned six new stables to be built, ready and waiting. I knew what I wanted, horses just like Beauty. I could afford them myself now, so why not? I'd ride them all, every day; maybe select one and start competing again, at least locally. I wondered what the equestrian scene was like around Anchorage.

But when I visited the AER headquarters, these

ideas vanished immediately. No – this is what I would do. I would take in these poor animals which had been neglected, abused, abandoned; I would give them care, attention, and – yes – love. I would give them all the love I had.

It's working out well. Alaska Equine Rescue is delighted to have an extra foster home, and I am delighted to be helping. To be fair, the horses are helping me too. Helping me to heal.

I am content now as I stroke Hero, looking across the cold, darkening fields at the other horses I look after, seven other wonderful animals I'm committed to rehabilitating until they can move on to new homes. Sometimes I have as many as ten horses here, and I've built more stables to accommodate them. I have twelve now – just in case – which is exactly the same number as we used to have, once upon a time, back in Westford.

The gunshot wound to my head didn't kill me; that was the good news, or so they told me. There was one hell of a lot of bad news to balance it out though.

For example: James Traynor and Tom Brooks were killed during the attack on the courthouse, along with a reporter for WABC who was hit by a stray bullet. James was hit by seven bullets, whilst Tom was crushed when the car rolled. He lived for two days in hospital before his shattered body finally gave up. Two other officers and three more reporters sustained serious injuries. And I was hit in the clavicle and just above the hip, before one of the assassins had moved in and shot me once in the head.

The wounds to my body were severe enough to impede my walking for the several months they took to heal; that didn't overly concern me though, as I was in a coma from the third bullet for nearly half a year.

By the time I *did* wake up, the rest of my body had healed fine; the doctors were the best my family could afford, which meant that they were the best in the country. But still, nobody really expected me to wake up – Paul sure as hell didn't, anyway – because of the damage to my brain. The assassin's bullet had entered above my eyebrow, the bone miraculously deflecting it away from deeper penetration and sending it up my forehead where it exited at the top of my skull. There was a tremendous amount of blood, bone and tissue spread out over those courthouse steps, but my brain received only a graze rather than being completely destroyed. Still, it was enough for discussions to be held about if and when my life support systems would be shut off.

Luckily for me (although in my dark times, I sometimes wonder), I woke up before those decisions were finalized. Two months of physical therapy and psychological counselling followed before I was allowed home. Such as it was, anyway; Paul had already moved out, leaving the big rooms feeling desolate, empty. I would have thrown my diamond engagement ring into the Hudson Bay, if he hadn't already taken it from my room when I was "asleep". Always on the lookout to make a quick buck, my beloved Paul.

A narrow escape, I guess.

As I walk, I subconsciously use my thumb to stroke my empty ring finger. My hands were never tanned enough to have a visible mark – I worked too hard, too many hours indoors under cold, filtered electronic lighting for that – but the mark is there all the same, within my mind.

I sigh inwardly, involuntarily, wondering if it will ever go away. Do I miss Paul? My mind says no, of course you don't; he's a thoroughbred bastard just like your father; he left you when you were in a coma, for crying out loud! And yet my heart refuses to listen. Stupid thing.

I suppose the only person I really miss – with both my head and my heart – is my middle brother Jack, and the sad truth is that he's been dead since he threw himself out of his apartment window fifteen years ago at the heart-breaking age of twenty. I close my eyes to the thoughts, blinking them away. Not now, I tell myself. Not now.

I check my watch, note the time, realize I'd better start getting ready soon. There is a party at Artie Jenkin's place tonight, and – after so long alone – I'm looking forward to it.

Artie is my nearest neighbor – although he lives half a mile away, his is the nearest house out of the six other ranches that are spread across this part of the valley, and he mentioned the party when I bumped into him in Palmer the week before.

He'd asked me to attend his party, claiming such

affairs were legendary around these parts. His brother was coming up from Seattle – it was going to be something of a meet-and-greet for him – and I'd forced myself to say "yes".

After all this time, I'd figured, why the hell not?

I'd later found out that he'd been telling the truth when he'd said lots of people would be there; according to the girls in Eagles Creek, Artie's parties *are* legendary. Go figure.

It's been the talk of Palmer over the past few days; the chief of police, school governors, the heads of Palmer's biggest firms, even the town mayor are going to be there.

After New York, I was a little nervous of being around people, but if anyone got out of hand, Ben Taylor would sort it out. The Chief of Palmer Police Department, Ben was a strong, decent man, a professional in every sense. He'd come to see me, aware of my background and my recent history, and made it clear that he could be called upon night and day if I needed him. I think he sees the possibility of another attack, Zebunac's goons coming back to finish the job. Part of him, I think, would welcome the change of pace. The other side – the more pragmatic, sensible side – would surely not.

There's nothing to worry about on that score anyway, I consider as I walk back across the fields to my farmhouse, checking on the large tracts of vegetables as I go, Molly my Border Collie – friend and loyal farmhand – close at my heel. If Zebunac wanted the job finished, he could have had me killed in hospital. Besides which, there was no point; he had gotten what he wanted. I was unable to continue with the case, a less prepared replacement was substituted, and the state lost. Zebunac went free. And – as if to add insult to injury – the gunmen were never found.

It pains me still, that lost court case. I wasn't even there, and yet I see it as a failure. It *was* a failure. How could he have escaped conviction? I sometimes wonder whether the DA's office was indeed intimidated, as Zebunac had clearly hoped, not tried hard enough as a result; but perhaps that was unfair.

The bottom line, though, is that I am under no threat; I'd been removed from the case as if I'd been dead anyway. Mission accomplished. It would serve no purpose to go after me now.

That's what I tell myself, anyway; but the fear that constantly eats away at my gut tells me something else entirely.

Back at the house now, I open the screen door to the kitchen and see Nero and Luna sat waiting for me, eyes up, ears pricked back, as if to disprove my previous thoughts. Black brindle Cane Corso, pure-bred Italian mastiffs a hundred and fifty pounds apiece. Guard dogs. Beautiful, but damn good at their job, which – yes, I'll admit it – is keeping me safe. Because although my conscious mind accepts the fact that Zebunac will have no interest in me now, out here in the middle of nowhere, my mind can play tricks on me. Sounds, shadows, feelings; I am often unnerved out here, used as

I am to the constant cacophony of a big city. Out here, the wind in the trees still makes me jump. And so – whereas Molly helps me around the farm – the two big guys keep me safe. They would protect me with their lives, and that gives me peace of mind. Maybe I'm not completely healed yet, after all.

The dogs sit up instants before the kitchen phone rings, almost as if they sensed the electricity racing through the cables. I wipe my hands on my work trousers and pick up.

"Jess?" the all-too familiar voice on the other end of the line says, thousands of miles away. "It's Paul. We need to talk."

My stomach turns, and I know Nero and Luna cannot protect me from everything.

2

I ring the doorbell, wondering if anyone will hear it; the noise coming from inside the house is terrific. The phone call from Paul, out of the blue after so many months, is playing on my mind, but I make a conscious effort not to think about it. I can't let it spoil my night.

Seconds later the door is opened, Artie standing there with a big smile on his face. "Jess," he beams, "you made it! Come in, come in."

He gestures me inside the big farmhouse, and I hand him a covered plate of shortbread as I go.

The house is already filled with people even at this early hour. Everyone has a drink in their hand, and one appears in my own as if by magic. "Rum punch," Artie tells me. "It's got quite a kick, so be careful. Now come on, I want you to meet my brother."

He takes me through the throngs of guests to the far side, where a handsome, bearded man is leaning against an oak counter, laughing with friends in between sips of bottled beer. Except for the beard, he's the spitting image of Artie. Then I spy the teeth, and realize that perhaps he's not quite as handsome as I thought.

"Pat," Artie says, "this is my neighbor, Jessica, she just moved here from New York a few months ago."

I see Pat lever himself upright, extending a hand. I take it gingerly, and he smiles. "A fellow Outsider," he says, and I'm not sure if I find it ingratiating or offensive – *outsiders* are how Alaskans refer to people from the "Lower 48" states. It's a party however, so I decide to go with ingratiating. "Delighted to meet you." He extends a hand and I shake it.

"Pat's wife and kids haven't been able to make it unfortunately," Artie explains, "so he's up here by himself this time."

Pat smiles. "A bit of freedom at last," he jokes, although I can't be entirely sure it is a joke. "No," he says, taking a pull of his beer, "Julia – that's my wife – she's snowed under with work right now, and my kids have both got exams coming up, they couldn't really afford the time off from school."

Nice, I think. His wife is snowed under, so he's left her alone with her work and the children. "Oh," I say, before realizing that something else might be required here. How do conversations work again? Damn, it's been a long time. "What does your wife do?" I ask eventually. That's the sort of thing people ask, isn't it?

"Oh, nothing world-changing," Pat says, and again I think: *nice*. It's just lovely how he values her. "She just works in a travel firm, and it's a busy time of year, people trying to get last-minute deals, you know." He finishes his beer, another one appearing instantly in his big dry hand. "She gets good prices for flights though, my ticket out here cost next to nothing."

I'm still thinking of what to say next, my social skills badly receded by months of solitude and introspection, when Artie touches my arm. Is he going to rescue me? I wonder hopefully.

"Sorry Jess," he says, disengaging himself, "I need to circulate, do the host thing, you know? But Pat here will look after you, won't you Pat?"

The brothers' eyes meet, both pairs twinkling with some unknown understanding. I feel faintly disturbed.

"You bet," Pat says, smiling at me. "Us Americans will stay right out of your way." I know now that Pat is *not* ingratiating.

I take my first sip of rum punch, and it hits my throat hard. I shudder involuntarily, and Pat laughs. "Strong stuff, yeah?" He shrugs his big shoulders. "Artie's made that crap for years, same recipe since he was a kid. It'll burn the stomach lining off all the bums in Seattle, that stuff, I guaran-damn-tee it." He raises his beer. "That's why I'm sticking to these."

He finishes off the bottle and grabs another, his third in as many minutes. I take another sip of my own, prepared this time. "It's not so bad," I say casually.

"So what brought you up here anyway?" Pat says. "Escaping from something?"

I'm amazed at the arrogance of the man, his utter lack of charm. But I'm here at a party, and he's someone to practice on, at least.

I shrug my shoulders. "Well, the Serbian mafia shot me in the head last year to stop me trying a case against them in New York. I was in a coma for six months, when I woke up I'd lost the case, my job and my fiancée. So you could say I'm escaping from something, yes. It's called my life. What's *your* story?" I keep my gaze levelled at him as I took another hit of punch.

Perversely, it feels good to say it out loud, get it in the open like this. Perhaps I'm not much of a charmer myself.

"Wow," Pat says now, holding up his hands, regret on his face. "I'm really sorry, I had no idea."

I soften in turn. "I'm sorry too," I say. "I'm not used to this, it's been a while since I've really had to speak to people I don't know, I'm still trying to get back into the swing of it."

"Well, let me get you a refill and we can start again, okay?" he offers, and I pass him my cup, accepting the invitation. It might help me get my mind off Paul, at least.

As he leaves with my cup, I feel a hand on my elbow and I turn, seeing the familiar, country-girl face of Larraine Harrigan beside me. We've met before, once or twice, but it's Artie's description of her that I remember best.

"Larraine Harrigan, yeah," he'd said. "Lives in the farm just over from me, near you, too. Amazing woman. Helps out at the shelter, amazing with the girls, really knows how to talk to them. And she still has time to look after the rest of Palmer, she's the go-to woman for advice, brings cakes around to the police department, campaigns for the mayor. And then she still finds the time to work on the farm," he'd continued, in open admiration. "Although I guess her boys help her out with the field work."

I'd met those boys too, I recall now; nice kids, polite and clean-cut, maybe about twelve and fourteen, maybe more. I'm not an expert on children's ages, and – sadly, I recognize – probably never will be.

But Larraine had seemed nice, and I'm glad she is here.

"Hi," she says, "Jessica, isn't it?"

"Larraine, hi," I say, and we both lean forward, kissing the other's cheek like long-lost friends. "It's so nice to see you."

She smiles back at me, and presses a glass into my hand. I look down, see white wine. "I thought this might be more your sort of thing," she says, and I know she is offering me a way out of my awkward situation with Artie's brother. I appreciate the save.

"Well, you're not wrong," I say, taking a grateful sip. It's not the best, but it's definitely better than seventy-proof rum punch. "Thanks."

Larraine gestures with her head. "Come on, there're lots more people here to introduce you to," she says. "Pat'll understand. After all, he'll be going back to Seattle before long, and you live here now. And these are the people you'll be living with." She puts her hand on my arm, a soft touch but strength seeming to be transmitted into me. "Now come on."

She is so right; so very, very right. Artie thought someone from Seattle would make me feel more comfortable, missing the point entirely. I came here tonight to make friends with people from my new home, right here. Larraine understands that, and I will be forever grateful to her.

I see Pat heading back over to me, and I gesture with my head to Larraine as she leads me away, shrugging my shoulders apologetically. *What can I do?* I try and say. *I'm helpless here.*

Pat smiles and shrugs himself, but – as he downs the punch in one go and casts the cup carelessly to one side before starting on his own bottle of beer – I can see another reaction entirely, barely restrained underneath.

I follow Larraine gladly from the kitchen.

3

Over the next couple of hours, I meet an incredible variety of people, my social skills being prized back out of my subconscious slowly but surely; the white wine helps, I'll admit.

She makes sure I know the rest of my neighbors first; they are all here at Artie's party, and they all tell me they wouldn't have missed it for the world, they never do.

Bill and Rachel Townsend are the old grandees of the valley, they've lived here for the past forty years or more, in the same house, which Bill built with his own hands; and then there are the Latimers, a solid nuclear family of four who moved here from Fairbanks just a few years ago; Tom Judd is a retired judge, a widower who splits his time between his farmstead here and an apartment in Anchorage; and Claude and Lea Eberle, French Canadians with six pre-teen children, make up the last ranch in our little hamlet.

Larraine is like a magician of some sort, leaving me

alone when appropriate, coming back to introduce me to others when it seems it will help. And all the while, she is making her own rounds of the party guests, always welcome, everyone happy to see her. Her children are here too, and I see them making conversation with the adults, especially the men.

I wonder if it's because they're looking for a male role model, living only with their Mom. Or do they? I realize I don't know. Is there a Mr. Harrigan somewhere? I wonder if I should ask, or try and find out, but I realize I don't know how. I used to be an Assistant DA for the whole of New York County, and now I can't even find out about one single aspect of a woman's life.

I feel my shoulders sagging as I realize just how much my life has changed. Where has the hard-charging woman gone? The woman who was willing to take on the Italian mob, the Triads, the East European gangs, the Balkan criminal underworld? The woman who had made her own way, refusing hand-outs from her father, who had just started to dominate the New York legal scene with a pair of figurative brass balls? A woman with a high-rise apartment in the Upper West Side and a handsome, sexy, charming, go-getting fiancée to match?

I put the glass of wine down, wondering if I've had too much. I start to zone out from the sounds of the party – the shouted bets from the poker tables in the dining room, the raucous laughter from the impromptu drinking games in the kitchen, the thumping music and dancing in the living room. All I can think about is Paul.

He called me, wanting to know if there was still a chance for us. He apologized, he poured out his heart, he begged for forgiveness. I put the phone down.

And yet . . . And yet . . .

"Honey?" I hear the voice next to me, see Larraine standing there, concern on her homely features. "Are you okay?"

I restrain the tears that want to pour down my face, but for some reason I can't lie to her. I simply shake my head.

She puts an arm around me and ushers me out of the room, cooing gently in my ear. "Come on," she murmurs, sheltering me. "Come on."

"So now you don't know what to do," Larraine finishes for me.

We're sitting on the end of a bed in one of the upstairs rooms, far away from the party. We can't even hear the music anymore, just the loud ticking of a clock on the bedroom dresser.

Tick, tock, tick, tock – I think I can hear my life, melting away around me, vanishing without a trace.

I've told Larraine everything; everything about New York, everything about my current state of mind.

Artie had said that Larraine was "great with the girls", and I remember now where it is they work; the Anchorage Street Shelter, a drop-in refuge center for runaways, beaten women, prostitutes and other people who are in trouble and have nowhere else to go. Artie helps run the place, and Larraine is one of the volunteer counsellors. I can see now why she is good at the job; she has a nature, a manner, which demands that you just pour out your heart to her.

I nod my head. "Yes," I manage, the tears having come and gone by now. "I guess I'm confused."

"And yet here you are. A strong, intelligent woman. Not in New York, pining away after your fiancée, desperate to get him back. You moved away. You moved on. No matter what he says now, the fact is that you've already made your decision. A strong, intelligent decision."

Tick, tock, tick, tock – still the clock counts down the seconds of my life. "Damn, that thing's annoying," I say, and Larraine smiles.

"Yes," she says, "it is, isn't it? Do you feel like your life is being counted down?" I nod, and she gestures towards the window. "Ignore it," she urges. "Get up, go over there." I do as I'm told, and Larraine is next to me, opening the window as I get there. The cold air hits me. Cold, but fresh. It reminds me that I'm alive. "Look out there."

The stars are bright here, and I can make out the great pine forest beyond Artie's farm, the huge jagged peaks of the Bald Mountain Ridge far beyond. Even at night, the sight is beautiful.

"This is where you live now," Larraine whispers, "where you belong. You've made that decision, you've left the other world behind, far behind. You just have to accept it."

I sigh, knowing she is right. It's the acceptance

that's so hard, the fact that things have changed. But they *have* changed, and there's no going back.

"Paul's a part of that past now," she says soothingly, closing the window, looking me in the eye. "The same as my own husband is a part of *my* past." She pulls me back to the bed. "Let me tell you a story of my own, it might help in some way." We sit down together again, and I wait for her to begin.

"I didn't have a very nice childhood," she said uneasily. "It was rough, it was unloving, it was lonely. My father left when I was little, my mother moved around a lot, bouncing from one new man to the next. And then I was thrown out entirely, tossed from one home to another. It was . . . bad. But I turned things around, got myself through college, earned a degree in psychology, got a job. Met a guy, a really fabulous guy, a doctor. He was part of the in-crowd, you know, took me places a girl like me couldn't have hoped to see otherwise. He took me to the fancy restaurants, to the private clubs, we even toured Europe. It was like a dream.

"We got married, of course. Had children, you've met them. Wonderful kids, aren't they?"

I nod my head encouragingly but remain silent, not wanting to interrupt; she is building to something.

"Well a few years ago, nine now I guess, I discovered the bombshell; my husband, my wonderful husband, the father to my wonderful kids, was a cheat. I discovered him with his girlfriend, in our bed one day. And she wasn't the first, it turned out, not by a long-shot."

She shrugs, and I feel my heart going out to her. How terrible it must have been.

"It nearly destroyed my life, let me tell you," she continues. "After the childhood I'd had, to feel that someone loved me, wanted to be with me, it was the best thing in the world. For a time, I even wondered if I could live with it, you know? For everything I had, could I forgive him?" She shook her head, and I felt the strength of her character emanate from the very core of her. "No, I could not. I just couldn't live like that, I'm not that sort of person. I dragged myself up from the gutter, and I did it myself, with nobody's help. My husband made me hit a low – and I mean a real low – but it wasn't the first time I'd been there, and I knew I was strong enough to haul myself up again.

"So I filed for divorce, got the kids, a big pay-out, and moved out here with them." She smiles at me. "So you see honey, you're not the only one. A lot of us here were outsiders at one time or another, and a lot of us rebuilt our lives here." It surprises me, this revelation. I was so caught up in my own life, my own problems, I had never really thought about anyone else here. I just assumed that everyone "belonged".

But Larraine Harrigan, one of the most respected ladies of Palmer, has only moved here a few years ago herself. Artie's brother lives in Seattle, and I realize that perhaps Artie wasn't born here either. I know Ben transferred from the San Francisco Police Department after a messy divorce. Who knows who else has similar stories? I am already starting to feel less of an interloper, less of an outsider.

She puts a hand on my shoulder, her gaze levelled at me. "I was strong enough to do it, and I know you are too, honey. I know it."

I smile at her, confidence building within me for the first time in months. I can't even hear the ticking of the clock anymore.

Maybe, I think, *I'll* start to know it too, soon enough.

And then – maybe – I really *will* start to heal.

4

I can feel the breeze even through my jacket. We're not far from winter, and night-time temperatures are already starting to drop.

After talking to Larraine, we returned to the party, and I actually enjoyed myself, even started to work the crowd a little; almost like I was back in the cocktail bars of New York after work, but more relaxed. Here, there was nobody who wanted anything from me.

There had been an ugly incident when Pat had allegedly been seen slipping a drink to an underage girl. It couldn't be proven, but the mood had soured considerably after that. The girl's parents were unhappy, Ben was unhappy, Artie was defensive, everyone else was keen to see what would happen. Larraine decided that it was time to leave with the kids, and I followed her lead.

She asked if I wanted a lift home, but I wanted to walk; the party had given me a lot to think about, and I wanted to do it in the fresh air, by myself. But I'm terribly grateful to Larraine for her timely words; perhaps more than she will ever know.

I walk down a narrow track which links some of these farmhouses, lost in thought. Larraine was right; I've made my decisions, moved on. It was – is – the right thing to do. I loved Paul, yes, that's true. But it's over now, and I have to face that.

The trouble is, I still love him. I know how stupid that is, I know he stole the engagement ring back off my finger when I was unconscious, in a coma; I know he moved his stuff out of my apartment, leaving it an empty shell to come home to, empty and heartless. I know he's a bastard, and yet I can't help myself.

But I must; there's nothing else for it. Larraine overcame an even worse betrayal and look where she is now. So Paul is coming crawling back, hat in hand. Let him. I can tell myself it means nothing to me.

Yes, I confirm to myself. It means nothing to me.

I survey the land around me, the post and rail fences of Artie's farm, my fields just half a mile further. The sweeping pines beyond, the mountain ridges beyond that. Beautiful. All I've ever wanted, before law ever reared its ugly head. Back when I was a girl, and my dreams were the innocent, sweet dreams of youth.

I remember Beauty, my first horse. I'd been riding a while, taking my lessons with the rest of the girls at Boston Equestrian Centre; and even back then, I'd wanted to be the best.

And then one day my mom and dad had taken me and my older brothers out to Westford. As we'd driven down that long, winding gravel driveway, I'd known there would be something special at the end.

Ted and Jack had been taken aback by the ranch-house, instantly running in to pick a bedroom for themselves, but I hung back. There was something else there, I could – literally – smell it.

My father took me by the hand and led me around to the far side of the house, and I saw them.

The stables.

My heart beating, I ran to the wooden stalls, instinct leading me to him. I ripped open a door and there he was; Beauty.

He was an American Quarter Horse stallion, seventeen hands and black. Not grey, black hairs on white skin, but black; true black, a real rarity. My father had remembered my favorite story, right from being a toddler when my nanny had read it to me over and over again. Anna Sewell's *Black Beauty*. It was what had made me love horses in the first place. And now here he was, right in front of me, his muscles rippling underneath the sheen of his incredible coat.

I have never loved anyone more than I loved my father at that moment.

But it had all come crashing down in the end, to be replaced by a life of harried academia and the sad results of criminal violence.

But now there is a chance – if I don't let Paul, or any other aspect of my past, interfere with it – that I can have it all back, the magic of the early days.

Maybe it is the thought of magic, but I notice it

then; a reddish hue, lighting the sky from the south-east. I turn my head, stunned by the ball of fire I see before me, raging across a sky which has already surrendered to the night. A huge, bloody, monstrous *moon*. A red moon, rising over the jagged horizon, as if set alight by a perverted miracle of nature, hell itself climbing over the mountain peaks to rule the night.

I am struck by the majesty of the image, the beauty, the magnificence. At the same time, I shrink from it, the size and scale of the thing scaring me; an indefinable, gut-instinct fear which seems to raise unbidden from the primeval marshes of my subconscious.

And then – even more than that – there is the déja vu, which I feel so strongly that I shudder. I feel it right down to my very core. This thing, this blood-red moon, is a part of me somehow, evoking emotions within me I had no idea even existed.

I stand still, drinking it in, awed and horrified at the same time.

I try to remember the reasons for such a thing happening. Dust in the atmosphere? Was that it? Something else tells me it is caused by an eclipse of some sort. And yet I've already seen the sun this evening, and they're not in the same part of the sky.

I find it hard to drag my eyes away from the fireball, bound to it in some strange unknowable way; afraid that if I do, I may lose a part of myself that I may never get back.

But finally I do look away, and continue on towards my house, the night sky lit up all the while by the blood-red moon.

Eventually I pass the heavy railings which mark the boundary of my land, and step into my own fields.

Some of my horses are in the stables, others are out at pasture. Later in the year they may all have to be kept inside, but for now, some of them prefer to be out.

I pat Lady's face, my hand running under her chin, stroking her gently. She turns her head then, bending to resume her feeding.

The others are further away and I briefly consider going to them before deciding against it. I'm tired, and I need to go to bed. I've had too much wine, and I still need to be up early to muck out the horses and walk the dogs. They won't listen to my complaints of a hangover.

I'm nearing the house now; simple, modest, perfect. It's home, and it finally really feels like it. The moon casts a strange crimson glow over the clapboard paneling and I look towards the fireball once more, wondering what it reminds me of.

And then I hear it. Panting; breath ragged. A horse? I stand stock-still, listening. I hear feet working over the fields, gasping.

A person.

I freeze, immobile. Who would be out here at this time of night? Have Zebunac's goons come for me after all? I wonder where my gun is, realize it's in a locked cabinet in the kitchen. A lot of good it's going to do me there.

But I understand then that the sound isn't

threatening; I can hear Luna and Nero growling in the house, but they're not barking.

No, the sounds are . . . frightened.

I continue walking towards the rough panting, passing the house now, and then I see her – lit up by the red glow of the moon, silhouetting her against the front fields.

I wonder for a moment if I'm seeing a ghost, the image is so strange, so disturbing; a young girl – fifteen, sixteen? – naked, bleeding, fighting her way through the tall grass towards my house. Seeking . . . refuge?

I break then, running to her, legs pumping beneath me as I cross the pasture to the bloody, naked girl; and then I'm there, and the ghost falls into my arms, eyes delirious with exhaustion and terror.

I'm shocked, horrified as the girl's brutalized, cut skin leaks fresh blood over me, her face puffed and bruised, her breath even more ragged now.

She lays in my arms and I tell her that it's okay, I'll get help for her, she's okay now; all the while wondering where she's come from, who's done this to her, what the hell is going on?

Her broken teeth appear as she tries to smile for me, to show me that she's okay, she feels safe now at last; then blood runs from her broken nose and she chokes violently. I hold her closer, her head to my breast so she can hear my heart beat, offering her comfort.

But I feel the breath becoming more and more distant, and I pull her head away, see the eyes rolling upwards into their damaged sockets, feel the body sagging deeper into me as she starts to let go.

"No," I whisper to her, "stay with me, stay with me."

Feebly she raises one pale, skinny arm and extends a finger. Pointing? I follow the finger across the fields, the farms, to the trees and mountains beyond. What is she trying to tell me?

The effort is too much for her and the arm drops, useless. It was the last of her energy and I know it is too late now for her; although I will spend the next twenty minutes trying in vain to restart her heart, I have felt the life leave her, a single rending breath which travels into the cosmos and leaves me crying over her dead body.

And high above, the red moon watches us both.

5

"Holy shit."

I turn my head to see Ben Taylor standing next to me; I must have missed the sound of his car, his footsteps on the gravel path which leads to the fields.

I'm still sitting in the wet grass, the dead girl's head cradled in my lap. As if I can still provide comfort to her in some small way.

I remember calling Ben on my cell-phone, knowing how close he was. I have no idea what I said to him.

I remember beating on the poor girl's chest, going mouth-to-bloody-broken-mouth with her.

I remember screaming, crying, tears of frustration and horror, tears which wracked me to the core.

And all for nothing. She is still dead. This poor unknown girl.

Still dead.

"It's okay," Ben says now, edging closer. "EMTs are on their way, guys from the PD." He stands and looks at us, runs a thick hand through his thinning hair, shakes his head in disbelief.

And then his professionalism takes over and he bends to one knee, checking for a pulse. I already know there won't be one.

"Shit," he says again, before placing a hand gently on my shoulder. "Come on, you've done enough here. Come on. It's okay." He takes the limp form of the girl from me, lays her gently on the ground, pulls me to my feet. I don't resist. "Come on."

He pulls me back, and I am still in a daze, but I let him; he's the Chief of Police, and I'm just in the way.

He kneels again, examining the girl more closely; and although I know I shouldn't, I edge forward too, really taking her in for the first time.

She's young like I thought, not yet an adult. Just a girl. Her skin is pale and she has the gaunt look of someone who's been on the streets for a while.

There are tears in her skin, rough cuts which are finally stopping bleeding. Marks on her wrists, ankles, neck. Ligature marks. She's been tied up. Strangled.

There are other marks too. Cigarette burns? Bite marks? Maybe both.

Her dark hair is greasy, speckled with dried blood, and it looks like clumps have been torn out from the root.

What the hell happened to her?

Ben's examination goes lower, but his body blocks out my view of her lower torso. "Ah shit," he says, and for a second I think he's going to be sick.

"What is it?" I ask

"Trust me Ms. Hudson, you don't wanna know."

He stands, wiping his mouth with a handkerchief, turning to me.

"Look, my guys will be here any minute. This place is a crime scene now, we'll have to get it cordoned off, okay? Then we'll wait for the State Troopers, they'll want to bring in their own investigators. These ranches are outside Palmer city limits."

He looks down at the body, turns back to me. "Why don't you go inside, get the kettle on? There's nothing more you can do here."

I nod my head, turn without thinking; his hand stops me, turns me back.

"You did good. You showed her a friendly face before . . . you know. You couldn't have done any more."

I nod my head again and turn to the house, my mind adrift on a sea of guilt and pain.

From the kitchen, I see the flashing lights outside, hear the murmured chat of people. My ranch is a crime scene, the streets of New York supplanted here to the Mat-Su Valley.

I clasp a cup of coffee in my hands, hoping the caffeine will sharpen my mind, bring me out of the dark hole into which I've fallen.

"So," Ben says, seated at the kitchen table, note book open before him, "the girl was alive when you arrived home, is that right?"

I nod my head, take a sip of coffee. Another

officer, Rob Kittson I think his name is, leans against the kitchen counter, eyeing the dogs warily. But they're in their beds, and they'll stay there unless I tell them to move.

"Yes," I say eventually. "I came across the fields, back from Artie's house, came around the side and that's when I heard the feet running through the grass. The panting, someone out of breath, struggling." I close my eyes.

"I know this is hard for you and I'm sorry," Ben says. "But the ABI won't get here for another hour or so, and they've asked me to do the prelims." He shrugs, and I know he would rather be anywhere else than here. I don't blame him.

The Alaska Bureau of Investigation will take the lead on this case, being the department of the State Troopers that deal with major crimes. And this looks like a definite case of kidnap and torture, and possibly murder too. But although we've already got the EMTs and the police department from Palmer, it'll be a while longer before the big guns get here.

I shrug too, showing Ben I understand his position. "When I saw it was a girl, I ran out to her, and she collapsed in my arms. It was all over so quick, I . . . But she pointed." I take another sip of coffee, nod my head. "Yes, before she . . . before she died, she lifted her arm and pointed."

"Where did she point?"

"Past the other farms, over to the woods, maybe the mountains," I say, although I'm not really sure.

Ben turns to Rob Kittson, and the two men exchange looks. "Doug Menders lives –" Rob begins, but he's cut off instantly by a quick shake of Ben's head. Rob looks at me and clams up.

"Okay," Ben continues, "then what happened?"

I sigh. "Then . . . she died." My shoulders sag, grief hitting me once more as I remember the breath, the life, leaving the young girl. But I refuse to cry until I've finished. "I called you from my cell-phone, then tried to resuscitate her with CPR." I shake my head, fighting back the tears. "But it was no good. I stopped trying just before you arrived, just laid her head in my lap and held her there." I wipe a tear away; I didn't quite manage to hold it in after all.

Ben nods, smiles. "Okay Jessica, thanks very much, I think that's all we need for now. Unless you saw anything else suspicious at all? Anyone walking around who shouldn't be here? I mean, not just now, but at any time recently? Anything at all?"

I think about Paul's phone call, but discount it. It's only troubling to me, nobody else.

"Just that damned red moon," I say, trying my best to be light-hearted, make a joke, laugh it all away.

"The what?" Ben asks from the doorway.

"The red moon," I repeat, "you know, the one tonight, didn't you see it?"

Ben looks at Rob, and both men shrug their shoulders. "There ain't been no red moon tonight Jessica," Ben says, almost apologetically. "Barely any moon at all, just a little crescent, and that's been as pale as it always is."

Not knowing what to think, I storm past the two officers, wrenching open my kitchen door. Molly barely stirs, but Luna and Nero bounce to their feet. I glare at them and they lie back down.

I walk out into the cold night air, barely taking in the crowd, the taped off areas of the fields, the dead body still lying there where we left it, waiting for the ABI crime scene unit to examine it *in situ*; the people from the party all here now, gathered behind the cordon, whispering to each other, pointing. Circling around the dead like damned vultures. But I ignore it all, looking up to the sky, expecting to see the great fireball of the blood-red moon.

But Ben is right.

There is nothing.

And then the stress of the evening finally hits me and I am felled as if I've been struck with a pick-axe, fainting clean away onto the cold gravel beneath me.

I lie in bed, still hearing the noises downstairs, outside.

I wasn't out of it for long, Ben and Rob helped me back inside the house and one of the EMTs gave me the once over and decided I could have a couple of pills and be put to bed. I waited up for the ABI, but they saw what kind of state I was in and said they would interview me tomorrow. The lead investigator gave me his card, and asked Ben if they could use the Palmer police precinct for interviews. Ben had complied readily, and I have an appointment to see them again at ten the next morning.

And now I can't sleep. How can I? With a dead, naked girl in my front yard and half the Alaska State Troopers camped out around my house, how am I going to get to sleep?

But I realize I need to if I'm going to be in any way coherent in the morning, and so I try and think of something else . . . anything else.

I decide to think about short-bread. Making short-bread. Perhaps the most peaceful part of my day, unrelated to things living or dead. I start to wonder if Artie will like it, if he's tried it yet, but I stop those thoughts in their tracks. No; I'm not thinking about people right now.

Butter, castor sugar, flour. Pre-heat the oven. Mix the sugar and butter together. Stir in the flour, get it nice and smooth; I feel myself starting to drift off.

Roll it out on the kitchen-top, not too thin. Get the knife, cut it –

Cut the girl, cut her skin, see how she bleeds, the knife passing through her soft, pale flesh, blood dripping, blood spurting

– I see the blood spraying over me, covering my eyes until I can't see.

I shoot up, bolt-upright in my bed. Sweating.

I shake my head, lie back down. This is hopeless, I decide, and swing the covers back. My feet hit the floor, and I'm on my way back downstairs.

Ignoring the sounds from outside, the bright lights, I grab a bottle of gin from the refrigerator and pour myself a tall glass. Wincing, I down it in one, pour myself another.

I set off back upstairs, my footsteps echoing through the house, making the hairs on the back of my neck stand up.

I laugh to myself; the gin is working. What am I scared of? With that amount of law enforcement outside, my farm must be the safest place in the United States right now.

I get back to bed, sipping on the gin as I go.

I let my mind wander freely, and it does, helped by the alcohol.

A fairground, bright lights beaming, children laughing; horses, I'm riding Beauty at a full gallop through the fields; snow and ice, sledging with my friends; heat from the gin in my throat, running down to warm my belly, rising up to dull my thoughts; a red moon, full and crimson, lighting up the night sky.

A red moon that never was.

Finally, I sleep.

Day Two

1

I wake thinking of Kenny D'Angelo.

My head is foggy, my brain hurting from too much alcohol. Why am I thinking about Kenny? I've not thought of him in years. A high-school boyfriend, he was a biker, a metal-head and – according to my parents – completely wrong for me. I guess that's what attracted me to him.

He was also best friends with my middle brother, Jack. My brother was Christened John, but he always preferred Jack. Thought it seemed rougher somehow; more honest.

Jack. That's right, I was dreaming about *Jack*. Three years older than me, he was still friendly; at least when I hit my teens. Which was about the same time I was forced to stop riding and started to rebel against my parents, so perhaps this is what appealed to him; he'd been rebelling from the day he was born.

But – whatever the reason – he *was* friendly, and when I needed someone, he was there for me. My older brother Edward was more of a cold fish, much like my father. In fact, he works for the same firm even now. And my mother was never that interested in us. In many ways she was typical of her class; moneyed Boston family, had children to look good and please her husband, but never let motherhood interfere with her charity work or her public campaigning.

No, Jack was my friend, the only person from my family I ever really connected with. At least up until the moment he killed himself.

The thought of death hits me like a bucket of cold water over the head. How could I have forgotten? Lying in bed in a dazed stupor, one half of me still in the dream-world, I had forgotten about last night. About what's lying out on my front lawn.

I hazily remember needing to get to an appointment at ten o'clock. Alaska Bureau of Investigation, using Ben's offices at the Palmer PD.

I roll over, check the time on my cell phone.

I gasp, shudder, leap out of bed, panic rushing through me.

It's already half past nine. How long have I been asleep?

Too long. I've not been up later than seven since I moved here.

Damn.

I start pulling on a pair of pants, hopping on one foot as I grab the cell-phone, dialing Alaska Equine Rescue. I'm half-way through buttoning a blouse when it's picked up.

"AER, how can I help you?"

"Dawn, is that you?" I barely wait for her to confirm before ploughing on. "Look, I'm really sorry, is there any way you can send someone over to look after the horses today? I need to visit the police department in Palmer and I just don't know how long I'll be. I'm already late."

I move over to the window as I'm talking, pulling back the curtains slowly. It seems quiet out there, but surely the media must have got wind of it by now. Young girl tortured, dying as she escapes across the farmlands of Alaska. No member of the press would ignore a story like that. They're probably waiting out there right now, quietly waiting until they see me, primed for the photo op.

I pause, hand on the curtain as Dawn speaks. "Oh no, what's wrong, is everything okay?"

I peel the curtain back, peer outside. Pull it back all the way, not believing my eyes.

There's nothing out there.

No dead body – not even an outline, no police, no medical personnel, no crime scene investigators, no ABI, no police cordon, no tape, no nosy neighbors trying to get a look, and no press. Nobody at all.

Maybe the ABI decided to clean it all up overnight, to avoid the inevitable sensation? But I know things don't work that way. Unless Alaska is different. I pause to consider. It might be, I suppose. It just might be.

The fact that there is no press presence out there makes me wonder if it's been reported at all. Surely one of the people from the party must have spilled to someone? But maybe the ABI is keeping a tight lid on it; maybe the case is bigger than the single body, they don't want anyone to get alarmed. Or maybe they have a suspect, don't want to get them spooked?

"Jess?" Dawn asks, concerned. "You okay?"

"Sorry Dawn," I reply finally, still wondering where everyone's gone, deciding not to tell her the truth, just in case the ABI *is* keeping a lid on it. "I'm fine, really. Please, don't worry. I just need to go in and make a report, but they've asked me not to say anything to anyone, I hope you understand."

I was already half-running downstairs, stopping by the door to slip into my sneakers. No time for fancy shoes today. No need.

I spot the dogs and let them out, pouring food into their bowls as I get my purse and car keys.

"Hey," Dawn says, "that's okay, no problem, just so long as you're okay. Of course, I'll send somebody over."

"You're a lifesaver," I say as I pull my jacket on. I let the dogs back in and they race over to their food, starting to devour it.

I leave through the front, leaving the door unlocked behind me. I say my thanks and goodbyes to Dawn, ignoring the accusatory glare of my horses as I get into my car, start the engine.

I pull forwards, checking the fields as I drive past. I was right. There is nothing here.

I check the clock on my dashboard. It reads *9:42*. I

should still make it on time.

Maybe they'll have some answers for me there.

I arrive with a couple of minutes to spare, frustrated by the radio show playing on the way over. No mention of any death, just the same damn songs they always seem to play. Can't they get any new ones?

I push through the glass doors, the reception space bright and cheery. I see officers working at desks through the glass partitions beyond. They're all working, but there's no urgency here, no hint that something terrible has happened.

Maybe the ABI has set up their investigation somewhere else?

"May I help you?" the woman behind the desk asks, red perm atop a bulbous head. The smile makes up for it.

"Hi, my name is Jessica Hudson, I have an appointment to meet . . ."

I realize I don't know the officer's name. He gave me a card though, I remember that, and I look uselessly through my pants pockets, my jacket pockets.

"I'm sorry," I say finally, "I can't remember his name, but he's with the Bureau of Investigation, he's dealing with the death that occurred last night."

Concern clouds the receptionist's large features. "Death?" she says, turning to the notes on her desk, leafing through papers. All the while, shaking her head. She looks up apologetically. "I'm sorry Ms. Hudson, I don't have any record of a death occurring last night."

I know she must be mistaken. "What time did you come on this morning?"

"Eight o'clock," she says, "but the Chief didn't make any mention of a death at the morning briefing, and there's nothing in the overnight paperwork." She shrugs, and I stand there, confused.

"It's being dealt with by the State Troopers," I say eventually. "It happened at Little Creek Farm, outside the city limits. The ABI are taking the lead, but they asked if they could use the precinct here as a temporary base, for depositions and interviews."

Again, the receptionist shakes her head. "No," she says with certainty, "I'm afraid not, Ms. Hudson."

I believe her, and it suddenly dawns on me what's going on. *Politics.* Either they know who the victim is, or they know who did those terrible things to her, and someone important wants it covering up. Maybe the girl is the daughter of a politician, and they want to use the tragedy for maximum public sympathy. Or else maybe the kidnapper or kidnappers are high-profile, and their gilt-edged lawyers have slapped a privacy suit on the whole thing.

Whatever's going on, my years in the "trade" tell me it's a cover-up, and my famed prosecutor's moral indignation flares violently. A young girl is dead – in my arms – after being held captive and tortured, and the authorities are sweeping it under the carpet?

"I want to see Chief Taylor." It is not a question but a demand.

"He's in a meeting at the moment."

"I need to see him, right now."

"I'm afraid that won't be possible, Ms. Hudson. If you'd like to take a seat, I'll find out when he can see you."

"I'm afraid that's not good enough. This is urgent. I want you to go and interrupt his meeting and tell him that Jessica Hudson is here to speak to him about the young girl who died last night." I don't say *murdered*; at the moment, there is no evidence that she was purposefully killed. She had been hideously abused of course, but she might have died of shock, illness, exposure, any number of things which wouldn't necessarily lead to a charge of homicide. But the case felt like murder nevertheless.

The receptionist looks at me, sees the resolution in my eyes, and nods her head. She levers her heavy frame out of the chair, smiles nervously, and pushes through the glass doors behind her, leaving behind a fog of candy and deodorant.

I take a seat, my foot nervously tapping out a beat on the tiled floor. I look around; still no activity, no sign of a major crime having occurred in the area. What the hell is going on? I know Palmer is not New York, but I'm still surprised with how this whole thing is being dealt with.

I check my pockets again for the ABI agent's card, and again my hands come up empty. What the hell have I done with it?

The door opens behind the reception desk, Ben Taylor standing there, a look of curiosity plastered over his rough features.

"Good morning Ms. Hudson," he says warily. "Livy says you want to speak to me about a murder that happened last night?"

I stand, shaking my head, moving towards him. "If it's a murder, that must have been established after I went to bed," I say.

Ben looks at me quizzically, hands on his hips. "I think you'd better come to my office," he says finally.

I take in the office as I wait for Ben to sit down; modern glass and chrome, a desk with two chairs on a shiny, tiled floor; a black leather couch in the corner under white bookshelves lined with procedural manuals; diplomas on the walls, the smell of disinfectant lingering in the air.

Ben finally sits, pushing across a mug of coffee as he takes a sip from his own. "Have you found out who she is yet?" I ask first, not giving Ben a chance to start the conversation.

My question surprises me; I had planned on demanding answers regarding the investigation, the cover-up. But I realize that it is the question of the poor girl's identity which is really uppermost on my mind. Above all else at the moment, I need to know the girl's name; I need to know who she was, in life. I felt her last breath, and I still don't know who she was.

The concern on Ben's face is disturbing. "Ms. Hudson," he begins innocently, "I really don't know what you're talking about."

I try hard to control my anger. "You know damn well what I'm talking about," I say. "I'm talking about that young girl who died in my arms last night, after staggering across the fields onto my farm. You remember, the girl who was naked, cuts all over her skin, burns, bite marks, chunks of hair torn out and who the hell knows what else. *You* examined her body, said 'Ah, shit', told me not to look. It's about the ABI investigation which doesn't seem to be happening. It's about why this thing is being covered up. It's about you being honest and levelling with me." I hold my gaze on him, piercing.

Ben holds up his hands; his surprise seems genuine. But I remind myself that he hasn't always lived out here; he was a detective with the San Francisco PD, and obfuscation is a way of life for big-city cops.

"Okay Ms. Hudson, I'll be honest with you." He levels his gaze at me. "There have been no reports of any deaths last night, in Palmer or anywhere else around here, not even in Anchorage according to the APD bulletin. You can check the paperwork yourself, we've got records of all activity logged overnight." He sips from his coffee mug, slurping; turns his eyes back to me. "But what you say concerns me a great deal. I know where you've been, where you've come from, what happened to you. I think maybe this is something related to your prior head injuries."

His face is serious, but I can't believe what I'm hearing. "You think I imagined it?" I ask, my body convulsing in anger, coffee spilled across the desk. I ignore the dark stains running freely across the glass. "Are you insane? I just imagined a girl dying, you showing up, the EMTs, the State Troopers, the ABI, my fields, my house turned into a damn *crime scene*?" I'm on my feet now, stabbing an accusatory finger towards him. "You're covering it up," I say, knowing it must be true. "And I'll tell you this now, I'm not going to rest until I get to the bottom of it."

I turn to leave, Ben still sitting in a state of bewilderment behind me. As I reach the door, I hear his voice, reaching out to me. I see the precinct's other officers staring through the glass at us, attention drawn by my raised voice.

"Okay Ms. Hudson, okay," he says, and I turn back round to him, sensing a certain level of acquiescence in his deep voice. "Come back to the table and tell me what you saw." I come back, sit down; pick up the mug, try to wipe the spilled coffee away. "Leave it," he says, clicking on a mini tape recorder. "Start at the beginning."

I nod my head. Ben already has my statement, but at least we're talking; that's the first stage, something I can build on.

"I was walking home from the party, as you know. Artie's brother Pat had spoilt the mood, you were busy calming people down, and everyone was starting to drift out." I see the look of confusion reappear on Ben's face, but ignore it. "Larraine Harrigan offered me a lift home, but I decided to walk. When I got near the house –"

Ben holds up his hand, interrupting me. "Ms.

Hudson," he says, grey eyes watching me warily, "which party was this?"

I sigh, exasperated at his question. "You were *there*, Ben," I say. "It was the party Artie had for his brother Pat, who'd come up to visit him from Seattle."

I watch as Ben shifts uncomfortably in his seat. "Ms. Hudson," he begins uneasily, "what day is it today?"

I look hard at him. "Sunday."

He shakes his head sadly. "I'm afraid not," he says after an uncomfortably long pause. "It's *Thursday*."

I feel chilled to the bone. Did I *sleep* for four days? That would explain why the crime scene has gone from my house, at least. But how would that be possible? Nobody could sleep for four days. And yet I was in a coma for *six months*. Could Ben be right? Is there still something wrong with my head?

I briefly consider the fact that's he's lying, but realize that he wouldn't do that; the date is simply too easy to independently verify.

I shake my head, trying to take it all in. "Maybe . . . maybe I slept. I had something to drink, and . . ."

"I think you misunderstand me," he says softly. "Today is the Thursday *before* Arthur Jenkins' party. It's October ninth. His brother Patrick is still in Seattle. The party hasn't happened yet. It isn't until October eleventh, this Saturday night . . . two days away." He raises his big shoulders, lets them drift back down, looks me in the eye. "It's not real," he tells me. "What you claim to have seen; it *can't* be real."

<u>2</u>

The doctor looks at me, asking the same questions, over and over.

"Have you been experiencing headaches? Any pains or sensations out of the ordinary?"

I am vaguely aware of being on the couch in Ben's office, reclined; my head on a white cushion, my feet draped off the arm at the other end. I try and concentrate. Have I answered any of the doctor's questions yet? Or have I zoned out, my body here but with nobody at home upstairs?

I shake my head, trying to think, get rid of the fuzzy cotton-wool feeling. "I don't think so," I manage finally.

"Nothing at all?" she asks again, and I see her now for the first time; late thirties, maybe forty, fit and trim, thick hair pushed back with a clip, rimless spectacles resting on her nose; safe, professional, reassuring. I wonder what sort of doctor she is.

"No," I say, more positive this time. And it's true;

I've had no headaches since coming to Alaska, except for the usual pre-menstrual symptoms I've always had. Severe migraines, severe cramps, but nothing out of the ordinary, and nothing related to the "accident".

I look across the room, see that we are alone; Ben has left us to it. Good for him.

I lever myself upright. "What's going on?" I ask the doctor.

"It's hard to say," she says. "I've contacted medical personnel back in New York, they filled me in on the basics of your case. I'm not an expert in this field by any means, but it seems to me that what you are experiencing is linked in some way to the damage you received to your brain. From the gunshot," she added unnecessarily. "The frontal lobes are obviously the location of our higher consciousness, they deal with how we interpret the world around us. A gross simplification of course, but an accurate one. Damage such as you received might well cause altered perceptions, difficulties in relating your experiences to reality."

"You're saying I might be going crazy?" I ask, too surprised to be scared yet; though I know the fear for my future well-being is hidden just around the corner.

The doctor smiles at me. "Not at all," she says easily, "not at all. It might mean nothing, just one aberration which scares us all, but then never happens again. *Or*, it might be symptomatic of some deeper problem, which might reoccur over the long-term. That's why I'll be referring you to Doctor Newholme at the Neuroscience Centre at Alaska Regional Hospital. He's the real expert around here, and he'll speak to the doctors back in New York and Boston who are familiar with your case."

She smiles at me again, puts one hand on mine. "Don't worry about a thing," she says. "We'll get to the bottom of this, and you'll be good as new. But for now," she says, reaching into a leather bag on the floor next to her, pulling out a bottle and pushing it into my hands, "I want you to go home and get some rest. Take two of these, three times a day, they'll help with the confusion and the anxiety you'll be feeling. Do you work?"

I look at the bottle, straining to read the label. I tell her about the horses, how someone is there covering for me.

She nods her head. "I'd suggest getting them to continue covering you for a few more days, just to be on the safe side. Do as much as you can yourself of course, but it's probably wise to have some back-up." She didn't need to say, *in case you have another episode.* The message was clear nevertheless. "I'll make the appointment with Doctor Newholme, see what he has to say, and then we'll take it from there."

I pocket the bottle of pills and nod my head, resigned to my fate.

Despite the reassurances of the doctors back home, the attack has caught up with me at last.

And I fear that I'm finally going insane.

***

As I approach my farm, the big tires of my SUV crunching the gravel beneath me, the sun high in a cloudless sky, the radio grinding out the same tunes as always, I am again unsure; but this time, I'm unsure of what I've been told by the doctor.

Could I have imagined the whole thing? The further I get from Palmer, the more convinced I am that what I saw last night was real. I turn down the long driveway to my property, see the fields stretching out on either side; the other farms, the forests, the mountains beyond. The girl had been pointing to those mountains. Why? Ben and his deputy seemed to have some sort of an idea last night, exchanging worried glances when I mentioned it, Ben silencing Rob when he mentioned someone who lived up there. Was it someone they suspected? Or perhaps someone they wanted to protect?

Or was everything happening only in my mind? Then I hear the radio DJ announce a competition, a fishing trip on the Kenai peninsula. His jocular voice offers, "*A superb opportunity for the world's best salmon fishing for anyone who can –*"

"Call in with the year the next song was originally released," I finish, just before the DJ says exactly the same thing. The station cuts to commercials, and I brake the car reflexively. How could I have known that? But the same competitions are run regularly on this station. Maybe it was just a lucky guess?

"Don't Go Breaking My Heart, Elton John and Kiki Dee," I say out loud. I don't know the year. 1976?

'77?

I pause with bated breath, halfway down my driveway, my fingers clenched around the wheel. I see my knuckles going white as I listen to adverts for Bob's Used Cars in Anchorage, Palmer Cleaning Services, a public announcement against littering; I loosen my grip, trying to relax.

The DJ is back. *"Welcome back everyone, we'll get right on with the next song, and remember, if you call in with the year of release, you can win a fishing trip to Kenai, compliments of King of the River! Here we go!"*

The familiar beat starts up, a rhythm I remember only too well; and not from the distant past, but just a few short days ago. The music pours out around me.

I don't believe it; I was right, it *is* the same song.

I shiver, my blood turning cold. Déja vu is one thing, but this? How could I have possibly known? *Because you've lived this day before.*

I shake the thought out of my head. It's impossible. The prosecutor in my head switches on, cross-examining me on the stand.

– Could you please explain yourself, Ms. Hudson? I thought you said that you've lived this day before?

– Err, yes. I think I've already experienced this Thursday.

– So you're saying that you've travelled back through time?

– I'm not sure, but yes, I think so, I must have gone through Thursday, Friday and Saturday, then when I woke on Sunday I had somehow gone back through time, Sunday was now Thursday again.

– I see. Have you recently experienced any significant head

trauma?

– *I . . . Yes. Yes, I have.*

As I play the scenario out in my mind, I know how it sounds. It sounds as if I'm crazy. But I *did* know which song was going to come on. I stop and listen again. I've not imagined it; it's still playing. But maybe I'm just imagining that it's playing? Can anybody else hear it?

I roll the car forwards, my mind in tatters. I pull up in front of the house, see a young girl out in the fields. For a split second my heart stops. But this girl is not naked, she is not bruised, she is not running for her life from

(the mountains!)

who knows where. She is fully clothed, blonde hair tied back in a ponytail, brushing down a chestnut gelding. She is the girl Dawn sent to look after the horses. She waves at me.

"Amy!" I call over to her. "Can you come over here please?"

"Sure!"

She puts down the brush, strokes Lara's cheeks, and trots over to the car. "Hi Jessica," she says when she gets here, young cheeks red as roses with the fresh air, "I hope you're okay, Dawn said –"

I hold up a hand to silence her. I feel bad about the rudeness, but I need a fast answer. "Can you hear the song on the radio?" I ask. Amy nods. "Do you know what it is?" I ask innocently.

I see Amy as she cocks her head to one side,

listening. "I'm not really sure," she says. "I think I've heard my dad listening to it though." She listens more. "I'd guess it's called *Don't Go Breaking My Heart* though, from the words, wouldn't you say?"

I nod my head, deep in thought. "Yes," I murmur quietly, "I think you're right."

"Is there a competition or something?"

"Yeah, but you need the year."

"Sorry, no idea about that. I could call my dad though, if you want?"

I shake my head. "No, it's okay. It doesn't matter really."

I vaguely realize that if my mind truly *is* rebelling, I could be imagining Amy, conjuring someone up in order to corroborate my fears. The prosecutor in me knows that this is a far more likely scenario than anything else, unpalatable though it is. Or if the girl's real, I could be intentionally mishearing her, changing her words in my head until I hear only what I *want* to hear.

I realize Amy has been talking. "Sorry Amy, what did you say?"

"I was wondering if you wanted me to stick around for a while?"

No! my mind screams. *I want to be left alone!* But the welfare of the horses always comes first, and I realize that – whatever the cause – I'm in no fit state to be looking after anything. I remember what the doctor said about keeping help around for the next few days.

"Yes," I say at last, "yes please. And will you be

around for the next few days? I might have some other appointments, and I'd rather someone was here to look after everything."

Amy smiles at me. "Sure thing," she says, obviously pleased to help.

I realize then that I'm still sitting in the car, talking to her through an open window. It must seem strange. I guess it *is* strange.

I close the window, turn the ignition off – John and Kiki mercifully quiet now, but making me wonder again if I just imagined the whole thing – and open the door, swinging myself out.

"How about a cup of coffee?" I ask. That's sounds normal, I think, although I wonder – deep down – whether I'll ever be normal again.

<u>3</u>

I sit in the fields, grass feather-light at my fingertips, warmed by the sun.

Amy is in the stables giving medicines to the horses that need them. I tried to act normally whilst I drank coffee with her, but I knew that the more time we spent together, the more suspicious she became that something was wrong. I can't blame her; my mind is set on one thing only, and everything else is extraneous. *What is going on?*

I checked the internet, just in case Ben *had* been lying to me, but there is no doubt about it; today is Thursday, October 9th, the Thursday *before* Artie's party. There's no information about any dead body, and I don't suppose there would be, given that she doesn't die until Saturday night. Doesn't she?

There are no red moons expected anytime soon either, according to various websites. And yet the image of that blood-red moon, towering above it all, watching with silent understanding, is still hard to put out of my mind. It sparked something – memories? – that I cannot grasp, although I keep trying. The memory is there somewhere, like those black lines that sometimes float in your eyes; it goes when you concentrate on it, forever out of reach.

And now I'm back outside, lying where the girl lay that night, broken head cradled in my lap. The feelings come back to me, so intense I cannot deny them. Seeing the naked body running through the long grass towards me, red light playing over her otherwise pale flesh, collapsing into my arms, her blood running over my own skin; her face bruised, swollen; teeth cracked, broken; her eyes, so terrified, so desperate, the most helpless eyes I have ever seen, eyes that must have seen unspeakable horrors, endured unimaginable suffering; eyes which finally went dark, the spark of life leaving them forever, leaving an empty shell where there had once been a beautiful young girl. I will remember those eyes forever, and instinctively I know – my internal prosecutor-self be damned! – that I imagined none of it. I'm not crazy. I am *not* crazy.

I get up and stagger back to the house, reaching for the telephone. I dial Artie's number, the house a blur around me. I know how to prove it. I *will* prove it.

"Hello?" Artie's voice answers.

"Hi Artie, I'm really sorry to bother you. I don't know why, but I was just wondering if your brother, the one who's coming up here, I was wondering if he has a beard?"

I've met his brother, I know I have. Tall and

strong, like Artie. Hair thinning, but he definitely has a beard, a full beard. And he was there alone, wife and kids left back in Seattle.

"And is he coming alone, or with his family?" I ask anxiously before Artie has even replied to the first question.

"Why," Artie laughs, "are you interested in him?"

Of course that would be what Artie thinks. I shouldn't be asking, of course, and yet I need to know. I laugh nervously. "No, nothing like that, I just have a . . . premonition, and I was wondering if I was right. Sounds weird, huh?"

Artie laughs again. "Yeah, it does kinda. But not as weird as some, I guess. Well, the answer is that Patrick has *never* had a beard, not so long as I've known him anyway, which is pretty much his entire life. And his wife and kids will be coming with him I'm afraid, so you'll have no luck there." His tone is playful, but I'm not in the mood.

"Honestly Artie, I am *not* interested in your brother. I was just wondering, that's all." I pause, my brain hurting inside my head. "I have to go."

"Okay, well, I'll see you Saturday night, yeah? You still coming?"

"Yes," I say uneasily, although I really don't know if I will anymore. "I'll see you then."

I put the phone down, cradle my head in my hands. I know I should have asked more questions. *Does his wife work as a travel agent? Is her name Julia? Do his kids have exams coming up?* But my first two had been shot down in flames, and I no longer have the heart to pursue it; Artie probably already thinks I'm one sandwich short of a picnic, and I don't want to make things worse. Rumors spread quick in small towns.

My mind goes back to the radio competition, and I start to realize that it must have only been a coincidence. A coincidence, fed by paranoia.

The doctor was right; I imagined the whole thing.

I open my bag, take out the bottle of pills and stare at it. Minutes go by, my eyes transfixed, the opaque glass pulling me in like a dream. I remember the doctor telling me to take two pills, three times a day.

I see the girl's eyes in the glass, looking at me accusingly, the red moon high behind her.

I unscrew the cap and take four, washing them down with three fingers of gin.

I hear a ringing in my ears; my head is fuzzy, confused, heavy.

I am in bed, and I know I've been here for some time. Not sleeping, but not fully conscious either. Drifting; just drifting. I don't know where.

It is dark outside, and I check the time. Just after eleven at night; still Thursday.

Still October 9th.

The ringing persists, and I finally understand that it is the telephone. I grope for it clumsily, knocking it off the bed stand.

I snatch it up from the floor, answer the call. "Hello?" I hear myself say, a voice outside of myself.

"Jessica? Are you okay?" It is Artie, and I become slightly more alert.

"I'm . . . yes, I'm okay."

"Sorry to call so late, but I just had to ring you, I don't know how you knew, but it's hard to believe."

"What do you mean?" I ask, levering myself up onto one elbow, curious.

"My brother. Pat. I just picked him up from the airport – by himself, his wife and kids decided to stay at the last minute, his wife's busy, his kids have got exams – and, get this, you'll never believe it – he's grown a beard. A beard! Never had one before, and there he is at the airport, and I barely recognize him. A beard! How did you know?"

I stare at the bottle of pills by my side, a quarter gone; the gin bottle is half empty too. "I don't know," I murmur, too many thoughts rushing through my head now, closing it down, darkness spreading across my vision. The mind can only take so much before it reaches its limit. Mine has been reached, beyond any doubt.

I pass out, the phone falling from my inert hand back to the bedroom floor.

DAY THREE

1

Noises filter through my slumbering consciousness.

Birds calling in the distance, their song muted; the scrape of metal on metal, piercing, shuddering; voices, drifting in from rooms beyond my own.

Still unable to open my eyes, inured by sleep, I try and listen to the voices. They are the voices of men, women; working voices; professional voices.

Was it just a dream? I wonder. Waking up, the crime scene gone, my visit to the police precinct, the doctor, the pills, the radio? I sigh. *Yes,* I decide, *it must have been a dream.* The voices are the voices of police officers. It is Sunday morning.

My eyes open finally, thick and crusty. I look up at a ceiling that is not my own.

Fully alert in an instant, my eyes wide now, I look around me, not believing what I am seeing, not understanding.

I am in a police cell.

The white walls seem to crowd me, reflective paint

disorientating me further. I am on a steel cot, bolted to the floor. A metal door bars my exit, thick steel with a long horizontal slot so officers can check in on their prisoners.

I am a prisoner.

I am fully clothed, but they are not the clothes I was wearing last night.

What happened?

I play the events back through my mind. Driving home, the radio contest, speaking to Amy, my call to Artie, taking the pills, drinking, Artie calling me back. Passing out in my bedroom.

Did I get back up, get changed, leave the house without realizing? I remember the bottle of gin. Did I do something stupid?

I am off the cot now, banging on the steel door. Moments later I see the grey eyes of a middle-aged man peering through at me.

"Yes ma'am?" the eyes say.

"What charge am I being held on?" I demand.

The eyes look at me strangely; the man beyond the door is surprised. "You were arrested last night on the charge of aiding and abetting a homicide, ma'am."

My blood turns to ice. *Homicide?* "Whose?" I ask quickly.

"We don't know the victim's name yet, but it's the young girl found on your farm last night."

Last night? My mind works frantically, trying to calculate time-frames, figure out what's going on. I was right about the day, at least; it is Sunday morning, the day after the girl died. My second Thursday must have been a dream, a product of an overactive imagination.

Which means I was arrested on Saturday night; after the party, after I found the body. It was just last night, but it suddenly seems so long ago. I struggle to remember what happened.

I went to bed, struggled to sleep, took the pills the EMTs gave me, drank some gin, finally managed to drift off. And then?

Nothing. My mind is a blank. But presumably I must have done or said something to incriminate myself? I see myself stalking down the stairs, throwing the front door open, announcing my guilt to the gathered officers. *It was me!* And yet, even with no memories to the contrary, I know that this can't be true. It is *not* true.

"How –"

"Save your questions please ma'am." The eyes cut me off brusquely. "Captain De Nares has been waiting for you to wake up. He wants to carry on your interview. I'll have breakfast brought to you."

The eyes disappear behind the sliding bar, leaving me alone once more.

Captain De Nares? I remember the name now, printed on the card given to me by the ABI officer last night. Yes. Captain De Nares.

My mind is so full, so tired, so confused; I think it will explode, and my hands grip my throbbing temples.

I sigh and sink back onto the metal cot. Whatever memories are in my head, they are as well protected as this cell. I'm not going to get any answers there.

And so I sit back, and wait for my interview.

"Case number two-four-six-alpha, second interview of suspect Jessica Elaine Hudson, held under the charge of aiding and abetting in the unlawful homicide of unknown female victim. Interview led by Captain Georges De Nares of the Alaska State Troopers, Bureau of Investigation, Major Crimes Division. Lieutenant Peter Michaels of the ABI, and Palmer Police Department Chief of Police Ben Taylor also present."

I watch from my collapsible metal chair at the man sat opposite me, reading off a crib sheet into the digital recorder on the table between us. Tanned skin, thick wavy hair, slim runner's body making him look younger than he probably is. I wonder if that is a help or a hindrance in his line of work.

In the corner of the room, Ben sits somewhat nervously, his large frame looking faintly ridiculous in the small chair. I can see he is uncomfortable with being here at all, and I wonder why.

"Okay Ms. Hudson, let's start from the beginning once more." The man's tone is smooth, easy. "We didn't really make much headway last night, so perhaps the morning will give us all a fresh perspective. Would you like some coffee?"

"Please," I say, nodding my head. Caffeine would be good. I have a million questions swimming around my head, and I feel the indignant rage of being imprisoned bubbling away just under the surface, but I keep a lid on it, knowing that it would do more harm than good to display it. They evidently already think I am involved in the girl's death in some way, and I don't want to appear aggressive. Added to which, I still have no idea how I came to be here; perhaps there *is* a reason, after all.

De Nares rises and steps out of the room for coffee, leaving me and Ben sitting awkwardly; he avoiding eye contact, me nervously drumming my fingers on the Formica table-top. I realize what I'm doing and stop immediately; it won't help my case to look nervous, I know that much.

De Nares returns, puts two cups down on the table and looks at me, smiling. Thirty seconds later he is still smiling, face otherwise unmoving. He wants me to speak first. Instead, I take the cup of coffee and start sipping at it. The harsh lights above start to hurt my head.

"So tell us again what happened," De Nares says finally.

I put the cup down, nod my head. "Okay. I was at the party at Arthur Jenkins' house, that can be verified by a lot of people. I left about eleven, half-eleven, and -"

"Sorry Ms. Hudson, I mean tell us what happened *before* last night."

"Before?" I ask, confused once more.

De Nares looks at me kindly. "Why don't we start last Thursday? You came into the police precinct, demanded to know what was going on. You told Chief Taylor about the death of a young girl on your farm."

I am shocked.

Beyond shocked.

I came in last Thursday? But didn't that just happen in a dream?

My mind starts to disintegrate as I fail to compute this new revelation, and De Nares continues, oblivious to the storm raging within me.

"Evidence item Twelve-B, recording of statement made by suspect last Thursday, October ninth, to Chief Taylor of the Palmer PD." De Nares places a mini-recorder on the desk, presses *Play*.

"The party hasn't happened yet. It isn't until October eleventh, this Saturday night . . . two days away. It's not real. What you claim to have seen; it can't *be real."* It is Ben's voice, the recording he made last Thursday, the Thursday I thought I'd dreamed. I know my voice will be next, and I prepare myself.

"But it is *real. I saw her, I held her head in my lap as she died."*

"Who is this girl?"

"I don't know!"

"Can you describe her?"

"She was young, a teenager. Dark hair, but some had been torn out. Pale skin, cut and bruised all over. She was naked, completely naked . . . She had green eyes, I think. About the same height as me, probably between five feet two and five feet four. She had . . . ligature marks on her wrists, on her ankles, around her neck. Burns, maybe from cigarettes. Possible bite marks. Her teeth and nose were broken . . ."

I hear my tears on the recorder, and De Nares clicks it off. He has made his point, and at least now I know why I am here.

"So could you please explain to us," De Nares says in his smooth, calming tone, "how it is you described the victim – *exactly* as she appeared when we saw her on Saturday night – *two and a half days before the event?"*

And there it is, as clear as day; I am being held because I reported a crime which hadn't happened yet, my description suggesting foreknowledge that such a crime was going to occur, which further suggests that I was directly involved in some way.

Which also means, even more disturbingly, that last Thursday was *not* imagined, I did *not* dream it; it really happened. But what does *that* mean?

"Why is it being treated as a homicide?" I ask next, trying to think professionally, keep all the other things at bay, unwilling to face them.

"Cause of death was confirmed as relating to injuries sustained over the course of several days, injuries inflicted by other parties. Specifically, complications from a compounded skull fracture, from what appears to be a blow to the head with a heavy blunt instrument such as a ball hammer." De Nares doesn't change his expression as he speaks, but his eyes twinkle reflexively; he wants to get a reaction from me.

"Other parties?" I ask. "How do you know more than one person is involved?"

"The victim was raped," De Nares says matter-of-factly. "Multiple times. Vaginally *and* anally. It was a mess down there." He says this last with only vaguely concealed disgust, and I finally realize that this man hates me. He is doing his best to be professional, but he thinks I know something, and he hates me for it. "We found traces of semen in the victim's throat and vagina, and inside and around the anus. Possibly from more than one man. So it's clear that there were others involved."

He pauses, sips from his coffee cup; waiting again, hoping I will speak, fill in some of the gaps. Yet how can I? What can I say? I don't know anything.

But I am hit again with the horror of what happened to that poor girl. I will never even know what atrocities she was subjected to, what kind of living hell she was forced to endure. Only the girl knew how it felt.

May God be with you.

I choke back my sobs, realizing that De Nares is speaking again. "What can you tell me about the vulva, Ms. Hudson?"

"Excuse me?"

"The vulva. Why was it closed like that?"

"I'm sorry," I say, "but I don't know what you're talking about."

De Nares keeps his gaze level as he throws half a dozen large photographs down onto the table-top. "I am showing Ms. Hudson photographs of the victim taken at autopsy," he says for the recorder.

My blood turns to ice once more as I look at the pictures.

The girl's pale, naked body is lying on a metal examination table, a hunk of meat to be dissected and examined. There is no life in her; none at all.

The cuts and bruises seem worse in these pictures, drawn out by the bright lights of the autopsy lab, the dark of night no longer covering them. I want to be sick.

I see the close-ups, photographs taken of the poor girl below the waist. I gasp involuntarily; her vulva has been sewn closed, the labial lips pierced crudely and tightened together with thick black thread.

De Nares watches for my reaction. "What purpose is being served by this?" he asks. "Why was it sewn closed?" He leans across the table, and I can feel the intensity of his gaze, eyes boring into me, and I feel myself coming undone, unable to speak. I can only look in horror at the pictures, listen to the captain's stark accusations. "Did you sew it?" he asks gently.

I see Ben over in the corner, quiet and uncomfortable. I still cannot speak. De Nares edges closer, his tone changing. "Did you watch them fuck her? Did you watch them fuck her, and then shove a fat needle through her lips, sewing her up closed? Watch as they fucked her again anyway?" His voice is strident now, rising in pitch.

"I . . . I . . ." But I cannot get any more words out.

"You know something!" De Nares shouts, banging his hand down on the table. "Look at the pictures! Look at them! You know who did this, don't you? Who are they?" He hits the table again, eyes boring into me. "Who are they?" he demands again, almost a scream.

I shake my head, at a loss to explain any of it. Then Lieutenant Michaels puts a hand on De Nares' shoulder.

The captain nods, rises, then notes the time for the recorder and turns it off; he leaves the room with the other man. Ben looks down at his shoes.

I gather my breath, struggling to come to terms with what I've heard. The girl was raped and then sewn closed? What sort of person would do that? And why? It doesn't make any sense. And that's not even to mention the other issue – how did I know on Thursday what was going to happen on Saturday? Because that is what seems to have happened, if you remove all known physical laws from the equation. Either I went through the days up to the event, then travelled back in time; or else I experienced some sort of incredibly lengthy, detailed psychic vision.

I try and ignore the other possibility – that I am hallucinating the whole thing, that I never recovered from the gunshot wound, that I'm still lying in a coma back in Mount Sinai Hospital, dreaming the whole thing from my electrically-adjustable hospital bed, connected to drips which alternately feed and extract waste from my body, my lifeless eyes covered by lids which flicker from time to time, providing a small measure of hope for anyone that still cares.

The door opens then, and De Nares strolls back in, Michaels trailing behind him. Ben's eyes flick up, rest on the two ABI officers for a moment, then turn away. I wonder what's going through Ben's mind. Does he agree with them? Does he think I'm involved in some way?

Michaels sits back down, still watching obliquely

from the side-lines. De Nares pulls his own chair out, legs screeching against the tiled floor. Sitting down, he flicks the recorder back on, notes the time, continues the questioning.

"What can you tell us about Paul Southland?" The question catches me off-guard. What does Paul have to do with any of this?

"I was engaged to him, before an accident I suffered back in New York."

"The attack at the courthouse?"

I nod my head, then remember the recorder. "Yes. I woke up from a coma after six months, Paul had taken the ring off my finger and moved out."

"Nice guy. Have you spoken to him since?"

I consider lying, but decide against it; they'll find out soon enough anyway. "He called –" I pause as I work out the time-frame; even though my last memory is going to sleep on Thursday night, I have to remember that today is actually Sunday; he called me on Saturday night, before the party – "last night, before I left for the party, about six o'clock, I guess."

"Excuse me, so you actually left for the party last night?"

"Of course I left, I went to the party, then came home about eleven, half eleven." I see the look of confusion on De Nares' face, and wonder if it's genuine.

"Well, let's leave that for the moment, we'll get back into that later." He writes on the pad in front of him, the first time I've noticed it. I wonder what he's writing. He looks back up at me. "Let's get back to Paul

Southland. Why did he call you?"

"To apologize. He said he was sorry about everything, he realizes he acted terribly, what he did was awful, inexcusable, but could I find it in my heart to forgive him, he still loves me, wants to be with me." I feel a tear forming in my eye, wipe it away before it appears fully. "He wanted to come and see me."

"And what did you tell him?"

"I hung up."

De Nares pauses, chewing on the end of his pen. "Really?" he asks in a measured tone, before seeming to change tack. "Do you know where Paul is now?"

"New York, I presume."

De Nares nods his head, seeming to weigh things up. "He's right here in Alaska. He's being picked up right now, as a matter of fact." He looks at me, examining me. "Did you really not know?"

I shake my head, shocked. "I had no idea whatsoever."

"So what we have is a woman who reports a crime which hasn't happened yet, a crime which involves one male accomplice at the very least; and on the other, we have your ex-fiancée right here, thousands of miles from home."

The implication is clear; De Nares is insinuating that we kidnapped, raped and killed the girl together. "But the girl had obviously been held captive for days, some of the wounds didn't look recent, she looked like time had been spent . . ."

"Yes, time *had* been spent abusing her. The doctors

think whoever's responsible took between three and five days doing those things to her."

"But Paul must have only just got here. If he called me at six, he couldn't have got to Alaska before this morning, after the girl was found, after –"

"The call originated from a payphone in Anchorage," De Nares says, cutting me off. "He was already here when he called you."

For the first time, I am truly nervous. "How long has he been here?" I ask, not wanting to know.

The answer comes too soon, the corners of De Nares' mouth turning up as he speaks, his tone accusatory, daring me to insist otherwise.

"Five days."

<u>2</u>

The three men have left me in the interview room to go for their lunch. A tray with a sandwich and a coke has been set in front of me, and I wonder if they are still watching me. I guess that De Nares is, at least.

They want me to stew in my juices for a while, make me think they know everything. They do seem to know more than me, but I realize that they are just fishing. They must be; I know I had nothing to do with it.

But Paul? Could Paul be involved in some way? Why is he here in Alaska? Why has he been here for a week without calling?

But I know Paul, and although he's not perfect, there's no way he'd be involved in anything like this. Why would he? He's successful, rich, attractive, charming. But wasn't Ted Bundy all those things? Well, maybe not rich, but attractive and charming, certainly. And what he did has gone down in history. Nobody ever suspected what he was capable of, not even those closest to him.

But Paul?

I'm sure there must be a reasonable explanation; he's probably here on business, wasn't sure whether to contact me, then finally decided to do it. He probably would've told me he was here if I hadn't put the phone down on him. Or maybe he came specifically to see me, then thought better of it, spent the past few days fighting an internal battle with himself, unwilling to admit to what he did, unable to apologize.

Yes, that's probably it. A man who never admits to doing wrong would probably take several days to work up to an apology. I bet he doesn't know anything about the girl.

I take a sip of the coke, a bite of the sandwich, not tasting either; my mind is too busy elsewhere.

Why had De Nares looked surprised when I'd told him Paul called just before I left for the party? Surely Ben must have filled him in on that? But he seemed to think I hadn't even been at the party.

I sigh. Just another bit of a puzzle I might never piece together.

I look down at my plate, see that it is empty. I pull the cup towards me, see that it's empty too. I push them away. I see paint peeling from the corner of the walls by the ceiling. From condensation. The sweet, adrenalin-scented sweat of the accused?

I shake the thoughts free. It's time to get my mind straight, before De Nares gets back.

What do I know? I go through the facts as I

understand them: my memories of Saturday night; waking up back on Thursday morning, driving to the precinct – *this* precinct – and asking about the case; realizing that the case wasn't even open yet, the event hadn't even happened, it was several days prior to Saturday night; taking the pills, the gin, waking up back here on Sunday morning, *this* morning. Not waking up at my house. Waking up *here*, at the police precinct, charged with aiding and abetting a homicide. Because of what I'd said on Thursday. The ramification was clear.

What I did on Thursday – my second *Thursday – has altered reality. Things didn't happen last night like they did the first time. So what* did *happen last night?*

The door opens, the three cops march in.

It's time to find out.

I decide to take charge and start asking questions of my own as soon as De Nares flicks on the recorder. I'm betting that they'll let me; interviewers always like interviewees to talk. They might say something incriminating.

"My memory of last night is a blur," I say. "It was a horrible night. I'm . . . confused. Did I go to the party at Artie's house?"

I can see the suspicion in De Nares' eyes. I know what he's thinking; he's thinking that I'm already trying to appear as if I'm not all there, in preparation for a future insanity plea should this ever see the inside of a courtroom. But I just want to know what happened.

"No," De Nares says eventually. "You did not.

Which is why I questioned you earlier when you mentioned leaving for the party. If you did, you never got there. According to your statement last night –" De Nares breaks off, pulls a sheet of paper from a file next to him and starts to read – "I was woken by my dogs growling. I moved to the kitchen and grabbed my gun – I'm still scared about things after what happened back in New York, you understand – and started looking out of the windows. Then there was a weak knocking on the door, and I opened it, gun raised, and saw the young girl lying there on the porch." He looks up from the paper. "You then claim to have pulled her inside, where she subsequently died. You then called Chief Taylor, who came directly from the party. Does any of this sound familiar?"

I shrug my shoulders. It does and it doesn't. It's not the same as I remember, but close enough. I try and think. If I was disturbed about what I thought was going to happen, perhaps I decided not to go to the party. Perhaps I thought I was going crazy, couldn't face other people? The trouble is, I don't know; it was me, but at the same time, it wasn't.

"According to Chief Taylor, last Thursday, before he clicked on the recorder to take your statement-slash-confession, you claimed to have attended the party. He says you spoke about the events of Saturday night as if they'd already happened. Would you care to comment on this?"

I can tell that this element of the case confuses him, and he is genuinely interested in what I have to say.

But again, I think I can guess what he suspects – it's all part of my pre-planned insanity defense.

I wonder what to say, decide quickly. To hell with it. I'll tell them the truth, at least as I understand it. Put it out there, see what they make of it.

"Do you believe in premonitions?" I ask as my opening gambit.

"No," De Nares says. "But please carry on."

"It's the only way I can explain any of it. I woke up on Thursday morning, convinced that it was Sunday, that I'd gone to the party on Saturday night, walked home and seen a girl running across the fields of my farm. The dream, the vision – whatever you want to call it – was so vivid that I was sure it must be true.

"That's why I turned up here on Thursday thinking it was Sunday, why I asked what was happening with the investigation. When Chief Taylor told me what day it was, how the party hadn't even happened yet, I freaked out. Who wouldn't? So I didn't go to the party, maybe trying to change my vision, but the girl staggered onto my farm anyway.

"So you see, if you think about it, it must have been a premonition. What else could it be? I don't even believe in that sort of thing myself, but what physical evidence do you have? You must have searched my home by now, and I know you won't have found anything. All you have is a statement I gave on Thursday about an event I thought had already happened. I don't think it would stand up in court."

I purposefully don't mention the fact that I have no

recollection of the new pattern of events between Thursday and Sunday. I reflect on the most obvious, yet utterly impossible scenario – that I've somehow moved through time, my days muddled, my actions affecting the outcome of each new day – and decide that staying with the premonition is my safest bet. There is a plethora of cases which deal with suspected psychic premonitions, it is one of those strange things regarded as being unlikely but "possible". Time travel, on the other hand? I don't think I could sell it; I don't even believe it myself.

"I have another opinion on this," De Nares says in his smooth, even voice. "One that doesn't involve a belief in the supernatural." He smiles at me, but it is the false smile of a predator. "I think you had prior knowledge of this crime. Either you were directly involved in the kidnap and torture of the girl, or whoever was, confided in you. Both possibilities mean that you know who else was involved. Perhaps it was your ex-fiancée, mysteriously here in Alaska. Maybe it's some weird kind of game you two play. Maybe he kidnapped the girl, raped her in front of you as a warning, a message – 'come back to me or this is what will happen to you', that sort of thing. Or maybe it was other people entirely, and Paul Southland's presence here is just a coincidence.

"The bottom line is that your statement on Thursday shows prior knowledge of an event which led to the death of a young woman. We have it on record." He smirks. "You were a prosecutor yourself, Ms.

Hudson. What would you have made of a 'psychic premonition' defense? You'd have been over the moon, knowing that no jury in the country, no jury in the *world*, would ever buy such complete nonsense."

He's right, of course. But I don't need to convince a jury; not yet at any rate. First things first, as always; I just need to convince someone in this room.

"But if I was involved in what happened to this girl, why would I have made that statement on Thursday? What would I have been trying to achieve? If I wanted to confess, why wouldn't I have just confessed? If I wanted to warn you, save the girl, why wouldn't I have just told you where to find her? Why this elaborate deception, to try and make it appear that I thought Thursday was Sunday?"

De Nares shrugs his slim shoulders. "I admit, I don't know. My initial feeling is that it's part of some sick game. You get yourself involved in the investigation, it gives you some feeling of control, of power. You're laughing at us." He sits back in his chair, dark eyes level with my own. "A girl gets kidnapped, raped, tortured, killed; you know who it is, maybe even got involved yourself; and you're sitting there laughing at us." The disgust was back in his voice, barely disguised.

"I know it sounds unbelievable," I say, trying to keep myself calm in the face of De Nares' brutal accusations. "Have you spoken to Arthur Jenkins?" I ask next, a thought occurring to me.

De Nares nods briefly. "Yes, we've spoken to

everyone at the party."

"Okay. Did he tell you that I called him on Thursday? After I came here, after I realized it was only Thursday, I wanted to know if I was going crazy, or if there was something else going on. I called Artie, asked about his brother. In my dream, or vision, his brother Pat had a beard. He looked like Artie, but with a beard. And so I called and asked him. He said no, Pat had never had a beard. I felt bad, like I *was* losing it; but then later on, Artie called back, he'd picked his brother up from the airport and he *did* have a beard." I level my own gaze back at De Nares. "How would I have known that? His own *brother* didn't know."

"Mr. Jenkins did share that with us, yes. And we are investigating the fact that you and Patrick Jenkins were previously acquainted. He has certain priors which make him of interest to this investigation."

What? I realize that now they're tying me to Pat, insinuating that he too had something to do with it. My actions on Thursday have incriminated myself *and* Patrick Jenkins, it seems. I wonder what prior convictions he has against him. I think back to the party, remember how he tried to get a young girl to drink. What was his motivation? Was it sexual? To get her drunk, take advantage of her? *Was* he involved in what happened to the girl on my farm? I think of another avenue to pursue.

"Last Thursday, I told Chief Taylor that Pat had been involved in some trouble at the party, something to do with giving drink to an underage girl, it caused a scene with Pat, Artie and the girl's parents. I'd seen the chief get involved, break it up." I turn to Ben, hiding away in the corner. "Did that happen?" I ask him directly.

"Yes," he says, nodding his head slowly. It was the first thing I'd heard him say all day. I see De Nares turning around, annoyed that Ben was answering the question. Ben saw the captain's look. Ignored it. "I thought it was weird when it happened. I remember someone telling me that Pat had been seen pouring some brandy from a hip flask into a girl's orange juice. I instantly thought of you." He looks at me with a combination of curiosity and fear. I think a part of him believes me. "You *knew*," he says, shaking his head. "You knew what would happen. I remember, I wondered what else would happen. I wondered if you were right about the girl." He clears his throat, clearly uncomfortable voicing these thoughts in front of De Nares and Michaels. "I wasn't surprised when you called me later. I think I already knew you would." His voice is unsure, but his eyes say it all. He believes me. Or at least he is open to the idea that all is not as it seems.

De Nares ignores Ben's words of support, choosing to interpret them in a different way. "This is just further evidence that you had prior contact with Patrick Jenkins. It seems that the whole thing was pre-planned; your statement on Thursday, your call to Arthur Jenkins, Patrick Jenkins then spiking that girl's drink, just as you'd 'predicted'. It's just another nail in your coffin, don't you see?"

Ben is sitting back, silent once more. No matter what he believes, what his gut tells him, this is not his investigation.

"It is entirely circumstantial," I say eventually. "There's absolutely no evidence to link me to Pat Jenkins *or* the girl."

De Nares just smiles at me, unperturbed by this absence. "Not yet," he says with total confidence. "But the evidence is there somewhere Ms. Hudson, and I'm going to find it. You can count on it."

<u>3</u>

It is later in the day, and I'm back on the couch in Ben's office. The same doctor I saw on Thursday is sitting across from me, peering at me through a pair of thick spectacles. I wonder if she needs them, or if they're just for show. I still can't remember her name.

De Nares' questioning had continued for the next couple of hours, but it was the same thing over and over again. Pretty soon even he realized we weren't getting anywhere.

It was then that I'd realized that I'd been sitting there all morning answering questions without a lawyer, which proves I'm not myself. What was I thinking? When I mentioned this, De Nares told me I'd waived my right to a lawyer the night before. Apparently, I'd been happy to answer questions with no legal counsel present. I didn't believe him, but he'd shown me the paperwork and – sure enough – it had my signature on it.

But that was then, and this is now; I immediately

pulled the plug on the interview, and had been escorted back to my cell. It was Ben who'd suggested having another chat with the doctor, and I'd agreed; after all, it can't do any harm. She can't reveal what we speak about without my permission. And it would also take my mind off thinking about who I want to represent me. Logic screams at me to call my father, but I'm doing my best to ignore that logic at the moment.

"So what do *you* think is going on?" the doctor asks me.

I shake my head. "I honestly don't know. You said the other day it might be related to the gunshot wound. Do you still think so?"

She shifted in her seat. "I don't know. We need to have a more detailed look at you, to be honest. I believe the ABI is looking at Thursday's statement as a confession of sorts, and this would certainly be the easier story to believe." She smiles weakly. "I'm sorry."

I persist. "But is the other thing, the alternative, is it *possible*?"

"If you're asking me if the damage to your brain has resulted in your developing what can only be described as some sort of *psychic* ability, I don't know. I will admit, there have been cases made for the same thing, but nothing has ever been verified. It's a fantastical claim, isn't it? But on the other hand, what we know about the brain is . . . limited, at best. We *think* we know a great deal, and of course, we know a lot more now than we ever did before, but I fear we've yet to scratch the surface. *Anything* is possible, Ms.

Hudson." She clears her throat. "But the balance of probability suggests that you had prior knowledge of the event, and that's the bottom line."

"That's the bottom line," I repeat pointlessly. I know she's right. Nobody's going to care about some out-there theory about psychic powers or time travel. Are such things possible? The best that can be said for them is that they can't be ruled out; they can't yet be *dis*-proven. But that's a long way from a water-tight defense, and I know it.

So who *will* I get to defend me? My father is the best I know, but this isn't really his thing. What I need is someone experienced in cases which deal predominantly with the psychological aspects of the defendant. But then again, with my father, it might not even get that far; he's an expert at finding fault with the prosecution's case. Most of his defendants don't even see the inside of a courtroom. And yet I don't trust him.

I settle back into the leather couch, my mind roaming; I can feel the doctor's eyes on me, but I do not engage her in my thoughts. I know what I will do; I'll speak to people in my old office, get a recommendation. I wonder for a moment who Paul's going to get to represent *him?* Maybe *he'll* hire my father.

There is a knock on the door. The doctor looks at me, and I nod my head. "Come in," she says.

Captain De Nares pokes his head through the door, a smile barely disguised on his handsome features. "Have you decided on your legal representation yet?" he asks.

I shake my head. "I'm going to have to make some phone calls."

"Well, you'll have to make them from Wildwood."

"Wildwood?" I ask.

De Nares nods, his smile widening. "Wildwood Pre-Trial Facility, Wildwood Correctional Complex. Nice little place on the Kenai Peninsula. I sent some of the case materials through to a judge this morning, seeing as you waived your right to legal counsel. He signed a warrant to have you moved to a more secure facility, confirming the charge of aiding and abetting a homicide."

I am too stunned to speak. I'm going to prison?

"I understand that you now wish to have a lawyer, and that's fine. But you'll have to arrange it all once you get to Wildwood, I'm afraid. Prison transport will be here to pick you up within the hour."

His smile breaks into a grin now; a grin that tells me my life will soon be over.

I sit in my cell in Palmer Police Precinct, pondering my immediate future.

Prison transport will pick me up in twenty minutes, and then I'm in the system, trapped. A judge will set bail, and they'll look at my assets and set a high price on my freedom. Too much? My father could probably pay it, but I'm not going to ask *him* for any favors.

So there I'll be, a prisoner in Wildwood. I'll get someone good to represent me, that's a given. But what then?

I shake my head, place it heavily in my hands. I just don't know.

A pain races through my heart, a sudden jolt of adrenaline as a realization hits me.

If they find who really killed the girl, they'll see I'm not connected to it. Yes, that's it. They need to find out who's *really* involved.

Names race through my head; Patrick Jenkins, Paul Southland, *Arthur* Jenkins. The name mentioned by Ben's deputy last night – *Doug Menders?* All are avenues to explore, and I hope that De Nares and his team are doing so. But I know De Nares already *has* me, and he believes I will lead him to the others involved. I wonder if this will make him lose focus, concentrate on questioning me when he should be actively looking for someone else.

The pain in my heart hits me again, and I know that *I* need to find out who killed the girl. I can't rely on anyone else; I need to do it myself.

And yet how can I? I will soon be trapped, unable to escape, locked in a steel and concrete box while I wait for my day in court.

But I also know it doesn't have to be that way. Instinctively, I *know* there is another way. Where this certainty comes from I have no idea, but the idea forces itself upon me with heart-rending surety.

I break down what I think has happened, clear to me for the first time.

I see a girl die in my arms. I go to sleep, and wake up on another day, a day from the past. I make a statement to the police, I think I'm going crazy, a doctor gives me pills. *I go to sleep*, and when I wake up, time has been rearranged once more.

I sleep, and time changes.

Does it sound crazy? Of course it does. And yet – unless I *am* crazy, and I'm hallucinating the whole thing, and I simply can't accept *that* – this is clearly what is happening.

Why it's happening, I have no idea. Is it linked to the gunshot wound to my brain? Is it linked to the horrifying experience of the girl dying in my arms? Is it something to do with the red moon, the one I saw that night, but no one else did? The red moon which stirs memories in me, which rise to the surface only to be dashed beneath the waves of consciousness?

But whatever is happening, and for what reason, one thing is clear to me at last; if I sleep, I might slip through time again, wake on another day. Which day? I don't know; I don't know how it works, or even if it *will* work.

Ten minutes left. Can I get to sleep in ten minutes, my mind on fire with its thoughts? But I must. I don't want to go to Wildwood. I don't. I'm not sure what it will do to my mind. Right here, right now, I feel I've got a chance. I don't trust my mind to cope if I'm in prison. I lay back on my metal cot, close my eyes.

I see the girl, face bloated, blood oozing from the corners of her eyes; I see my father in court, shouting, arguing, pointing, winning; Paul bent over a dead body, blood dripping from vampire teeth; a masked gunman,

107

rifle exploding towards my face; the tears of a small girl, her dreams ripped from her; the screams of my brother as he throws himself from his apartment window, falling to his death; the hideous glow of the red moon watching it all.

A bang on the cell door breaks my reverie completely, and I sag, hopeless. So close. *So close.*

The door opens and De Nares comes in, accompanied by two armed prison guards. "It's time," he says pleasantly, as if he's picking me up for a date.

The guards approach me, handcuffs out. "Hands please, ma'am," one of them says, and I know this is it. My last chance.

I raise my hands as the men approach. I smile, watch as they relax slightly.

And then I turn and run, run straight for the wall on my right, head down.

My head connects hard with the concrete and I see stars, my vision swimming, everything around me a blur. There is one second of final consciousness as I fall backwards, look up at the ceiling.

And then I am gone.

DAY FOUR

1

Jack smiles at me, and I smile back.

His handsome face changes before me, the fullness of youth bleeding out of him; I see him in his black leather jacket, studs in his nose and eyebrows, older now. I see him in jail, my father there also, spit flying out of his mouth as he shouts violently at my brother, shaking him by the shoulders, their faces just inches apart.

The flesh on Jack's face wastes away further, leaving him gaunt, a pasty skull atop skinny shoulders. We are in a dingy apartment and the jacket is off now, his t-shirt sleeve hitched up, his teeth pulling tight on the cord around his bicep. I see the relief in his eyes as the needle enters his scarred upper arm, the pain leaving him in an instant as he presses the plunger.

I hear a noise outside and open the door to see Beauty running down the corridor towards us, galloping, his muscles rippling. I back away but he crashes through the door and rears up in front of us. I hold Jack in my arms while Beauty's hooves hover above us, threatening to crush us. Then he lets out a feral shriek, and I see his eyes for the first time, blood-red and fear-crazed. His hooves crash down in front of us, blood-spittle flying from his mouth, teeth sharp and deadly, coated in foamy blood. He shakes his head and the blood is cast loose, spraying the dark walls from one side of the apartment to the other.

I pull Jack's head into my shoulder, protecting him, but then he wakes and I feel his body jerking. He cries out in blind panic, pulling away from me, and then he's gone, running the other way.

I reach out after him but he's too fast, he's at the window already.

He doesn't stop, but just keeps on going, right through the glass. The window shatters and Jack disappears into the night beyond.

I race to the window, see Jack below, his eyes looking up at me as he falls, his arms extended. I reach out for him, but he's gone too far already. It's so far down I hardly see him hit the sidewalk; I just see the halo of blood around his body, highlighted by the sodium glow of half-broken streetlights.

I turn back inside the apartment, but Beauty is gone. I turn back to the street, and Jack is gone also.

I look up at the sky, and watch as a red moon rises above the horizon. I watch that moon, and realize that it is watching me right back. I feel it as it watches us all, seeing everything, knowing everything.

Hopeless, all I can do is fall to my knees and cry.

Half asleep, I think about the dream.

I never saw Jack the day he died, was never in the apartment, and yet for years I've dreamt that I was there, unable to stop him, unable to help him. I know it's suppressed guilt. He was troubled, he was involved with bad people, into drugs, I could see it was taking its toll on him, he was losing control, and yet I never said anything, never *did* anything.

But I've never seen Beauty there before, never seen the red moon. I wonder what it means.

I sense movement next to me, and my eyes open, fully awake in an instant.

And I gasp as I realize I am in bed with a man.

A naked man.

His back is to me, wide and muscular. I have no idea who it is. Slowly, my hands search my own body, and I feel that I am naked too. I can smell the sweat on both of us, sickly sweet.

Unwilling to move, my eyes scan the room. It is still dark, and I wait for my eyes to adjust. Slowly – so painfully slowly – I start to be able to make out the basics.

We are in a king-size bed in the middle of a small bedroom, a door directly opposite. There is one night-stand, on *his* side of the bed. No pictures of a wife or family. A digital alarm clock which tells me the time is just after six in the morning; a shame it doesn't tell me the date. One old wooden wardrobe in the corner, a half-open chest of drawers, socks sticking out at odd angles.

A part of me breathes a sigh of relief. Whoever I'm in bed with, at least he's probably single. My eyes keep roaming, but I see nothing else.

I concentrate on my breathing, trying to get my heart-rate down. Who the hell have I slept with?

The good news, I suppose, is that I'm evidently not in Wildwood. Not unless Alaskan prisons are *very* liberal, at any rate. Which means that my theory must be correct – I go to sleep, I go through time.

Unless you're just crazy.

I ignore the little voice in my head, however much sense it makes, and begin to formulate my strategy.

Even more important than finding out who I'm in bed with, I need to find out what the date is. Have I travelled forward or backward? Has the girl died yet? Have I been arrested yet? Have I been to the police precinct to make my statement/confession yet?

I roll over in the bed, away from the strange man, and look down on the floor. *Yes*. My clothes. Slowly, carefully, I reach down to them, feeling around for the hard shape of my phone. I find it, pull it out and flick the screen on.

It's Thursday. I'm back on Thursday again? I check the exact date, and see that it's not the same Thursday. Instead, it's October 16th, four days *after* my visit to the cells of Palmer Police Department, five days since the girl died at my house. I wonder, helplessly, what's happened during those days.

I decide to become pro-active and slide my naked

body out from under the sheets, gather up my things from the floor and head for the bedroom door.

As I creep across the unpainted floorboards, my eye catches something on top of the drawers, and my head turns to get a better look.

I stifle a cry as I realize what it is.

A gun.

My heart leaps up to my mouth, but then I notice something else lying next to it.

A badge.

It is a golden shield, held fast to a black leather wallet.

I hear movement behind me, and turn to see the naked man turn over in his sleep, closed eyes looking sightlessly up towards the bedroom ceiling. I gasp in surprise.

The man is Ben Taylor, Chief of Police.

<u>2</u>

The bathroom is mercifully easy to find, directly across the small hall from Ben's bedroom, and I slip inside, lock the door behind me, and hit the lights. I saw stairs off to one side of the hall, so I guess I'm in a house rather than an apartment. I wonder if he lives alone, or if he shares with anyone.

I get changed quickly, nervous about exposing my body in this strange place. Pants on, I sigh with relief as I button my blouse. I feel protected.

I turn to the mirror and look at myself. As if the headache and booze-smell didn't already give the game away, my face tells the tale that I had too much to drink last night. Bags under my eyes, hair wild. I see I have make-up on, wonder why. Did Ben and I go out on a date?

I look closer. Even though I've slept in it, it's not run too much. Amazingly, it doesn't look too bad. *I* don't look too bad, all things considered.

But what the hell am I doing here? What's been

happening the last few days? Am I seeing Ben Taylor now? Or was it a one-off, something we should try and forget?

I realize that it's going to be difficult to find out without my sanity being called into question. The fact that I'm not in a psychiatric ward after knocking myself out on the cell wall indicates that I'm being perceived as sane, at least for the time being, and I don't want to jeopardize that by asking too many strange questions about things I should already know the answer to.

But I'm also not in prison; not in Palmer, Wildwood, or anywhere else. Which might mean that they've already caught whoever did it, or else at least have further evidence which has cleared me. Or else it means that my bail has been posted, which might also therefore mean that my father has become involved.

The fact that I'm in Ben's house hopefully indicates that I've been completely exonerated though. Would the Chief of Police take home a woman who's out on bail for aiding and abetting a homicide just outside his city limits? It seems unlikely.

I want to have a shower, but decide against it; I don't want to use the towels. It's strange, but I have no idea what my relationship is to the man in the next room. I've never been the type to go out, get drunk and wake up next to a stranger. It's just not me. Even when I was younger, rebelling against my father, the guys I slept with were all boyfriends. Bad, inappropriate boyfriends perhaps, but boyfriends nevertheless. This experience is entirely new to me, and I don't really know how to handle it.

I look at the toiletries on the sink and around the shower though. Just one of everything; one toothbrush, one tube of toothpaste, one soap, one shampoo, one shower gel, one razor. So at least he lives alone, and I'm unlikely to run into anyone else; I have to take small comforts where I can.

I turn back to myself. The clothes I'm wearing are nice; I might be wearing jeans, but they're my best jeans, and the blouse is a Chanel. It's as if I've dressed up for something low-key but special. Did I? Do I like Ben Taylor? It pains me, but I just don't know.

I think about the choice of clothes, wondering what they mean. I'm not wearing a dress, so I know we weren't at the theater, or dining out at a fancy restaurant. Jeans and a top. Almost casual, and yet I selected the best I've got in that department. I know how my mind works. I will have arranged to meet Ben, or he will have asked to meet me, to informally discuss some aspect of the case. I dressed up in an understated way, presumably because I was (*am?*) attracted to him, and wanted him to notice me as something more than a suspect. It obviously worked.

Unless I was trying to get information from him, and wore something nice to encourage him? Perhaps then drank a bit too much, and one thing led to another?

A sickening feeling hits me as I wonder if he drugged me. How would I know? But he's the police chief, and I can't believe he'd do that. He seems like an honest, good man. But then again, he's been through an acrimonious divorce, so presumably can't be entirely perfect. Although perhaps that's unfair; my fiancée broke up with me, and that was hardly my fault.

But you never can tell about people, my years in the courts taught me that much at least. What if *Ben* is the killer?

I shake my head, clearing it. *No*, I tell myself clearly, *no. That's paranoia talking.*

On the other hand though, paranoia is probably reasonable given my situation.

A thought occurs to me, and I fish my phone out of my pocket. Flicking it on, I check the call log.

Apparently I've been busy the last few days. There are several numbers I don't recognize, as well as some that I do. AER Headquarters. My own home number (whoever's looking after my horses?). My father's cell phone, mom's cell phone, and their home number back in Boston. The New York DA's office. And two other numbers – Ben Taylor (Cell) and Ben Taylor (Home). The first call came on Tuesday morning.

There are two interesting things about this, I think as I start to try and deduce what has been going on. The first is that I didn't have either of Ben Taylor's numbers on my phone prior to Sunday, at least as far as I remember. The second is that I've entered his first name *and* surname, something I normally do if it's for a formal relationship. Friends I normally just put in as a first name. I wonder if this confirms my previous suspicion that we were originally meeting up to discuss the case,

119

or in some sort of other, non-dating capacity.

On the other hand, it might just be because Ben is a common name and I've already got one or two in the phone book.

I groan inwardly. Damn, this is impossible! I'm trying to piece together the events of four whole days from my choice of clothes and a call list.

I access my text messages in the hope that I'll find something else.

Again, there are a lot, and I trawl through them. Most are from friends asking after me, and my replies reveal some useful information. In fact, a picture gradually begins to emerge.

It seems that most people don't know why I was arrested, and now appreciate that it was some sort of mistake anyway. It also becomes apparent that my father *has* become involved, getting the charges dropped due to lack of evidence. There are a couple of texts from him, wanting to meet up, presumably after he'd already negotiated my release. I haven't replied, and I wonder if I *have* met up with him, if he's still here in Alaska, or if he's already flown back to Boston. I wonder if Mom came with him. There are no messages from her; but then again, I might have spoken to her instead.

There's no news in the texts about Paul, and I wonder what's happened to him. Was he arrested, and if so, is he still in custody, or has he been released too? And if so, where is he now? It's strange that there are no calls or messages from him. Does this mean he's locked up, unable to use his phone? Or have I just deleted anything he might have sent me?

It also looks like Amy is staying in my house now, a semi-permanent guest whilst I sort things out. I hope I haven't been too unpleasant to live with.

The messages between me and Ben are fairly low-key and innocuous – "You still ok for tonight?" – "Yes" – "Okay, see you at seven" – and don't give me much to work with. There are no declarations of undying love, at least.

I note that this seven o'clock tryst was being arranged for *Tuesday* night, so at least I had the good grace to get a second date out of the man before I slept with him. I hope. There were calls, but no messages from yesterday.

I search for a Wi-Fi connection, but can't find one; just my luck. I won't be able to find out if there's been anything on the news yet.

I run a little water, splash it on my face, turn off the light and open the door.

It's time to see if there's anything to find in his house which might help me get a grasp on what the hell is going on.

3

I creep slowly down the stairs, careful to test each step for creaks. The floorboards are bare throughout the house, which seems old enough to have plenty of noise hardwired into it by the years.

In the dark, I put one hand on the rail and one on the wall to guide myself. There were three other doors upstairs, but I don't want to go rummaging around so close to Ben. At least when I make it downstairs and turn the lights on, I'll be able to relax a little.

The stairs lead straight down into the living room. I wonder whether the light will travel up the stairs to Ben's bedroom, but decide it's worth the risk – his door is closed, and it's further down the hall anyway. I fumble for a light switch, and when the place is lit I see the living area is open plan, an archway leading to a dining area and kitchen beyond.

The place isn't massive, but it's homely and comfortable. There's a beaten-up sofa to one side, a leather recliner having pride of place in front of the big-screen TV. I'd bet it has a beer cooler under the armrests; bachelor's paradise.

The floorboards are bare down here too, but in the light I can see why; it's oak hardwood, very pretty. There's a rug under the recliner and the coffee table next to it, and I guess it's to keep Ben's feet warm for those long nights in front of the TV, watching the game. I wonder if friends come around to join him. I hope so.

The dining table through the arch is nice, a family heirloom perhaps. It looks old, but barely used. I see the kitchen beyond, stains on the breakfast bar indicating this is where Ben does most of his eating. There and the recliner, anyway.

I notice a dark shape in the corner of the dining area, and turn to examine it. An upright piano, cheap but serviceable, its stool worn and well-used. Surprised, and immediately hating myself for that, I stroll over, looking at the sheets on the music rack. I see Chopin's *Scherzos No. 2 Opera 31* pushed to one side, the Duke Ellington Orchestra's *Take the "A" Train* lying victoriously atop it. With a twang of guilt, I check the box next to the piano, seeing a mix of classical and jazz pieces. I sense the classical is how he was trained, and how he feels he needs to practice, but his heart is pure jazz.

I am starting to understand what I might see in him.

I see a vinyl deck in the other corner; no i-pod for this man. Hundreds of albums are crammed into a sturdy pine bookcase, and I sift through them, learning about the man I slept with. John Coltrane's revolutionary 1965 album, *A Love Supreme*. The masterpiece *Time Out* by the Dave Brubeck Quartet. *Ellington at Newport*, with Gonzalves' 27-chorus saxophone solo. The relaxing bossa nova of *Getz/Gilberto*. Dozens more, a collector's collection. There are classical albums here and there, a few blues, some country, a little rock. But it's clear that jazz is Ben's passion.

My hand strokes the albums, fingers tracing the covers. I'm beginning to get some more of an idea of Ben Taylor, Chief of Police. Loneliness is the first word that comes to mind. A chair he sits in to eat his meals, listening to jazz by himself, maybe heading over to the piano to practice a few bars of his own from time to time. Losing himself in the music. My heart beats a little harder in my chest; I try and ignore the sensation.

I would guess loneliness is typical of a divorcé who's moved from his home town. I wonder why he got divorced. Work? A common problem with cops – they work terrible hours, and even when they do come home, they often bring it back with them. When you see some of the things people do to each other, it can make normal family life hard to cope with.

So if Ben is a police "lifer", will he bring his work back here with him? It's possible. I enter the kitchen, fill the kettle and turn it on; aimlessly leaf through a stack of mail by the bread bin. Through the windows I see it is still dark outside, although what little light there is gets reflected off the crisp layer of snow which must have fallen overnight.

I remember the coffee table and wander back to the living room, ignoring the dining area. The coffee table is littered with papers, and I sit down on the sofa to look through them. Strange really – I'm able to check through Ben's private papers with almost no guilt at all, but I'm loath to violate the sanctity of his leather recliner.

On the top there is a copy of the Anchorage *Daily News*, yesterday's edition. Open at the sports pages. I leaf back through it, examining each page closely. I find it all too quickly; five days on, and the poor girl still makes page two.

I read on, nervous.

Enquiries are ongoing into the death of a young girl on the grounds of a farmstead in the Matanuska-Susitna Valley. The authorities have yet to release the identity of the victim, but she is believed to have been in her teens, and to have died of injuries sustained through assault, aggravated by exposure.

Ex-New York District Attorney's Office prosecutor Jessica Hudson was released without charge two days ago after helping the Alaska Bureau of Investigation with their enquiries. Ms. Hudson relocated to Alaska after an organized crime shooting left her in a coma for six months back in New York. It is not believed the death is connected. However, Ms. Hudson's father – prominent Boston defense attorney Charles Hudson – has recently been in Palmer, and it is suspected that he negotiated his daughter's release after she was initially charged in connection to the girl's death.

Even more interestingly, Ms. Hudson's ex-fiancé, Paul

Southland, was also detained and charged in connection to the girl's death, although he too was recently released. He travelled to Anchorage from New York ten days ago, apparently in order to seek a reconcilement of some sort with Ms. Hudson. It is not known whether Mr. Southland and Ms. Hudson have seen one another since their release, but it is believed that Mr. Southland has now flown home to New York, although he is not allowed to leave the United States, pending the outcome of the ABI investigation.

The ABI has been quiet about the case, but it is believed that Captain De Nares, who is heading the investigation, has called in behavioral analysts from the FBI's Investigative and Operations Support Section, a unit of the National Centre for the Analysis of Violent Crime. This is often done in cases of serial murder.

Unconfirmed reports of the state of the dead girl's body may indicate that she was kidnapped and tortured, and parallels have been made with several outstanding cold cases where bodies of young girls were discovered dumped in wilderness areas in the locality, including Chugach State Park. Remains of several victims were discovered in 2010, although it is unknown how long ago they had been dumped there.

When asked about a possible connection between the cases, Captain De Nares said "At this stage, we are keeping an open mind about the case. It is being treated as a standalone crime, and any attempts to link it to previously unsolved cases are inaccurate, misleading, and seriously unhelpful. We are viewing this as a local crime at the moment, and have absolutely no evidence to suggest it is anything else. But I can assure the public that we are exploring every avenue available to us, and we will do everything in our power to bring justice to this girl and her family."

At the time of printing, it is believed that another non-local is helping the ABI with their enquiries and is currently being held at Palmer Police Precinct, where the investigation is based. Patrick Jenkins, a resident of Seattle, Washington, was visiting his brother Arthur when the girl's body was discovered at a nearby farm. He is apparently of interest to the investigation due to previous misdemeanor convictions of an unknown sexual nature. Authorities have refused to comment further on his involvement.

I put the paper down, run a hand through my hair. Well, *damn*. Great reporting. I didn't do a thing, I've been released without charge, and they still manage to make it look as if I'm involved in some way.

My mind turns to the other things suggested by the article, specifically the involvement of the FBI. Is this the work of a serial killer? I consider the state of the girl, her injuries. What De Nares told me, the fact she had been raped and then had her labial lips sewn closed. I wonder if there was any evidence of similar mutilation on the remains found in Chugach State Park. I know it would depend how long they had been out there; it's possible there won't have been a lot left. But the involvement of the FBI's IOSS suggests that someone in the investigation suspects there's more to the case than they're letting on.

I think about Pat Jenkins. Prior convictions for sexual felonies don't surprise me; he seems the type, unfair as that might be. But I know he only arrived in Palmer the night before the girl died, which – bearing in mind De Nares told me the girl would have been kidnapped and held for several days – must mean that he's got nothing to do with it. Unless Artie already had her, and waited for his brother to come and play his part? Or else Pat was here longer than Artie was letting on, maybe covering for him. Still, the ABI would be able to find that out pretty quickly.

What seems obvious is that the girl was kidnapped, tortured, but then managed to escape somehow. She was staggering across the fields *towards* my house though, in the opposite direction than if she'd been escaping from Artie's farm.

I think back to the poor girl's quivering arm as it raised up, her finger extending in defiance of the cold that was slowly killing her, to point towards the distant woods. I remember the name Ben's deputy mentioned, Doug Menders. I wonder what, if any, role he might play in the proceedings. His name isn't mentioned in the paper, at any rate. Although maybe he featured on another day; I've missed four of them.

I look at the article again, seeing Paul's name. I wonder why I didn't let my thoughts settle on him straight away. Instead, I've left him for last. Him and my father.

It appears that Paul's gone back to New York, and the implication is that my father's also left. It figures; his work here is done. And Paul would want to get back as soon as he could, to engage in serious damage limitation. He wasn't charged in the end, but he's unable to leave the country, and the residual stain on his reputation just by mere association with this case won't do his chances of making partner any good. I try not to feel happy about this.

But perversely, I'm a little bit upset that Paul has gone. A part of me, I suppose, wanted to see him. I sigh, wondering if I'll ever grow up.

I put the paper back down and my eye is instantly drawn to something else, a sheaf of white foolscap paper nestled under a dog-eared copy of *Sports Illustrated*.

I glance towards the stairs, nervous I will see Ben there watching me as I go through his things, but it is quiet, nobody there. I reach forward, pulling the papers out.

Jackpot.

I can see Ben is definitely the type of man who takes his work home with him, even when he's not even on the case. What I have in my hands is the ABI case file, or at least significant parts of it; interviews and depositions, victim profile, autopsy report, VICAP entry, crime scene analysis along with photographs. I wonder where to start, but it's really no contest.

With one last look up the stairs, I open the file at the victim profile. Despite the newspaper report indicating otherwise, the ABI knows who the girl was.

And now, at last, I will too.

4

The girl's name was Lynette Hyams.

She was only fifteen years old. But from the little information the police have on her, it seems her sixteenth birthday would have been far from sweet. The profile is thin, but manages to draw a tear from my eye nevertheless.

The last place she was officially registered as living in was Seattle, which immediately suggests a link to Pat Jenkins. But then again, Seattle is also the last major city on the mainland, and plenty of people arriving in Alaska come from that area. Especially those escaping from something, and although the police don't have the specifics, it definitely looks like she was running.

The first time she appeared in connection to Alaska was when she was picked up for soliciting in Anchorage, a little over six months ago. It's suspected she worked for Dennis Hobson, a pimp working the Spenard red light district. I wonder if he's been questioned yet.

One of the first jobs I had for the DA's office was

working cases for the Special Victims Bureau, Child Abuse Unit. I've seen the pattern before; an abused girl finally breaks and runs, finds herself in a new city where she doesn't know anyone, and immediately becomes the target of predators who know exactly how to use them. Offer them comfort, security, hope, sometimes even love; often get them hooked on drugs, make them dependent; and then force them into prostitution. Often at this stage, they believe the pimps are doing them a favor. It's a cliché for a reason; it is so often true.

I can see poor Lynette's life, destroyed before it had ever truly begun. I wonder if her death was linked to the industry in which she worked; was she tortured by Hobson for some sort of infraction, as an example to his other girls? Or did whoever she was running from back in Seattle finally manage to track her down, her past catching up to her? Was she running from Patrick Jenkins?

Her mother is listed as Kim Gaskell, her father as Sydney Baker. Stanley Gaskell, Kim's current husband, is her fourth. Lynette's surname came from her mother's third husband, Bill Hyams. I guess she was fed up with changing her name by the time Stanley rolled by, and decided to keep it as it was. Although, as I look through the list of dates, I see it more clearly now – Lynette's mother reported her missing just over a year ago, just after she'd married Stanley Gaskell. But the truth was that Kim hadn't seen Lynette for six months prior to this – just before her fourteenth birthday – and it was only when pressured by her daughter's school liaison officer that she admitted that Lynette had run away.

So she hadn't been around for her mother's fourth wedding, not lived with them, and not taken Stanley Gaskell's last name. I wonder if there is some connection. Did Lynette run because she couldn't face living with this new man?

Stanley Gaskell has something of a rap sheet on him, but nothing that would overtly suggest child abuse. Larceny, assault and aggravated robbery don't make him a nice guy, however.

Kim Gaskell has quite a sheet of her own. Mostly narcotics misdemeanors, but also driving under the influence, being intoxicated in public, supplying alcohol to minors, shoplifting, and even grand theft auto. Most had been pleaded out, but she'd spent two years in the Washington Corrections Centre for Women when Lynette was just six years old.

It's different people, different places, but I've seen it so many times before that Lynette's lifestyle in Anchorage was almost inevitable. Some kids manage to rise above the horrors they see, but most just get sucked into the same kind of abusive lifestyle they've known all their lives. Still, I can never get over the sadness of such situations, the gross wastage of human life. I wonder what sort of life I would have had in Lynette's place, and doubt I would have done any better.

Whether Lynette travelled directly to Anchorage after she ran away from home, nineteen months ago at the age of thirteen, is unknown; until her first arrest for prostitution six months ago, she could have been anywhere. Done anything. Met anyone.

Did she cross paths with Pat Jenkins?

I shake my head; I won't find that out just by reading this brief profile. It's something to bear in mind though, definitely.

The list of suspects is growing, slowly but surely. I think I can rule out Paul, but don't; you can never be sure. Pat Jenkins, and his brother Artie. Kim Gaskell, Stanley Gaskell, and Kim's three ex-husbands; who knows how many ex-boyfriends, who will also need to be investigated. Dennis Hobson, and any associates. Doug Menders, whoever he is.

There is also the possibility that Lynette's murderer is a serial killer, unconnected to her in any way. Perhaps she appealed as a victim due to her age, appearance, or vulnerability; or perhaps some other factor we will never know. The fact that Lynette was working the streets is problematic; prostitutes are the most popular choice of victim for serial killers for good reason. They are already on the edges of society, they often have no fixed address, their colleague are reluctant to talk to the police, and it is part of their job to get into cars or go to unspecified locations with men they don't know.

I hope it is not a serial killer. I know that criminal behavioral profiling helps, and the FBI's VICAP program is first-class, but the sad fact is that most serial killers are caught by accident. Police stop drivers for traffic violations and find rape kits in the trunk. The killer catches his leg on a nail and leaves a trace of blood, which is found to correspond with a DNA record for someone previously charged with a drink driving offence.

They keep on doing it until they die, get arrested for some other offence, or run out of luck and get caught. The careful ones are sometimes never caught at all.

Again, I hope it's not a serial killer.

I go to the kitchen and make myself a coffee, return to the sofa with the mug warming my hands.

I pick up the autopsy report, ignoring the attached photographs for now. She was petite, I see immediately from the statistics. Barely over five feet, and under a hundred pounds. Just a little girl. Living the life she was, I'm sure she could present a street-tough persona when she needed to, but deep down she was just a little girl, lost and alone.

I see the formal identification was made by Lynette's mother. I wonder how she felt when she saw her daughter lying on the cold metal table in the morgue. Did she feel any responsibility for what had happened to Lynette? Or did she not see any causal link, did she just blame her daughter for being too headstrong, for running away?

I scan the report, fixing on the external examination. It's not long before my blood runs cold, the clinical language of the coroner only hinting at the hell the little girl must have seen in her final days on this earth.

Severe head trauma, including three indentations of the cranium consistent with the repeated heavy impact of a blunt instrument such as a ball hammer. The nose has been broken recently, and the left cheekbone is fractured in three places. Bleeding is evidenced from the ears, consistent with brain trauma. The lateral incisor, canine and first molar of the left side of the victim's upper jaw are all missing, and residual damage of the gums indicates that this was a recent injury. They appear to have been forcibly removed. There is a hairline fracture to the lower jaw. Swelling underneath both eyes, on the cheeks, and across the forehead are indicative of impact injuries, either with the fists or some other hard object. Traces of semen have been found between the victim's teeth, under the tongue, and inside the throat. Samples have been removed for analysis.

A ligature mark is visible on the victim's neck, crossing the anterior midline, just below the laryngeal prominence. The skin above and below the dark red ligature mark shows petechial hemorrhaging. Severe abrasions are also present, indicating that the ligature was perhaps used to drag the victim from one place to another.

The victim's right collarbone is fractured adjacent to the midline, and there are fourteen separately identified bruises on the right arm, sixteen on the left, again indicative of being struck with fists or other hard object. Ligature marks are also present around both wrists, with abrasions. Fingernails of all ten fingers were short with unidentified dirt underneath, indicating the victim had been scratching something hard, such as the floor or walls. The foreign material has been removed and sent for analysis. The distal phalanges of the last two fingers of the right hand are fractured.

In addition to impact injuries, there are twenty-two incisions on the victim's lower trunk, covering an area from the genitals to the navel and from hip to hip. The deepest cut pierced the lower intestine, causing internal bleeding. The wounds are consistent with a sharp-bladed weapon such as a razor-blade or box-cutting knife.

The victim's genitalia are that of an adult female.. There is evident bruising and soft tissue damage to the area around the genitalia, and the labia minora have been sewn closed with black thread. The prepuce has been mutilated with a sharp implement, and the glans clitoris has been crudely removed, perhaps with scissors.

After removal of the stitches, an internal examination indicates that the victim was subjected to forced sexual intercourse, with evidence of semen found both internally and externally. There is also evidence of foreign object insertion, consistent with a lengthy cuboid made of a hard material such as wood or metal, which has left residual damage to the vaginal walls.

Damage to the anus indicates that the victim was violently sodomized, with deep abrasions to the anal canal and bleeding evidenced . . .

Bruising is evident on both legs, concentrated on the inside of both thighs, consistent with violent sexual assault . . .

I am just skipping through it now, the details too gruesome to read in their entirety. But where is the cause of death . . .?

I skip to the conclusion and read on.

Although death could have resulted from any combination of the injuries sustained by the victim, in addition to the weather conditions which led to frostbite and hypothermia, the damage to the skull was by far the most lethal of the victim's multiple injuries. The cranium was indented, and the force of the skull against the brain from injury 2-14 (see accompanying diagram) in particular, caused severe bleeding of the brain which ultimately resulted in the victim's death.

Cause of death has therefore been established as brain bleeding from a depressed skull fracture, exacerbated by the victim's other injuries and exposure to climatic elements.

I put the report down, the urge to vomit passing only after several seconds. The savagery, the ferocity of her attacker is overwhelming. What kind of person are we dealing with here? To keep someone captive and *torture* them, it is simply inhuman. Quite simply, the kind of person we're dealing with is a monster.

I'm glad it wasn't me.

The thought enters my brain before I can catch it, and I immediately feel the familiar guilt. It was always the same back in New York; I'd see victim report after victim report, crimes that defied belief, people doing things to each other that simply didn't seem possibly. And every time, despite my best intentions, the thought would always be there, my inner instinct for survival screaming out at me, daring me to contradict it.

I'm glad it wasn't me.

And although I feel bad about such a thought, the truth is, I *am* glad. The suffering endured by that poor little girl in those few days before she died was more than anyone should have to deal with in a hundred lifetimes. It cannot be comprehended by anyone who hasn't been there, nor should it be. It can destroy minds just thinking about it.

I remember Lynette just before she died, before the life sparked out of her; the look in her eyes, asking me just to be with her. I feel a love for her more powerful than anything, a love which can never be returned; and in that same moment, I also feel *hate*. Hate for whoever did this to her, hate for Kim Gaskell and her husbands, hate for the terrible circumstances which led to the destruction of Lynette's young life, a process which started long before she ever moved to Alaska.

I sigh.

I'm glad it's not me.

Would I trade myself for her, my life for hers, endure what she went through if it meant I could save her? I wish I could say yes, but the truth is, I don't know. Sadly, if I'm honest with myself, I don't know if I could. And now I hate *myself*.

I notice the dim sunlight then, which is only just starting to filter in through the living room windows, and in that instant an image flashes before my eyes. It is a face I don't quite remember – a man, early fifties perhaps, grey moustache atop a kindly, patrician smile, a full head of hair swept back over a creased forehead, bright blue eyes behind steel-framed glasses. Despite the friendly smile, the feeling that hits my gut for that split-second is one of pure terror; I feel powerless, helpless, alone. A secondary image, a blazing red moon, enters my vision then, wiping his face out completely.

The red moon disappears an instant later, and the

feeling of terror goes too, just as soon as it appeared. I remember him now; a man I've not thought of for years, since I was girl, back in Boston. Desmond Curtis, a friend and business associate of my father's; they played golf together, I think.

But why am I thinking about him now? And why did his face make me feel like I'd been violated in some way, hitting me with that cold, dread fear?

I shake my head, trying to clear it. The autopsy report must be affecting me more than I thought. I think that I'd better take a break before looking at any more.

I take a sip of my coffee, lukewarm now, and relax back onto the sofa, closing my eyes.

Then I remember De Nares mentioning that there was evidence that more than one perpetrator may have been involved. I wonder what that evidence is. Does he think the autopsy indicates that one person held the victim while another raped her? She had ligature marks on her wrists and neck, and was obviously tied up; it doesn't necessarily mean there was anyone else involved. Unless De Nares was just trying it on, get me to start talking?

Maybe I'm missing something. I put the coffee down and pick up the ABI's preliminary crime report. I wonder if they've put together Lynette's movements prior to her abduction? Or *suspected* abduction, I suppose it should be; nothing has been proven yet except the girl's death. Was she abducted? Did she go willingly with her killer? Where did they go? Where was she held?

I open the file, and then freeze. There is a noise from upstairs; a door opening. Creaks on the landing. Creaks on the stairs.

Quickly, I put the file back as I found it, hiding it beneath the *Sports Illustrated*. I grab the paper, open it to page two. Then I think again. It's yesterday's paper; have I already read it? If so, it might seem strange if he sees me reading it again. Or would it?

It's too late anyway. I see his feet on the stairs, then the rest of him. He sees me on his sofa and smiles. Is it relief he feels?

I put the paper down casually, smile back at him.

"Morning," he says as he reaches the bottom. "Have you been down here long?"

I wonder if it's a test of some sort. "Not really," I say.

Ben runs a hand through his hair. "Sorry, not much of a host, am I? Guess I had a few too many last night, I slept like the dead." He winces. "Sorry. Bad choice of words."

Two *sorries* in the space of a few seconds. Is that a sign of something? Does he feel bad about last night? I wonder how *I* feel, decide I still don't know.

"Don't worry about it," I say, smiling again. "I'm a light sleeper, and a bit of an early bird."

Ben nods his head as he passes me on the way to the kitchen. "Me too, normally at least. I'm gonna make myself a coffee, you want another?"

"Sure," I say. "White, no sugar please."

Ben grunts an acknowledgement, and then he's

gone, leaving me to my thoughts. I think about following him, but would that be too pushy, too needy? He's got a hangover, needs his space. Besides which, he probably *hasn't* done a lot of entertaining, living along here with just his memories. I don't want to crowd him.

I'm still thinking about what to do when he appears at my side, pushing a coffee mug towards me. "Thanks."

"You've not tasted it yet," he says, face deadpan. He's a hard one to figure out, I'll say that much for him.

He starts to sit down in the recliner, stops himself. Passes the coffee table and plops down on the sofa beside me instead. "You hungry?" he asks.

"Yes," I answer honestly, "I guess I am."

"Well, I'm not much of a cook," he says, making me wonder why he asked me in the first place. Does he want *me* to make something?

He must see the look on my face, and another smile crosses his own. "Hey, I'm not asking *you* to make anything," he says, the smile widening. "I was wondering if you wanted to go out for breakfast with me?"

I don't hesitate. "Why not?" I reply, strangely happy.

It's the first time I've been asked out on a date in months.

5

The Noisy Goose Café isn't the most romantic place in the world, but its blueberry pancakes more than make up for it.

It's convenient too, stationed just outside the center of town, off the Glenn Highway, just a five-minute drive from Ben's house. Ben and I sit at a table by the window, and outside – beyond the highway – I can see railroad tracks and the site of the state fairground, empty and barren at this time of year. In the distance, I can also see the mountains towering over everything.

There's a heavy layer of snow covering the world outside, and it's nice to be in here where it's warm and cozy. It's wall to wall pine, with models of ducks and geese everywhere. A sign on the wall reads, *Flying is the 2nd greatest thrill known to man. Landing is the 1st.* There's even a model walrus hanging around on the floor next to the illuminated cake cabinet.

I like it.

"I've been coming here since I moved to Palmer," I hear Ben say, drawing my attention back to him. The winter sunlight filtering through the café window shines warmly on his face, and I look at him as if for the first time. He has a square jaw on a rectangular face, all hard edges; weather-beaten skin stretched over a sharp frame. His grey-blue eyes are hooded slightly by folds at the corners, and they soften his face nicely. His salt and pepper hair is kept Marine-short, and he has the wide-shouldered body of a manual laborer. With his heavy checked flannel shirt, I could definitely buy him as a lumberjack. He's handsome, I decide finally, in a Philip Marlow tough private-eye kind of way.

Handsome, into jazz, and he doesn't seem to think I'm a lunatic; that's a lot of positives, in my book. I look at him, raising my eyebrows, asking him to continue; I'm sure he wants to say more.

"My first day here in fact," he carries on, jaw muscles tightening and relaxing as he feasts on his bacon and eggs. "I didn't know anyone, got a transfer out of the San Francisco PD and just chose the furthest place I could, turned up in Palmer on a Saturday with work starting Monday. There was a mix-up with my things, so they weren't gonna get delivered 'til Wednesday, so there I was, stuck in a new house with just the clothes on my back and my carry-on bag, wondering what the hell to do. So I just wandered around until I found this place. When I got here I was so hungry I ate three of the lunchtime specials straight down." He stops to eat more of his bacon and eggs, and

I have no trouble believing his story. "Been coming here ever since. Never was much of a cook. My ex used to do all the cooking, I guess." He looks sheepishly into his coffee mug.

I nod my head in understanding. "I know just how you feel," I say, conversation with Ben feeling natural, not at all stilted as my efforts have typically been over the past few months. "I never used to cook either. When I was a girl, we had a lady who used to cook for us."

I check Ben's expression for any sign of distaste; the image of cooks and servants doesn't sit well with some people, even if I was just a girl at the time with no control over my parents' lifestyle choices. His expression remains interested and non-judgmental; he probably knows all about my background from briefings written up for the investigation. I'm probably not telling him anything he doesn't already know anyway. Still, I continue.

"And then when I went to college, I found I just didn't have the knack for it. And, awful as it sounds, I was just too used to good food to put up with my own, you know? So I ate out. A lot. And then I shared a house with a girl who was really good in the kitchen."

"You're still friends?" Ben asks.

"Her name's Kate. Still my best friend," I say with a smile.

"Do you miss her, living up here?"

"Yes. I guess I do. But you know how it is when people start work, we only got to see each other a couple of times a year anyway, busy schedules and all that. We still talk on the phone." A beat pause. "Are you still in touch with anyone from San Francisco?"

He shakes his big head. "Not really. I left a bit of a mess behind if I'm honest." He pauses as we hear a gust of wind shrieking along the railroad tracks outside, and we both look out of the window, seeing the snow begin to fall again, slanting at an angle with the cold breeze. A passing car wobbles dangerously in the cross-winds. We turn back to each other.

"Gonna be a cold one," Ben says seriously. He moves his mug away from him, spreads his hands on the table. "But as I was saying, I left San Fran under a bit of a cloud. When I got hitched to Dana I was like a love-struck teenager, you know? Now I can see she never really felt the same way, not really. Like her friends; she kept her circle of friends, got me to drop mine, and I'd lived in the Bay area all my life, but she fluttered her lashes and I forgot all about them." He shrugs his big shoulders again. "But what you gonna do, right? That's just how it is. So I never really saw any of my old friends anymore after that, her friends became my friends, although I could tell they didn't like me too much. I don't think they were used to cops in their little clique, I made them nervous. Probably for good reason, most of 'em were on coke or were misusing meds of some kind. I think the reaction from them is one of the things Dana wanted from me; I was a bit different from the guys her and her pals usually went for, which was doctors, lawyers, businessmen, you know the type."

I *do* know the type; I was engaged to one of them myself. But Ben isn't being judgmental; it's almost as if he doesn't see *me* as that same type. I wonder how he *does* see me? I nod my head, keeping contact with those hooded grey-blue eyes, urging him to continue. He moves his mug further up the table, and eventually does.

"So I'm there doing my thing, working hard, long shifts, and eventually, I guess, my wife followed the same pattern as all her friends. She started drinking too much, doing a bit of coke herself on her Saturday nights out with the girls." He shakes his head. "I suspected what she was doing, tried talking to her about it, but she denied it, and I dropped it. Carried on with my work. We'd been married eight years before I realized she'd been cheating on me." The muscles in his jaw tighten, his hands on the table balling into fists. "And not once, not just with some other guy she'd fallen in love with." He shakes his head sadly. "When I first heard the rumors, it was from another guy in the PD, telling this story about some girl he'd heard about getting . . . being caught in a delicate situation, in a nightclub bathroom with one of the barmen. Some people thought it was her, I discounted it, but then I started to pick up on things, things I'd missed before, maybe intentionally, I don't know. But I started to get crazy, I started to follow her, I even started to use other cops to trail her. Misusing departmental resources, my chief called it when he pulled me into his office to give me a warning. The first of many, as it turned out.

"Anyway, one thing led to another, I found out

Dana had been putting herself about all over the city, I confronted her about it, she told me it was my fault, I'd driven her to it, you know the usual cop routine, I was obsessed with my work, didn't show her enough affection." He moves his head, cracks his neck. "Who knows, maybe she was right? Anyway, so I'm at home during a work shift, getting it all out in the open with her, when there's a knock on the door, a guy's turned up with a bottle of Jack Daniels and a smile which fades just as soon as he sees me there." His hands open, palms up. "And I just lost it. I took that bottle and near beat him to death with it, right there on my front porch.

"My department did its best, and I ended up not being charged, but the damage had been done. Me and Dana filed for divorce, which turned really messy; she claimed *I'd* cheated on *her*, she took some of her own coke to the station, saying it was mine, I even got tested but came up clean as a whistle, I asked her to get tested but she refused and the claims were thrown out, but it was a real nightmare. My reputation in the department was going downhill rapidly, and I knew I had to get out of there before things got even worse. So I started looking for jobs elsewhere and when I saw the position of Chief of Police come up here, I jumped at it. And you know what?"

"What?" I ask.

"It's worked out perfectly. The big city was never for me, too many people, I just never knew it. The outdoors is in my blood, and this is my true home." Once again, he shrugs those big lumberjack's shoulders up and down. "I guess things always happen for a reason, you know?"

My hands move across the table as if they have a mind of their own, covering Ben's, squeezing them. I stare into those grey-blue eyes and nod in complete understanding. "Yes," I say. "I *do* know."

Silence follows, and it is a few moments of bliss, just a feeling of pure contentment with another human being. Ben breaks off first, reaching for his mug of coffee. "So I'm gonna try calling Doctor Sandwell today, see what we can find out about what happened to you."

"Doctor Sandwell?" I ask before I can stop myself. Ben nods, a look of curiosity appearing across his face. "Doctor Alistair Sandwell," he says slowly, "remember?"

I nod eagerly. "Of course I do." I smile. "Doctor Sandwell."

Ben smiles back. "You have no idea, do you?"

Should I try lying to him? But if I tell him I have no idea what's happened for the past few days – including sleeping with him – will he think I'm crazy? Hell, maybe he'd be right.

I shake my head. "The last thing I remember is running head first into the wall back in the cells on Sunday." I watch him closely for his reaction, but he doesn't even bother to hide it.

Ben laughs, shaking his head from side to side. "Well I'll be damned," he says and – unbelievably – slaps his thigh, as if it's some sort of comedy show. "I'll be damned. I knew it," he carries on, still shaking his head. "I knew it. When we were talking just now, I could tell from your eyes, you know? You were seeing me as if for the first time, as if the past few days hadn't even happened." He composes himself. "So you don't remember last night?"

I shake my head. "No. I woke up next to you this morning and freaked out."

Ben starts laughing again, and it's starting to annoy me. "Do you mind?" I ask. "This isn't funny to me."

Ben sits back in his chair, head bobbing. "Okay. I'm sorry. Really. It's just – *damn* – it must be weird. I can't get my head round it, I really can't."

"What's there to get your head round?" I fire back. "I'm crazy. Insane. Okay?"

"No," Ben says evenly, "I don't think you are." He leans towards me. "Ever since that first night, you know what? *I believe you.* De Nares thinks *I'm* crazy, but there you go. I don't know what's happening, or how it's happening, but there's something going on in that fantastic brain of yours, that's for sure."

I sit there in stunned silence. He believes me? For a moment, I consider that this is some sort of set-up, entrapment to try and get me to make a slip-up, reveal something the ABI wants to hear. But Ben seems genuine. I can't be sure for certain, but I believe him. And that makes me feel good.

"Thank you Ben," I say, my hands finding his over the table again. "Thank you." A thought occurs to me. "So who *is* Doctor Sandwell?" The name seems familiar in some way, but I can't seem to put my finger on it.

"First things first," Ben says. "Let me tell you what's been going on for the past few days. You must be dying to know."

Ben's right, and I smile. First things first. I have three days to catch up on.

6

What I hear is interesting, to say the least. Weird too, being told what you've been doing for the past few days, with absolutely no recall whatsoever.

After I knocked myself out by head-butting the cell wall, I was transferred to the Palmer emergency room where I was treated for a concussion. Doctor Elaine Mumby, the lady I'd seen twice before and apparently an eminent clinical psychologist, interviewed me in my hospital bed and reported that – in her professional opinion – I wasn't lying, I actually believed what I'd told the ABI. Which is true, of course.

I was then transferred to the Neuroscience Centre at Alaska Regional Hospital, where I finally entered the care of Doctor Claude Newholme and his staff. According to Ben, I underwent brain scans, x-rays, MRIs, any test they could think of. Files were received from Mount Sinai detailing what happened in New York, the coma, the damage to my brain.

Ben says that while the tests were going on, De

Nares was busting his nut, furious he wasn't allowed contact with his prime suspect. And then my father arrived – nobody seems to know how he found out, but he must have haul-assed from Boston to get here so quickly – and broke De Nares' case apart in minutes. Ben says he was impressed, and glad he wasn't on the receiving end. Long story short, the judge rescinded the charges completely, although apparently De Nares still has his eye on me. When I asked Ben what De Nares would think about the two of us, he laughed and said it wasn't a problem; I'm free, and Ben isn't officially on the case.

Due to a complete lack of evidence, other than his presence in the general area, Paul was released without charge too, and – as far as anyone knows – flew straight back to New York. I never saw him. My father didn't stick around either, and Ben's not even sure if he stopped by to see me. Probably just came to ensure I didn't embarrass him and his practice; his son committing suicide was bad enough, without his daughter being charged with aiding and abetting a homicide.

Although I had appointments to keep, I was let out of Alaska Regional on Tuesday morning. Ben had spent a lot of time with me, feeling bad about the whole affair, and we'd gotten to like one another. And so, on the pretext of Ben filling me in – confidentially of course – about the case, we'd met for dinner on Tuesday night. We'd hit it off well, arranged to see each other again on the Wednesday, hit some bars after dinner and one thing had led to another – two lonely people with a lot of stress and a few too many drinks – and we'd ended up in bed together. I couldn't tell if Ben was disappointed or relieved that I couldn't remember that part.

His description of our brief courtship is strange, as if it happened to someone else entirely, but after spending time with him this morning that I can actually remember, I can easily see how it could have happened. In fact, I think I might even like him.

Back to the case, Ben tells me that De Nares is trying his best to bust Pat Jenkins' balls, but Ben doesn't buy it; the times and dates just don't add up. They can't establish that Pat knew Lynette back in Seattle, but that doesn't mean he didn't. Either way, De Nares is still hanging in there.

My house has been turned upside over, with everyone from crime lab technicians to the canine unit riding roughshod through it. Not just mine though – they'd done a thorough job of Artie's and Larraine's too, as well as our other neighbors. The Townsends, the Latimers, the Eberles, even Judge Judd – they've all had their properties searched, from top to bottom. Given the state of the girl's body and the cold weather conditions that night, the experts have decided that she couldn't possibly have made it more than a few miles. It's suspected she was being held somewhere in the immediate vicinity. Nothing was found anywhere though, and Ben says they're still putting things back together. Maybe they should check further afield; the human body is sometimes capable of a lot more than we give it credit for.

The ABI and Anchorage PD are still trying to locate Dennis Hobson, and Kim Gaskell and all her partners and ex-partners are being brought in for questioning, preliminary enquiries being carried out in their home states, not even De Nares wanting to drag them all the way up to Alaska if there's no need. Kim and her current husband seem to have strong alibis, but there are several question marks over some of the others, including Lynette's biological father.

All of which brings us up to our fifth cup of coffee, and a new question I have for Ben. "Tell me about the unsolved murders from a couple of years back." Maybe it's more of a demand than a question, really.

Ben gestures to the waitress for a sixth cup. Looking at the weather outside, a blizzard starting to foul up the rush-hour traffic, we're not in a hurry to go anywhere.

He purses his lips, brow furrowed as he thinks. "It was a bad time," he reflects eventually. "A real bad time. Couple of hikers up in the Chugach State Park stumbled across some human remains. A femur first, uncovered after the snow and frost finally began to thaw, they weren't sure what it was at first, but then they found a jawbone, definitely human. The rest of the skull was right next to it, just under the topsoil. They stopped looking then, the lady was sick and the guy called in the PD.

"Well, everyone but the army got involved, you

couldn't move for people in those hills, all departments got roped in, we scoured I don't know how many square miles of that damned place, animals had carried the bones all over. Eight bodies in all, all decomposed beyond recognition, you know what the weather conditions here are like, forensic examiners had no idea about time of death. Depressed skull fractures might have indicated cause of death, but in the cases where the hyoid bones were found, they were broken, which might indicate that the victims were strangled.

"It took months to track down the names of the victims through dental records when we could find teeth, facial reconstruction and comparison to missing persons' photos when we didn't. In the end, we only managed to positively ID three out of the eight, with a strong idea about two more and absolutely nothing to go on for the remaining three."

Ben shakes his head, obviously still upset by the events, and understandably so. "Prostitutes, the girls we identified," he continues, "working the Spenard area, just like Lynette." Another shrug of the shoulders, an audible sigh. "ABI and Anchorage PD pulled in hundreds of people, the FBI got directly involved too, making up offender profiles, you know, every john, sex offender and ex-con in the area was interviewed, but nothing. Just nothing. The girls we identified had been reported missing at the back end of two thousand nine; experts guessed the other bodies had probably been there longer than six months, but that was the best they could do. Trying to link them to outstanding missing persons was a real sonofabitch too, you know how it is with street girls."

I nod my head; I do know how it is, and it goes back to my previous thoughts about why they make appealing victims. If one goes missing, it rarely gets reported to the police. More often than not they move to another part of the country, maybe running from an abusive pimp, maybe because they think there'll be richer pickings elsewhere. The bottom line is that they are a group of people forgotten by society.

"It reminded some people of a couple of girls who were found in some woods just outside Anchorage, back in two thousand six, two thousand seven," Ben starts up again. "Before my time, but we all learned about it. Bodies were ID'd as runaways, young women, girls really, you know, fourteen, fifteen years old. Found strangled to death, probably on-site. Evidence of violent sexual assault."

"Rape?"

Ben shakes his head. "No evidence of semen, possible the killer used a condom but no clear evidence to suggest that. Forced insertion of a blunt instrument, vaginal and anal. Anchorage PD suspected a branch had been used in one of the cases, they found it discarded near the body, blood and feces on it. They found a cross near the other."

"A cross?"

Ben nods. "Uh-huh. A crucifix, big one – hardwood, square end. Possible the killer dropped it by mistake, maybe tripped and lost it in the dark. Didn't seem to have been left on purpose anyway. And again, evidence up and down the lower shaft." The disgust is evident on Ben's face.

I can't help thinking about Lynette's autopsy report, the damage reportedly caused by a blunt instrument. Could it have been caused by a wooden crucifix? I guess it could have, but it could have been a thousand other things as well, and sexual assault with such objects is quite a common occurrence in these cases. It suggests a link, but far from proves it. Still, it's the sort of thing which gets the investigative instincts on full alert.

"So what happened then?"

"Well, they looked up and down those woods for weeks, never found any more bodies. Never got a conviction."

Ben smiles at the waitress as she pours his coffee. I wait until she leaves.

"Was there a feeling that the cases were connected?"

"Oh yeah, we all thought there must be some connection, but there was no real evidence to suggest it. The Chugach bodies were too decomposed for anything like that. Still, a lot of us thought they must be linked – I mean, could there really be two people that crazy out there?"

"Yes," I say, knowing it is unfortunate but true.

"Yes," Ben agrees, "we both know anything's possible, right? But we couldn't even match the signatures between the cases. We're not even sure the

Chugach women were sexually assaulted. Still, we looked up those old cases, brought in anyone we suspected back then, re-interviewed them. Still nothing."

"Do you think this latest case is connected?" I ask gently.

Ben's brow furrows in thought once more as he considers his answer. "Yes," he says at last. "I'm pretty sure of it. Call it a gut instinct, I don't know. But yes, I'd say they're connected. Those early murders looked quick, on-the-spot. The bodies dumped in Chugach were hidden more carefully, I think the killer spent more time with them. And then those bodies were found, an investigation starts, so maybe the killer refines his method again, you know? Maybe now he takes girls somewhere even more private, murders them and then hides the bodies. Maybe even his own house, under the floorboards, in the garden. Easy to do out here, right?"

I nod. "I guess so."

"And Heaven knows, there are a lot of people go missing, especially girls living on the streets. But how many have just run away, left town to escape pimps and boyfriends, and how many might have been . . . taken?" He shrugs those big shoulders, regretful. "It's just impossible to say, and the killer probably knows that.

"So, what we have is someone who might have been killing girls for years, since at least two thousand six, constantly refining his methods. But eventually he gets a bit sloppy, like they all do."

"How?"

"He let Lynette Hyams escape before he could kill

her."

I nod in understanding. Terrible as it sounds, letting Lynette escape *was* sloppy. But what does that mean? "Is he getting tired of it?" I ask. "Do you think he *wants* to be caught?"

The shoulders move again, up and down. "I'm not sure. I'm not even on the case, remember? But it happened right there, less than a mile from where I was having a good time partying and drinking beer. I want to help clear it up, officially or not."

I nod again, gesture to the waitress. I'm about ready for *my* sixth cup. A thought occurs to me then, and I turn back to Ben. "Who's Doug Menders?" I ask.

Ben can't disguise the look of shock that instantly hits him. "How do you know that name?" he asks, and I wonder if there's a hint of suspicion in his tone.

Still, Ben tells me he believes my story about the strange way I've been experiencing time, and I decide to tell him exactly how I heard the name. I tell him about the first time I saw the girl – the time when she died in the field, and not in my kitchen – and how she had pointed across the fields, towards the mountains. How I'd told Ben and Rob Kittson, and how Rob had indicated that a man called Doug Menders might live in that direction. How Ben had told Rob to stop talking.

"Why would you have told Rob that?" I ask.

Ben opens his mouth to speak, then closes it as the waitress returns with the coffee urn and pours me another cup. Waiting for her to leave, he then looks at me seriously. "I would have warned Rob to stop talking in front of people," he says, "because Doug Menders was the prime suspect in both of those previous cases we've just been talking about."

I look at my coffee cup, and wonder if they serve anything stronger at this time in the morning.

I think I need it.

7

The Glenn Highway isn't quite so bad once you're on it, although the blizzard's no better. The snow's coming down like an Arctic monsoon, and the windscreen wipers are working overtime to keep even a little visibility. But rush hour is over and traffic is lighter now, meaning our progress can be measured in miles, rather than just feet, per hour. I know how it can be; it once took me four hours to travel two miles through town.

Ben's police cruiser is a Dodge Charger; pretty nice, although I can't help thinking an SUV would be a better choice around here. Still, if catching crooks is your business, sometimes it pays to have something a bit faster.

I wonder, for the first time, where my own SUV is. I didn't see it at Ben's house, so I presume it's at home. Or maybe the police station? Did Ben pick me up before our date last night? I realize I still have no idea.

We travel north through the city, the highway

turning into North Cobb Street. There are people out on the streets, but most are hiding inside. Those citizens brave enough to be outside – or those with no other choice – are huddled up against the cold, multiple pullovers and huge jackets, hoods covering face masks that keep just the eyes showing. It reminds me of the steps of the courthouse in New York and I look away.

And then we're out of the city again, taking a left off the highway onto the Farm Loop. My farm is a few more miles away, Douglas Menders' cabin just a bit further than that.

"The ABI have already interviewed him, of course," Ben says, talking to me but keeping his concentration focused laser-like on the road ahead. An icy country road and a three hundred horsepower rear-wheel-drive car aren't a match made in Heaven, and I'm happy for Ben's attention to be kept right where it is. I can feel my heart rate rising as it is.

"In fact, he was one of the first people we pulled in." Ben changes down a gear as we approach a bend in the road. My hands grip the seat reflexively, but we glide round smoothly. "But there was nothing concrete we could hold him on."

"His name wasn't mentioned in the papers," I say.

"He sued a lot of people after the last time, caused a lot of trouble. During his first interview for this latest thing, he gave everyone a warning, and I guess it must have worked. Nobody's gonna rag on him in public unless there's some very clear evidence for doing so."

"Tell me about those other cases."

"Well, he first came to police attention when those bodies were found in the woods near Anchorage. You know the protocol, we pull in anyone with prior convictions of a similar nature. Menders was a registered sex offender, served a fifteen-year term down in Florida for three cases of raping a minor. A related homicide charge was dropped, but the cops down there were pretty sure it was him. Ligature strangulation, but nothing could be proved, you know how it is." The car rounds another bend, my hands grip tight again. Thirty-foot pines rear up at us from both sides, and I wonder if we're going to get to see them close-up. But then the road straightens out again and I relax. For the moment, anyway.

"Anyhow, he moved to Houston after that, got another ten-year stint there for another couple of rapes. Only did three years though – he got religion, opted for surgical castration and early release."

"Surgical castration?"

Ben nods as he drives, eyes still dead ahead. "Yep, one of those schemes they try out from time to time. Not sure if the research backs it up, but the idea was that it would reduce his drive, you know, 'cure' him of his problem."

"But it didn't?"

"I'm sure you understand the nature of these crimes from your own work," Ben says as he skillfully navigates the car around another series of bends. I find I'm gripping the seat less and less tightly, and I nod my head. Yes, I do understand the nature of such crimes.

Although the criminals often have high sex drives, the effect this has on their behavior is negligible to say the least. Mostly it's about control and power, things which don't really get sorted out through castration. It's like saying the genitals are a rapist's weapon, and without that he's harmless. Unfortunately, time and again this has been proven to be untrue.

"The operation went a little bit haywire anyway," Ben continues. "Nobody's sure if it was an accident or not, but they ended up severing some of the nerve endings in the penis too, cutting some ligaments. Bottom line is, he couldn't get an erection even if he had the desire. Not anymore."

"Is that why he was the prime suspect? Because those first girls weren't raped?"

"Yeah, pretty much. That and the crucifix anyway. Like I said, Menders got religion when he was inside. But in terms of those first attacks, you've got to ask yourself why they weren't raped. Sexually assaulted, yes, but not raped, not as far as they could tell. Could indicate someone early in the cycle, maybe not quite graduated to the full act yet, or else they were interrupted before they could do it, or else they just couldn't get it up and weren't able. But you'd usually see some sign of masturbation at the scene, evidence of ejaculate. But there wasn't anything. Why not? Like I said, could be a number of things, maybe even the physical evidence had been washed away by the rain, but Doug Menders had just moved to town about three months before, and I guess he looked like the top candidate. Ligature strangulation too, just like the case that got dropped back down in Florida."

We pass the turn-off for my house and the other farms. Strangely, I don't feel the need to go there, to check on the place, see how Amy's getting on. I feel disconnected in some way, like my life is on hold, I won't go back to normal until this whole thing is straightened out. I wonder if that will ever happen.

We follow the road, rounding more bends as the terrain becomes steeper. We're climbing into the forested hills now, and suddenly I'm nervous. Ben might be used to confronting people on the streets, probably gives it no more than a second thought. But for me, even though I've dealt with many of the worst kind of people over the years, it's always been in a guarded, air-conditioned office, or in a courthouse under the watchful eye of the guards and sheriffs. I'm not used to meeting suspected killers on their home turf, and I'm surprised to find myself so unnerved. Maybe it's something to do with the attack in New York.

I was surprised at first at Ben's decision to go and see Menders alone, rather than passing it up the chain of command. But then again, what would he have said? He only knows about the girl pointing because of the fact he believes it happened in what can only be described as an alternate past. Who the hell would believe him? Added to which, he isn't even supposed to be on the case in the first place, and Menders has already been interviewed at length, and subsequently cleared. He has an alibi, albeit a weak one, but there's no proof that he had anything to do with it. Ben wants to talk to him directly, get a sense for the man. As he said earlier, he has a gift for these things.

I feel colder as the car climbs the mountain, and I don't think it's just the altitude. I wonder why I asked if I could go with Ben, but of course I know. I want to see him too, get a feel for the guy. I feel so involved in this whole thing that anything I can do to help, I'll do.

"He was the prime suspect for the Chugach murders too?" I ask.

"Hell, Menders is the prime suspect for most things round here. His reputation isn't exactly good."

"You were saying earlier about his religion?"

"Well, nobody knows for sure if it was a genuine conversion or just a ruse to get out of prison early, but to hear him talk about it he's a reformed character, an evangelical, deeply into it in an unhealthy fire and brimstone way. We thought he might have used a crucifix due to some sort of terrible internal struggle, you know, he's conflicted, a religious guy who's still got these urges he can't suppress, so when he can't take it anymore he takes a symbol of that religion and uses it to help him commit the crime, almost making that religion an accomplice with him. Or else we thought he might have just been using it as a sick joke, a kind of big 'fuck you' to the whole system, excuse the language."

"But there wasn't enough evidence to hold a case together?"

"Not enough evidence to *start* a case against him,

never mind hold one together."

"Do *you* think it was him?"

"I'm not sure," Ben says uneasily. "He's such an obvious suspect, you know? And he's definitely a very, very bad man. Weird, crazy, I mean bat-shit crazy, the whole bit. But the fact was that there *was* no real evidence against him, so all you've really got is a gut instinct. And with this current case, obviously there's been evidence of direct sexual assault, so that works against him as a suspect, unless he's grown it all back, and I think we can rule that out. The other option, of course, is that this time he's been working with someone else." I immediately think of Pat Jenkins, but that's probably unfair. Or is it? "He's guilty of *something*," Ben continues. "With someone like him, there's no doubt about that, but guilty of what? That's the question no one can answer."

We're off-road now, ploughing through deep snow on a seldom-used single-track lane cutting a swath through the thick hillside forest. If not for the snow storm, in the gaps where the trees cleared I guess you'd probably be able to see my little farming neighborhood in the valley below.

We travel like this for another couple of miles, and then I see faint lights up ahead through the snow.

"That's it," Ben says. "Menders' cabin."

"Well I guess that means we're one step closer to answering that question."

"Which question?" Ben asks as he pumps the brake, taking us to a safe halt on the unpaved road.

"Finding out what Doug Menders might be guilty of."

8

Ben knocks on the door as the wind whips the snow up around us. I pull my coat tighter around me as we wait for an answer.

Seconds go by, the time dragging, and Ben knocks again, harder this time. We wait again, but again there is no answer.

"Son of a bitch is probably playing games with us," Ben says, brow furrowed.

I don't know why – maybe just because it's so damned cold – but I reach forward and push at the cabin's thick wooden door, and I'm not even surprised when it swings slowly open.

Ben's arm instinctively goes across me, holding me back, at the same time as he draws his handgun from the holster underneath his jacket. I can see from the look on his face that this is unexpected.

"Doug's careful," he whispers to me, "he never leaves the place unlocked, even when he's home."

"Are we going in?" I whisper back.

"*I* am," Ben answers, "*you're* going to stay right here."

I look around the snow-swept landscape, hemmed in by thick trees on all sides, the feeling of claustrophobia bearing down hard on me, and I grip Ben's arm, glaring at him. "I'm not staying out here," I say in a voice that I hope will convince him. "If you're going in there, then so am I."

Ben takes a second to decide, and although his eyes roll skyward, he nods his head and gestures for me to move behind him.

I do, and a moment later he's through the door, into the cabin, and I'm following him so closely we might as well be attached.

The cabin is small and homely, while still managing to keep an air of the sinister about it. Religious paintings hang on every wall, alongside crosses and crucifixes of every shape and size imaginable. I don't know if it's the darkness that comes from a lack of light – the windows are shuttered against the cold and a single bare bulb illuminates the inside space – but the Christian paraphernalia, cloaked in shadow, is far more disturbing than uplifting. Again, I wonder if Menders is a believer, or if it's all for show. At any rate, I can see how the discovery of the crucifix in the woods might have people peg the man as a prime suspect in those crimes. I wonder what his alibi was.

Ben moves further into the room, and a moment later I hear the breath catch in his throat.

"Shit," he breathes, shoulders sagging, and I'm

reminded of the first time he saw Lynette, dead outside my house, and I fear the worst.

Has he found another one?

"Shit," he sighs again, and I move past him, peering around the old sofa that's been blocking my view.

I inhale sharply as I see the sight before me, as shocked as Ben.

There, on the floor of the cabin, is the dead body of a man, congealed blood spread out across the pinewood floor in a gruesome halo that reflects the religious iconography with vicious irony.

"Menders?" I ask Ben, unsure.

"Yeah," he says, moving forward. "It's him."

I see Ben turn away from the body then, obviously aware that the killer could still be here.

He checks the room quickly, then turns to me. "Stay there," he orders me, and this time I don't argue; and a moment later, Ben is gone, off to check the cabin, room by room.

I look around the room nervously, the fear rising again, ice chilling my veins. I try and look away, but I don't know which is worse – the dead body on the floor, or the paintings and crucifixes on the walls.

Eventually, despite my fear, my eyes turn back to the dead body of Douglas Menders, a thousand thoughts running through my mind. Who killed him? When? Why? Was it connected to Lynette's death? Was it another captive, who'd killed him trying to escape? Or if Menders wasn't the killer himself, did he know who it was? And had the real killer murdered him as a result?

I look again at the body, my stomach queasy.

Is he even dead?

I edge nervously forward, staring at the man on the living room floor. At first glance, I am surprised. I think I must have been expecting some sort of frightening, sinister caricature of a man, with missing teeth and crossed eyes. But on first account – except for the bloody wound to his head – Douglas Menders seems entirely normal.

The man looks to be in his fifties, trim and fit for his age. He still has most of his hair too, and while he isn't exactly handsome, he's definitely not the horror show that I was expecting. A pair of small oval-framed spectacles – dislodged by the blow that presumably killed him – hangs down on his chest, linked to a thin chain around his neck. Combined with his woolen cardigan and leather slippers, he has more the look of a slightly eccentric college professor than a serial killer. And yet I have to remember that, whether he has any connection to the Hyams case or not, he has been convicted of a string of violent sexual offences, and is – was? – a dangerous man.

I bend over the shape, looking for any sign of life while still keeping my distance, all too aware that he might be playing possum. Ted Bundy used props such as arm casts and crutches to appear injured, to get his victims to lower their guards – and when he dropped his keys and they bent down to pick them up for him, he'd crack them in the back of the head with a tire iron and haul them into the boot of his VW Bug. Menders might look dead, but I'm not taking any chances.

From this distance, he doesn't appear to be breathing – I watch for a full minute or more, looking for the tell-tale rise and fall of his chest. I consider putting my fingers to the blood, to check if it's real; but who am I kidding? I'm no expert, despite my years working for New York County. It was all prosecutorial, paperwork-based, interviews and paper-pushing. I've never investigated a real, live crime scene before.

But the blood *smells* real, and I gather up the nerve to kneel beside the body, extending my fingers toward the man's neck to check for a pulse.

I jump as a hand claps down on my shoulder, my fingers jerking away from Menders' exposed neck like they've just touched a bare electrical wire; my heart leaps in my chest, and my pulse triples in an instant.

"Jessica," I hear Ben's voice say from behind me, "what are you doing?"

"What am *I* doing?" I exclaim, heart still pounding as I turn my face to Ben's. "What the hell are *you* doing, sneaking up on me like that?"

"Hey," he says, hands raised in surrender, "hey, I'm sorry, I didn't mean to scare you, okay?" He peers down at me, brow furrowed. "What *are* you doing?"

"Checking that he's really dead," I say, realizing how stupid the words sound.

Ben's eyes rove across the body of Douglas Menders and he shakes his head. "He's dead," he says with grave finality; but he bends at the knee anyway, his own fingers going to Menders' carotid. They dig into the folds of skin and he waits for a few moments before shaking his head again. "He's gone, Jessica."

I don't know whether I'm relieved or upset; on reflection, maybe I'm a little bit of both.

"What happened here?" I ask as I stand back up.

Ben shrugs. "A struggle, maybe," he says, indicating a small table that's been knocked over, magazines and books scattered on the floor. I'd missed it before, the result of the room's poor lighting.

My first thought was that another victim must have escaped – bashed her captor over the head and high-tailed it out of there. Even now, she might be cowering half-naked somewhere, out there in the ice and the snow.

There were no tracks outside, but there's been so much snow that it might have covered any footprints. There *could* still be someone out there; someone like Lynette.

"Do you think it was another victim?" I breathe to Ben, and I watch as he looks around, taking in the scene, his finely-honed detective's instincts probing silently.

"I don't know," he offers in the end. "I've checked the house, there doesn't seem to be any place a victim could have been secured or tortured. There's just a kitchen, a bathroom and a single bedroom, and that's it."

"The bathroom?" I ask, remembering a case I'd worked back in New York, prosecuting a sick sonofabitch who'd strung his girlfriend up from the shower pipe over his bath, beating her black and blue for over a week before neighbors had alerted the police to the screams. It had taken them a week, but at least they'd done it in the end.

I wonder, though, if a victim like Lynette Hymans could have been strung up over Douglas Menders' bath, been kept there, tortured there?

"I don't think so," Ben says, "there's no sign of blood or anything else in there. If a girl had just escaped, it's not likely she would have cleaned the place first. Plus, police have been up here a few times since we found Lynette – both Palmer PD and the ABI – and we didn't see anything going on, and believe me, the place was searched from top to bottom."

I shrug my shoulders. "Then what?"

Ben looks around, taking it all in again. "Could be a vigilante attack," he says thoughtfully. "Maybe people got wind of Menders' name, despite it being kept out of those news reports, decided to take matters into their own hands. Wouldn't be the first time something like that would have happened . . ."

"With Menders?"

"Well, I think old Doug was beaten up a few times during his early years here – one of the reasons he didn't really leave the cabin, he was too damn scared, another reason why I don't think he was involved too directly. He was just too scared to drive around and troll for victims, you know? But no, what I was really thinking about was when I was still with the SFPD, I worked a

175

couple of real nasty cases where suspects had been beaten to death by vigilante gangs. One guy had been called a pedophile by the press, and was dead within the week. Turns out he wasn't even guilty anyway. Another one *was* guilty, a rapist, and while I didn't have much sympathy for the guy, what they did to him was pretty sick. He was unrecognizable, he had a face we knew well, but we had to go off fingerprints and dental records for an ID in the end."

I nod with understanding; I've seen similar cases in New York myself. "Can I take a look around?" I ask, not really sure why.

Ben looks quizzical, as if asking himself the same question, then he nods gently. "Okay," he says, "but don't touch anything, this is a crime scene. And be quick, I'm gonna have to call this in, and I want you gone by the time the ABI gets here. It's gonna be bad enough explaining why *I'm* here, never mind you."

"Okay," I say, knowing that he's right. Ben could conceivably come up with a story about calling in to check up on Menders, or some other little white lie, but me? What would I be doing here? And why would Ben be with me? Even though my father has waved his magic wand, I'm sure Captain De Nares still sees me as a suspect. Ben shouldn't even be working the case, never mind *me*.

Ben pulls out his radio and starts to call it in to the PD, and I finally move away from the dead body of Douglas Menders and head for the thick wooden door that leads to the kitchen.

I remind myself not to touch anything – the last thing I need is for my fingerprints to be found here when the lab boys arrive on the scene. That would *really* mess with my day.

With a sense of trepidation, I push open the door using the back of my hand and slowly enter the kitchen.

The space is small and – like the living room – eerily dark, a tiny, solitary window allowing some of the cloud-dulled sunlight from outside the cabin to pass through.

There is a sink, a worktop, a small cupboard and a simple iron stove, all clean and serviceable. I put my gloves on and open the cupboard, see a small range of cooking and eating utensils stored there, stacked neatly. There is also a small wooden table and a single chair, and I start to try and imagine Douglas Menders' life here – day after day, week after week, month after month spent alone here. Waking – maybe in the morning, maybe not until the afternoon – and making himself something to eat, sitting down alone at the table to consume it. Washing and drying the pans and plates, putting them away, making the place clean and tidy again before moving onto . . . What?

Did he ever see anyone? Did he ever *speak* to anyone? I hadn't noticed a telephone in the living room, and there isn't one here in the kitchen either. Such isolation would be enough to drive anyone mad. What had it done to Douglas Menders? Would he have craved company of some kind, and if so, what would he have done about it?

Standing there in the dark kitchen, his dead body lying in the very next room, it is an unsettling thought.

What am I looking for here, anyway? What am I hoping to find that the police or the ABI would miss?

Maybe I don't know what I'm looking for, but I know *why* I'm looking, at least. It's because Lynette Hyams died in my arms, it's because I'm being hurled through time and space on some quest I don't even fully understand, it's because of that damned red moon that only I can see, it's because – if only I can manage to solve this crime – maybe I can prove to myself that I'm not crazy.

I push the thoughts away and push through another door that opens out onto a tiny hallway, two more doors leading off – the bedroom and the bathroom, I suppose.

As I hear Ben's muffled voice on the radio back in the living room, I open the nearest door and enter the bathroom.

Like the rest of the cabin, the room is small. There is a sink, a toilet and a three-quarter-size iron bathtub. No mirror. No cupboards. A crucifix and a couple of pictures in their place. On closer inspection, the pictures are two of the fourteen Stations of the Cross – the first showing Jesus carrying his cross on the procession to Calvary, the second an image of Jesus crucified on that same cross. This particular artist seems to have drawn inspiration from the most gruesome parts of the tale – there are streams of blood coursing down Christ's face from the crown of thorns, and a river pours from the spear wound in his side. I wonder what Menders would have been thinking as he studied those pictures from his iron bathtub, and I shiver involuntarily.

With no cupboard, there are just a few assorted toiletries arranged neatly around the sink. And now I notice that there *is* no shower pipe that he could have hung any victim from, although I suppose he could have kept someone tied up in that bathtub. But, as Ben said, there is no sign of blood or anything else that might indicate that someone had been kept there, and it was unlikely that if someone *had* killed Menders and escaped that they would have taken the time to clean up the place before they left.

In the dim illumination afforded by the bare lightbulb, I once again note how clean this room is. Maybe that was how he spent his days? Scrubbing the bath and the floorboards? Maybe trying to wash away the sins of his past.

The crucifix and the pictures on the wall support the religious angle, although I still don't know if is all for show. But if so, who was he showing? He clearly had very few visitors, and he could have stopped trying to convince the police long ago.

So perhaps Menders *was* a reformed man?

I see cleaning products stored between the legs of the bathtub and examine them. Nothing special, mainly bleach.

Of course, such ruthless attention to cleanliness might not be the result of a tortured soul; it could also be the signs of a man trying to hide something.

I back out of the room, still searching. Not for evidence so much as a . . . feeling.

I was scared in that bathroom – the religious paraphernalia, the thought of the dead body, my knowledge of the kind of man he was, all combined to bring the fear out in me – but it's not the feeling I'm looking for.

I move down the tiny hall and open the bedroom door with my gloved hand. The curtains are drawn in there and my other hand feels along the wall until it hits a light switch.

Another single, bare lightbulb flickers on above me and I take in the single bed, made up with hospital corners, sheets starched; the side table, stacked with books, a small reading lamp next to them; a pine wardrobe, closed tight; and by the window, a table and a chair . . .

I see a pair of binoculars lying carelessly on the tabletop, a large telescope set up right next to it. I look more closely, see that they are high-grade items, semi-professional stuff. There are a few astronomy journals open on the table, pinned down underneath the binoculars, and another look at the bedside table shows that most of the books there – except for a dog-eared copy of the King James Bible – are about astronomy and star-gazing.

I know the night skies around my own home are incredible; I'd literally forgotten that the heavens contained that many stars, I'd been in New York so long. What you could see at night from up here, I can only guess, but it was no wonder that Menders had taken it up as a pastime. It answers my question of what he did out here on his own, at least.

I bend toward the eyepiece of the telescope and aim it upwards with my gloved hands, but I am met only with a cloud of snow-swirling grey-and-white. I leave it, pick up the binoculars and aim them out of the window.

I don't even aim them skyward; instead, I point them out to the small garden, adjusting the focus. They're good, and I calculate that – between the binoculars and the telescope – Menders' interest in astronomy cost more than everything else in his cabin put together.

It is then that the snow clears slightly and I see something, out beyond the trees. I adjust the focus again and my heart starts to beat a little faster.

I put the binoculars down and go back to the telescope, not aiming it upwards now, but outwards, away from the house, through the trees that border the cabin's garden . . .

And that's when the feeling hits me, and I know I've found what I've been looking for.

<u>9</u>

"De Nares is on his way," Ben calls from the hallway as he approaches the bedroom, summoned by my shouts. He arrives at the doorway with a furrowed brow. "So, what have you found?"

I point at the table by the window, and his eyes follow my finger. "The binoculars?" he asks for confirmation as he enters the room, and I nod my head.

"And the telescope," I add.

"So Menders was a star-nut," Ben says. "So what? He had to do something up here, right?"

"Look through the scope," I tell him, and – although he has one eyebrow raised in question – he does as I tell him. "Tell me what you see."

"I can't see anything," he complains, "the thing's not focused, there's too much snow –"

"Look further out," I insist, "the focus is fine if you're looking at the right distance. Just wait for a break in the snow."

Ben sighs, but continues looking as I wait. And,

after a few more seconds, realization dawns. "Son of a bitch!" he exclaims. "I can see your house from here! And Artie's place, and Larraine's . . . hell, I can see the whole lot of you through this thing." I wait for the next step in his thinking. "And so could Doug," Ben says eventually, head coming away from the scope. "Son of a bitch." Ben looks at me closely. "You think he knew who did it, don't you?"

"Don't you?" I ask, everything clear in my mind. "He doesn't get visitors, he craves human contact, so what he does is *watches* us. You said yourself, he hates – *hated* – leaving this place, so he watches from a distance. And then he sees something. At the very least, he might have seen the girl running across those fields, they're right in his field of vision. He might have known where she came from, at least."

"Did he record it?" Ben asks, thinking with me now. "Did he make notes? Keep a journal?" He is already rooting around, searching through the man's books and papers.

"Do you think he knew the killer?" I ask.

Ben stops searching, looks at me, shakes his head. "I don't know," he says sadly. "I just don't know. It's possible . . ."

"Maybe he was working with someone," I suggest, the idea forming unbidden in my mind. "He couldn't do it anymore, so he hooks up with someone who can?"

"It's possible," Ben says again, "but I don't think so. More likely that he was engaging in a bit of voyeuristic viewing and saw something he shouldn't.

Maybe he contacted the killer after the fact though?" he says thoughtfully, rubbing his chin. "Either for blackmail, or to work his way into the killer's operation somehow?"

I nod, going with it. "And the killer didn't like it, came up here and dealt with the threat." I look back at the table, notice a gap in the mess for the first time. I point at it. "Is that from you moving things around?" I ask Ben.

He shakes his head. "No," he says, "I put everything back where it came from. But you're right, it looks like something's missing."

"Yeah," I agree, "something about the size of a book – or a *journal* – placed about right for a guy looking through the scope to write notes in."

"But it's not here now," Ben says, and I know we have jumped to the same conclusion. No firm evidence perhaps, but we both have the *feeling*.

"So we have a dead body, a surveillance set-up that would have allowed him to see the girl, and – possibly – one missing journal."

Ben nodded. "A journal that could maybe help ID the killer."

"But it's gone now, if it ever existed in the first place."

"It might still be here. Maybe Menders hid it."

"It's worth a shot," I say. "Let's get started."

But Ben shakes his head. "No," he says firmly. "De Nares and the ABI will be here soon, and you've got to get out of here. We think Lynette's killer did this, right?

And you were one of the prime suspects in that case. Can you imagine what De Nares is gonna do if he catches you here, or if he suspects – for even a moment – that you were here?"

I *can* imagine, and the thought isn't pretty; even my father might not be able to get me released so easily, if I was to be found here.

"Okay," I agree uneasily. "I'll go. But you promise you'll look for that journal, okay?"

"You bet," Ben says with conviction, before looking at me with concern. "Hell," he says, "I forgot – I drove you up here, didn't I? How the hell are you going to get back down by yourself?"

Damn. It was a good point, too. But you could see my house from here. It would be a hike, but I could get there.

"I'll walk," I tell him.

"You'll what?" Ben says in surprise.

"I'll walk down," I tell him. "The snow's not so bad now, and there must be some trails leading down."

Ben shakes his head gravely. "No," he says, "no, I don't like it, I don't like it at all. These are bad conditions to start with, and you're not dressed for hiking. Added to which, there's still a killer out there somewhere, and we know he was here recently." Ben points outside. "What if he's out *there?*"

"But I can't let De Nares see me here," I respond, "and I can't really take your car, otherwise how would you explain how *you* got here?"

Ben thinks for a moment, trying to figure things

185

out, but I stop him short. "Look," I say, "I'm going. I'm walking. I'm a grown woman, okay? I can make my own decisions. I've got boots, gloves, a jacket, a hat, what else do I need?"

Ben's gaze is leveled at me, and he knows this is an argument he won't win. I know he's torn between the logical and emotional centers of his mind, one telling him that it's the sensible thing to do, the other questioning how he can let me go out there on my own.

Eventually, he bends a knee and pulls up the right leg of his pants, withdrawing a small snub-nosed .38 revolver from a brown-leather ankle holster.

"This," he says in answer to my question, holding the weapon out to me in one giant hand. "Take this, at least."

I extend my own hand and take it, putting it into my coat pocket, the weight unfamiliar yet oddly comforting.

"You know how to use it?" he asks, and I nod my head. I'd learned to shoot at the family ranch back in Westford, and I'd been back on the range a few times since my "accident" . . . just in case.

Our heads both turn at the sound of sirens in the distance, then Ben turns back to me. "Okay then," he says. "Go." He leans forward, kisses me once on the cheek, and looks away.

Immediately, the sounds of the sirens growing louder, I do what he says.

And a moment later, I am gone.

10

An hour passes, maybe more, and I am regretting my decision.

What the hell had I been thinking? Ben was right – I *am* freezing to death out here in the woods, and my hat and gloves aren't doing a whole lot to help.

But that's not even the main problem. Back in the house, with the smell of death in the air, surrounded by crucifixes and sinister artwork, I had held no fear of the snow-crisp beauty of the great outdoors beyond. And with De Nares and his troops about to descend on the scene, I had absolutely no wish to get into a confrontation with him that might get me sent back to jail.

That much is still true, at least; I have no wish to return to jail. I *am*, however, rather less enthusiastic about my surroundings than I had hoped to be.

In fact, I am terrified.

An hour away from Menders' cabin, on the steep, heavily wooded slope that will eventually wind its way down to my own farmstead, the isolation is devastating. I know that Ben, alongside De Nares and an ABI crime scene team, are only a relatively short distance away, and yet I can see nothing except for the trees and the snow, and can hear nothing except for the whistle of the wind and the sigh of the branches.

I pause and look about me. Do I even know where I am? With the wind and the snow blocking out sight and sound, it is hard to be sure. I've been heading downhill steadily since I began, in what I hope is a straight line, but what had seemed like an easy task back in the cabin now seems much harder.

Impossible?

No; not impossible. Nothing is ever impossible. My father, for all his other faults, taught me that, at least.

I know I can't let the conditions get to me, can't let the isolation confuse me; if I continue just making my way steadily downhill, I *will* come out near the small hamlet of farms that holds my own home.

I *will*.

But it's not just the fear of getting lost that affects me. Out here, all alone, I am suddenly all too aware of the danger I am in. The killer of Douglas Menders, the killer of Lynette Hyams, *might* still be out here somewhere.

Is he somewhere in the trees, watching me right now?

The thought brings a chill to my spine stronger than the snow or the wind ever could, and my hand reflexively moves to my jacket pocket, feeling the reassuring heft of the .38 through its lining.

My eyes dart about the place, settling for just a moment on each gap between the huge trees, searching wildly for anything out of the ordinary. On a conscious level, I know that – under the circumstances – it is entirely possible that my mind will start making things up, seeing shapes or movements that simply aren't there. On a subconscious level though, I'm already doing it, and seem unable to stop.

I can feel my heart rate rising as I look around me, eyes scanning, gun held tight in my pocket.

I know I'm being paranoid, but what if Ben is right? What if someone *is* out there? I remember the body of Lynette Hyams in my arms, I remember what the killer did to her, the damage he inflicted to that poor girl, the pain she must have felt, I remember the light of life blinking out of her eyes, leaving nothing but an empty shell. I remember the dead, bloody body of Douglas Menders, back up the mountain. I remember that we still don't know if it's a single killer, or multiple *killers*, and my heart races faster as I imagine people all around me, watching me, waiting for the time to move in on me, to attack me, rape me, torture me, kill me . . .

In a flash, the .38 is out of my pocket, aimed out at the trees in a two-handed grip as I turn wildly this way and that.

"Come on, you sons of bitches!" I yell, without conscious control, unable to stop myself, but knowing somewhere deep inside that it is the attack on the courthouse steps, being shot by Zebunac's hired assassins, that is driving me to this; the fear eating away at my insides, day in and day out as I wait for them to return and finish the job. *This is it, dammit;* I've had enough, out here in the snowy woods, surrounded by potential enemies, *I've had enough!*

The fear has eaten away so much of me that I don't know what's left, and I'll be damned if I'm going to let it continue any further.

"Come on!" I scream into the wind once more. "Fucking come on! Show yourselves, you cowardly bastards, I know you're out there!"

I turn and turn, the cold-steel barrel of the .38 swinging with me, trained on the gaps between the trees, the places where the men are hiding, watching, lying in wait.

Well, I'll fucking show them.

"What are you waiting for?" I shout, still not knowing where the words are coming from. "I'm right here! Come on out here!" My voice starts to weaken, and I choke on my own tears. "Come on," I sob, falling to my knees in the thick, deep snow. "Come on . . ."

I see movement ahead of me then – I'm sure of it – and the revolver comes up of its own accord, my body stiff, tense, the tears freezing on my face.

Then I see what it is and almost smile as the shape glides out of the trees, imperious and regal, unperturbed by the wind and driving snow.

It is a gigantic elk, its huge, sweeping antlers not yet shed for the winter, and I watch in awe as it parades before me.

I drop the gun to my knee, comforted by this natural beauty, the elk's strength seeming to radiate from its beating heart to mine, filling me with warmth and a feeling of security that moments ago had seemed forever unattainable.

The beast moves closer toward me, and all thoughts of watchers in the woods are gone as I stare at its graceful head, at the way its antlers sweep back over its shoulders, spikes pointing forward near the tip, its immense, powerful body wrapped up in a cloak of warm greyish-brown.

Then I see its eyes, huge within its furred skull, black pinpricks in a sea of curved, shining brown, and I rise from my knees, our faces just inches apart now, our frozen breath meeting in the middle.

And then I see something else in the elk's eyes, something deeper, something hidden away, buried far beyond where I can see . . . and yet I *do* see.

A burning red moon, imprinted on the black pinprick in the sea of brown, a burning red moon in each eye that taunts me, that threatens me, that is forever watching me . . . a red moon that will never leave me, and I know that the feeling of being watched isn't the killers, waiting for me in the trees, it is this same red moon, the red moon that watched as Lynette died in my arms, the red moon that stalks my every moment, chasing me, pushing me, challenging me to . . .

Yes.

To solve the crime.

And then the spell between us is broken and the

elk turns and runs back for the trees, snow churning up behind it from its stamping hooves.

11

I don't know how long I've been walking for, but the hazy sun is low in the sky now and my body is exhausted. I cannot even remember much of what happened up there, my freezing journey down through the deep snow and ice of the thickly forested slopes. It all seems like a dream.

Out of the woods – even though I am now much further away – I can hear the sirens wailing up at the top of the mountain, outside Menders' cabin. Within the huge walls of trees, enclosed within the forested slopes, I could hear nothing except the wind; the experience had been unnerving, at least until I'd seen that giant elk. But had I really seen it?

I just don't know; it could have been a figment of my imagination. Maybe the cold, the wind, the driving snow, the fear, all combined to make me hallucinate back up there. After all, did such animals normally appear so close to humans? And that wasn't even to mention the twin red moons that shone within its eyes.

I am pretty sure that – even if the elk was real – I must have imagined *those*.

But what does that say about me? What does it say about this whole thing?

Am I just imagining everything?

It had all seemed so clear back in the woods, staring into the eyes of that magnificent animal.

But what I fear is the real answer taunts me from the edges of my consciousness.

You're crazy.

You've imagined it all, including the murder, including the party, you've imagined everything.

Or else I'm dreaming it all, asleep in Mount Sinai, still not awake from the gunshot wounds.

Or maybe I'm already dead? Like the kid in that movie with Bruce Willis, he's dead and he doesn't even realize. Is that what I am?

Am I a ghost? Am I –

"Jessica?"

The sound hits me like a rifle shot, startling me. I turn, and see Pat Jenkins leaning against a fencepost, whisky bottle in a gloved hand, smiling crookedly at me. He's in one of his brother's fields, although at first glance I cannot see why.

But he is drunk, I can see that immediately.

"Pat," I manage, not knowing what else to say; our last meeting didn't exactly go too well.

If it ever happened at all, an unwelcome voice in my brain fires back.

"Jessica?" he asks again, and I can smell the whisky

on his breath even from the other side of the fence, several feet away. His beard – previously so neatly trimmed – has been allowed to grow, and I get the sense that it has probably been a while since he last had a shower too. "What are you doing out here?"

"Going for a walk," I answer immediately, without skipping a beat.

Pat looks around him, eyes quizzical, and I can see that he's wondering – even in his whisky-addled state – *where* I've been walking.

"Hiking in the woods," I add, hoping to forestall any more questions.

He takes another swig of the whisky, looks thoughtfully at the nearby trees, then gives a low whistle. "Shit," he says, "you believe in playing with fire, I guess. Don't you know there's a killer out here?"

My body gives an involuntary shiver as I remember the fact that Pat was seen trying to spike the drink of an underage girl at that party

(*the party which never happened*)

even though he has a wife and kids back home, and that Pat is also one of the suspects in the death of Lynette Hyams.

Does De Nares have a good reason to suspect him?

Do I?

I recall how he had approached me at that party

(*it* did *happen!*)

and how uncomfortable he'd made me feel, how awkward; how grateful I'd been when Larraine had

195

rescued me. Maybe I'd misjudged him, but now I'm not so sure; I'm not so sure at all.

And then I realize that – in *this* reality, at least according to De Nares – I didn't attend the party at all. So how the hell does Pat Jenkins know who I am?

"How did you recognize me?" I ask him, better late than never.

"Photo in the papers," he answers easily. "And who the hell else is gonna be walking around here, anyway? That's your house over there, right?"

"Yeah," I say in agreement.

"Well," he says, lip curled, "aren't you gonna ask who *I* am?"

Damn, I should have asked earlier – but earlier, I'd forgotten that we'd not met. "I don't have to ask," I say confidently – more confidently than I feel. "You're Patrick Jenkins. You look just like your brother, whose field you're standing in. And who the hell else is going to be stood in Artie's field, looking like him?"

The curled lip turns into a smile, of sorts. "I guess you're right," he says

But what the hell *is* he doing out here in the fields, dressed in a heavy parka, gloves and hat, leaning on a fencepost and drinking whisky?

Who *does* that in a snowstorm?

Reflexively, my hand touches the gun, which is now back in my coat pocket, and I feel very slightly reassured by its presence.

"Sirens," he slurs, answering my question before I've asked it, pointing up the hill. I turn, see the reflection of the blue flashing lights high up, far away, and realize he's come out here to investigate.

And that concerns me – what if he links me coming out of the woods with what happened up at the cabin? It'll be on the news soon enough, and I hate to think what he'll do with the information.

Act innocent, I tell myself.

Act normally.

"Yeah," I say, nodding, "kind of crazy, huh? I couldn't hear any of it when I was in the woods, trees must have blocked it all out. How long's it been going on for?"

He regards me coolly for several moments, and – reluctantly – I meet his gaze until he turns away and shrugs. "A few hours now, I guess," he mumbles, before taking another swig from the bottle. "Came out here to check it out in the end. Fucking cold though, should have stayed where I was."

"What do you think's going on up there?"

Pat shrugs, eyes drooping. "Hell should I know?" he mumbles, then seems to perk up a little before continuing. "But my brother reckons there's some crazy old pervert lives up there, a fuckin' sex monster, you know?" He spits on the floor, on his own side of the fence. "There's a convicted fuckin' sex killer up there," he says, angry now, "and those sonsofbitches arrest *me*! I'm just here visiting Artie, and I get dragged into this whole fuckin' mess."

He shakes his head, drinks from the bottle, and turns his eyes like a hawk up toward the faint lights flashing away up the hill, before shifting them back to me.

"Arrested you too, huh?" he asks. "Before Daddy came to the rescue," he adds scornfully.

"I didn't ask him to," I say, before I can stop myself, the words an instinctive response to such accusations; I know it's pointless defending myself, but I've had a lifetime of people accusing me of having it easy, of "Daddy" helping me out at every turn. No matter what I do, it's hard to get out from under his shadow, even now.

"Uh huh," he says doubtfully, and I find myself hating him even more. He shakes his head. "I still don't really get what happened."

"Me neither," I agree, meaning it. I mean, I *really* don't know what happened; I might not even really know what's happening right now.

"No," he slurs, "no, I mean I don't understand how you knew."

"Knew what?"

"How you *knew.*" His eyes bore into mine, accusation flaring within them. "You knew about that girl before you 'found' her."

"And who told you that?" I ask, surprised that he knew the reason for my arrest; I didn't think it would be public knowledge. But Palmer is a small place, and people talk; I suppose rumors were bound to surface, sooner or later.

Pat shrugs again. "It's the word around the campfire," he says, still leaning his weight heavily against the fencepost. "Is it true?"

I don't know what to do, what to say. How can I possibly explain it?

Yes, I knew that she was going to die because I'd already seen it, I'd already been there, she'd already died in my arms.

I went to the police because I didn't even know what day it was, I didn't know that the murder hadn't even happened yet.

I'm traveling through time as we speak; I have no idea what day it will be tomorrow. Will it be the day of the murder again? Before? After?

But we're *all* traveling through time, I tell myself; it's just that most people are traveling forward.

Which direction *I'm* traveling in, is anyone's guess.

"That's none of your business," I say at last, wanting to cut the conversation off. "You of all people should know better than to listen to rumors."

The best form of defense is, so I'm told, to attack; it seems like as good an idea as any.

"And what the hell is that supposed to mean?" Pat asks, levering his body off the fencepost at last, eyes fierce.

Why am I upsetting this man?

I finger the gun in my pocket once more, made nervous by his proximity. There's a fence between us, but it isn't much.

"There are rumors about you too," I say, before I am able to stop myself. "Spiking drinks. Things in Seattle." I'm fishing with the second claim, but I know the ABI must have had some reason to push him up their suspect list.

"What things?" he asks, eyebrows furrowed.

I shrug my shoulders. "I don't know. I don't listen to rumors."

He continues to stare at me, then grins his crooked grin. "Touché," he says. "Touché." He sniffs hard, rolls phlegm into the back of his throat then hawks it out onto the snow. I watch in disgust as it melts through the upper crust and disappears. "Anyway, I've heard what I've heard, there ain't any un-hearing it. You went in to the Palmer PD and asked about that girl, several days *before* she died. Then when the body was found – on *your* property – you were arrested for aiding and abetting a homicide, am I right?"

"I've already told you," I say, trying to keep my voice steady despite my rising anger, "that's really none of your business."

"Oh really?" he asks, the venom back in his voice, in his eyes. "Well, it *is* my fucking business when I get arrested too, when they try and make some sort of connection between us, like we're some sort of sicko, child-killing Bonnie and Clyde pairing, what do you think? They think we're in this together."

He drinks some more whisky, then I see the anger flash through him and he smashes the bottle down on the top of the fencepost, the glass shattering everywhere. I back away, hand halfway to the gun in my pocket.

"I had to explain this shit to my wife," he shouts, "my *wife!* I'm not allowed to go home, I'm not in jail, but I'm not allowed to leave Alaska, can you believe that shit?"

Suddenly he breaks down, his fury replaced by helpless sobs. "She's gonna leave me," he cries, "I just know it, I just know it . . . after last time, she . . . she . . ."

He starts to cry again, body wracked with the sobbing, and my hand comes away from the gun.

I wonder what he means by "after last time", but decide not to push it, to merely file it away for future reference.

He's bent over now, crouched down in the snow, the tears continuing to stream down his dirty, bearded face. And then a finger comes up, points at me accusingly.

"But you know something," he hisses, "don't you? *Don't you?*"

"No," I say, backing away, "I don't know anything. Whatever you've heard, it's not true."

"Bullshit," Pat fires back, "you're fucking that cop too, aren't you? Screwing the chief of police, a great way to get away with murder, you fuckin' little whore, you –" I'm moving toward him before I know what I'm doing, hand flying out to slap his dirty, lying face; but then I feel a hand on my shoulder, a reassuring voice in my ear.

"No," Larraine Harrigan says gently. "No. It's not worth it."

At the same time, Artie Jenkins appears from the same direction as Larraine, jumping the fence and pulling his brother away.

"I'm sorry," Artie says, "he's struggling to cope

with . . . well, with everything that's been happening, you know, he –"

"Fuck you," Pat responds angrily, "I don't need you to make excuses for –"

Artie cuts his brother off with a single look, and hauls him away across the fields, looking back toward us. "I'm sorry about this," he says again, "I'm sorry."

And then the brothers are gone, away across the fields on their way back to Artie's farmhouse.

I turn to Larraine, see her SUV parked nearby, front doors open. I'm surprised we didn't hear it arrive, but I guess we were too involved in our little "debate" to concentrate on anything else.

"We were just coming home from the shelter," Larraine says, "I was just dropping Artie off when we saw you two talking over here. Given everything that's happened, we thought it might not be a good idea."

I nod, recognizing that she is right; and what's more, that this is the second time that she has rescued me from the unwanted attention of Patrick Jenkins.

Although in this reality, it's just the first, an inner voice reminds me.

"You look terrible," Larraine says, eyes concerned. "Are you okay? Do you want to come to my house for a cup of coffee?"

I wonder how I look. *Do* I look terrible? A part of me is offended by the suggestion, but then I realize that she is probably right. I've stumbled across a dead body, hiked down – maybe for several hours – through a mountain in a snowstorm, and then had a near-violent encounter with one of the suspects in a young girl's murder.

I probably *don't* look my best.

I wanted to get home, to visit Amy, the dogs, the horses.

But do I want her to see me like this? What sort of message would that send about my state of mind, my health?

Eventually, I nod in agreement.

"Yes," I say to Larraine, trying out a smile. "I think that would be nice."

12

Larraine's home is lovely; unlike most of the pioneer-style interiors found throughout the area, her farmhouse is almost like a little English cottage. We are in the kitchen, and from the Aga stove resting against one whitewashed wall, to the checkered cloth that lies on the turned-leg wooden table, the room is both cozy and functional.

I sip the hot, milky tea she has given me, taking in my surroundings. In some ways, it perversely reminds me of Douglas Menders' cabin – that could have been cozy and homely too, had it not been for his almost demented obsession with religious iconography. There is a cross on the wall here too, I notice, but it is simple and seems to fit in with the rest of the décor instead of overpowering and dominating it.

It makes me think of my own home, which is perhaps just a little austere in comparison. I suppose it reflected my mood when I moved here from New York – empty and barren. I've made an effort to give it a homely feel, but I can see now that – in comparison to this – my own farmhouse is still a work in progress.

"There you go, Jessica," Larraine says as she puts a large slice of homemade apple pie in front of me, smothered in cream.

"Thanks," I say, before gesturing to the house. "Beautiful place you have here."

"You like it?" Larraine asks as she sits down at the table with me, pouring herself a cup of tea. "It wasn't like this when I first got here, believe me. I was in such a state after leaving my husband, the house was half-empty for about a year, maybe two. But I eventually got a grip, and . . . well, yes, I'm quite happy with it now, I guess."

"It looks amazing," I confirm, thinking it funny how similar my situation is to Larraine's own past. She has kids, of course, and I've been shot in the head; but other than the details, the essence remains the same – we are both women seeking refuge here in Alaska, escaping from a life that had threatened to finish us.

"Thank you, dear," Larraine says, adding spoon after spoon of sugar to her tea before taking a sip. She puts the cup down, looks at me curiously. "If you don't mind my asking, why were you at Artie's farm today? Given . . . what's happened, I wouldn't have thought it a good idea to fraternize with his brother."

I shake my head. "No," I say, "it was just a mistake, that was all. I was out walking in the hills, the snow started to come down hard and I decided to get back home the fastest way possible – so I came out of the woods and walked past Artie's fields. Pat was there when I got there."

"Oh? And what was *he* doing there?"

"He'd heard the sirens," I say, "he came out to investigate."

Larraine seems to think things through carefully for a while, taking a bite of her own apple pie and chewing it slowly.

I use the time to take a bite too, and it tastes just as good as it looks. "Delicious," I say, and although Larraine smiles, it is clear her mind is elsewhere.

Finally, she looks up from the pie. "I suppose he had something to say about those sirens up the hill, and you walking in the woods at the same time?"

I wonder if she is actually considering what Pat thought, or voicing her own opinion of the "coincidence".

"Yes," I answer after a moment's thought, deciding to be honest, "he did. He was drunk, so he probably didn't know what he was saying, but he seemed suspicious."

"Hmmm," Larraine murmurs through another mouthful of pie, "it figures. Man like that is *born* suspicious. Treats everyone like they operate the same way he does."

I am glad that Larraine seems to disregard the possibility of my involvement in anything. Or at least, I am glad that she is making the effort to pretend, anyway; it makes me feel better, whether it's true or not.

"How *does* he operate?" I ask.

Larraine shrugs her shoulders. "I don't like to gossip," she says – which is always the telltale sign of someone who *does*, of course, "but I've heard some bad things about Pat, things from back in Seattle."

"Oh?" I say, feigning disinterest, disguising my eagerness for more information – all part of the gossip game. "What sort of things?"

"Well," Larraine starts, conspiratorially, "those 'sexual misdemeanors' the papers talked about? Turns out Pat used to be a teacher, until he was caught . . . having *sex* with one of his students."

She says the words with obvious distaste, which begs the next question. "How old?"

"Fourteen," she spits. "Rotten son of a bitch . . . *If* it's true," she adds, as if to cover herself from a charge of slander. "Apparently works as a dog-catcher for the local council now, can't get a job in a school anymore, had to beg for *that* job, by all accounts."

I nod along with her, wondering where she gets her information. But she *does* work with Pat's brother, I remind myself, and that would certainly be as likely a source as any.

Wasn't Dennis Rader, the infamous BTK serial killer, working as a compliance officer or dog catcher when he was eventually caught? I ask myself, wondering about the parallels. People like Rader are drawn to those sorts of jobs, experts suppose, because they are positions of power, positions where they can exert their influence over others. Is Pat the same?

I guess this explains the "last time" Pat had

mentioned back on the farm; he must have been referring to this incident . . . mustn't he? Unless there is more to Pat Jenkins that we still don't know . . .

"I suppose that backs up the rumors about him spiking that girl's drink," I say. It's not gossip, I tell myself; it's fishing for relevant information.

Larraine finishes another bite of pie and nods. "It sure does. Little Sophie's not even fourteen yet, not 'til summer. Sick bastard, with a wife at home as well."

I can see she is angry, that she obviously has a strong dislike for this man, and I imagine that it is perhaps because he reminds her of her own errant husband.

"But they released him," I say, cautious about how I phrase things. There are some things that I presumably should know about the case, which – given that I've missed out on a couple of days, during which anything might have happened – I might *not* know. I need to try and get additional information without revealing too much about my own situation. It seems that Larraine is a great person to get this from – she is, after all, the "community den mother" as Artie describes her, and she seems eager to exchange stories.

I just need to be careful what I say.

"They released him, sure," Larraine says, "but I don't know, he seems . . . suspicious, don't you think? It might just be his background, and I guess we shouldn't judge anyone too harshly on *that*. But I don't know what you think, but I get an uneasy feeling whenever I'm around him." She pours me another cup of tea from the china pot, then another for herself. "Oh, I get on with his brother just fine, we work over in Anchorage together, you know. Artie's pretty nice, I've known him a long time. But even he has doubts about his brother, I think."

"What sort of doubts?"

Larraine shrugs uneasily. "Oh, I don't know, just the way he talks about him sometimes, I guess. But maybe it's nothing."

"Do you think he might have been involved?"

"In that poor girl's death?" She drinks some tea, pushes her empty plate away as she thinks. "I'm not sure," she says. "Reports say that she must have been held for several days before you found her, and Pat only got to Alaska on Thursday evening. I suppose it would be impossible for him to have abducted her."

"Unless he got here earlier than he claims," I suggest, but Larraine shakes her head.

"No, I think the police checked that out, they definitely have him on the Thursday flight from Seattle, people back home corroborated the fact he was there until then."

"I guess if he abducted her late Thursday night, early Friday morning, it's still possible. Or else . . ." I say, wondering if Larraine will jump to the same conclusion as I did, when I'd thought about the matter back at Ben's house that morning.

"Or else," she says, "another person abducted her before Pat arrived."

"If that is the case," I say, knowing that more than

one person was probably involved, but also that this fact hadn't been in the newspaper article and so wasn't public knowledge yet, "then who would he have been working with?" I paused, pretending to think. "I suppose the most likely person would be . . ."

"Artie," Larraine finished for me, nodding uneasily. "Yes, I've been thinking about that." She drinks her tea, not taking her eyes off mine; the effect is unnerving. "He was arrested too, you know."

"Really?" I ask, surprised; that wasn't in the article either, and Ben had never mentioned it. "I didn't hear about that."

"Well," she continues in a conspiratorial whisper, "he was brought in for questioning really, but held there for quite some time. The police – or the ABI, or whoever's in charge – must have been following the same train of thought."

"But they released him without charge."

"No evidence. House was clean, nothing at all to tie the girl to him in any way."

"What do *you* think?"

"I like him," Larraine starts, her voice unsure now, "but I know his job doesn't do him any favors in a case like this."

"What do you mean?"

"Well, he runs the shelter, of course. You know, for runaways, drug addicts, we get a lot of working girls there too. The police haven't released the identity of that girl yet, but from what they've said, it looks like she was from this sort of group, if I'm not out of turn saying it. So, the cops probably know that the girl might have come across his path there. Makes sense, from their point of view."

She is right, and I am amazed I've missed it until now. Yes, Lynette Hyams was exactly the sort of girl who could have turned up at Anchorage Street Shelter, and it turns my suspicions immediately more toward Artie Jenkins. It would be an ideal cover, a perfect place for scouting helpless, vulnerable victims. Lynette could have been spotted by him, selected as a victim; possibly abducted by him, kept in some as-yet unknown location for his brother.

Just because his house was clean doesn't, I remind myself, cross him off the list completely; it is entirely possible that he has a secondary location somewhere. We live in the vast semi-wilderness, there must be countless places where a cabin or small hut could lie undetected; and if it was an underground chamber, then it might never be discovered.

I think about walking back down the forested mountain and a chill goes down my spine as I think about what – or who – might still be out there. *Is* there an underground chamber somewhere? And if so, does that mean there might be more victims, still held there?

I shake my head to clear it; I can't think about those things, not now. It is a rabbit hole, and if I go down there, I may have difficulty getting back out.

"Are Pat and Artie under police surveillance?" I ask, making a note to ask Ben about it as well. He's not on the case, but I'm sure he will know; and if he doesn't, he can certainly find out.

"Yes," Larraine says, nodding her head, "I think so. Oh, nothing obvious, of course, but on the journey back from Anchorage, Artie was going hell for leather on the theory, he's convinced his phones are tapped and people are watching him. Probably the ABI, if they're doing their job right. Another slice of pie?"

"Yes please," I say, watching as she levers herself up from the kitchen table, returning with the pie. She places a large slice on each of our plates, pours the cream and sits back down. I wait until she is seated, then say, "Of course, if Pat's involved, Artie doesn't *have* to be. There *is* another possibility."

"Menders?" Larraine asks, her mind razor-sharp. I nod my head, and she contemplates the idea. "Could be," she says. "And I get on with Artie, so I'd be delighted if he wasn't mixed up in all of this." She thinks some more, eats some more. "I guess people discount Menders because of the surgery," she says, "but there's nothing to stop him abducting someone. He'd just need a 'friend' to . . . well, you know . . ."

I've read the autopsy report. I *do* know. Menders could have used his crucifixes, he could have tortured her, he could have sewn her up, he could have done many of the terrible things I've read about; but someone else would have had to rape her.

Pat Jenkins and Douglas Menders?

It's possible, certainly, but how on earth would they have known one another?

But I make a mental note to talk it over with Ben

later. It might have already been checked out, but any form of communication between the two men – email, letters, chatrooms, *anything* – would be highly incriminating.

"I guess they're checking DNA," I say, wondering why I hadn't asked Ben earlier. But it has been a long time since I was involved in anything like this, and the coma has obviously taken its toll. I know that semen was found with the body, and I am sure that De Nares is trying to match it to his suspects. I realize that I don't know what the rules are for this in Alaska. Does the suspect have to give permission? Can you only take samples from people arrested for a crime? Charged for a crime? Is the ABI even *allowed* to cross-reference Pat's DNA with the semen found with Lynette Hyams?

I realize then that there are no details in the papers that I've read about the attack, no indication that there was any sexual assault, and decide to be more careful with what I say.

"Maybe they managed to find something under her nails or something, you know?" I add to my first statement, not wanting to appear to know more than I should.

Larraine nods. "Maybe," she says, "and that would be a real breakthrough, wouldn't it?"

Maybe it would, maybe it wouldn't; in these cases, things are rarely so clear-cut. Sometimes the evidence is excluded on legal grounds, other times it is spoiled before it even reaches the crime lab, and it is often not quite so incontrovertible as many people believe.

"Yes," I say half-heartedly.

"I mean," Larraine continues eagerly, perhaps perceiving my own lack of enthusiasm, "this is the first time a 'fresh' body has been found, if you'll excuse the term."

"A 'fresh' body?" I ask, momentarily confused.

Larraine nods her head sagely. "Those bodies up in Chugach were too badly decomposed for there to be any evidence left, if I remember correctly."

I am surprised, yet I try not to show it. So Larraine thinks the crimes are related too? "You think there's a link?" I ask.

"Don't you?" she responds as she pours us both some more tea. She looks up at me and shrugs. "It just seems like common sense, you know. How many people like that are out there? And whoever it was that killed those poor girls before, he was never caught. So why wouldn't he be back?"

"Why wait so long?" I ask, wondering if Larraine will come to the same conclusions as Ben and I had.

"The killer might have been arrested for something else," she says, "and was unable to do anything until now. Or else he's just moved to a different area, maybe another country altogether. Or maybe, he's been hiding the bodies somewhere more effectively. Maybe he's never stopped, it's just that no more victims have been found until that girl escaped. Heaven knows, it's difficult to get reliable information on some of these girls. I help out in the shelter, remember? Girls come and go on a near-daily basis, we help them when we can, but what happens to them after they leave is anyone's guess. As horrible as it sounds, they're non-people, as far as the system is concerned. I've been worrying about them for years, warning them to be careful."

"You're convinced it's the same person?"

"Or people," she says, nodding. "But I guess I just don't want to think about there being more of them out there. It's too scary to think about, isn't it?"

I nod in return. "It sure is," I agree. "What do you think motivates somebody like that?"

"Hate," Larraine answers almost immediately. "What else can it be? This guy, he *hates* women. Why?" She shrugs her shoulders. "Who knows? Maybe his mother beat him as a little kid, maybe his wife cheated on him, maybe the girls laughed at him at school, saw him in the changing room, you know the sort of thing. Hell, maybe all of that and more. But I think anyone who kills women – and from the press reports of those earlier crimes, they all seem to be a part of the same sort of group, teenage girls, young women, on the streets – well, I think anyone who targets that group *must* hate women, for whatever reason."

"I think you're probably right," I agree with her, thinking about Pat Jenkins, about those young girls he's been linked to. Thinking about Douglas Menders too, someone who could *definitely* be said to have a problem with women.

My eyes must have strayed subconsciously toward the mountain, because Larraine follows them, making the connection. "Do you know what's going on up there?" Larraine asks, gesturing up the forested slopes, where the lights and sirens still come from, her eyes like a hawk's.

I've enjoyed our conversation here in this homely kitchen, and I genuinely like Lorraine; but at the same time I'm all too aware how easily she is sharing information – *gossip* – with me. I cannot be sure if she'll relay our entire conversation to Artie in the car on the way to work in the morning – *Hey Artie, you'll never guess what that nosy-parker Jessica Hudson thinks! I like her, but you should have heard . . .*

I get the feeling that her experiences with men might make her more easy sharing such intelligence with women, but you never know; and I'm not entirely happy to think of her talking to *anyone* about what we've discussed, male *or* female.

Consequently, I know I need to be *very* careful about what I say here.

"No," I say, "I've got no idea, it's hard to tell exactly where the lights are coming from. I suppose the two most likely options are, they're raiding Doug Menders' cabin for some reason, or else maybe they've found something in the woods up there."

"Another body?" Larraine asks, and I know my suggestion has successfully engaged her.

I shrug. "Could be," I say. "Or maybe a secondary location, like a cabin, or a chamber or something," I continue, remembering what I'd been thinking about only minutes before.

Larraine nods her head, deep in thought. "Yes,"

she says, "yes, I guess it might be." She looks up at me. "Terrifying, isn't it? This whole thing, I mean, we can make educated guesses, but we've got no *real* idea who's doing it, or why. We don't know if there are more victims out there, we don't know if it's the same person that killed those other girls, or if it's a new monster altogether. Whatever the answer, it doesn't help me sleep at night."

"Yeah," I sigh in agreement, "me neither." *Although at least when you finally go to sleep, you wake up the next day like a normal person.* "How are your kids handling things?" I ask, the thought just occurring to me. "They're just young boys, surely they must be frightened to death?"

"They're getting older," Larraine reassures me, "they're not scared of the boogeyman hiding under the bed anymore, you know. They're growing up big and strong, Adam's nearly twelve now and Rich has just turned fourteen. And whoever this psycho is, I think it's clear he's only interested in females. No," she confirms, as if to reassure herself, "there's nothing for them to be frightened of."

I hope she's right; but the presence of *any* sort of killer in the area must surely be a worry?

"Are they at school?" I ask, and she quickly turns to a clock on the mantle of the small kitchen fireplace. She stands quickly, an apologetic look on her face.

"I'm glad you reminded me," she says with a guilty smile, "I should be on my way to get them. They've got soccer practice after classes finish, but they should be done soon and – Heaven knows – the school buses don't come anywhere near here. But I just feel terrible leaving you like this," she says, genuine sympathy in her eyes. "Would you like to stay here while I'm gone? You can help yourself to more tea and cake."

"No," I say, standing from the table and stretching my aching legs, "I should be getting back myself, see how the horses are doing."

She seems disappointed, as if she has let me down in some way, then nods her head. "Okay," she says, "but at least let me give you a lift. I think you've had enough of walking in the snow for one day."

I smile. "It's a deal," I say.

"And who knows," she says as she gets her coat from a rack on the wall, "maybe we'll hear something on the news about what's happening up there?"

I put on my own coat and nod in agreement, only too aware of *exactly* what is happening up there – the ABI is processing the crime scene of Douglas Menders' homicide.

"Maybe," I say with a hopeful smile as I follow Larraine out of the door toward her SUV and – at last – home.

I wave goodbye to Larraine as she pulls away from my driveway, and rap on my own front door. It feels strange, but I know that Amy will be there and – even though it is my own house – I don't want to just barge in, unannounced.

I note that my SUV is parked next to the house, answering the question I'd had back in Ben's car earlier that day. He'd obviously picked me up from here the night before, to go on our date together, and I feel slightly relieved that I don't have to track my own car down.

The dogs respond first, Molly pawing frantically at the door while I hear Luna and Nero padding heavily across the kitchen floor and whining in high-pitched tones that bely their size and appearance.

Moments later, the door opens and the dogs burst forward, Molly's paws clamping onto my thighs as she desperately tries to lick me while the other two circle happily around me, wagging tails hitting me so hard, they hurt.

Amy is in the doorway, and although I can see she is smiling, it seems somehow not quite genuine and I wonder what is going on, what the problem is. Have the police been here again? Have they already called, trying to find me, to connect me to Menders' cabin?

"I'm sorry," Amy says, "I didn't know who he was, honestly, I –"

I wonder who she is talking about, what's been happening, when an all-too familiar face appears behind her, grinning sheepishly.

"Hi, Jess," Paul Southland says, and my heart momentarily skips a beat and sinks in my chest at the exact same time.

13

Despite the shock to my system (*what is he doing here? – was he involved in the Hyams' death? – what does he want from me? – why isn't he back in New York?*), I speak first to Amy about the horses, make sure they're okay; I feed and fuss over the dogs; I even check the news websites for any information about Doug Menders (there isn't any). Anything to avoid confronting Paul, who stands silently waiting for me by the door to the hallway, leaning nervously against the painted wooden frame.

If he looks nervous, then I've got no idea how *I* look; I don't even know how I feel. I woke up this morning in the bed of a man I'd slept with, a man who I'd been on dates with and presumably have some sort of relationship with, without remembering any of it; and now here in front of me is the *other* man, the man who – once upon a time – I'd decided to spend the rest of my life with, the man who left me unconscious in a hospital bed, the man who'd taken the engagement ring from my finger while I lay in a coma and moved all of the things out of my apartment, the man I'd moved thousands of miles to avoid.

The man a part of me still loves.

Finally, Luna and Nero close by my side, I turn to him and give him my full attention.

"Do you want me to stay?" Amy asks, although I barely hear the words.

"It's okay," I say. "Thanks, but I'll be okay."

She retreats upstairs, where she's got a spare room while I need the help.

I still haven't taken my eyes off Paul.

"Surprised to see me?" he asks, obviously hoping his boyish charm will still work on me.

I try hard for it not to.

"I heard you'd gone back to New York," I say, trying to make it sound as if I would have preferred it if he'd done just that.

He shakes his head. "No, I've been staying in a hotel in Anchorage. My firm hasn't exactly kicked me out, but I think 'partner' is now a long way off, that's for sure. I'm keeping a low profile for now, until this whole thing blows over."

He tries to make light of the situation, but I can see that it pisses him off.

"You got arrested?" I ask, maybe trying to piss him off even more.

"Brought in for questioning," he says awkwardly. "But it still doesn't look too good for a senior defense attorney in one of the big New York firms to be involved in a case that might involve rape, torture, murder, not to mention serial killing." He shakes his head sadly, though I am far from feeling sorry for him. "No, it doesn't look good at all."

I look at Paul again, see that some of the old arrogance (*confidence*, I'd thought at the time, when I'd been in love with him) is gone now; it's in his posture, the slump of his shoulders, the way his head now seems to hang down between them. Gone is the chest-out, chin-up look of the young prince, out to conquer the world.

And suddenly, a part of me *does* start to feel sorry for him, at least a little.

I think for a moment about what to say, then decide to get straight to the point.

"So what are you doing *here*?"

He seems to think about the question deeply, as if he doesn't even know himself. "I don't know . . ." he starts gently. "I guess I . . . just wanted to see you. After all, it's been so long, and I've come all this way, gone through all this shit, and I still haven't seen you, not really *seen* you . . ."

At least that answers one of my questions; in the muddle of days that I'd missed, or rearranged, I *haven't* seen Paul already, not here in Alaska. That would help, I was sure; much less chance of saying something that would seem out of the ordinary. If we *had* already met up, I wouldn't have a clue as to what we'd said, how we'd left things.

As it stands, I might just be able to get through this.

"You want to see me now?" I ask, unable to help myself, all of this having been bottled up inside me for months. On the telephone, I'd been caught completely unawares by his call, unprepared for how I'd respond to him. Now, I am ready. "I was in hospital for months, how about coming to see me *then*?"

I keep my voice cool, but laced with venom. "Oh, that's right," I continue, snapping my fingers as if just remembering, "you *did*. You came into my room, reached over my unconscious body, and pulled the damn ring right off my finger."

"That's not fair," he responds, although he cannot keep looking me in the eye. "I . . . I . . ." He staggers to the kitchen table, across the stone-flagged floor, and grabs hold of the back of a chair for support. "I'm sorry," he gasps, and I am shocked, not used to seeing weakness of any kind in this man. "Can I sit down? I've not . . . been sleeping well, I . . ."

I go to him, helping him down into the chair, noticing for the first time how his brow is sweating, his armpits too. I wonder if he is ill, or if it's something else.

"Thanks," he says, still weak; then his eyes flash for a moment and my entire body tenses and moves away, the dogs by my side instantly, and I have no idea if Paul is really suffering, or if it's some sort of act.

But why?

I keep my distance now, edging round to the other side of the table before taking a seat, the dogs still close by.

"Why *are* you here?" I ask again, more softly this

time.

Paul raises his head and looks up at me through hooded lids. It looks like he's been drinking and – like he says – not getting enough sleep.

"I needed to see you," Paul says, and it sounds genuine enough. "I . . . after speaking on the phone, despite what you said, I could tell you still felt something. I guess I thought if I could just see you in person, I could convince you that I'm sorry, I'm really sorry for everything, I really am. But then all this shit started happening – you were arrested, I was arrested, who knows what the hell is going on. You're released, I'm released, and I just know it's a bad idea to see you, people are talking already, we're probably under surveillance by the ABI but I'm using what little influence I have left to shut down any of that sort of shit, but I knew it was dangerous coming here, but I knew I couldn't just fly off back to New York without at least seeing you once. And so I waited in that damned hotel room, waited, and then just said 'fuck it', got a taxi and came over. And that's that, that's what happened, that's why I'm here."

He'd really got into a roll there, the words just spilling out, and I'm convinced even more than ever that he's been drinking, maybe since he arrived in Alaska, maybe since before he left New York. He really is a shadow of his former self, and I know it is not just the accusations from the Hyams case that are going to scupper his chances of making partner.

I decide to ignore the fact that he'd contradicted

himself – *you got arrested, I got arrested*, he'd said, in stark opposition to his prior claim that he'd only been brought in for questioning. But I file it away for later; it will be easy enough to check with Ben, if it comes to it.

I look at him across the table, still keeping my voice soft. "What do you think will happen?"

I am conflicted, confused; I want to scream at him, yell at him – *Get out of here, you son of a bitch! Get out!* – and hit him, slap him, grab him and haul him out into the fields; but I also want to go to him, to hold him close, to feel his skin against mine, and the dichotomy of my feelings threatens to shut down my system entirely. There is such a plethora of different emotions darting about within me. It would be bad enough for Paul to be here on any *normal* week; a direct, physical presence was bound to test my mettle, the barriers I've built up to help protect me from the psychological scars he's inflicted on me. On *this* week, with my mind already messed up from Lynette's death and my subsequent, unexplainable bouncing around from day to day, his presence here threatens to overwhelm what little sanity I have left.

"I don't know," Paul mumbles, and the whole situation seems suddenly very surreal; Paul doesn't mumble, he *never* mumbles; he doesn't drink either, he gets up early to hit the gym before racing to the law office and impressing the hell out of everyone he meets.

But people change, I guess.

I've changed.

Lynette Hyams changed; she used to be alive.

Did Paul have anything to do with it? The thought sends a shudder through me, and I don't even hear his reply to my question.

"Sorry?" I say. "I missed it, what did you say?"

"I said, I just want things to go back to the way they were, you know? You, me, the apartment, New York, everything just how it was."

I observe Paul, how he has changed; his sallow skin, his eyes deep in their sockets, and it's clear that he's been suffering since long before he came to Alaska. Maybe he *does* feel guilty? Maybe he desperately *does* want to get back together with me, to make it up to me? He doesn't make excuses for the ring, for the apartment, for what he did, and – to a certain extent – I respect him for that; at least he's not trying to weasel his way out of it, at least he seems to recognize that there *are* no excuses.

But the thought hits me again.

Did he have anything to do with the death of Lynette Hyams?

The way he looks, the way he's acting, I just don't know; he doesn't seem to be the same Paul Southland that I knew and loved, once upon a time. Who can say what he's capable of?

And yet if the serial killer theory is to be believed in this case, then the same perpetrator was also active here several years ago which would – on the face of it at least – seem to rule Paul out entirely.

I recognize now that this same argument could also be used for Pat Jenkins. Where was *he* living, back in

2010? 2006? Did he ever come to visit his brother during that time? And did Artie have alibis for that period too? It's worth checking, but I'm sure that De Nares and the ABI are tracking down those leads, if they haven't done so already. I know that De Nares sees me as the main suspect, but I trust that he is not fixating on me and allowing it to ruin his professional judgment. Other leads will surely be followed up properly.

I hope.

But I think again about the circumstances, the possibility that more than one person is involved in this. What if Menders *was* responsible for those earlier murders, the ones found in Chugach, and the ones before that, found just outside Anchorage? The bodies were so decomposed that it couldn't be proved if they were raped, at least not conclusively. The use of blunt objects might well indicate someone who was *unable* to rape someone.

But Lynette *was* raped, brutally so. Could Paul have some connection to Menders, could they have been working together? But I believe that even less than I believe that Pat Jenkins was involved.

But, I remind myself, Douglas Menders is now dead, and Paul is now here in my home, only a short distance – relatively speaking – from Menders' cabin.

Is it a coincidence?

Or is it something more?

I shift uncomfortably in my chair, and the dogs' ears twitch in response; my friends are tensed to act quickly if they are needed.

"I'm not sure there's any going back," I say, trying to keep strong. "Not anymore."

"Too much water under the bridge, I guess?" he says, eyes downcast.

"I guess."

His eyes look up at me at last. "How are you holding up, anyway?"

"I . . . I don't know." It's the truth, at least. How *am* I holding up? For the first time, I consider, maybe I'm not holding up so well?

"It's weird, right?" Paul says.

"What is?" There are so many weird things going on, which one does he mean?

"You know, I heard about what you told the police, I know why you got arrested, you said that girl got killed before it actually happened, am I right?"

Paul seems animated, for the first time since being here, and I guess it's because he feels he's onto something, his professional instincts aroused.

But how does he know? Did somebody at the ABI leak the information? Palmer PD? Anchorage? I sigh; it could be anyone.

But I don't want to admit anything to him, not right now, maybe never; I still don't know his real agenda here.

"You know better than that," I say to Paul. "I'm never going to comment on an ongoing investigation, whether I've been exonerated or not."

"Ah," he says with a tone that borders on satisfaction, "still the Assistant DA, right? Even out here, even after all this time."

I shrug. "I guess it never leaves you, even if you want it to."

"I guess not. But still," he persists, "it's kind of strange. And – if you didn't have anything to do with it, and I really don't think you do, not in a million years – it's a little like what you told me, you know, a few years ago."

What the hell? Predicting a murder – or seeing it first, or whatever you want to call it – is similar to something I'd told Paul about before?

My brain clouds over as I struggle to imagine what that might possibly be; but I know my memory hasn't been the same since the attack in New York, I know that the bullet left my head a mess.

What is he talking about?

I need to know, and yet I have to be careful about how I find out.

"And what was that?" I ask, acting as if I know exactly what he is talking about but playing the game, as he might expect me to do.

Paul smiles at me, although – in his current state – the effect is more disturbing than charming. "You know," he chides, waiting for me to admit to whatever it is that we discussed before. Instead, I continue to look at him until he speaks again. "You know," he persists, "that problem you used to have, those doctors, that whole thing back in Boston."

That thing back in Boston? Wow, I have no idea what this man is talking about, absolutely none at all.

So what am I going to do about it?

"I don't know what you're talking about," I say, deciding in an instant to be honest, to simply level with him; I need to know, and I don't care what he thinks.

I can see he doesn't believe me, that he's about to give me the *Oh yeah, right* routine, and I put up a hand to stop him. "I'm serious," I say. "After the attack, my memory, it's . . . not what it was. I really don't know what you mean." I hold his gaze for a few moments, then ask the question I so desperately need answered. "What happened in Boston?"

14

"Even without that attack in New York," Paul begins, "I guess you might not remember too much about it. According to your Mom – your Dad would never talk about any of this – you were treated with electro-shock therapy and hypnosis, when you told me a few years ago, you only remembered very vague details."

This was already starting to freak me out. Electro-shock therapy? Hypnosis? And my mother had provided details to Paul? It was already starting to get a little hard to take in.

"What did I tell you?" I ask him.

"You . . . how do I put this? You had episodes where you claimed things had happened . . . bad things, things that couldn't be proved. But apparently you were convinced these things had really happened, and it was very hard for your parents to deal with, your Dad was afraid that his 'crazy daughter' would ruin his chances of promotion within his firm, right? The only person who believed you was your brother."

"Jack?" I ask, breathless, unable to know what to believe.

"Yeah," Paul says with a nod, "I guess. Although I never met him, you know . . . ah . . ."

That's right. Jack died long before I met Paul, and the thought of my brother threatens to send me over the edge. And so I cut it off, forcing myself to concentrate on what Paul is telling me; what I'd apparently told *him*, a lifetime ago.

"Well anyway, you couldn't remember any of the actual cases that happened, you know, those incidents which you thought had happened, when you told me about it, you just remembered the basic outline, seeing the doctors, being treated, that sort of thing."

I pick up the hidden inference. "But you looked into it yourself?"

Paul looks embarrassed, as if I've caught him with his pants down. "Well . . . uhh . . . yeah, I looked into it. I'm sorry, but I guess I knew what your Dad meant. I was going to get married, and I thought I had to know if there was . . . something wrong with you, you know?"

"You didn't want me spoiling your chances of making partner," I say, trying to keep the bitterness out of my voice.

He shrugs his shoulders. "I know you must hate me for what I did to you anyway, so why lie now, right? Yes, I checked into it because I didn't want something from your past rocking up and spoiling my chances of making partner. I'm sorry."

"It doesn't matter anymore," I say, shaking my

head and – finally – meaning it. "Go on. What did you find out?"

"Well, I couldn't get any real details, but it all seemed to revolve around your perception of time, from what I could find out anyway."

"What do you mean?" I ask, my curiosity aroused to fever-pitch.

"Like your days became muddled up, you thought it was one day but it was really another, that sort of thing." My heart almost stops in my chest as he talks, the thought that this might not be the first time that this has happened a real, genuine shock. "You went from one doctor to another, but nobody believed you."

"Nobody?"

"Well, there was one apparently, but he was hounded out of the profession by all accounts."

"As a result of believing me?"

Paul nods. "Pretty much, yeah. The best doctors in the country finally decided that you had . . . now, what was it now, what do they call it? 'Acute tachypsychia'? Is that it?"

"I don't know," I say, never having heard of it.

"Yeah, I think that's right, acute tachypsychia, it's something to do with how you perceive time, they thought that there was some sort of imbalance in your brain, that sort of thing. That's why you got treated in the end, they targeted your brain, zapped it this way and that according to your Mom. You barely remembered any of the details in the end, I guess it's no surprise you don't remember any of it now."

"How old was I?"

"Eleven, twelve, that sort of age I think," Paul says.

"How long did it last?"

"I'm not sure, I think a year or two, but I'm not sure."

"What was the name of the doctor that treated me, the one who believed me?"

"The name of the doctor? Come on, I really don't know, I have no idea."

"But he was in Boston?"

"At the time I guess, yeah."

I know I need to find that doctor, to ask him for the details of my case. What really happened? *Why* did it happen?

Or maybe it never really happened at all, maybe it's just a psyche game by Paul; maybe he found out what happened here in Alaska, and has made up all this other bullshit to get me talking to him again, to get me to trust him?

But what if he *is* telling the truth?

"Do you know anything else?" I ask, desperate for more information.

"Not really, no," Paul says with a tinge of regret – real or pretend, I can't say. "Only that your Mom said you used to say something about a red moon, right around the time you'd have what she called an 'episode'."

"What did she say?" I press, trying not to sound too eager but almost certainly failing. "What, exactly?"

"Well, apparently you'd see this great, big red

moon anytime you'd have this weird tachypsychia thing, although nobody else ever saw it. Red moons, or blood moons, are generally associated with lunar eclipses, but none were ever recorded when you claimed you saw them."

My heart is beating so hard, so fast in my chest that I think I might pass out. Maybe the red moon that I saw – that I keep seeing – *does* have some sort of significance?

But what?

What?

Another thought dawns on me then, and it is far from pleasant.

Is there something wrong with me?

My parents, and – it seems – most of my doctors, all thought I was making things up, that I was confused, that I had some sort of mental condition that caused me to act out, to imagine things that weren't really there. Were they all correct? The only people who believed me were my brother – who ended up killing himself – and one single doctor, who was hounded out of the profession as a result, at least by Paul's account.

Not for the first time, I wonder if I *am* crazy. Maybe this whole thing wasn't caused by the gunshot to my head after all, maybe it goes deeper?

Is anything real? Or have I imagined everything?

And yet – despite checking out my history, to help protect his precious career – Paul must have still given me the all-clear. He had proposed to me, after all, had agreed for us to get married, so he must have decided that my mental health wasn't a liability.

Unless he loved me so much that he was willing to ignore it?

I might once have believed that; but, knowing what I know now, I doubt it.

If I'd been a liability, he would have dropped me like a bad habit.

I breathe out slowly, trying to get my thoughts together. From what Paul is saying – if he is to be believed – my mysterious, sanity-questioning experiences here in Alaska are *not* the first things that have happened to me in this way. Apparently I have been "out of time" before, when I was younger; an "illness" for which I was treated.

I am curious – more than curious – about the details of these earlier experiences. What were these things that I claimed to have seen? What happened when my perception of time changed? Did I manage to change these events, like I am hoping to do now? And what is the red moon, is it just a symbol? Is it a way that my mind tries to make sense of things?

I wonder, again, if Paul is telling the truth. The detail about the red moon is convincing, but I remind myself that this was in my original comments to Ben, right here in this same kitchen on the night I found the body. Paul might have come across that information, reported somewhere along the way. Then I catch myself – no, I decide, that would be impossible; because I only mentioned the moon the *first* time I found the body. My current situation is predicated upon the *second* time I experienced Saturday, the time I only know about from listening to De Nares reading my statement in the police interview room, the version of events when I *didn't* go to the party, when I'd found Lynette Hyams on my front porch and not in the fields outside, the version where she'd died right here on the kitchen floor.

Damn, the whole thing is so confusing, it threatens to overwhelm my all-too-fragile mind.

But if I didn't go to the party, I didn't go outside, I didn't see the moon, and so Paul couldn't have heard about it from anybody – and this must lend credence to his story, surely?

But the only trouble is that the only Saturday I remember is the first one – the one where the 'I' that I am now existed, not the secondary 'I' who experienced the alterative version of events and made that police report. I don't actually know what that 'I' saw, what that 'I' experienced.

Damn, if my brain didn't hurt before, then it sure as hell does now.

What I need to do, I realize, is find that doctor. *He* will have the details of what happened to me when I was younger.

When I was younger? I think suddenly of those flashbacks to my father's friend, Desmond Curtis, the terror I felt as I remembered. Is it connected somehow? I shake my head. The *doctor*, I remind myself. He is the key. He is the answer.

But how the hell do I even find him?

"Are you sure that you can't remember that

doctor?" I ask Paul, trying not to appear too desperate. "The one who believed my story?"

Paul shifts in his chair, and he peers across the table at the dogs. Molly is off in the corner, spread-eagled and minding her own business, but the two guard dogs are doing their job, keeping their wary glare fixed on our uninvited guest.

"Can you get rid of those guys?" he asks nervously, and I remember that dogs scare him, city boy that he is. "They're really freaking me out."

"That's their job," I reply, although even I admit that Luna and Nero might be a bit of overkill – two Italian mastiffs, nearly three hundred pounds of muscle and sinew between them, compared to the sorry shell of a man that sits at my table.

I relent and nod my head. "You can let them out," I say, gesturing to the kitchen door.

"Thanks," Paul says, and the relief on his face is palpable as he pulls himself to his feet and pads across the kitchen.

They were meant to protect me from Zebunac's armed assassins; I think I can handle Paul. After all, we lived with each other for three years.

Paul opens the door, but the dogs don't move. I click my fingers and point, and they reluctantly get to their feet and trot out into the front yard.

Paul and I both look at Molly, sprawled on the stone flags, and shrug our shoulders at the same time; she's not moving for anyone. I watch as Paul closes the door, then I turn to the counter and reach for the kettle.

"Coffee?" I ask, chastising myself for not asking sooner. Paul may have stung me – to put it lightly – but that's no reason to be rude to a guest.

Hey, I think, maybe living in Alaska is already having an effect on me?

And then the sound of a click confuses me momentarily, before I realize what it is.

I turn from the kettle and confirm my fears, and my heart sinks even deeper.

The dogs are outside.

And Paul has locked the door.

15

"What are you doing?" I ask, my mind turning somersaults. I lived with this man for three years, yes; but do I really know him? What do I know? The last few days are making me seriously doubt whether I know anything at all.

But he didn't set my danger radar off at all, he didn't appear dangerous, and – after the New York attack – I'm a bag of nerves when it comes to this sort of thing. If he's got bad intent, how did he mask it before?

Maybe it's just my residual feelings for him, maybe I've been duped again into trusting him?

Dammit, why did I let Nero and Luna leave?

Molly's stirring on the floor, but I know she won't do me much good. But I'm in a kitchen. Plenty of knives. My gun somewhere, too. Damn, where is it? Shit, why don't I keep it somewhere obvious, why is it locked away in a drawer somewhere?

Shit, shit, shit.

"You look nervous," Paul says, surprise in his voice as he walks slowly across the kitchen toward me. "Why?"

I back away by instinct; I don't want to show him that I'm afraid, but I can't help it.

"Why did you lock the door?" I ask, trying to keep my voice even.

"I told you," Paul says, glaring at me through those hooded eyes. "I don't like dogs."

I see a change in those eyes then, a lethal change, and I turn, yanking open the nearest drawer and reaching for a knife, a fork, *anything* to stop Paul from getting to me; I pull out a paring knife and turn back, but it's too late, he's there already, hand gripping my wrist, pinning my knife-hand to my side as his other hand goes to my throat, gripping tight; I try and scream, but his fingers close tighter and tighter, and all that comes out is a choked cough.

"You fucked my life up," Paul whispers close in my ear, and – beyond his words – I can hear Luna and Nero barking outside, slamming their paws against the thick wooden door, desperate to get back in; even Molly is up, running toward us and, despite the pain, despite the fear, I am appalled when Paul kicks her straight in the chest, the toe of his boot slamming hard into her and sending her flying back across the kitchen with a helpless whimper.

I convulse with anger, straining to move against Paul's grip; I am whipping my body up and down, left and right, but it is not enough, Paul's grip is too tight, his high school and college athleticism still with him; he squeezes my wrist tighter and the knife drops to the floor; I try and hit him with my other hand but the blows are weak, they just bounce off him; my fingers snake out toward his eyes, but he turns his head and squeezes even harder on my throat, and my arm goes slack, without the strength to mount the attack.

"First you go and get yourself shot," he spits, "despite your father telling you to drop it. How did that look for my chances at the firm? You think they want a partner with an invalid for a wife? How would that fucking look at all the dinner parties, answer me that, huh? But I still loved you, you bitch, you don't know how hard it was for me to end it, to take back that ring, to end it all. It almost killed me." Through my hazy vision, going black as I balanced between consciousness and sleep, I can see his face soften, his grip lighten ever so slightly; I know I should take advantage of it, but I can't, it's all I can do to get some oxygen into my lungs, to stay alive. The dogs outside are going crazy, Molly cowers, terrified, in a corner, and I know I've made one of the biggest mistakes of my life, maybe my last. But I can breathe again, if only a little, and I know I still have a chance.

"And then I follow you out here, try and get you back. Stay in a hotel, can't bring myself to ring you, to call you, to see you, anything, I can't do anything. Do you know how that made me feel?" He almost cries as he says the word, "Weak. Powerless. A man like me, can you imagine that?" He laughs, a short, ugly bark. "A man like me can't be weak." He shakes his head, as if to convince himself. "Can't be. Not in my position, not in my world. But I call anyway, and you stop me dead, stop me cold. Nothing, just nothing, no chance of us getting back together, no chance of anything."

His face is close, I can smell the alcohol on his breath now, can see the way his pupils dilate wildly, and wonder if he's been on the coke again. He was keeping his eyes away from me before, but now they're right here in front of mine, and I know he's been on it, I'm certain. I know he did it when he was younger, he claimed it made him sharper, better at his job. He gave it up for me, but now I can see it's made a return, and I am scared, scared beyond all reason. A sober, clean Paul might not hurt me seriously, but *this* Paul? This Paul, I don't even know.

"Please . . ." I manage from my burning throat.

"Please?" Paul whispers, mocking me. "Please? You want to hear about 'please'? How about I'm only out here in this fucking shit, forsaken wilderness, for you? Fuck 'please'! I'm here, and I get fucking arrested, brought in for some shit that's coming out of your sick mind! You've ruined my job, you've fucking ruined my life! Fuck 'please'! *Fuck you*," he spits, right next to my ear; and then he licks that ear, traces his drink-soaked tongue across my cheek, my lips. "I'm not coming out here for nothing," he tells me, and I feel him growing hard against my leg, and I try again to break free, to fight against him as it becomes clear what he wants from me – one final conquest, one final abuse, the ability to look at himself and know he got the last word, the last say, to know that he *won*, that he's still a winner; and in that instant, I see Paul for what he is. He is not the clean-cut, all-star, straight-A guy that everyone thinks he is, that everyone loves; he is cruel, hard, driven to win at all costs, driven to possess, to control; I suddenly see the college jock that doesn't take "no" for an answer, the type that doesn't classify date-rape as a crime, but as a right.

I see a monster.

He drops his weight and – with his grip still around my neck – I come crashing down to the kitchen floor, the impact driving the air from my lungs, leaving me winded, out of breath, savage pain wracking me; outside the dogs are barking, and I feel Paul once more hard against my leg; see Molly running toward him, latching her small jaws around his arm; watch as Paul shouts in pain, in anger, and tries desperately to shake her off as Luna and Nero threaten to break the door down behind us; look on in sheer terror as Paul's hand slips off my neck and reaches for the knife that I dropped on the floor next to us, sure he will use it on her; and then I scream, my throat free now, I scream at the top of my voice, and I hope someone – anyone – will come; and then I remember that Amy is in the house, she will come here, and then I feel guilty, horribly guilty, and stop screaming instantly. *No, no*, I don't want her here, I don't want her to be in danger, I don't –

And then there is the sound of a door breaking, being kicked open, and I hear Nero and Luna even louder now, and I also hear boots bounding hard along the floor, see human legs alongside the dogs'; feel as Paul's body is twisted this way and that as the dogs attack him, hear a voice, somewhere near, somewhere distant, a voice . . .

"Call them off!" the voice yells, and I can hear it is Ben; I can also hear the screams as Paul is mauled by the animals, and Ben's words finally register and I click my fingers, click my tongue, use my burned throat, my damaged cartilage.

"Enough," I manage to gargle, and it *is* enough, the trained command stopping Luna and Nero in their tracks, mouths thick with blood, Paul a tight, dense ball on the floor next to me, curled into the fetal position, whimpering helplessly as the dogs retreat.

And then Ben is there, handcuffing Paul, pinning him to the floor as he looks at me, fear on his own face. "Shit," he breathes, "damn, are you okay?"

I gag as I try and breathe properly, my dogs surrounding me now, licking me, fussing over me. "Shit," I say, as an echo of Ben, as I finally allow myself to relax slightly, my limbs spreading out across the floor, looking at the man who saved me. "I am now."

But deep inside, I am starting to believe that I might never be okay again.

<u>16</u>

Once again, I am in the bed of Ben Taylor – only this time, it is no surprise.

We are finally back from Palmer Police Precinct, where our statements were taken and Paul now sits in jail, facing charges of battery, attempted rape and – because he grabbed the knife, even though I think he was probably intending to use it on Molly – attempted murder.

I am exhausted, mentally and physically, and it is no surprise at all. I still can't quite believe what a day I've had, it seems totally overwhelming. The adrenaline I felt when Paul attacked me had started to ebb from my system at the police station – the "parasympathetic backlash", Ben had called it – and I'd had to ply myself with coffee to stay awake.

"Do you think it's him?" I breathe, taking comfort from Ben's strong arm around me; feminism be damned, it feels good, and I need that comfort now more than ever.

"You mean the man who killed Lynette?" Ben asks.

"Yeah," I say. "Killed her, or whatever. You know, if he was involved in some way, did it himself, or assisted someone else, that sort of thing."

Ben breathes out slowly. "I don't know," he says, "I just don't know. But I guess I don't buy it, no. No, I don't. I mean, what are the chances? We're looking at a potential long-term, deranged, mission-oriented serial killer, right? He wants to rid the world of prostitutes, or something. Maybe. Could be a lust-killer as well, especially with the latest evidence of sexual torture. But either way, we're looking for someone with a cause, a reason to do this, an organized sort of killer, at least that's what I think. And I *don't* think Paul Southland qualifies, it just doesn't fit. I mean, what are the chances that he comes to see you in Alaska – about three thousand miles from where he lives, right? – and somehow manages to either kidnap, torture and rape a local citizen, or else hook up with someone else, get in on their game, so to speak?" He sighs again. "It could be, it just could be, but I don't buy it. Do you?"

I sigh too. "No," I say, "no, I guess I don't. Even after tonight, what happened, I don't think he's capable of that sort of sustained torture, that pathological hatred, psychopathy, whatever you want to call it. And as you say, I don't think there was the opportunity either." I think for a few more moments, mentally in pain from the thoughts I am having about my ex-fiancé, the man I was prepared to marry just a few short months before. "No," I continue, "I think he's more the date-rape type, I guess. Doesn't like rejection, doesn't understand the word 'no'."

Ben kisses the side of my head, and it feels good. I'm still on edge from what happened back at the ranch – the reason we're here again, and not at my place – but I find myself melting into his arms nevertheless.

"Unless he was doing the same thing in New York," I say, thinking about it for the first time. "Maybe Lynette's murder is unrelated to the Chugach killings, unrelated to those earlier ones, the bodies left near Anchorage. Maybe it's just coincidence. If Paul *is* Lynette's killer," (I can't believe I'm thinking this, let alone saying it), "maybe he's been doing it for a while."

I think for a few more moments, goosebumps appearing on my skin as I consider the facts. "He used to get up early, real early, be gone sometimes before I'd wake up. Sometimes not get home 'til late either, I put it down to work at the office, but who knows where he was, what he was doing? I had my own work to think about, I guess I just believed what he told me. But who knows?"

I breathe out slowly once more, gathering my thoughts. "Maybe he came here to see me, but – if he's that type – maybe he couldn't help himself, couldn't go too long without another victim. Maybe it's just a coincidence, Lynette and those other girls."

"Do you really think that?"

I sigh. "No," I admit, "no, not really. But we can't rule it out either, can we?"

"No," Ben agrees in that deep, gravelly voice of his,

"we can't rule *anything* out. But if it's any help, I don't think it's him. Think about tonight, the way he went about things. The man who kidnapped and abused Lynette is organized, *highly* organized. He can trick people, charm them, fool them into going somewhere with him; obviously, he also has somewhere to take them. If the same man who killed Lynette had wanted to . . . rape *you*, or whatever, you know . . . then he would have abducted you, taken you to the same place, right? But Southland was disorganized in the extreme; except for locking the door, he probably had no real idea what he was doing. Alcohol, weed *and* cocaine in his system, come morning he probably won't remember half of it. Complete bastard, yes. Obviously. Serial killer? I'm not so sure. But as you say, we can't rule it out."

"I still can't believe it," I say, my voice weak with emotion, and I feel Ben's arms pull me in tighter.

"Me neither," Ben says. "I just wish I could have gotten there earlier." There's guilt in his voice, and I won't allow it.

"Don't say that," I say, "don't you ever say that. You did everything you could. You *saved* me."

Ben doesn't know how to respond, perhaps never learned how to accept gratitude, and an awkward silence ensues.

"So what's the latest on Menders?" I ask, changing the subject. We were at the station together for most of the evening, but only in the capacity of chief of police and victim/witness; and we both knew not to discuss the Menders case in front of anyone else anyway.

"Confirmed cause of death was severe head injury, we have the murder weapon as the brass lamp that we found on the floor next to the body, bits of hair, skin and blood found on the base."

"A weapon of opportunity?" I ask, surprised.

"Looks that way, and I'm not sure what sort of spin that puts on things."

"No," I agree. "If someone had gone there with the intent of killing him, they would surely have taken a weapon with them."

"Yeah, unless he couldn't get it into play for some reason, had to go for something else."

"Or maybe he just went there to talk to Menders, and one thing led to another . . ."

"Yeah, maybe the guy didn't initially plan to kill him, maybe it was a mistake, or he just took an opportunity when he saw it."

"Does that tie in with our feelings about this killer? The organized type?"

"But the situation was different. For the female victims, he trolls for them, selects them, takes his time. With Menders, we have some other options. Maybe he was a partner of some sort, they knew each other – a very different kind of scenario then. Or else, like we thought, maybe Menders managed to identify the killer through the telescope, and wanted to blackmail him – calls him over to the house, they discuss the deal, the killer decides there's a better way and beats him to death with the first thing he finds."

I consider the matter for a while, before deciding

that we still don't really know anything. "No prints?"

"None," Ben confirms, "nothing that the crime scene guys have found so far that we can use. Medical examiner estimates time of death as yesterday, somewhere between eleven in the morning and two in the afternoon, give or take."

I breathe out, recognizing how close we are to the killer. If we'd just been here yesterday . . .

"My tracks?" I ask as the thought occurs to me, suddenly nervous.

"Covered by the snow by the time anyone looked." The cramp in my stomach eases up a little. "Any sign of the missing journal, or whatever it was?"

"No," Ben says, "unfortunately not. From the space, dust, that sort of thing, they reckon it was a book about eight inches by five. Could be a diary or journal."

"Could just as easily be a paperback novel," I suggest, and Ben grunts in agreement.

"Yeah, could be anything," he agrees, before shifting slightly, as if he's just remembered something. "Hey, I never called Doctor Sandwell. Dammit, it just slipped my mind completely."

Doctor Alan Sandwell, I remember now, Ben mentioned it this morning. Thought I would know who it was, but we never got a chance to go through it.

Maybe it's connected to my previous problems, the ones I never even knew I had, until Paul told me? *So I'm gonna try calling Doctor Sandwell today, see what we can find out about what happened to you*, that's what Ben had said. What happened to me? My heart beats faster as I grasp at this opportunity. Maybe Sandwell is the doctor who believed me?

"Who is he?" I ask; Ben already knows that I don't remember anything from the last few days, so I don't mind asking now.

"He's an old doctor of yours from Boston," Ben says, and my heart rate goes up once more. "Does the name ring a bell?"

"No," I admit, "not really. But my memory of that time isn't too great either, apparently." I pull away from Ben, sitting up in the bed. "Do you have his number?" I ask, trying to keep the excitement out of my voice.

"Yeah, home and office. Why, you're not thinking of calling him now, are you?" He shifts around, looks at the bedside clock – it reads *1:24am*. "Shit, it's only half-past one in the morning, he'll think you *are* crazy if you bother him now."

"Half-past five in Boston," I respond, "maybe it's not too early to get ahold of him?"

"You're joking, right?"

"No," I say, my voice firm. "I'm not." I then proceed to tell him about what Paul said to me, and I am glad that he listens to what I have to say.

"He might have been lying," Ben says, and I nod my head.

"Yeah," I say, "he might. But what if it's true? I *have* to know. What if he can explain what's happening to me?"

"Yeah . . ." Ben says, noncommittally.

"What's his number?" I press.

"I don't think he'll thank you," Ben says, but – to his credit – he doesn't even try and talk me out of it any further, seeing that my mind is set. Instead, he reaches over for the cellphone that rests next to the clock, flicks it on and scrolls through the contacts list. He gets the right number and reluctantly hands it over. "There," he says, "but be prepared for him to be a little bit grumpy at least, yeah?"

"Yeah," I say, then hit the call button.

Grumpy, it turns out, was an understatement – Doctor Alistair Sandwell was a volcano, exploding all over me. Apparently he had to be up early enough anyway, and didn't like his traditional six-thirty reveille being interrupted for any reason. But after some sweet-talking, he had given me the information I'd been after, although it wasn't actually the news I wanted to hear. Turns out that Dr. Sandwell was one of the medical experts that *didn't* believe me, and he was unwilling to discuss cases over the telephone anyway. I could make an appointment to see him in Boston, to see him in person, but that was a seven-hour flight and I doubted I'd still be awake after that time – and if I wasn't awake, then when I *did* finally wake up, it would be a different day and the appointment would probably be of no use anyway.

But – after much prompting, and the intervention of Ben, who claimed my request was of a vital, life-or-death nature – Dr. Sandwell did give me one piece of significant information. Apparently, the doctor who had backed me up, who had believed my unbelievable story, is called Glen Kelly and – as far as Sandwell knows – he now lives in a retirement village in Florida.

Five minutes later, a badgered Ben turns to me and presents me with a new telephone number – main reception at Pine Hills Retirement Village, Gainesville, Florida.

"But the guy's eighty-one," Ben says pleadingly. "Leave it until the morning, okay?"

A part of me seriously wants to ignore Ben's advice and call the man right away, but then another part tells me that he might just be right; what would be served by calling now? Kelly would probably be only semi-coherent at best, and I might learn nothing. No, I decide, better to wait until morning – or later in the morning in Florida – before I approach him. I want to find out all the information I can, and it's important that I have Kelly on my side from the start. For all I know, he might hold some sort of resentment against me, a grudge for his being struck off, for being forced into semi-retirement.

But at least now I have a name, an address, a telephone number – whenever I wake up tomorrow, no matter what day it is, I won't forget those details, and I can contact him then.

It's not only Dr. Glen Kelly who needs his rest either, I think as I finally relax back into Ben's arms – I am exhausted myself, literally on my last legs. And, as I decide to leave Kelly until tomorrow – whichever day tomorrow might be – I feel myself relaxing immediately, the tension easing out of my body, my mind.

And, while still wondering what tomorrow may bring, I fall into the merciful embrace of a deep, wonderful sleep.

DAY FIVE

1

The blood runs down the windows, streaking the glass, pitter-pattering off the torn, thinning curtains onto the threadbare carpet of the hotel room.

It runs down the walls too, in torrents.

Torrents of blood.

Whose blood?

My brother's.

Jack's blood.

I look out of the window, down, down to the streets below – at first I can see nothing, the lights are too bright; I turn away, think again, turn back . . .

And then I see him, what is left of him, broken pieces of my brother's body smashed apart over that concrete sidewalk, and I feel vomit rising in my mouth as my eyes zoom in toward his broken, bloody face, the world around me a blur, and now I see only his face, cracked apart, bones and flesh rendered open.

And then, just as I am about to scream, to pierce the air with my fright, my horror, my sorrow, I hear the trample of hooves behind me, the crashing of a door, and I turn, turn to see Beauty rearing up in the doorway, blood all around him – it's falling from the ceiling now as well as the windows and the walls, it drips from his flat teeth, his eyes, it is everywhere –

And I fall backwards as his hooves come crashing down over me, and I close my eyes as I feel a colossal weight press down hard onto my chest, open them and see –

Paul above me, forcing himself *inside* me, his teeth fangs in a vampire's mouth, his eyes twin red moons, and finally I scream.

I scream and scream, and I do not know if I will ever stop.

"Jess," I hear a voice say to me, near me, so soft I can barely hear it; then I feel a hand on my shoulder, shaking me awake, and I hear the words more clearly now, "Jess, Jess. Jessica, wake up! Wake up!"

And then I do wake up, and stare into the frightened eyes of Amy Reiner, the girl who has been staying and helping me in my home. My head is foggy from the dream, from everything that has happened, but I begin to understand that if Amy is here, then I am once more in my own house.

I look around, check the bed and confirm it – *yes*, yes I am home, home in bed.

But what day is it?

"You were screaming," Amy says apologetically, "I didn't know what to do, I'm sorry for coming in, I just wanted to make sure you were okay, it sounded horrible, really horrible."

"It's okay," I manage, as I turn over to look for my cellphone, grabbing it off the night-stand and flicking it on, ignoring Amy as I search for the day, the date.

I look at it, and it takes me longer than it should to work it out.

Wednesday.

It's Wednesday, the day *before* Ben and I go to Menders' cabin, the day before Paul attacks me, here in my own home.

"It must have been really terrible," I vaguely hear Amy saying, "a real nightmare, are you sure you're okay?"

"Yeah," I say after a few moments, remembering Dr. Glen Kelly – Pine Hills Retirement Village, Gainesville, Florida. "I'm okay." I turn and smile at her, grateful but at the same time wanting to get rid of her, to concentrate on what I should be doing. "Thank you," I say, hand resting on her forearm.

"Do you want anything? Cup of coffee? Tea?"

"Coffee," I say automatically, needing the caffeine but also wanting Amy out of the room. "Thank you."

"No problem," she says, turning to leave. "Are you sure you'll be okay?"

"Yeah," I say, "I'm okay now. Can't even remember what it was about," I lie.

"That's good," Amy says, and then retreats outside, closing the door behind her.

I look at my phone again immediately, checking the

time.

Damn, it's already half past ten; I must have really needed the sleep.

That makes it about half past two in the Florida afternoon, not a bad time to call . . .

And then it hits me.

Wednesday.

It's the day Douglas Menders is killed. Which means that the killer will be at his cabin today.

Which means if I can get back up there in time, I might find out who the killer is.

Excitement races through me as I see my chance, then I check the time again.

10.34am.

I think back to my conversation with Ben the night before, and I am already out of bed and pulling my jeans on.

Medical examiner estimates time of death as yesterday, somewhere between eleven in the morning and two in the afternoon, give or take, he'd told me.

Damn, that doesn't give me much time.

I pull on my shirt at the same time as I call Ben, reminding myself that he hasn't experienced tomorrow yet – he doesn't know that Douglas Menders dies, or anything else about it. But he believes my story about flitting about from day to day, so maybe he'll believe this? If I call him, he can meet me up there, we can find out who the killer is, together.

But his cellphone just beeps lifelessly back at me, and it is clear that either his phone is turned off, or else he's not in a cellular service area.

Shit.

I pull on a sweater as I leave my room and race down the stairs, calling Palmer PD as I go.

"Is Chief Taylor there?" I ask as soon as the receptionist answers.

"Can I ask who's calling?" she answers, and I can hear that it is the same woman who took my initial inquiry last Thursday, the one who smells of candy and deodorant.

"Jessica Hudson," I answer as I get to the bottom of the stairs, negotiate my way into the kitchen.

"Hello, Ms. Hudson. Unfortunately, Ben's out at the moment, we're not expecting him back until late this afternoon."

Double shit.

I rack my brains, trying to remember if he mentioned yesterday

(tomorrow!)

where he'd been, but I can't.

"Can you tell me where he is?" I ask.

"Not specifically, Ms. Hudson, I'm afraid. But he said it's out of the area, somewhere up around Chugach State Park. Bad cell coverage up there, I can try him on the radio though, if it's an emergency?"

What do I say? What *can* I say? If I ask for another officer, or for someone from the ABI, if I tell them that the killer might be going to Doug Menders' cabin, then the obvious question would be, *How do you know?*

And how the hell would I answer *that?* De Nares

for sure would take it to mean I have knowledge of, communications *with* the killer.

So what do I do?

And, I suddenly think, what the hell is Ben doing over in Chugach anyway? He doesn't mention it to me tomorrow, I know that much.

I smile as Amy holds out the coffee mug for me, take it from her as I pick up my keys, shove my feet into my boots, and head right on out the door. She tries to speak, but I gesture to the phone, shrug my shoulders in apology, and leave the house behind.

"Can you just get him to call me, if you get through to him?" I ask as I blip my car, pull the door open and jump inside, sipping the first layer of coffee as I start the engine.

"Yes, ma'am, I'll do that," the lady at Palmer PD says. "Is there anyone else here who can help you?"

I wonder about this for a moment as I pull out from the driveway, then make my decision. "No," I say, "no, thank you. Have a nice day."

"You too, Ms. Hudson," she says, and I cancel the call, throwing the phone onto the passenger seat next to me and taking another hit of caffeine from the coffee mug as I turn past Artie's farm, accelerating off up the semi-paved road on my way toward the highway, and Menders' cabin.

The time on the clock in the dashboard reads 10:42, and I struggle to come up with a viable plan. I check for the .38 in my coat, curse as I realize that I don't have it yet – Ben doesn't give it to me until tomorrow. Then I realize that I could have – should have? – used it on Paul, gone for it as soon as I'd heard him lock the door. I'd only thought of the gun locked away in the kitchen cabinet, I'd forgotten all about the one in my coat pocket.

I sigh, thinking how typical that is – when I had it, I didn't use it because I didn't *think* to use it; and now I remember about it, I don't have it.

I consider turning back, getting the gun out of the locked cabinet, but think better of it – I'm tight for time as it is, and I don't want to risk missing out on my opportunity to identify Menders' killer.

I wonder then – strangely, for the first time – if I might even be in time to *save* Menders. And then an ugly thought enters my head – do I *want* to save him?

I am disgusted with myself for thinking it, know for fact that if I *can* save him, I *will*, but the existence of such a thought is perhaps understandable; after all, this is a serial rapist and – on the balance of probability – a killer. Maybe not of Lynette, but probably of victims back in Florida. What was it that Ben had told me? Fifteen years for three cases of raping a minor, and a homicide charge from ligature strangulation that he narrowly avoided.

Does a man like that *deserve* saving?

Of course he does, I tell myself – everyone deserves a chance.

And yet I haven't called the police, or the ABI, only Ben. If I *really* wanted to save him, I'd pick up that phone, call them, and get them up there with their sirens blaring, scare the killer off.

But then we will lose maybe our only chance of identifying him, and the killer can go on to torture, rape and kill other victims. And if he runs away, not caught – and there is no evidence in the minds of the cops that anyone was ever there, that Menders was under any sort of threat – then there is nothing to stop the unidentified killer from going back and murdering Menders at some other time anyway.

I'm trying to justify myself, and I know it; but I've obviously decided to use Menders as some sort of bait. I know the killer is on his way there – is maybe there already – and I don't want him scared off.

I have to know who it is.

I'm skirting around the base of the mountains now, coffee mug empty and dashboard clock reading *10:56*, and I pick up my cell and try Ben's number again.

Still nothing, just that hollow, empty beeping to remind me that I'm on my own.

I'm off the Farm Loop now, on the service road that winds its way precariously up the hillside toward Menders' cabin. I'm glad that the snow isn't so bad today, and I remember it doesn't really get started in earnest until tomorrow morning; it makes driving a lot easier, that's for sure.

I'm nearing the cabin now, the snow slightly more apparent as the car snakes upwards, and fear – horrible, gut-churning, naked *fear* – suddenly sweeps through me. My muscles tense involuntarily and I feel the car swerve across the road as I pull on the wheel, my pulse high, my stomach roiling.

Breathe, I tell myself, *breathe!*

I need to get this under control, I need to sort myself out, but I cannot rid myself of the knowledge that I'm purposefully putting myself in harm's way.

The best guess that Ben and I could come up with is that either Menders and the man who kills him are partners, possibly working together on abduction-murders like the Lynette Hyams case, or else Menders is trying to blackmail the man responsible. Either way, I am about to put myself right into the crossfire of two very dangerous people, with no real idea of what I'm doing.

Surveillance, a voice somewhere in my head tells me, and I know it is right, surveillance is my best option, perhaps my only option if I don't want to get picked up by these people and become a victim myself. Because it also occurs to me that *nobody knows where I am*.

And then it also occurs to me that – if I am killed out here, if Menders is killed – then Ben won't come up here tomorrow, he won't find us, nobody will find us, maybe for a long time; because the only reason Ben *does* come up here tomorrow

(*the tomorrow that has already happened*)

is because I mention Lynette pointing up the hill toward the cabin over breakfast at the Noisy Goose. But if I'm dead, we don't have breakfast, and he has no reason to come up here.

Wow, if I'm not crazy already, thinking about this stuff will soon sort that out, I think as I reach the last mile of road before the cabin.

I'm running out of time, and I ease off the accelerator without even thinking, then stand on the brake and come to a sliding stop, angled up the hill, just before another long, looping bend.

I wonder what made me stop here, and then I see it, a tiny trunk road off to the right, its entrance partially covered by the spreading branches of several fir trees.

Perfect.

Even if I leave any tire tracks, I know the snow will have completely eradicated them by tomorrow.

I move the SUV slowly forward, pulling off the main road and hiding the vehicle deep inside. The last thing I want is to pull up right in front of the cabin, drawing anyone's attention straight onto me.

I look around the car for something I can use as a weapon, find a tire iron in the trunk and a can of de-icer in the glove compartment. Not exactly ideal, but better than nothing. I pocket the can, and take a secure grip on the tire iron. Yes, I think again, feeling its solid weight in my hands, it is definitely better than nothing.

I feel the icy tension of fear slice through me once more, and it makes me doubt what I am doing, doubt whether I am capable of this.

Then I remember the elk, the giant elk that I saw in this same forest

(unless you just imagined it)

and the memory – real or not – gives me strength.

I *can* do this.

I *can.*

I look at my watch – *11:12*.

I know I might already be too late.

Dammit, I *will* do this!

And then I move, legs pumping through the thin covering of snow as I make my way to Menders' cabin, and whatever – or whoever – I might find there.

I pick a position from where I can see the cabin, but I cannot be seen myself.

I hope.

I am hidden in the trees, crouched down behind a fallen trunk, eyes focused like a laser on Menders' homestead.

There are no vehicles outside, that is the first thing I notice, and I hope this means that I'm not too late, the killer is not already there.

I then realize that perhaps the killer isn't using a car or – like me – he parked it further away and hiked in the rest. Which means, of course, he could be somewhere close, and a shiver runs down my spine as I realize he could already be watching me.

I take a deep breath, tell myself that there's no use in thinking that way, if I do that, the fear will almost certainly stop me from doing *anything*.

And so I grit my teeth, and wait.

An hour later, it's already past midday and I still haven't seen any sign of Douglas Menders in the cabin, and I am starting to wonder if he is even there.

It's possible, I suppose, that Menders was/is killed

elsewhere, and the killer comes back to place his body here, framing it as some sort of struggle.

But why?

I start to become anxious, check the time again – *12:12* – and suddenly wonder if he's already dead. Maybe I arrived too late? Maybe the killer has already been and gone?

Is Doug Menders already on the floor of his living room, head split open by the brass lamp?

Sighing heavily, I know there is only one way to find out.

I'm going to have to go over and take a look.

I arrive at the cabin, tire iron in one hand and can of de-icer in the other, out of breath from my half-crawling approach, as well as the sheer stress, the fear of discovery.

But there is nobody out here, it is just a cold, crisp day with a mere hint of tomorrow's snow in the air.

I take another step toward the wooden structure, off to one side of the window I have identified as that of the living room. I hold my breath, count to four, and breathe slowly out.

I'm going to just slide my eyes across the bottom of the window, check inside, see if the body is already there, and then get back to a safe distance and decide what to do.

Before giving it another thought – before I can chicken out – I move slowly across, keeping my head low, letting my eyes pass the window pane. I stop, my eyes focus, trying hard to penetrate the dark interior. I can see the space lit by the single bulb, and I look to the floor, trying to find the place where Menders fell. Or *falls*.

My heart is in my chest, and I know this is already taking longer than it should, I'm too exposed here, the killer – if he's out there – can see me clearly right now, and all I have is the tire iron and the de-icer.

I sigh, move away from the window, and turn back to the woods.

At the same instant, my head snaps back, a rope or cord around my neck, the hot stink of onion breath close to my face, whispered, hate-filled words in my ear.

"You little whore," the voice taunts. "I've got you now."

2

I sit in the dimly-lit living room of the cabin, the still-living form of Douglas Menders right in front of me, regarding me like an animal in a zoo.

Or like a predator looks at its prey.

I suddenly consider the fact that Menders wasn't just observing through his telescope, wasn't just trying to blackmail the real killer. Maybe my first instinct was right, Menders is the leader, the instigator; whoever raped Lynette was just a moon in his orbit.

But where is that second person, the one I assume is coming here to kill Menders?

I am scared, frightened beyond all measure. Before long, I am sure, there will be two dangerous men in this house, in this room – men who hate women, torture them, rape them, kill them. And I'm tied to a chair, helpless.

And nobody even knows I'm here.

My neck still hurts from where he wrapped the rope around my neck and pulled me from the window;

it had been so tight, I'd dropped my makeshift weapons without even trying to use them, and by the time he'd brought me inside, the lack of oxygen had made my body weak, compliant. My mind had wanted to resist when he'd tied me to this chair, but my body had not been able.

And now here I am, in the den of the predator.

The fear is back with a vengeance, and I am not sure if I can control it; everything around me is suddenly hyper-real – colors are brighter, contrast is sharper, smells are stronger. I can even smell the adrenaline in my own fear-sweat.

I try to put a positive spin on things – perhaps the man who kills Menders is not his partner-in-crime? Maybe it *is* a vigilante, or group of vigilantes, come to seek revenge on Menders, believing him to be responsible? Is it possible that he/they will save me?

I laugh, gagging slightly, knowing that I am grasping at straws. It is far more likely that whoever it is will kill me too, or worse. Maybe the two of them *are* working together, and I have very stupidly entered the lion's den, unprepared and unprotected. And my earlier thoughts come back to me, how nobody even knows I'm here, and I gag again.

"Jess," Menders says soothingly, and – despite the pain and disorientation – I am still disturbed by his use of my name. I know it will have been in the papers recently, but he uses it with such familiarity that I wonder for how long he has been spying on me, down in the valley below. Has his voyeurism created some sort of relationship between us in that twisted mind of his? "Jess," he says again, "what were you doing outside my cabin? You spying on me?"

He says it good-naturedly, almost as if it's funny, and I can see he appreciates the irony; he's been spying on all of us, and for who knows how long, and then he catches *me* peeking through *his* window.

His face seems relaxed, jovial even, but I notice that in his hands he still holds the short length of rope that he used to strangle me with, that he dragged me into his house with, and the effect is chilling.

"Someone's coming here to kill you," I say, trying to make myself valuable to him, already bargaining for my ongoing safety.

"Who?" Menders says with a dark chuckle, pointing toward the floor. "You?" he asks, and I see the tire iron and the de-icer there.

I shake my head vigorously. "Protection," I mumble softly.

"Protection?" he asks. "Against who?" He smiles. "Me?"

"You," I say, "and whoever you're working with, or whoever you're trying to blackmail." My eyes dart nervously around the room, still waiting for the arrival of the other person, whoever it is, the killer I am looking for, the man who smashes Menders over the head with the big brass lamp.

"Is that who you're looking for?" Menders asks, following my roving eyes. "My 'partner'?"

I shrug. "I don't know."

Suddenly, Menders' demeanor changes, and in his eyes, I see something different, something terrible, something I imagine those women he raped would have seen, as he moved in. "That's right," he growls, "you don't know *shit*, you stupid little whore." He sits back in an easy chair just across from me and smiles, playing with the rope in his hands. "But *I* do."

"I know that you're about to die," I say, as bravely as I can.

"You know *what?*"

"I see things," I tell him, thinking that if anyone will believe my crazy story, it's another crazy person. "I saw the girl die, days before she did. And I've seen your dead body, right there on the floor in front of you." I see a clock on the mantelpiece, check the time. "You've got an hour and a half left," I tell him, "maybe less."

Menders looks angry, but he doesn't yell, doesn't shout, doesn't even move, he just keeps on looking at me with those dark eyes.

"Bullshit," he spits.

"There's someone coming here," I press.

"There's someone already here," he says, pointing at me; then he licks his lips, reflexively, like a reptile might, and the chill down my spine comes back, even worse than before.

"I'm serious," I say, still trying to sound cool, like I'm in charge. But Menders knows better, and I get the feeling that this isn't the first time he's had a woman tied up.

I panic again, crazy with fear that – at any moment

– someone else might turn up, and then both of them will do what they want with me. I'll know who the killer is – maybe – but I'll be the next victim, and there won't be anything I can do with the information.

Unless, I think to myself, the same magic that sends me around time when I *sleep*, will also do the same if I *die*?

It is unlikely, of course, but I take comfort from the thought anyway; it gives me succor, like the thought of Heaven for a devout Christian, it makes me believe that – whatever happens here – it might *not* be the end.

I decide to attack, to go on the offensive; if the other person turns up, so be it, but I will see what I can get from Menders first.

"Did you kill her?" I ask, matching my gaze to his, determined not to be the first one to look away.

Menders matches my gaze and looks at me in wonder. "What," he says, "that girl who died on your farm? You think I had something to do with it?"

"Before she died," I say, "she pointed up here. The last thing she did."

"She pointed up here?" Menders responds with a barking laugh. "From all the way down *there*, she pointed up *here*? Shit, lady, that's some pretty fucking accurate pointing, ain't it?" He shakes his head. "Let me tell you what I think – you've been told stories about me, the big bad monster up in the cabin. No other leads, must be me, right? And then all of a sudden, you remember the girl pointing where? At my *house*?" He laughs again. "What bullshit. And even if that girl *did* manage to point at anything before she died, there must be half a dozen other ranches down there between your house and mine, why couldn't she have been pointing at one of them?"

"*Was* it you?" I ask again, ignoring his words. If I am going to die here anyway, I might as well try and find out some information before I go. I would hate to die, still not knowing.

"Shit, what would I be doing with that girl anyway?" Menders explodes, rope tight between big, strong hands. "You think she was here? You think it was me that took her? *What the fuck for?*"

Suddenly, Menders jumps to his feet, and I tense in my chair, ready for the blows, for the rope; but he stops, grunts heavily, and pulls his pants down around his ankles, tottering uneasily in front of me. He looks at me with hate in his eyes, and I once again imagine that this is what those girls might have seen back in Florida and Texas; maybe the girls here in Alaska too.

Then he pulls his shirt up and reveals himself to me, a small dark shaft hanging limply between his legs, testicles removed, the scrotal sac shriveled behind it. Menders' eyes bore into mine. "Just tell me *Jess*, just tell me what the *fuck* I'm going to do with that?"

I can see the bat-shit crazy now, that's for sure.

"Okay, okay," I say uneasily. "I . . . get the picture. I'm not saying you raped the girl."

For several long moments, Menders just stands there in front of his easy chair, pants around his ankles with his small, darkened penis exposed, his eyes glaring hatefully at me. And then he seems to come to his senses, bending to pull his pants back up. He spits on the floor – his own floor – before he sits back down.

"You're not saying I raped her. Just that I killed her, huh?"

I don't answer, unsure of what to say and still aware that our time is running out, the other killer must be here already, maybe waiting outside, wondering what to do.

Menders shrugs. "I'm sorry," he says eventually. "I'm sorry. Sometimes I . . . get angry, I guess. But hell, I've been like this since I moved here nearly twenty years ago, with prison before the operation, I haven't had sex for twenty-four years, and I still get this shit." He sighs. "And nobody believes me about finding Christ either. But it's true. I've told everyone a million times, it's true. I found Him back in prison, and I've lived with Him inside me ever since. Believe me, I'd have killed myself before now if it wasn't true. He saved me then, and he's still saving me now. You think I'd have kept up this charade for two entire decades? They already let me out, why would I carry on pretending if it wasn't true? I'm a reformed man, but still people blame every crime that happens around here on me." He sniffs. "But I don't care. Peter Chapter One, Verses Six and Seven, 'Rejoice, though for a little while you may suffer trials, so that the testing of your faith, which is more precious than gold which is tested and purified by fire, may be found to result in praise, glory and honor when Jesus the Messiah is revealed'. You're just fire, sent to test me. That's all you are. But I'm already saved."

"Good," I say, as evenly, as calmly as I can. "Good. If that's true, how about one more test? Another chance for you to prove your faith to God."

Menders is immediately suspicious. "What sort of test?"

"Untie me," I say. "If everything is as you say, you don't need to tie me up. *Trust me.*"

Menders chuckles. "Trust you?" he says, mockingly. "Trust you, the person who thinks I'm a killer, some sort of sicko rapist-killer? You, the person I found outside *my* house, peering into *my* window, with a damn tire iron in your hand?"

"I know it doesn't look good," I try again, keeping the dialogue going, "but I'm here to help, really. You've got to believe me. I've *seen* your dead body, right here in this room, I've seen this day before."

"Don't bullshit me."

"It's not bullshit," I fire back, "it's real, as real as it gets. At some stage between now and two o'clock, someone gets in here and smashes you over the head with the brass lamp."

Menders looks to the side table. "This brass lamp?" he asks, eyebrows raised.

"Yes."

"Who kills me?"

"I don't know."

"You don't know? I thought you saw it?"

"I saw your dead body, I didn't see you die. That's

why I came back."

"To see me die?"

"To find out who did it."

Menders murmurs something under his breath, then chuckles again. "You spin a pretty interesting yarn."

"It's not a yarn," I insist. "Someone's on their way here now to kill you, they might even already be out there, waiting."

"You trying to scare me?"

"I'm trying to help you."

"Why do you want to do that?"

I test the ropes that bind me, shift in my chair. "I don't know," I say honestly, then shake my head sadly. "I really don't know."

I notice for the first time that there is some give in the rope, a small amount of space – tiny, infinitesimal really, but there all the same – and I immediately start to work my hands and wrists, twisting and pulling to create more space. I know Menders might pick up on this, know I need to get him engaged in conversation, but – in between the fear, the action of my hands, my anticipation of the arrival of whoever kills Menders – I find that I cannot think of anything to say.

I lock eyes with Menders instead, trying to get the image of this man's shriveled, ruined penis out of my mind. How much anger would that create in someone already prone to violence? It's an unhappy thought, and as the man himself watches me from his neat little chair across the room, my eyes take in the sinister forms of the crucifixes which hang on the walls, cloaked in bands of shadow and candlelight. Could such a man use an object like that on a woman? Yes, I decide sadly, of course he could. But did he? I sigh. That's another question entirely.

"So Jess," Menders says, "before the boogeyman gets here, I've got a question for you." He settles back into his chair, obviously not worried at all about the possibility of his upcoming death. He smiles, and the sight is not a pretty one. But at least he is going to engage *me* in conversation, it seems, which will hopefully distract him while I try and loosen my bonds. "My question is," he continues, "how does it feel to be here? Here in my *lair*. Are you frightened?"

The thought seems to genuinely excite him, but I decide not to lie, to give him what he wants. "Yes," I say.

"Did you even know I was here, before this all happened?"

I shake my head. "No, I had no idea *anyone* lived up here."

"And how does it make you feel now, knowing that I'm up here?"

"As you might expect. Uneasy, I guess."

Menders nods his head. "I guess it would. But don't you believe me about being reformed? Do you believe that reform is even possible for people like me?"

The question gives me pause, despite the situation. To be fair, it's a good one. What *do* I believe about the issue? I certainly used to believe in reform; but then years in the prosecutor's office seeing the same criminals pass in and out of jail made me change my ideas. Can a leopard change its spots? "I don't know," I answer truthfully.

"I think I can believe that," Menders says in return. "Yes, I can believe that. Eight years in the New York DA's office has probably created some measure of cynicism in you, and that's only to be expected. But I think you're a fair person at heart, you want to believe the best, and so you're conflicted. Is that about it?"

"I guess so." I try not to show my concern about how much Menders knows about me; it's probably nothing he hasn't picked up from the papers.

Menders settles back deeper into the old chair, steeples his fingers and rests his chin there, eyes watching me. "The first one I did, I was just fourteen," he says eventually, and even though the words chill me to the core, I don't say a word. But my stomach turns immediately; it is the casual way he speaks that is the most horrifying thing, as if he is talking about walking the dog, or gardening. But I will let him speak.

"I'd seen her around the neighborhood," he continues, "she looked good, you know. About my age, but thought she was too good for me, ignored me. Most people ignored me back then. Didn't realize at the time how nice that could be. Didn't feel nice at the time, believe me. Pretty little rich girl like you, probably always been noticed, right?" He doesn't wait for an answer, just nods his head vigorously. "Right. So there I am, cruising the neighborhood on my bike, always seeing this girl, Sally her name was, Sally Jessop I think. Great little tight ass, I used to whack off over it every night, right? Then I started following her, found out where she lived, watched her from the bushes outside and whacked off right there. There were a few close calls, but no one ever caught me. But it wasn't enough." He pauses, breathes deep to control himself.

"I tried talking to her," he says, fidgeting in his chair, "I tried to get to know her, for real, right? Right. But she wouldn't talk to me, I was the local geek, freak, whatever. She and her friends just laughed at me. Laughed at me! Fucking bitches. So anyway, one day I waited for her outside her house, then I just dragged her into her own garage, right? Put my hand over her mouth, and I just did the bitch right there. She knew who I was, I strangled her a bit but couldn't bring myself to kill her, it was just a warning, you know, just my little way of telling her she best not fuck with me. And then I told her straight, if she said anything to anyone I'd come back and slit her fucking throat." Menders leans back again, a half-smile on his dark face. "Guess she got the message. She never did tell anyone. Or if she did, nobody ever spoke to me about it." Those dark pools that should be eyes look eerily into my own. "I was just a nervous, scared fourteen-year-old boy. Nobody ever got me for that one, or for the dozen more I did before I graduated high school. Now I know you got a bee in your fucking bonnet over finding whoever killed that girl who ended up on your farm. But answer me this, pretty lady – if people didn't find out what I'd done, just a kid, just how the fuck are you gonna have any chance finding a professional serial killer, someone who's perfected their craft over years, maybe even decades? Huh? Answer me that, Ms. Jessica Hudson, ex-hot shot Assistant DA, current fuck-buddy of the Chief of Police?"

I don't answer right away, don't even think about how he knows I'm seeing Ben Taylor. My mind is focused not so much on the story itself – I remind myself it might not even be true – but on why he's told me it. What purpose does he feel is being served by the story? Perhaps he just wants to scare me; it's an indelible part of his character, he wants women to fear him. But is that all? Did he tell me this just for his amusement, or is there something more behind it?

"So you think that a serial killer is responsible for the girl's death?" I ask, ignoring most of what he told me and concentrating on what's connected to the actual case at hand.

Menders snorts. "What, you don't?"

"I think it's open to debate at the moment," I reply evenly, before I hone in again. My work with the rope is working, I can feel it loosening, and already I am getting mobility back into my elbows and shoulders. A little more time, and I might be able to get my hands free. I wonder about what I will do *then*, but decide to cross that bridge when – *if* – I come to it. "What makes you so sure?" I ask, continuing to take his attention away from my arms.

"It was too controlled to be a crime of passion,"

Menders says thoughtfully, "or even a crime of revenge. Whoever did it – and it's *not* me, I can tell you that much – has had a lot of practice. And I mean a lot. Obviously, you must have considered the link between this girl and the bodies found in the Anchorage woods, and those others found out in Chugach State Park? Of course you have. I know Ben has, which is why he's over in Chugach today, right? Everyone was hot for me for those crimes, so they're hot for me again for this one. Makes sense when you've got nothing else to go on." He turns his head, looks towards the shuttered windows. "You know, on a good day there's a gap in the trees out there which lets me look right down the valley. I can see all of those little farms down there, the ranches. I can see a lot." He carries on staring at the shutter, his eyes dreamy. "I see you working in the fields with those horses of yours, your little doggy. Stroking them, feeding them, riding them. Playing with your vegetable patch, doing your best to grow them like everyone else but not knowing what the fuck you're doing." He turns back to me. "Right?"

A chill runs down my spine, but he doesn't wait for me to respond, just nods his head and confirms his own suspicions. "Right. But you shouldn't worry," he says with a grin, "even if my cock was working, you're not my type. Too old." He stretches back, smile widening once more. "That girl you got living with you at the minute though, helping out with the horses? Amy Reiner?" My blood runs cold as he says her name. Menders sees my reaction and the dark pools of his eyes

285

flicker with pleasure. "Yeah, little Amy is more my type. That little ass. If I could, I'd fuck her in half, you know that? Right? Right?" I open my mouth to speak out, to shout at the evil man in front of me, to threaten him, but he cuts me off with a shrug of the shoulders. "But I can't," he says with regret. "I can't." He points to the shutters again. "And I suggest you concentrate your search a little closer to home."

The implication hits me immediately. "You saw something?" I ask, remembering the binoculars, the telescope, the missing journal. "You saw her? You know where she was running from? You know who did it?" The words rush out of me. What does he know? He can see the houses below, in the valley. My farm. Artie's farm. "Was it Arthur Jenkins?" I ask frantically. "Pat Jenkins?"

Menders just shakes his head sadly. "I've already said too much. Me and whoever did this, we're birds of a feather, fuck together. There's no way I'm telling you who did it. Even if I do know, which maybe I do, and maybe I don't."

I look around the room, see the artwork, the crucifixes. "You're a reformed man," I say urgently. "Don't you want to stop whoever's doing this? It's evil, can't you see that? It's the work of the devil, and you have to help us if you can."

Menders smiles that eerie smile once again. "Cop whore, I don't have to do jack shit. I know, and you don't. That makes me happy, makes me feel like I've still got something left, something I've got control over.

Right?"

"Yes," I say instantly, "you've got control, you've got the power over life and death. Who knows how many more victims there could be? If you've changed like you say, why not choose life this time? Life for those poor girls?"

"You're right, I could say something, maybe save people, maybe not. But the Lord helps those who help themselves. Maybe I'm a liar. Maybe I've not changed. Maybe I'm happy someone's doing what I still want to do. Maybe I think that all those stinking fucking whores should get what's coming to them, and rot in Hell." He says this last with fire in those black pools, and a vehemence that leaves me in no doubt about the man. He is the devil himself, his soul as black as night.

I'm still dealing with the fact that the man-beast in front of me probably knows who killed Lynette Hyams, and potentially many more victims besides, when he stands up and starts to move slowly toward me.

Panic hits me, threatens to overwhelm me; I feel sick, my stomach flies up to my chest, my heart lurches toward my gut. What is he doing? What does he want?

Where the hell is the other person?

Please let it be vigilantes, please let it be vigilantes . . .

Come on! Where are you?

"What are you doing?" I whisper as Menders approaches.

"Oh, nothing," he says with an uncharacteristically coy smile, before bending down to the floor and retrieving the tire iron and the de-icer from where he'd dumped them earlier. "But you know," he says softly, trying out the weight of the tire iron, "it occurs to me that nobody knows you're here." Another chill goes through me, and my hands work faster. "Now, to put your mind at rest, I didn't kill that girl, and I don't have a partner, I'm not part of some whacko, mutual-masturbation kill squad, or whatever your little fantasy might be." He breathes out slowly as he appears to read the list of ingredients on the de-icer. "I might very well know who's behind it all," he says, eyes still on the can, "but I've not been in contact, they don't know I know. And if I have no partner, and I'm not trying to blackmail anyone, then I guess nobody's coming here to kill me, either."

"Vigilantes," I say desperately, and for a moment, I see a flicker of doubt in Menders' eyes; but it is only a flash, before it is replaced by those twin black spots that speak only of evil.

"I don't think so. No, Jess, I don't think so. I don't think anyone's coming. And as I said before, I don't think anyone knows you're here. If you'd mentioned it to Ben Taylor, no way in hell he'd have let you come up here alone, no way in hell. And, let's face it, who else is there?"

"I left a message with the ABI," I say, my eyes nervously darting between Menders, the door, the window. I don't know who his killer is, I just know that I want them here, now. I don't care what happens afterward, I just know I don't want Menders getting any closer.

His eyes, they remind me of those eyes behind the woolen masks that day on the courthouse steps. Cold, merciless, evil.

"No, you didn't," Menders says, onion-breath once more close to my face. "You don't want to be connected to this thing any more than I do. De Nares has a hard-on for you already, and you don't want to make it any worse."

"What do you want?" I say breathlessly, the words an effort, my voice shaking.

"I want to use this on you," he says, raising the can of de-icer to my face. "See what it does to you." He shows me the tire iron next. "Then maybe try this out. See what *that* does to you."

I can see in his eyes that he is serious, that he *is* going to use these things on me, that he truly believes that nobody knows I am here, he has complete confidence in himself, knows that he can abuse me, kill me and bury me in the woods, somewhere I might never be found.

I watch in slow-motion as the can comes level with my face, nozzle turned toward my eyes.

No! my mind screams, terror flooding my system.
Nooo!

Without even knowing what is going on, I feel my hands come free at last, come free and make a grab for the can; he spits in anger, drops the can and swings the tire iron at my head; I move to one side, the iron whistling by my ear just before it connects with the side table, sending it crashing to the floor, and then he kicks me sharply in the leg and I collapse in agony on top of the brass lamp; I can hear him shouting obscenities above me and, without thinking, I roll to one side as the tire iron comes down toward me, grabbing the lamp as I move, jumping to my feet, heart racing, breathless, mind a blank as I see Menders stumble with the force of his blow; and then I am swinging the lamp down as hard as I can toward his head, watching in disbelief as it smashes down into his unprotected skull with a dull, wet *thud* that reverberates through me with a sickening chill. I carry on watching, heavy brass lamp still in my hands, as the body

(*dead body, he's dead, dead, dead*)

of Douglas Menders crashes to the floor, silent and helpless, and still and . . .

Dead?

I check the clock on the mantelpiece – *12:43*, right between eleven in the morning and two in the afternoon, exactly as the medical examiner thought.

All the breath leaves my body and I drop the lamp, fall to one knee, eyes on Menders as I check for any sign of life, but I know, I know it is too late, I've seen this scene before – tomorrow, today, yesterday, whenever – and I know that there *is* no partner, no blackmailer, no vigilante.

I know that *I* am the murderer, the secret killer of Douglas Menders.

3

I stand over the dead body of Doug Menders, still trying to make sense of what I've done.

I don't know if there is any point checking him – when Ben and I find him tomorrow, he is definitely dead. But if he is still alive, still breathing *now*, can I save him? Or doesn't it work like that?

I take a deep breath, lean forward, and – copying Ben's technique – feel for the pulse at his throat.

There is none. No breathing either.

Nothing at all.

I shiver, horrified by what I have done; then twitch as I look at the doors, the windows, wondering if anyone is there, before I remember that the person or people I was expecting are not coming; they don't exist. Nobody's coming. In the reality I've experienced, Ben and I don't arrive here until late tomorrow morning, and there was nothing to suggest that anyone else had been here in the meantime.

I have no idea if that tomorrow will still happen the

same way or not, but I have to assume something similar will occur – the body will be discovered, and the ABI will surely descend on the scene.

What do I do?

I can't help staring at the broken, lifeless body of Douglas Menders, lying on the floor in front of me. Moments ago, he was alive; now he is dead, at my hand, and I do not know how to deal with it.

What was I thinking?

Survive, a voice tells me. *You were thinking* survive.

Yes, I agree with the voice, that's right; survival was my only thought. I reacted, did what I had to do, and the result is that I am still alive. A man is dead, but I am still alive.

And yet I don't feel victorious, don't feel that I have won.

Instead I feel weak – perversely, even more powerless than I'd felt when I'd been tied up.

I reflect, for the first time, on the possibility that Menders might have only been trying to scare me, had probably not even been going to hurt me in the first place. He'd already explained how he liked the power, the control he could exercise over others, how he wasn't in a position to do anything physical anymore, but could maybe get his rocks off just by scaring people. Was tying me up, his talk of nobody knowing where I was, threats that he could do anything to me he wanted, just talk?

I wonder how I would have reacted, had Paul not attacked me the night before. But he *did*, and I was already on the edge, full of nervous energy. And if you add the whole Zebunac affair into the mix, I am a live-wire, someone who could only be pushed so far. I'd had enough, taken enough, been hurt enough.

I was the wrong person to attack.

But did I overreact?

No, I tell myself, *you only hit him once.* It was just a lucky (unlucky?) shot.

And maybe he *did* he intend to follow through with his threats?

It was a risk you couldn't take, the voice in my head tells me, and I decide to listen to it. It's right, after all – who the hell was Douglas Menders, to put me in that position? I feel guilty, but he brought it on himself, didn't he?

I should turn myself in, I know that much. It was self-defense, right?

But what the hell was I *doing* here? I know that's the first question De Nares will ask, and I know that there's no answer I give that will cast me in a good light. Menders was right – the detective has a hard-on for me as a suspect in Lynette's death, and my inexplicable decision to go alone up to Menders' cabin would be almost impossible to explain. I could claim that he abducted me, but Amy saw me leave the house under my own steam, obviously with a destination in mind. Would anyone believe that I'd been kidnapped?

But on the other hand, Menders was practiced in the art, known by the authorities as someone with a record of this, and perhaps the story wouldn't be too farfetched? But it would cause everyone to look toward

Menders as the killer, and – despite what he said he was going to do to me, my gut instinct insists that he was telling the truth when he said he had nothing to do with it. I don't want the police, the ABI, chasing shadows.

I want them to find out who was *really* responsible for Lynette's death.

Of course, Menders could have been lying about not being involved, could have been lying about not having a partner; certainly, after my recent experiences, I'm reluctant to rule out any of the main suspects. Menders and Paul have both shown themselves to be violent, and Pat Jenkins' behavior did him no favors.

Unless they were *all* in it together?

I wonder for the first time if they knew each other. Paul was – is – a defense attorney. Did he ever work cases in Seattle? Texas? Florida?

It's a disturbing thought, but worth checking. What if he'd previously defended one, or both, of the others? Could he have put them in touch with one another, facilitated some sort of "mutual-masturbation kill squad", as Menders called it?

The trouble is, I am starting to understand that almost *anything* is possible.

If I can travel through time, why can't Paul have previously known Douglas Menders and Patrick Jenson?

I'm sure that De Nares have checked it out, but then again, maybe he hasn't? Maybe he's not as professional as he likes to think he is? Small things like that can get missed, and it is often the small things that break cases wide open.

And this is yet another reason I don't want to turn myself in. If I'm in jail, I'm not looking into the case. Sure, I might "escape" again by waking up on a different day, but what if I wake up next week, and I'm still in prison?

No, I realize I've already made my mind up about that – I'm not handing myself in, I'm not telling the authorities that I killed Menders.

I'm going to get the hell out of here.

I look at the body again, and go instantly weak at the knees, feel vomit in my throat. But I choke it back, not wanting to spread my DNA all over Menders' carpet.

I can't believe I'm already thinking like a criminal.

But I know that – if I'm not admitting what I've done – that's exactly what I need to do.

Think like a criminal.

Cover my tracks.

I feel terrible to be thinking like this – like a criminal, like a killer. But I also know that I do not want to be investigated, I do not want to be imprisoned, I do not want my search for Lynette's real killer, or killers, to be stopped, or impeded in any way.

I remember my conversation with Ben as we lay in bed – tomorrow night's conversation – and how he told me that the crime scene guys hadn't found any evidence. Which tells me now, that – if I'm careful – I might just get away with it.

I shudder as I wonder if this is how a lot of killers feel – they've committed a crime, maybe by mistake, maybe a worse crime than they intended to commit, a homicide instead of a rape, or a robbery, and then they are left terrified, desperate to cover up all evidence of their activities.

The thought makes me feel sick, dirty and sick, like it's against everything I've ever fought for, I've become what I've always fought *against*. But at the same time, I know that thinking like this is doing me no favors; life has moved on, my situation has changed, there is no way I could have ever foreseen any of *this*. But this is my situation now, and I have to deal with it as best I can. Maybe I'll be caught at some stage, maybe punished for what I've done; but as long as I've found Lynette's killer, I will accept that punishment gladly.

Until then, though, I am going to do whatever it takes to remain free.

I pull gloves out of my jacket pockets, put them on, and leave the body behind, heading for the kitchen. I see a dish towel on the back of a chair, immediately recognize that it was not there when I was last in the kitchen, and grab it.

I return to the living room – doing my best to ignore the corpse that lies there – and start rubbing the cloth over all the surfaces and objects that I fear I may have touched with my bare hands, especially the brass lamp, the "murder weapon". I realize that other DNA evidence might be left behind – stray hairs, skin cells and the like – but I figure that as long as I get the major items out of the way – like fingerprints, the tire iron, the de-icer, my car – then it will at least give me a few days' grace.

I wipe the place clean, from top to bottom, and I find it ironic that the lack of fingerprints and evidence was one of the reasons I'd previously believed that Menders had been murdered by a professional killer.

I wonder what to do next, how I'm going to spend the rest of my day, realize that I'm supposed to be out on a date with Ben tonight. But how the hell am I going to be able to talk to him, having done what I've done, knowing what I know?

And then I remember something, and my heart leaps in my chest, my feet moving before I've given them a conscious demand.

Moments later, I am in Douglas Menders' bedroom, staring at his desk.

There are the binoculars and the telescope.

There are the astronomy books.

And there, where previously there was only an empty space, is a journal.

A journal which could reveal the true identity of Lynette's killer.

4

The journal sits on the car seat beside me as I wind my way back down the hill, eyes ever-watchful, mind on high-alert as I look for other people, other vehicles, anyone who might be able to place me on this road when the police finally go canvassing for witnesses.

I still don't know what's inside the journal, what I might find there. The desire to open it, to read it, devour it, is overwhelming, but my desire to escape is even more powerful.

Back in the cabin, I'd suddenly had a feeling of crushing, irresistible fear, worse than anything I'd already felt; the dead body, the smothering darkness, the crosses, the crucifixes, the paintings, the surveillance gear, the musty, cloying atmosphere that seemed to be closing in on me with every passing second, it all added up to a scene from Hell, a scene I had to get out of before I lost what little sanity I had left.

And so I'd grabbed the journal and ran, leaving behind the same eight-by-five empty space on Menders' cluttered little desk that Ben and I find tomorrow.

I pull out onto the Farm Loop, relieved that I've still not seen any traffic. I know I've left tracks back up there – tire tracks, boot tracks – but I know they will be gone soon, obliterated by the snow.

I want to keep on driving, but there are two competing instincts within me, fighting hard – the desire to get to safety, and the desire to pull over, rip that journal open, and find out exactly who the *real* killer is.

I'm away from the road winding up to Menders' cabin now, and at last I feel that maybe – just *maybe* – I can risk having my first look inside.

After all, if there is evidence in there that reveals who murdered Lynette, and maybe others besides, I need to get it to the authorities immediately; the sooner they know, the sooner they can do something about it. The killer, or killers, could be out there looking for more victims right now, as I mess about here in my car.

I'm scared, but the truth is more important and I pull the wheel to one side, sliding the SUV off the road, no longer caring if anyone sees me.

I reach for the journal, heart rate increasing steadily as I open it.

There are a lot of pages – hundreds? – and I scan them, looking for names, dates, any solid information that might be relevant.

Names, names, names . . .

But try as I might, my first scan yields no names.

No days or dates, either.

Shit!

It is just a rambling monologue, on the face of it offering no indication of when it was written, over what period of time.

I sigh, stop flipping through, and read the first page I come to, somewhere right in the middle.

give me something to do – maybee, maybee, maybee.

what do I want? I want. I want to. I dont know. what the fuck do I want? Want. want. want. want. Do I know. No. why? I do not know.

It is barely intelligible, his scrawl indecipherable in places. Sometimes he uses capitals, other times he doesn't; sometimes the spelling is good, other times it is not; sometimes his sentences seem to make sense, and other times I have no idea what it is he is trying to say.

But why would I? I presume this journal was only for him, perhaps was some way of dealing cathartically with his feelings and emotions.

I flip to another page, read some more.

Stars, tests, me, me, me, wat am I doing here…

I do not no her name yet, I wil find out yes

yes, yes, yes

Ursa Major is a constellation in the northern celestial hemisphere, one of the 88 modern constellations

– and so it goes on, listing more facts about the star system, and from the difference in writing, I can see that he had tried hard to spell everything in this section correctly, had perhaps even copied it out of some textbook.

But who is the girl he mentions? Is it Lynette Hyams? Amy Reiner?

Is it *me*?

There is no other point of reference, no way of getting a time-frame of any kind.

But it hints at the voyeuristic tendencies that Menders had, suggests that – even if he was not directly involved in Lynette's abduction, torture and death himself – he might very well have seen something relevant, just as he'd told me he had, something that might be right here, in these pages.

I flip through again, page after page, looking for names.

Where the hell are the names?

I sit back, upset, angry, horrified. There is something in this journal that will lead me to whoever killed Lynette, I am sure there is . . .

There has to be, hasn't there?

But *where*?

I know I am going to have to read the whole thing, cover to cover, maybe more than once, to try and translate the text, interpret it, seek the evidence that I am sure is there. But that will take time, time I might not have.

Should I take it to the police? Show Ben? The ABI would hand it over to a team of experts, they would be able to extract all the information that it contains. But then how would I explain how I came by it? I know that I would be arrested in a heart-beat.

No, I need to read it myself, digest it. I open it at the beginning, but a car passes by at that exact same moment and I nearly have a heart attack, right here in my car.

I slam the journal closed, gun the engine up and pull out back onto the road, panicking now, desperate not to be identified, not to be caught.

Damn.

Despite my relative safety, my heart is still thumping in my chest, hard enough to hear. Not only have I been subjected to two physical attacks in the last twenty-four hours, I have now killed a man and am paranoid about being found out. Combine that with my near-death experience in New York, and it's too much for me to take.

I need to get away from here, get away, get away. . .

But where?

And then suddenly I remember something, grab the cellphone off the seat next to me, dial a number that I memorized the night before.

"Pine Hills Retirement Village," a young, chirpy female voice says after only a single ring. "How can I help you today?"

Her bright, airy manner relaxes me slightly, so at odds with my experiences in the mountains. Just minutes before, I was in an old cabin in the woods, staring at the dead body of a monster; now I am in the air-conditioned comfort of my SUV, chatting to a nice young lady on the telephone, half a world away.

The feeling is surreal.

"I . . ."

And suddenly, talking is hard, and I am not sure if it is from the damage to my throat from the rope which

Menders used to drag me inside his house, or if it's just the stress and fear that have left me like this.

I concentrate, try harder.

"I . . . I'd like to speak to one of your residents there, if I can?" I finally manage.

"Oh, no problem," the lady says. "Are you a relative?"

"No," I say, "I'm an old friend."

"What is the name of the resident, please?"

"Glen Kelly," I say, as I get onto the track that leads back to my ranch.

"Dr. Glen Kelly?" she asks for confirmation.

"Yes," I say, surprised that he is still known by the title. "Would it be possible to speak with him, please?"

"Oh, I'm sorry, Dr. Kelly isn't available at the moment." My heart sinks, thinking he might be ill, or out of town, that I might not get to speak to him in time. But then she says, "He's competing in our annual tennis tournament," and I relax at the news. He's there, and he's obviously still fit and healthy. "It's a real hit with our seniors here, and Dr. Kelly still has a terrific serve, he'll probably make the finals."

"That's great," I say.

"Do you want to call back later, or can I take a message?"

"Does he have a direct line to his room, or house, or whatever?"

"He does, but we're not authorized to give that out without his permission, I'm afraid."

"Okay," I say, almost without thinking, the words

coming of their own accord, "can you pass on a message?"

"Yes, of course. What's your message?"

"Please tell him that Jessica Hudson is coming to see him."

5

I am in the departure lounge of Ted Stevens Anchorage International Airport just ninety minutes later, waiting for the early evening flight to Minneapolis.

I have a plan, of sorts.

I'd raced back home to grab my passport, not telling Amy exactly where I was going, what I was doing, only that I'd be gone for the rest of the day. She hadn't objected in the slightest, glad to be looking after the horses, the dogs, the house. She is a saint, that girl, I think as I look nervously around the lounge, journal hidden in my carry-on bag, my eyes scanning for cops, still fearful that they are coming for me even though I know that this is highly unlikely. After all, I know I don't wake up in a jail cell tomorrow, I wake up in Ben's bed, and he knows nothing about Menders.

But still, I am nervous.

I think again of Amy, how I need to find some way of thanking her, when all this is over. If it's *ever* over.

I scrub the thought from my mind, looking up as

my gate is called.

I still haven't managed to get through to Ben, but have left him a voicemail, cancelling our date tonight. I haven't given a reason, or told him where I'm going, or why I'm going; with everything that's happened to me lately, I am sure he will understand if I just want a bit of space.

Not telling people where I'm going is a part of the plan, in a way; I will be free, for a while at least, free of Alaska, the people here. It will give me time to get my head straight, to sort myself out.

The only problem is time; I need to stay awake for the entire twelve-hour journey to Gainesville, otherwise I'll probably be zapped to another day before I ever get there and I'll never speak to Dr. Kelly, never find out what's wrong with me.

And I *need* to find out.

I need to find out for sure, once and for all, if I'm crazy or not.

Hopefully, Dr. Kelly is the key to that.

All I need to do is stay awake.

My flight leaves at 17:10, which is 21:10, Florida-time. After changing at Minneapolis, and then again at Atlanta, I should arrive at Gainesville Regional at 9:26 tomorrow morning, local time.

I stand, finishing off the super-size cup of Starbuck's Blonde Roast and throwing it in the nearest trash can. The leaflet said that it had the highest amount of caffeine – 475mg for the Venti – and that was good enough for me. I can already feel my eyes opening a little wider.

Which is good, because I am starting to come down from the massive burst of adrenaline I'd experienced at Menders' cabin, that had been sustained as I'd fled the scene. It has left me wrecked, empty, and absolutely exhausted; and I still have a half-day journey and jet-lag to contend with.

I walk toward my departure gate, taking a last look at the local news on the TV screen as I go.

Still no news on Menders, and I breathe a sigh of relief.

Hopefully, I'll keep awake on the plane through the extreme over-abuse of coffee and energy drinks, and it will give me a chance to have an initial read-through of Menders' journal. By the time I reach Gainesville, I should have some idea if there's anything of use in there; and then after I've spoken to Kelly, I hope I will also have some more information on my medical condition – if you can call it that.

I've booked a return ticket (if my departure is investigated, a one-way ticket would look highly suspicious), but I know I won't have to travel back the same way; my aim is to speak to Kelly, call Ben if I find anything of use in the journal, then book myself into a hotel and go straight to bed. If the past few days are anything to go by, I'll wake up on another day again, probably back in the Mat-Su valley.

If the past few days are anything to go by.

But by now, I know that there are no guarantees with this thing.

I gladly accept the cup of black coffee and the can of Red Bull from the stewardess, smiling in the friendliest way I can manage.

We are cruising at thirty-eight thousand feet now, a blanket of clouds obscuring the outline of Alaska below us.

"Tired?" she asks with a smile of her own.

"More than a little," I agree, the initial kick of the Blonde Roast desperate now to be topped up.

"If you want, I can bring you a pillow and a blanket? We've got five hours until we land at St. Paul."

"That's okay," I say, tapping the journal which lies on my lap. "I've got some work to do before we land."

"Are you getting off at Minneapolis?"

"No," I say. "Atlanta." I don't tell her that I'm then taking a regional flight from Atlanta to Gainesville; the less people know about my movements, the better.

"Atlanta?" she repeats with a raised eyebrow. "You're going to need a few more coffees and Red Bulls, I guess."

I laugh. "Don't I know it."

She leaves, and I nervously thumb the journal. I've got an aisle seat, and the middle-aged couple next to me are minding their own business. The woman by the window is reading an e-book, and the guy in the middle is watching one of the in-flight movies. Looks like some sort of horror flick, and I don't look for long; I've had enough horror for a lifetime.

I'm mindful, however, of how I angle the journal, to make sure that nobody else can see it. I might be paranoid, but with good reason.

But I've got five hours to kill, and I finally open the journal and get down to work.

By the time the plane starts its decent into Minneapolis-St. Paul International, I'm about two-thirds of the way into Menders' book.

Two-thirds in, and I still don't really know what to make of it. The way it is written – not only his scrawled, barely legible handwriting, but also the irregular spelling, the sometimes-nonexistent grammar, as well as the barely coherent structure – makes it far from an easy read. Most of my time has been spent trying to decipher parts of it that seem to defy explanation.

There are a lot of passages that deal with the stars, mixed in so deeply that sometimes they are hard to separate from the rest of it. More than once, I've been reading a sentence about Menders' daily habits, or about a book he was reading, or his thoughts on women, and don't immediately realize when he has gone off into a diatribe about astronomy.

Thinking about his attitude toward women, I re-read a section from just a few pages back, still trying to get my head around what might make a person *hate* so much.

fucking whors shood all fucking die, die, die, yes fucking bitches DIE I hate them so much they stink so bad I wish I coud just get rid of you all why why why why why do you do it you Whors. I dont no why you dont all fall into HELL and DIE if I coud I woud FUCK you all to HELL and back. I woud

STRANGEL and KILL and BLAST you all to the Crab Nebula, a supernova remnant and pulsar wind nebula found in the constellation of Taurus –

Bizarrely, the passage then goes on – in very neat, perfectly-spelled writing – to describe the Crab Nebula in exquisite detail, possibly a passage copied from a textbook or website.

But it makes me wonder about the man, makes me wonder if he was just sat there at his desk reading and writing about astrology, then got hit by an irresistible urge to commit his hatred of women to paper, to purge it from his system, to let it all out into this journal.

It makes for severely uncomfortable reading, as I am drawn into the dark netherworld of Menders' disturbed mind, but so far, I have found no details of anything he saw down in the valley. There are vague mentions of other women, possibly from Palmer or Anchorage, but no names, no details. It is clear that he was still stalking people on occasion, would follow them, but it is hard to ascertain how far this went. It is clear that – even in the most crazed phases of his writing – he was reticent to give up any details, anything that might incriminate him in a court of law, if the journal was ever found.

My mind is hurting, but not just from the turgid handwritten notes I have been concentrating on – I am on my eighth coffee and my sixth Red Bull, and I am fearful that my skull is simply not big enough to take the pounding of my brain against the inside of its shell.

I have been fighting sleep for the past hour – really

fighting it – and I close the journal as the big Boeing 757 touches down on the St. Paul runway, grateful for the chance to go for a walk, maybe visit the airport restrooms and splash some water on my face.

The rest of the journal will just have to wait.

We are in the air over Illinois when I see it, eyes bleary, mouth as dry as if it has been stuffed with cotton balls.

I miss it at first – for a long time now, the words on the page have been floating in front of me, forcing me to read, then re-read, then re-read again before anything truly sinks in, my exhaustion threatening to overwhelm me, to destroy me, despite the several grams of caffeine I must have ingested over the past several hours.

But finally it sinks in, something . . . something . . .

I blink my eyes, trying to moisten them so I can see straight; my vision clears, blurs again, then clears, and I read the section again.

component stars remain near 100 solar masses, making them among the most massive stars recorded and the star arrives at the base, it is a little star, a young star taken into the base not struggling maybe sleeping so they have another one, Another littel star for their constellation what shoud I name this one??? ab3-7 I think. yes that is right definitely right. I wonder what they do with this littel star I woud love to be there I woud love to help them I woud love to try it myself oh yes yes yes

– and then it switches back to more information on something called Pismis 24, which again is clearly something copied out of a textbook. I wonder if he is genuinely interested in this part of his writing, or if it's just a way of hiding the other passages; was Menders hopeful that if someone ever found his journal, if they were to give it just a cursory glance, they might think it was only an astronomical notebook? If so, he was even crazier than I thought – there is such a huge difference in style, spelling, layout and appearance between the sections that you would have to be blind not to see it. Another alternative is that he was sitting at his desk, copying notes, when something occurred to him or – as in this case – caught his eye, and he immediately jotted his thoughts or observations down into the same book.

I can imagine him there alone at his desk, writing about Pismis 24, when he sees a vehicle approach, somewhere down in the valley. He checks his telescope, sees a "little star" – ab3-7, Lynette Hyams, someone else? – being taken "into the base", and I have to assume that he is talking about one of the ranches he can see down there in the valley, I have to assume that he was witnessing the passage of a victim into the murder-house.

Which means that it *is* someone down in the valley, someone within the little hamlet of homesteads which surround me.

I think of Larraine Harrigan and Artie Jenkins; retired Judge Tom Judd, alone in his big house; the Eberles, with their large house and even larger family; the solid and dependable Latimers, the old Townsend couple . . .

Could any of them be involved in this? One of

them? Some of them? *All* of them?

Menders says "they", an indication that – as De Nares suspects – there is more than one person involved. But who *are* "they"?

And could Douglas Menders see anywhere else from his desk? I reflect now on how I should have carried on looking through the telescope, tried to find out if he could observe any other areas of the Mat-Su valley from his cabin. But I was too wrapped up in what I'd seen, was too terrified by the fact that he could see *me*, to investigate further.

And why did he label the girl – if that's what the "little star" refers to – by the title "ab3-7"? What does *that* mean? Are those her initials? Is the number an age, or range of ages? Is that the number of suspected victims, somewhere between three and nine? Thirty-nine?

Hell, I still don't know anything, and I order another coffee – with milk this time, to help soothe my churning stomach – as I race back through the journal from the beginning, trying to find any similar references that I might have missed before, tired as I am.

And then I do start to see reference to other "littel stars", appended by Menders' unknown system of coding. There are ab3-3, ab3-4, ab3-5 and ab3-6, all lost within the tangle of genuine astronomical information. Some of that stuff was so dense, I must not have noticed when Menders' true voice interceded. So maybe his method of keeping his secret diary worked?

But I know why this final one stood out over the

others, it is because he interjects just a little too much of the personal with this one – the fact that he wants to help them, his excitement at the idea. The previous entries lacked this element. Perhaps by the time of ab3-7, he'd had time to consider what was going on down there, to work himself into a fever pitch about it?

Except for this personal spin, all of the other entries reveal the same information – references to "they", to the "base" and to "their constellation". I have to think that he is witnessing the result of abductions, girls taken off the streets, maybe from their homes, and brought back to one of the farms that make up my little area of the world.

An area I'd thought was safe.

I remind myself that there *are* other options – maybe he was monitoring other areas, maybe it describes something else altogether, maybe it means nothing at all, just another part of Menders' twisted psyche?

But I know I am onto something, and speed-read my way through the rest of the journal, now I know what I am looking for.

And sure enough, I see entries for ab3-8, then – twenty pages later – another for ab3-9. I keep scanning through the pages, nearing the end now, and then I see something else that I missed before, once more lost in the technical jargon of the amateur astronomer –

An O-type star has a temperature in excess of 30,000 Kelvin, and is a hot, blue-white star of spectral type O and what is this ab3-9 is moving acros the void free of the base its owners are in the cluster the littel star is down down the littel star is down. gone? essence uplifted to the true constellations? gone gone gone how did they let this happen is this the end for them I wonder I cannot believe what I have seen the pretty littel star free for just one beootiful moment, racing acros space like a comet, a meteor, a falling star. a dead star and I wonder wat will hapen now, O-type stars are located in regions of active star formation, such as the spiral arms of a

– and then it ends, segues into more information on O-type stars, and I am left stunned, for here in my hands I am holding an eye-witness account to what I believe must be the escape of Lynette Hyams (ab3-9) across the void (the fields) to my own home. But the eye-witness is dead,

(*murdered*)

– no, killed in self-defense –

(*murdered, by you!*)

– shut up! –

and can add nothing more to the account. But it seems to be the implication that the "owners" (the abductors, the torturers, the killers) were at Artie's party that night (isn't that what the "cluster" must mean?).

There is so much information here, and yet I barely understand any of it.

What does it all mean?

Was Lynette being held somewhere in the valley? At someone's house? In an outbuilding? In an underground chamber of some sort?

And who the hell are "they"?

Everyone from the hamlet was at the party, most

of Palmer too, so that doesn't narrow down the field much.

But I have to believe that Lynette *was* being held somewhere near my own house, maybe another eight "littel stars" alongside her. And what became of them?

The coffee and Red Bull threaten to rebel in my stomach and I grab for a paper bag from the seat-back in front of me, holding it up to my nose and mouth and taking in big gulps of air to stop me from vomiting – in, the bag collapsing; out, the bag expanding; in, out, in, out.

Finally – the couple next to me giving me no more than a cursory glance – I am okay, I can breathe again, I am not going to be sick.

But the horror remains, as I struggle to come to terms with the fact that there might be a further six victims out there. I don't know where they are, or what has happened to them, but the only thing I am certain of is the horrifying reality that – if the body of Lynette Hyams is anything to go by – they might be better off dead and buried.

<u>6</u>

Eyes clenched tightly shut, I vomit violently into the toilet bowl in the restrooms of Gainesville Regional, the caffeine finally catching up with me and causing my stomach to rebel.

But I have made it, I am still awake, and I am here in Florida; at times it was close, I was half-asleep, but each time I managed to catch myself.

And now here I am, sick and tired, but here.

I open my bleary eyes, see a black pool in front of me; see the toilet bowl as my eyes focus, see the vomit turn to blood in front of me, a bowl full of thick, clotting blood; I pull away, scared and frightened, and reach for the flush, but what comes out is yet more blood, blood to wash away blood, and I watch in horror as it pours out of the toilet onto the floor around me, and I yank open the door and run from the cubicle, but the blood follows me, sweeping across the tiled floor after me; I collapse against the sink, hands braced on the edges and open my mouth to scream, when –

I look into the mirror, see everything is normal around me; there is no blood, nothing chasing me; just the face of a tired, exhausted woman looking back at me from the mirror, bags deep under her eyes, lines crisscrossing her features where there were none before.

What is happening to me?

The horrible taste in my mouth tells me that I *have* been sick, but the rest must have been some sort of vivid hallucination, brought about by lack of sleep. And stress too, I guess.

But I'm okay now, I tell myself as I look in the mirror; I'm okay now.

I ignore the curious looks of the two other women in the restroom and splash water on my face, then some more, and more again; the feeling is refreshing, rejuvenating, invigorating. It doesn't make up for a good eight hours' sleep, but it makes me feel better anyway.
I wash the sick out of my mouth, then buy some mints from a machine on the wall and immediately start work on two of them.

My stomach still feels queasy, acidic, but I don't think I am going to be sick again.

Finally, I straighten up and check my appearance in the mirror; and then I'm hit with heavy déja vu as I vividly remember checking myself in the bathroom mirror of my West Side apartment, the morning I was shot.

It's only now, that I realize how different I look, how I've changed over these last months. Back then, I was concerned with a stray hair being out of place, everything had to be just-so, as perfect as it could be; it was all part of the image, the job, it was all about an impression of exquisite professionalism I was trying to project. Now, I'm just happy not to have vomit on my hair and jacket.

How times change.

I splash a bit more water on my face, think briefly about adding make-up, but decide I don't have either the time, or the inclination. That side of me is gone now, perhaps forever.

Only the truth remains, and my quest to find it.

I get a taxi into downtown Gainesville, then another to Pine Hills; I avoid a direct route, in case anyone is following my tracks, and I think about how easy it is, how simple, to fall into the authority-dodging behavior of the inveterate criminal.

I booked myself into a hotel in the city center when I was there, preparing for later; I know I'll need a safe place where I can fall asleep, hopefully save myself a twelve-hour journey home.

I've left my overnight bag there, along with the journal, and now I feel naked and unprepared as I approach the house of Dr. Glen Kelly. The journal ties me to Palmer, to Alaska – in a way, to Lynette Hyams – and now, in this strange place, I am confused, as if I have lost my purpose, my reason to be here.

The house is right in the heart of Pine Hills Retirement Village, next to the tennis courts, gymnasium and open-air swimming pool, with the three on-site restaurants only a stone's throw away too. The village is landscaped with lakes and lawns and flowerbeds, and consists of neat individual homes like Dr. Kelly's, low-rise blocks of "independent living" apartments, and – in a separate, hospital-like building – what are labelled "assisted living" apartments.

The lady in the plush reception hall by the parking lot wasn't the same person I'd spoken to on the phone yesterday, and didn't know if my message had been passed along, but – when she'd put a call through to Kelly's home and told him that I was there – he had agreed to see me.

But now that I am right outside, I am starting to have doubts. Why am I here? What am I hoping to achieve? What do I want to find out?

The truth; you want to find out the truth.

But what if the truth is something I don't want to hear?

Grow up, I tell myself. *You're a big girl now – just do it.*

I do as I'm told, before I think better of it, and reach for the doorbell. It echoes in the house beyond, and it is not long before I hear the pad of feet in the hallway beyond, hear the *snick* of a lock, and watch as the door opens to reveal Dr. Glen Kelly.

He is a small man, neat and trim, with a white mustache and short, silver hair; despite his age, he doesn't wear spectacles, and there is a youthful vigor in those dark brown eyes that I instantly like. He seems familiar, like a distant relative seen at a funeral, but I do not consciously recognize him.

"Dr. Kelly?" I ask tentatively.

"Yes," he says, and his face breaks into a warm, friendly smile. "Jessica. It's been a long time." And then he holds up a copy of the Anchorage *Daily News*, open at a page that shows my name, my picture, in connection to the investigation into the death of Lynette.

He nods his head slowly, knowingly. "Yes," he says, smile still on that friendly, familiar face. "I've been waiting for you."

7

We sit in his living room, drinking weak coffee and eating biscuits. He lives alone, I've already discovered, his wife having died of cancer years before; he freely admits that part of living in this retirement community is to find someone new, and I get the impression that he is not short of options in that department.

Turns out he won that tennis tournament yesterday too, and I can only imagine that this will have increased his standing with the retired ladies even more.

"It was the *veteran,* veteran category though," he says self-deprecatingly. "Over-seventy-fives, so the competition wasn't too fierce. Not the US Open, anyway. Do you still play?"

I shake my head. "No," I say. "Not for years."

"A shame," he says, "you used to be quite good, as far as I remember. Saxon courts you played at, wasn't it?"

"Yeah," I say with a laugh. "It was. So, I guess you *did* used to know me."

"Oh, I did, Jess. Yes, I certainly did. And it doesn't surprise me that you can't remember any of it, not after what they did to you."

I can hear some bitterness in his voice, and I can tell that – whatever "treatment" I received back then – Dr. Kelly was not a fan of it.

"What *did* happen to me?" I ask. "And why did you think I'd come and visit?"

"I'll deal with that second question first, if that's okay; that one's a bit easier to answer, the first will . . . take some time."

"Okay," I urge, rubbing my dry eyes, trying to get some blood flow back into my face.

"You're tired," Kelly comments. "Of course . . . You've been trying to keep yourself awake, haven't you? Scared that if you sleep, you might . . . *travel*, unexpectedly."

I nod my head, scared but at the same time relieved that there is someone who might actually understand my condition, what I am going through.

"When did you last sleep?" he asks with concern. "I'm not sure, I guess . . . thirty hours ago, maybe more."

"Jet lag too," he says. "I'm sorry I didn't think about it sooner. Wait there."

I begin to protest, too keen to hear what he has to say, but then he is gone, and I am left sipping at the light-brown coffee, eyes starting to droop despite all the caffeine that must still be in my system.

He returns, and my eyes open. Did I fall asleep?

I'm not sure, but if I did, then it wasn't deep enough to have any effect.

"There," he says, passing me what looks like a smoothie. "Drink that."

"What is it?"

"Oh, a natural mix, it'll help keep you awake, for a while at least. Bee pollen, ginger, maca root, yerba mate tea, lemon juice. Tastes pretty bad, but try some."

I do, and it's not as bad as it sounds. In seconds, it's all gone.

"Good," he says, like a doctor happy with a patient who has taken their medicine.

"So," I say, already feeling the effects of the drink, "you were going to answer that second question first . . ."

"Yes," he agrees, "okay. Well, after I was . . . dissuaded from pursuing my profession by some of my contemporaries, I followed your subsequent career from a distance, I guess I was . . . *curious*, perhaps, to see if any of the peculiar characteristics of your condition were ever to resurface. But I couldn't keep in touch, not directly – if the treatment was effective, I wouldn't have liked to upset the applecart, so to speak. But I monitored your career, watched as you took off in New York. Followed the press coverage of that diabolical situation outside the courthouse. When you woke up, I couldn't help wondering if . . . the bullet might cause some . . . how do I put this? Cause some *regression*.

"But you moved to Alaska, everything seemed to be okay, and then . . . I read this." He taps the newspaper article. "I've had it sent to me since you moved there." Suddenly, he looks awkward. "Sorry if I sound like some sort of stalker, but your case has had a pretty profound impact on my life, and I'm a curious man."

I suddenly feel terribly guilty, thinking about how I might have ruined this man's career. "I'm –"

But Kelly holds up a hand, cutting me off. "No," he says firmly, "I'm not looking for an apology, I don't want sympathy, I'm just explaining to you, making you understand why I've been monitoring things, even at my age. I guess I'm one of those people that just can't let go, right? Like a dog with a bone.

"Anyway," he continues, tapping the paper again, "I read this, that you've been arrested over some sort of homicide, I naturally look into it in a bit more detail, then I find out the reason, that you gave details of a murder to the police before it even happened. ABI naturally assume you must have had some sort of foreknowledge of it, right? Aiding and abetting right there, minimum." He shakes his head in seeming disbelief.

"How did you get those details?" I ask, knowing the reason for my arrest was never made public, at least not that I am aware of.

"Ms. Hudson," he says with a smile, "I'm eighty-one years old, I've been around long enough to know plenty of people, in *all* lines of work. And some of 'em owe me favors."

He winks conspiratorially, and I smile, a little girl

again.

"Well, I immediately had to ask myself the question, *did she see it again*? Has it started again?"

"Has *what* started again?" I ask quickly, desperate to know what *he* knows. "Did I see *what* again?"

"The Red Moon," Kelly says gravely. "It always starts with the Red Moon."

We are sitting outside now, discussing my case over lemonade and cucumber sandwiches at a café that overlooks the tennis courts; even when he's not playing, he likes to keep an eye on the competition.

"The problems started when you were eleven," Kelly says, just before taking a bite of his sandwich. The sun is in my eyes as I look at him, but the warmth is a welcoming change from the snowy wastes I have come from. I was going to order a coffee, but he thinks that the citric acid in lemon juice might be better for me. "Around about the same time you started menstruating, if I recall."

"What?" I say, surprised – shocked – by his knowledge of such information.

"Jess," he says with a wave of his hand, "I am – well, I *was* – a doctor. *Your* doctor, for a certain amount of time. These are just medical facts."

I sigh; I know he is right, it is just strange to talk to this man about this subject. He might well have been my doctor, but I still do not remember him, and after everything that has happened recently, I have a hard time trusting strangers.

"Well anyway," he continues, undeterred, "I only mention it because some of my colleagues believed it was important, that your mental image of the Red Moon was linked to it in some way, a mental projection, if you will, of your emergence into womanhood."

There is an underlying implication in his words, something I don't immediately grasp. "Why would I project something about that?" I ask eventually. "Did it scare me?"

For a moment, Kelly looks uneasy, and he takes a short break to sip lemonade through a long, green straw before looking back at me.

"Jessica," he says, "do you remember a man called Desmond Curtis?"

Desmond Curtis? I do know that name, in fact I only thought of him the other day, for the first time in years. Blue eyes behind steel-framed glasses . . . grey mustache . . . a friend of my father's? And then I remember the terror, the *horror* associated with that name, and my stomach cramps up and – for just a moment – I feel terribly alone.

"I . . . yes, vaguely. The name makes me uncomfortable though, I don't know why."

Kelly looks at me carefully, as if judging how I will handle what he has to tell me. "That makes sense," he concedes finally. "Because the first instance of your . . . unique problem, let's call it . . . was directly related to Mr. Curtis."

"How?"

"You claimed that he sexually assaulted you."

"What?" I gasp, not believing him – but the way he holds my gaze, the honest and nonjudgmental way he looks at me, makes me wonder if he is right. And if he *is*, what does it mean? Why can't I remember?

"Nobody believed you, of course, and with good reason," Kelly continued. "Because you made the complaint *before* you'd actually met him."

"What?" I repeat, stunned.

"Mr. Curtis was a business partner of your father's, played a bit of golf with him too. But he'd never been to your house, you'd never met him at the club, at your father's office, anywhere. You claim he assaulted you in your bedroom in Westford, during a birthday party held for your mother. A party that hadn't happened yet."

The parallels with my current situation are incredible, and I want to ask questions, but don't dare interrupt his story.

"Anyway," he continues, "you then claimed that you'd gone back in time, he *had* assaulted you, but in the *future*. And you can just imagine what your parents thought, what the *doctors* thought."

"They must have thought I made the whole thing up," I say instantly. "So what happened?"

"Well, you never did meet Desmond Curtis in the end – the police had been called in because of your complaint, and it rather soured his relationship with your father. He never went to that party."

"So I *wasn't* assaulted?"

"Well, yes and no. In the reality most of us exist in, *no*. In *your reality* – at least, *I* believe – *yes*."

"But," I say, "I remember him, remember what he looked like . . . and yet you say I never met him."

"That's what everyone else believes. I believe you *did* meet him – and I think he *did* assault you, just as you claimed – just not in the same reality as the rest of us."

"You believe that I traveled back in time, that I changed my own history?"

"Yes," Kelly answers simply. "I do. You changed it in a way, but in actual fact, for you, it was too late – the damage had already been done. You'd been assaulted, but nobody else would ever see it."

"But couldn't I describe him? Tell people what he looked like?" I say, thinking about Pat Jenkins, how I'd known he had a beard without ever "really" having met him.

"He was a society figure," Kelly says, "had his picture in the papers regularly, on the local news, that sort of thing. It was assumed you'd seen his picture, perhaps become fixated on him, and come up with the whole story as some sort of way of making a connection with him."

"Accusing someone of rape is one hell of a way of making a connection."

"People have done much stranger things, believe me. And nothing you said, no 'evidence' you supplied was good enough. Nobody believed you."

"You know, I don't really remember what happened, not exactly."

"That's not because it didn't happen; you remembered for a long time afterward, believe me. It was your treatment that finally made you forget."

"You didn't agree with the treatment?"

"Oh, there was probably nothing wrong with you forgetting that horrific incident, it wasn't that I argued against *that*. It was just that I wasn't sure if your condition could actually *be* treated. Or if it even *should* be."

"What do you mean?"

"As a young girl, you remembered what happened to you, what Desmond Curtis had done to you, and it was very difficult for you to handle. You'd gone back, changed the circumstances, stopped him ever coming to the house. But for you, the attack had still happened. But during other episodes –"

"There were more?" I interrupt, amazed at what I am hearing.

"Yes," Kelly says, "several. And in those cases, you were able to actually help others – people who had no recollection of their 'alternate' fates, and couldn't possibly remember what you had saved them from. Simply because, due to your intervention, what you saved them from had no longer happened, the circumstances no longer existed."

"What do you mean?"

"Well, let's take one example. Marie Langford. Do you remember her?"

"Yes . . . vaguely." I remember the name, maybe a face, a friend from school maybe?

"Well, at the time you were best friends. And then you saw her killed by a car, hit her square on and drove off without stopping."

My mind is a blank; I remember none of it.

"So anyway, you woke up the next day crying and moaning about Marie being dead. It really frightened everyone, as you might imagine, especially when they realized that she was alive and well. Then you found out that it was two days before you thought it was, and so you claimed that you must have fallen asleep and woken up two days earlier, that you traveled through time as you slept. But whatever the reality, you spent those two days making sure you did everything you could to stop Marie going near that road."

"And?"

Kelly shrugs. "And she didn't. She's still alive and well today, married with three kids in Connecticut."

"So I saved her?" I ask, the implication clear.

"You did," Kelly says with a proud smile. "You did. Of course, nobody except you ever realized what you'd done; not even you, in the end."

"*You* realized," I say.

"Yes," Kelly agrees, "but I came rather late to your case. You were thirteen by then, you'd had many episodes and I think your parents were at their wits' end. They just didn't know what to do with you, they were being pressured into the electro-shock therapy approach by some of the biggest names in the industry, you know, and I think they didn't want to go down that road but were running out of options."

"So they brought you in."

"Yes. Your parents were a real mess, they'd already

331

sold the house at Westford, moved the whole family to the city, mainly so that you could have constant access to medical help, psychiatric help, counselling, everything you needed. He didn't want you riding anymore either, he was terrified that if you had a fall, you would be even more damaged, even more disturbed."

I put my drink down, things falling into place for the first time. Suddenly, my father's decision to sell-up, to move us to Boston, to get rid of the horses, at last makes sense; and the realization sends another huge surge of guilt through me, as I understand, for the first time, that maybe he is not the monster I have always thought, that perhaps he *did* only want the best for me. First this, and then Jack killing himself not so many years later, it must have been too much for him to bear; my mother too, what must she have thought, what must have been going through *her* mind? Perhaps my father's workaholic lifestyle and my mother's vapid, gala-obsessed social obsessions, were just evidence of how they were struggling to cope?

"And then I ruined everything," Kelly says, interrupting these revelations, "by believing you."

"But why did *you* believe me?" I ask, getting back to the subject at hand, putting aside those thoughts of my parents, for the time-being at least.

Kelly pauses, watching the tennis for a long while before continuing thoughtfully. "To this day, I'm still not entirely sure, to be honest." He pauses again, watches the action on the courts, and frowns. "Well, actually, that might not be true," he admits. "Your memories of the events you described, they were so intense, so detailed, that they *demanded* to be believed."

"And that was good enough for you?" I ask, amazed.

"No," he says with a smile, "I have to admit that it wasn't. But then something very interesting happened. You had another episode, just after I'd been assigned to your medical assessment team. A man had a heart attack just outside the tennis club house, you watched it happen, you saw the Red Moon, you knew that tomorrow . . . well, you knew that tomorrow would be a different day. And, maybe because I was new to the team, I'd not built up a defensive wall about your stories yet, I was relatively open minded, apparently you came to my office afterward, asked me some interesting questions."

"What sort of questions?"

"Personal questions," he says. "Private questions, of the sort that an adult might not usually answer from a thirteen-year-old girl. My first sexual partner, what happened, details, that sort of thing. Apparently, you claimed that it was an experiment; you believed you would soon be 'beamed' forwards or backwards in time – sometimes it was forwards, sometimes backwards, sometimes both, you'd be bounced around until you could figure out how to fix things. But anyway, I guess you were convinced that sooner or later you'd end up on an earlier day, hopefully to help the guy, or whatever. And you thought that if you knew things about me that you couldn't possibly know, then my earlier self would be convinced that – at some stage – you had asked an alternative version of me those questions."

"Is that why you say 'apparently'?" I ask, understanding now. "Because *this* version of you never answered those questions?"

"That's right," he says. "I only heard your answers, when you came to me, a day before that man would have died. This version of me, well, I never heard you ask those questions, that 'me' is gone forever, I guess. But this me, *this* me, you gave it to straight, all the sordid details of me and Lucy O'Shea in the back of my '59 Caddy, at the drive-through movies. Down to all the little details, including what I'd done before the date even started. The only thing you didn't know was the name of the movie . . . and that was the thing that really convinced me."

"Why?"

"Because to this day," he says with a smile, "I have no idea what it was. It was my first time with a girl, why would I give a two-bit damn what movie was playing?" I laugh, and he joins me; the sound relaxes me and I can see why I might have trusted this man, all those years ago.

"People claimed that a lot of your information – because you had tried to prove it to people before – well, they claimed it might come from research, available facts, you know. It's amazing what you can find out, if you're bright enough, if you're determined enough. But anyone researching that night would have found out the name of the movie, that's for sure. You had the day, the date, why not the movie, right? And it's the little details like *that* – sometimes not just what you know, but what you *don't* know – that really count, in a case like this. But there was something else," he says, eyes flicking back now to the tennis match. "Something even more convincing, for me at any rate."

"What was that?"

"You took me to the tennis courts," he says. "You needed a doctor anyway, right? You knew the guy was going to have a heart attack, so you dragged me down there. And sure enough, it happened just as you said. I had my gear with me, I'd even got a portable defibrillator; he started going down and we got to him real fast, you and me, and we saved him. Started that heart back up, got him to a hospital, and saved him."

I can sense the pride in his voice again, know now why he believed in me when nobody else did.

"I tried to convince people, of course," he says sadly, "but they'd already made their minds up about your condition. Acute tachypsychia, they called it, an inability to experience time properly, in certain circumstances; it's like the time distortion that you get during high-stress situations like car crashes, you know, that sort of thing, when time seems to speed up or slow right down, it's there in all the literature. They figured it was brought on by your inability to cope with your first menstrual cycle; apparently you had bad cramps, lots of blood, it was apparently very hard to cope with; so the general feeling was that this psychologically led to a fear of your approaching womanhood, leading you to accuse

Desmond Curtis of sexually assaulting you. Your visions of the Red Moon were ascribed to being representative of that first period, that first cycle, and essentially this is what most of the doctors focused on. They said that, after the fallout from the Curtis incident, you couldn't admit your guilt, couldn't admit that you'd made the whole thing up, and so you then had to carry on the charade by pretending to have more episodes, more 'visions', more incidents of logic-defying time travel."

Kelly sighs as he finally looks back toward me, shaking his head. "It's no surprise you weren't believed," he says. "Visions? Time travel? Who in their right mind would ever believe such a thing?"

I think for a minute, my own gaze wandering to the tennis game beyond. "You," I say at last, turning back to Kelly. "You believed."

"Yes," he admits, "I believed; and look what happened to me as a result."

I must look guilty, because once again he is shaking his head vigorously. "No, no," he says, "you can't feel bad about it. You didn't know what would happen. You trusted me, how can I blame you for that? But people believed I was naïve, others that I was out-and-out stupid, while others made insinuations that our relationship wasn't ethical, that it was more than the usual doctor-patient relationship."

"But why –"

"That time at the tennis court, people wondered why I was there, why we were 'meeting up' outside regular hours. They didn't even care that we saved that man," he adds angrily, "they only asked what I'd been doing there with a thirteen-year-old girl." He sits back and sighs. "I suppose they meant well though," he says in resignation, "they did what they thought was right, I guess I may have jumped to the same conclusions in their position. But your father wasn't happy, wasn't happy at all, he used his influence to get me drummed out of the profession for good."

"I'm sorry," I say, before I can stop myself.

"I've already told you," Kelly says, "there is no 'sorry' here, you weren't at fault, you weren't at fault at all.

"So what happened next?"

"What happened next, was therapy. I objected, of course, but I was no longer of interest, no longer had a say in the debate." He smiles as a waitress comes and clears the sandwich plates, and orders us another couple of lemonades. "You were zapped, blasted, everything that was available, they used on you," Kelly continues when the girl has gone. "Your brain was plugged into all sorts of things, they believed that if they targeted the part of the brain that deals with the processing, the sensation, of time, then they might be able to 'cure' you. They used hypnosis too, to help you forget."

"And it worked?" I ask, knowing that it must have – for a time, at least.

Kelly simply shrugs. "Maybe it did," he says. "I guess it *did*," he says more emphatically, "yes. It stopped your episodes. At least up until recently."

"You think the gunshot may have loosened things

up in here again?" I ask, pointing at my head.

"Well," Kelly says with a laugh, "I guess that's one way of putting it, but . . . yeah, I think the gunshot wound, the coma, the damage to the brain, I think it reopened this . . . *ability* you have, if you want to call it that."

"But what *is* the red moon? How does it . . . *work*?" I ask, for wont of a better word.

Kelly shrugs those shoulders again, as if he's asked himself this same question a thousand times, and still hasn't come up with any sort of answer. "The simple answer is, I don't know. I just don't know. All I know is that it is real, however it works. Whatever the red moon is – whether its supernatural, or just how your mind deals with your condition – we'll never know. But maybe it doesn't even matter. Why are any of us here in the first place, right? How was the universe created? All we have are theories and guesses.

"I've thought about it for years, trust me. The 'me' that you asked those questions of, back in my old office. What happened to him? Is he still there, in an alternate reality somewhere? How many *me's* are there? How many *you's*? Who's to say if our present reality isn't dependent on someone else's time travel? Or is it a matter of alternative dimensions? Are they, in fact, the same thing, one affecting the other?

"As I say, I've spent a long time thinking about it, maybe twenty years or more. And you know what I've discovered?"

I shake my head, and he smiles.

"I'm better off playing tennis," he says. "At least that's got rules that I understand."

I laugh, and so does Kelly.

"My point is serious, though," he says after a moment's pause. "Maybe the *how* doesn't matter at all. Maybe there *is* no explaining it. Maybe the *why* is of more importance – or should be."

"What do you mean?" I ask, before thinking back to something that Kelly said earlier, seizing upon it. "You said that perhaps my condition *shouldn't* be treated," I remind him. "Why did you say that?"

Kelly takes a long pull of the new lemonade that has appeared before him, then meets my eyes. "Think about it," he says. "Think about what a gift you have, think about what it can be *used* for."

I guess I've already been thinking along these lines myself, but I want to hear Kelly say it. "Go on," I urge him.

"Okay," he says, "I'll tell you what I think. In previous incarnations of this condition, you would be faced with some form of trauma, and – if it was severe enough, if it affected you badly enough – pretty soon you'd see that big red moon, and you'd know, you'd know it was starting again. And then you'd bounce around from day to day – and if you want me to be more specific, you'd bounce around the days very close to the event, or close to important days related to the event, you know? A very limited time frame I guess, very focused. And anyway, you'd bounce around time until you'd solved the problem, helped whoever needed

339

helping. And all for no reward, no thanks, nothing except electro-shock therapy and a 'crazy' label. But you *would* help people; with this ability, you *could* help people. And hell, I think you still *can*. I think that – if your past is anything to go by – then the only chance you have of ending this thing, of bringing things back to normal, is if you erase the event that started it."

"Save the girl?" I ask, then watch as Kelly nods his silver-topped head.

"Yes," he says slowly, gravely. "If you ever want this nightmare to end, you need to *use* time, use this skill, this ability, use it to find that girl *before* she's abducted, *before* she's killed. Find her . . . and save her. And by saving *her*," he adds, "you'll save yourself."

8

I lie on the bed in my hotel room, trying to sleep.

Ironic – I've been struggling to stay awake for the entire day, and now I can't sleep.

And I *need* to sleep – not just because I crave it physically, but also because sleep is what will send me to another day, perhaps another day when I can help Lynette, when I can *save* Lynette.

My talk with Dr. Glen Kelly is one I will never forget; and it isn't so much the history that he gave me, the missing pieces of my life, the explanation for countless events – no, it is for the hope he gave me, the renewed sense of purpose in my life.

Before, I was scared, alone, afraid, I was confused by my "problem", thought I was going crazy; now I see that maybe it's not a problem at all, but a gift.

Yes, I think as I stretch out on the double bed, it *is* a gift.

And it is a gift I want to use.

Dammit, why can't I sleep?

I want to get back to Palmer, get back and help that girl; I don't know which day I will wake up on, but I swear that – whatever day it happens to be – I will do everything I can to help her, dead *or* alive.

Then something occurs to me, and I reach for my cellphone, dial Ben's number.

He answers after only a couple of rings. "Jessica?" he says, and I like the sound of his voice, think that I might even be starting to miss him. I hear the sound of a saxophone in the background – John Coltrane, I think – and I imagine Ben sitting in his easy chair with a beer in his hand, crime scene reports scattered across the table in front of him; looking for answers, just like me.

"Hi Ben," I say. "Sorry to stand you up last night."

"That's okay," he says, "at least you left a message. Sorry I was out of town all day. Where are you, anyway?"

"Florida," I tell him.

"Florida?" he says, his voice louder. "What the hell are you doing down in Florida?"

"One of my doctors is here," I tell him, "someone that used to look after me."

"Oh," Ben says, voice softer now. "Okay. Okay. I guess the ABI haven't banned you from traveling. De Nares might not be too happy about it though."

"Screw De Nares."

Ben chuckles. "Yeah, I guess you're right. Screw him."

"Anyway, the . . . ah . . . reason I'm calling is, because I need a favor."

"A favor?" he asks warily. "What sort of favor?"

"You believe me, don't you?" I ask. "About . . . you know . . ."

"Your visions?"

"Yeah," I agree. *We can call it that, if you want.* "Well, do you?"

"I . . . yeah, I guess I do. Yeah," he adds with more conviction. "I do."

"Then you need to help me," I say, remembering the police reports spread over Ben's coffee table, most of which I didn't have time to read. But I have suddenly realized that they might hold the key to helping Lynette.

Ben sighs. "Okay," he says. "What do you need?"

"Tell me everything you know about the day Lynette was abducted."

I've finished a bottle of champagne from the minibar and two beers, so I decide to get started on the shorts. The Malibu looks tempting, and so I open it and down it with one long swallow.

I was right – it *is* good.

My hand wavers as it automatically selects something else, and I tell myself that it is all for strictly medicinal purposes. I have so much caffeine in my body that I still cannot sleep, and what I need is a dose of depressant – and alcohol fits the bill nicely.

It's certainly having an effect, as the room spins wildly around me; I lose my grip on whatever bottle my hand has pulled out of the fridge, my legs go from under me, and I end up in an unsightly heap on the carpet.

Not very ladylike, I appreciate that, but who cares? It's not every day that you learn what I've learned today – that I was sexually molested at the age of eleven, made to forget nearly two years of my life through controversial therapy and treatment.

No, I think as I claw my way across the floor, try to pull myself up onto my bed, *it's not every day you learn that, at all.*

Jack is gone, gone once more out of the window, nothing left but the blood, and the silent screams inside my mind as Beauty crashes into me, knocking me breathless to the floor; his body rampant over mine, muscles flexing, nostrils flaring; I see the face of a man above me then, mid-fifties, grey hair, cold blue eyes under steel-rimmed glasses; he pins me to the ground and I feel helpless, powerless, afraid, alone, terrified, and I cry out as he touches me, grabs at me, my hands and feet try and lash out but he is too strong, too strong . . .

The face changes then, melts like a candle, flesh running, eyes lost in running blood before reappearing as the face of Paul, above me, crushing me, forcing himself on me, his face sweaty, eyes red, evil, his breath coming out like hot steam . . .

I am crying, screaming, begging for mercy, and then the face changes again . . . it is Beauty, it is Dr. Kelly, it is Ben, Artie, Pat, it is Douglas Menders, it is my father . . .

It is a man in a woolen mask, green eyes boring

into mine . . .

And then he is gone too, replaced by an unknown form, an unknown face, a shadow, a wild beast astride me, I try and see who it is but can't, I can't, I can't . . .

And then I am in the street outside, neon lights shining bright over Jack's dead body, and I cradle his shattered, broken head in my arms, try desperately to push the oozing jelly of his brain back into his jagged skull, blood over my fingers, my hands . . .

Lynette's blood, all over me, and now I cradle her head in my hands, see once again the spark of life leave her, scream up into the night sky, up at the moon, the huge, blood-red moon that seems to grow, and grow and grow, until all I can see is that moon, the moon that has controlled my life for so long, that controls everything, and I feel pulled toward it, see my soul pulled from my body, the red moon wanting to devour it, as it devours everything, but I won't let it, I won't, not this time, and then I understand that the red moon is not fighting me, it is allowing me to merge with it, to become one with it, to use its power . . .

I hold Lynette in my arms, look into those dead eyes, shallow in that pale face; watch in wonder as they light back up, life flooding her body, rejuvenating her, revitalizing her, and I am hit by a wave of relief and awe, excitement and amazement.

Because Lynette Hyams . . . is alive.

DAY SIX

<u>1</u>

My eyes open slowly, painfully; it takes several moments to gather myself, for the inner world to fade away, for the outside world to take its hold.

And when it does, I fly out of bed like I've been scalded.

There are so many questions, I am overwhelmed.

Where am I, what time is it, what day is it, what date is it?

I'm no longer in the hotel, I see that instantly; no, I am in my own room, back in Alaska, back in Palmer. I hear birds cheeping outside, look out of the window and see a clear blue sky, the late autumn sun low on the horizon, just rising; no snow anywhere.

I check my phone, look at the screen, take several moments to process the facts.

It is October 8th, nearly an entire week before Lynette Hyams dies on my doorstep.

October 8th – the last day anyone sees her, the day she is abducted.

She is still alive on October 8th.

She is still alive.

And this might be perhaps my one and only chance to save her.

I get in the shower, glad that I don't have a hangover, glad that I'm waking up in my October 8th body and not the one that would have woken up in that Gainesville hotel room; that one would have been in a world of alcohol-induced pain. But mentally, I still had a long, long day yesterday, and a shower – turning the temperature from scalding hot to freezing cold as I go – is exactly what I need to blow the cobwebs out.

I towel myself off, blow-dry my hair, and change into fresh clothes, suddenly feeling like a million dollars.

As I make my way downstairs, I try and piece together what Ben told me the day before (or more than a week in the future, to be more accurate).

There are several witnesses that place Lynette in the Spenard district on the 7th, working the streets for her pimp – and on-again, off-again boyfriend – Dennis Hobson.

She'd had several "dates" that night, some of them in the cars of her customers, others in a motel room that Hobson rents for the purpose. As far as could be done, Ben assured me, these customers had been identified and chased up by Anchorage PD and the ABI.

She normally lives in an apartment on West Benson Boulevard – again, paid for by Hobson – but apparently, she wasn't there last night. Further witness statements suggest that she had an argument with Hobson over payment for her last trick of the evening, a car date. She claimed that the guy never paid her, Hobson claimed that she was holding out on him and gave her a couple of slaps, right there in the middle of the street.

Follow-up ABI investigation showed that instead of going home, she had spent the night at . . . the Anchorage Street Shelter.

Run by the one-and-only Arthur Jenkins.

Did he know her?

It's hard to say, because apparently, she signed in with a false name; it was only the testimony of a couple of friends that alerted the ABI to the fact, and – on following it up – it was confirmed that she *did* stay there. Signed in at 03:21, was out by 07:23.

I know that I'm already too late to catch her at breakfast – witnesses had seen her eating at Kay's Family Restaurant on Spenard Road with two of her girlfriends between 7:30 and 8:15, and it is already past nine.

Past nine . . .

Damn! It's been so long since I've had a normal routine, I've completely forgotten about my horses, my dogs. Amy's not here – in this reality, I've had no reason to call the AER yet – and I've completely forgotten my responsibilities.

I race downstairs, let the dogs out, and pick up the phone. Dawn answers, and except for mention of the police – I substitute "medical problem" – it is almost a facsimile version of the conversation I had/have with her in a few days' time. She promises to send someone over, and I ask if Amy is free; I already know she'll do a good job.

I feel guilty, but there are more important things to do; the horses are all out at pasture, and it's mostly just grooming and caring-time I'll be missing out on. A couple of them have meds to take, but not until dinner. And it's not as if I could have set my alarm – how did I know I'd be waking up on this day? The last time I lived October 8th, I was up with the larks, my own personal body-clock getting me up just after six-thirty, like it always does; always *did*, anyway. I don't think my body-clock is working at all anymore.

I grab some toast, pour food into the dogs' bowls, and wonder about exactly where I'm going to go first.

Lynette's girlfriends corroborated having breakfast with her on Spenard Road, and they are the same girls who told police that she'd spent the night at the shelter. They knew what Hobson had done the night before, and their statements said that Lynette's face was slightly bruised on one side from being slapped. She hadn't wanted to talk about it, but had admitted to spending the previous night at the shelter.

There were two interesting things here already – Dennis Hobson is a proven abuser, a man who almost certainly recruited Lynette into her life of hooking for dates on Spenard, and who uses violence to keep her there. He is an obvious suspect, although Ben says the reports exonerate him to a large extent – he's over in Anchorage, and enough people have seen him there in the week leading up to Lynette's death to give him a pretty good alibi. It is assumed that Lynette must have been being held close to where she died – and even if it is further than people give her credit for, it is unlikely in the extreme that she would have made it, naked and half-dead, from quite so far as Anchorage.

And that's not to mention the fact that – unknown to everyone except me – Douglas Menders claims to have seen the killer or killers in the direct vicinity of the hamlet in which she was found.

But Artie works at the shelter – helps *run* the shelter, actually – and he also lives right there in the community. His brother gives me the creeps, and I still can't rule Menders out entirely.

I feel a wave of nauseating, gut-wrenching guilt as I think of Menders, of how I killed him, then remember that I didn't – he's actually still alive, at this point in time, anyway. I *can't* have killed him, if he's not dead. Can I?

I wipe the thought away, getting my mind back onto Lynette, and what happened to her. I need to concentrate on the facts, nothing but the facts. That's what's going to help, not wild suppositions.

So, what are the facts?

Lynette left the restaurant at about a quarter-past-eight according to the girls – security cameras have it as 08:17 – and then her whereabouts are unaccounted for, at least for the rest of the morning. Again, cameras have her heading north on Spenard after leaving her girlfriends, but there is nothing else on record until she signs back into the Anchorage Street Shelter at 12:21, using the same false name that she supplied the night before.

She eats lunch there, briefly sees a doctor about her facial injuries, and is gone by 13:56.

Ben's notes indicate that the doctor tried to help her with other issues – she admitted to having symptoms of venereal disease, and was clearly a drug-user – but Lynette distrusted the medical services, and left before help could be given.

Larraine was off that day, but Artie – in subsequent interviews – admitted to having met her, although he only knew her as "Jermaine Tracy", the name she'd given at the time; according to Ben, he was as surprised as anyone when the police told him that the dead girl was the same one who had eaten lunch at his workplace only days before.

Her exact whereabouts after leaving the shelter are unknown, but several witnesses have her back looking for dates along West Northern Lights Boulevard. She was seen outside the Spenard Roadhouse in the early afternoon, and again by the Billiard Palace Bar at about five o'clock. According to friends and colleagues, these weren't her usual hangouts, and might indicate that she was avoiding her pimp-boyfriend, who reportedly runs his girls along the main drag of Spenard Road.

The last time she was seen, was by one of the girls working Northern Lights, who claims she saw a young woman of Lynette's description getting into a silver SUV – make and license plate unknown – at about six o'clock that evening.

This evening, I remind myself, the urgency a burning pain in my gut.

I think about the ranches in my hamlet outside Palmer, think about where she could have been taken.

Obviously, not to my own house.

Then there is Larraine's, but she lives with her two sons and – from talking to her – I know she doesn't have a boyfriend at the moment.

There are some other farmsteads nearby, but – I have to admit – I don't know much about them.

I know Tom Judd is retired, and – as well as the ranch – he also has an apartment in Anchorage; but even though that is where Lynette went missing from, it doesn't necessarily mean anything.

The Eberles have six children, and I find it hard to imagine that they would have the energy or time for anything else, especially as they are one of the few families in the area to run their farm on a full-time basis.

Phil and Nancy Latimer also have children, but they only have two – twins, a boy and a girl, in the final year of high school. I wonder, briefly, about the boy; he'll be about seventeen, more than capable of overpowering someone like Lynette. Could he be acquainted with Menders? Could Menders be controlling him? Or is it a father-son thing? Sick, but certainly not unheard of in cases like this.

But I am sure the ABI and Anchorage PD would have turned up something, if they *were* involved. Wouldn't they?

I almost forget about Bill and Rachel Townsend,

who live in the hand-built ranch at the furthest edge of the valley. They keep themselves to themselves, and are rarely seen; it might seem suspicious, but they are both in their late seventies and it is entirely understandable that they are not constantly racing around anymore.

And then, of course, there is Artie's house – a man who knew the victim, and who was one of the last people to see her alive, and whose brother has been in trouble for sexual misdemeanors with underage girls already.

But, I remind myself, all of the homes in this area were searched, from top to bottom – and not just by the Palmer PD, but by the Anchorage cops, and the ABI too. If there was anything to find, they would have found it.

Which makes me wonder about two possibilities – either Lynette walked a lot further than we thought, and Menders was just making things up; or else there is some hidden site out here, a chamber in the woods, or buried in a field somewhere.

I look out of the kitchen window, into the sun-bleached valley, and the thought chills me to the bone.

Those cryptic entries in Menders' journal come back to me – *ab3-3, ab3-4, ab3-5* . . . how many bodies might be buried out there?

Another littel star for their constellation . . .

But how many *littel stars* are there?

The thought is sobering, and I bring my mind quickly back to the matter at hand; I've started speculating again, and that's not going to help Lynette.

No.

Fate – or the Red Moon, whatever it is, whatever it wants – has brought me back here on this day, at this time, for a reason.

I already have the one important fact that might save this girl.

She is going to be at the Anchorage Street Shelter from 12:21 until 13:56.

I am going to be there too.

And I am going to convince her to leave Alaska forever.

Before it is too late.

2

It is strange, I think, as I park my car in the big lot that borders the shelter; the people I have met over the past few days, the experiences I have gone through, none of it is real anymore, at least not in the conventional sense.

There has been no party, I've not been in jail, not slept with Ben, not been to Florida, not been attacked by Paul.

None of it has happened . . . and yet it has.

I try and clear my mind of these thoughts, knowing that they cannot help me, can only serve to obfuscate my sense of mission, my sense of purpose.

I need to find Lynette Hyams, get to her before the predator does.

Nothing else matters.

It is half past ten, and the sky is still blue overhead, although a chill in the air heralds the arrival of next week's snowstorms.

The drive to Anchorage took under an hour, and I know I now have about two hours until Lynette arrives at the shelter. Out of my car, I look around the lot, notice that every other vehicle is an SUV. Lynette could literally have gone with anyone; or the last person she was seen with might *not* have been the person who abducted her anyway, might just have been another trick. Her real abductor could have taken her at a later time, at a different location.

The shelter has *got* to be my best shot of getting to her, I tell myself. Hasn't it?

I wonder what to do until she gets here. Hang around? Wander about this area, get a feel for it? Head on toward Spenard Road? The shelter is located on 3rd Avenue in the northern downtown area, near Buttress Park; I know that if I head west, then drop down south on the Parkway, I'll eventually get to Spenard. It's more than three miles though, would probably take me at least an hour, and there's no guarantee that I would see Lynette on the way. If she's walking – which is possible, given the time – then she might not use the main road, might use all sorts of alternate routes; and she might not be walking anyway, she might still be meeting up with customers or friends, might have one of them drop her off at the shelter. And then there are taxis and buses to think about too.

No, I decide, the chances of coming across her as she makes her way to the shelter are slim at best; I'm probably better off hanging around the immediate area. But I don't want to go inside the shelter, don't want to take the risk of Artie seeing me, asking me questions. How would I explain what I was doing there?

"Ms. Hudson?" a voice says, surprising me. "What are you doing here?"

What the hell?

I turn, see the Latimer twins just two cars away from me.

What am I doing here? I think. *What the hell are you doing here?*

They might be boy and girl, but I'm not even sure which of them spoke; the voice was neither particularly male or female, perfectly neutral. It was what I'd noticed when I'd first moved to Palmer, when I'd gone door-to-door to meet my neighbors with a handbasket of homemade food and a bottle of wine, and had met them for the first time. It was what I'd noticed again at Artie's party; although I had to remember that, as far as they were concerned, we'd still not had that party yet.

"Hi," I say eventually, trying my best to sound relaxed; I even attempt a smile, and hope it doesn't look too forced. "Do you work here too?" I ask, ignoring their question with one of my own.

"No," the boy – Mike, is that his name? – replies, as both of them walk across the lot toward me, "we're just here as part of a school works project, social care stuff, you know? Larraine said to come down, they can always use another set of hands."

"Is Larraine working today?" I ask, thinking that it was her day off.

"No," the girl answers. I'm pretty sure her name is Victoria, but I could be wrong. "But Artie knows we're coming in. Just to help over lunch, give us an idea of how places like this operate."

"You here to see Artie?" the boy I think is called Mike asks.

"No," I say, maybe too quickly. "I'm meeting someone at Buttress Park about a horse that needs taking in, this was just the closest place to leave the car."

"Oh," the girl says, smile fixed on her face, unreadable. "Okay then. Well, I hope it goes well." She turns to her brother. "Come on Mike, we need to make a move, we've only got a few minutes."

"Sure," he tells her, before turning to me and shrugging apologetically. "Sorry, but we've got to help set up for lunch," he says. "Hope your meeting goes well."

"Thanks," I say. "Hope your lunch goes well too." It is a poor response, I realize, a bland platitude that means nothing, and I am embarrassed that I can find nothing better to say. How did I ever manage to fight off the best defense attorneys money could buy, in the highest courts of New York County? Back then, my words were weapons; now they are empty and weak.

Like me.

No, my inner voice fires back immediately.

Not like you. You are strong. You have a mission. You are strong, and you are going to do it.

Yes.

Hell, I *am* strong, I *am* going to do it, and doubts be damned.

Before I realize, the twins have waved their farewells, turned on their heels and already started on their way to the large, red-brick building that houses the Anchorage Street Shelter.

They pass their car on the way, and I notice that it is yet another SUV, a silver Toyota. Does anyone ever buy anything else these days?

The presence of the twins here is troubling, to say the least. They hadn't even really figured into my considerations before. Yes, I'd realized that Mike – that *is* his name – was certainly old enough and strong enough to have carried out the attack on Lynette, but at the same time I had discounted him very quickly. After all, he was only seventeen, and there was such a brutality about Lynette's torture, I find it hard to accept that someone so young could have had anything to do with it.

And yet is it just a coincidence that he is here, on the same day that Lynette is here, the same day that she goes missing?

Slowly, I wander away from the shelter, following West 3rd toward Buttress Park; they might be watching me, and I don't want to appear too suspicious. They are bound to tell Artie about me being here, and I suppose my presence at the shelter might be no more suspicious than theirs. After all, both Artie and Lorraine – neighbors of the Latimers – work here, and work placements *are* normally arranged through personal contacts, aren't they?

But there is something about the confluence of events that seems strange. I am not a believer in coincidence at the best of times, and certainly not at the moment.

Could Mike have some sort of relationship with Artie that we don't know about? Could Artie be leading the boy down a dark path, using him in some way? And was the girl involved? I've been concentrating on male suspects, but is Victoria – if that *is* her name – also involved in some way? Does she have a relationship with Artie? I already know that his brother is interested in underage girls, but does Artie also like the younger type?

Mike seems polite and clean-cut, but I don't know what to make of Victoria; she seems colder somehow, but does that mean anything?

Damn, I know I'm wasting my time. What did I tell myself earlier? Stick to the facts – Lynette is going to be at the shelter for lunch. I am going to intercept her, make sure that she is kept safe. Working out who was *going* to abduct her is beside the point, if she never gets abducted in the first place. I'll leave the Jessica Fletcher bit to the real detectives.

I leave the parking lot and head west, and soon start to pass single family homes and low-rise apartment blocks, covered parking lots and small businesses, as I approach Buttress Park. I wait to cross an intersection, industrial buildings rising to the south, and check my watch.

10:46.

I wonder if I will see Lynette walking this way, if it will be easier if I speak to her here, or at the shelter. On the street, I will be able to speak to her away from the prying eyes of Mike, Victoria and Artie; I can say what needs to be said, without fear of being overheard.

And yet, out here, she will have no point of reference, I will be nothing more than a stranger, why would she even stop and listen to me?

But if I speak to her at the shelter, she may assume I work there, it may give me the "in" I need to get her to listen.

I realize that I am thinking about her as a victim, as *my* victim, and the thought makes me very uneasy. Why don't I just club her on the back of the head, throw her in the back of *my* SUV, and take off with her?

A sudden chill goes down my spine as I realize that maybe it *is* my SUV that she is seen in, at six o'clock this evening.

But then again, I consider, the police report that states those facts was written when I'd already experienced October 8th the *first* time; and I was nowhere near Anchorage then, I was just looking after the horses at my ranch.

I breathe out a sigh of relief; at least I've ruled *myself* out as a suspect, anyway.

I pause then, still not having made it as far as the park. What's the point of going, I ask myself? What good will it do me? Better to retrace my steps to the shelter, maybe just sit in my car and watch the comings and goings, see if anything seems out of the ordinary, if there are any more faces that I recognize. We've already had the Latimer twins, I wonder if anyone else from the valley will turn up? The Eberles and their six children?

Judge Tom Judd, whose apartment is less than a mile away? Hell, will I see Douglas Menders – the man I killed, still alive – come down from his mountain retreat, will he be here too?

I sigh, long and hard.

Maybe I do still have a little bit of Jessica Fletcher left in me, after all?

<u>3</u>

My watch reads 11:23, and nothing much has happened since I came back to my car.

There have been various comings and goings – people visiting and leaving the shelter, other people using the parking lot in much the same way as the story I gave the Latimers, leaving their cars and going elsewhere – but nothing of great importance, nothing that stands out as different, or in any way suspicious.

Still no sign of Lynette.

I start to yawn, but it catches in my throat as I notice something on the other side of the road, some sort of movement that is familiar to me, somewhere in my deep subconscious.

And then I see that it is not some*thing*, it is some*one*.

It is Paul.

It is Paul Southland, ex-fiancé, soon-to-be-attempted-rapist.

And what the hell is *he* doing here?

But he is just walking along the sidewalk, in a daze, minding his own business and all but ignoring the shelter on the opposite side of the street.

Ignoring the parking lot too, luckily.

I watch him, entranced, like a voyeur, and I am reminded of Menders and his telescope – and suddenly I feel dirty, and ashamed. And yet I don't stop watching him.

Instead, without thinking, I turn on the car's ignition and ease my SUV out of the parking lot, creep out onto East 3rd, and begin to follow Paul from a discreet distance.

I remind myself that this might be yet another coincidence, that Paul was known to have been in Anchorage for several days before he called me, and I can't believe I didn't factor in the possibility that I might see him here.

But then again, I tell myself, this is a city of three hundred *thousand* people, a city which spans a huge area of land; what are the chances of Paul just happening to be on this street, at this time? Especially as this is a man pulling down a six-figure salary, and there seems to be a definite dearth of five-star hotels in this immediate locality.

So what *is* he doing here?

I don't know, and so I follow him, understanding that he is a man who is willing to use violence on women, a man who is walking past a location that a murder victim has recently stayed at, that will soon be revisited by that same murder victim, only hours before her final abduction.

There is little traffic on the streets, and although this makes following Paul easier, I am concerned that he might see me; but he never looks upwards, his gaze instead fixed on the sidewalk as he shuffles along, a shadow of his former self.

I know that he has not even been charged with a crime yet, should still be filled with the arrogant zeal of a New York lawyer, and I wonder why he is so downtrodden. Is what he told me true? *Is* he struggling with guilt over what he did to me? *Has* he only come to Alaska to try and make up with me?

We turn south on Eagle Street, and I am thankful when other vehicles start to filter down, making me not so obvious. We pass the intersections for East 4th and East 5th, before Paul – head still down, feet shuffling – makes a slow right turn onto East 6th.

The one-way street wants me to make a left-turn, away from the direction Paul is heading, but I stay at the lights long enough to see what must be his destination, a Sheraton hotel right there on the corner. It might not be five-star, but it's good enough, I figure.

And sure enough – as I sit patiently at the lights, watching like the good voyeur I am – just a few moments later, I see Paul passing through the glass doors into the hotel lobby, and I finally allow myself to make the left turn away from the high-rise building, before hooking north on Fairbanks Street and heading back to the shelter, quickly checking the time on my dashboard clock as I go.

11:42.

Not long to go now, not long at all, and I pull back into the shelter's large parking lot at a quarter to twelve, hoping that I've not missed anything while I've been following Paul.

Could it just be a coincidence? He looked troubled, alone, depressed. Maybe he'd just been out for a walk? I know he'd been struggling to build up the courage to call me, the courage to apologize, but what are the chances of me seeing him right here, right now?

I shake the thought out of my mind, knowing that it doesn't matter; not right now, anyway.

What *does* matter is Lynette, and I know she will be here soon.

Unless, I think desperately, she is already here?

After all, I suppose I don't actually know what the healthy, living version of Lynette Hyams looks like. All I have seen is the pale, beaten girl that died in my arms in the red, moonlit night, and the autopsy pictures taken after she was already dead.

But what does the *real* Lynette look like?

With a helpless shudder, I realize the truth of the matter.

And the truth is, I don't know *what* she looks like.

4

12:14, and I see a girl on the far side of the street.

A girl that *could* be Lynette Hyams.

But I've thought that about every teenaged girl I've seen for the past half an hour – whether they were going in or out of the shelter, or whether they were just minding their own business somewhere nearby. For a few moments, at least, I've thought that they might all be Lynette.

But this girl is different, I see that immediately. There is something hesitant about the way she moves, as if she is unsure where she is going, *if* she should be going there at all.

She is petite, about five feet two, her build very small, child-like. Her hair is light brown and shoulder length, as the medical report described Lynette's to be – although to me, when I saw her that one time, her hair was a dark, torn, mangled and blood-filled mess. She wears a short denim skirt, tights, dark vest and a leather jacket that is a couple of sizes too large for her; different from what she was dressed in this morning, according to the statements from the girls she'd shared breakfast with, but very similar to what she was/is seen in this afternoon, the last time anyone saw her. I guess the change of clothes means that she went home after having breakfast, which perhaps accounts for her not being seen. Unless she got changed somewhere else, which means that she might keep clothes at someone else's place. Did she have another boyfriend somewhere? I remind myself that the police reports don't offer any evidence to back this up, but that doesn't mean it's not true. And if it *is* true, is it possible that Dennis Hobson knows about it? *Could* he still be involved?

I shake my head, clearing the thoughts as I examine the girl as she crosses the road, comes closer.

I see a livid bruise on the left side of her face, know that this matches the damage supposedly done by her "boyfriend" the night before.

This girl's physical appearance matches Lynette's, along with her clothing, her injury, and she is making her way toward the shelter for roughly the right time.

It *has* to her, hasn't it?

I sigh, as I reach for the door handle.

There's only one way to find out.

"Lynette!" I call out as she meanders through the parking lot toward the shelter's main entrance.

The girl turns to me, surprised and suspicious. Perhaps a little nervous too. And why not? She is fifteen years old, ran away to escape an unhappy home life at the age of thirteen, only to be recruited and exploited by a violent and abusive pimp, made to turn tricks in Spenard to fund the drug habit he's given her.

I have to remind myself that her view of life is going to be seriously affected by what she has done, what she has seen, and I need to be careful in how I approach her, what I say to her. Girls like Lynette have a sixth sense for cops, and treat most people with outright suspicion.

I think back to my time in the Child Abuse Unit of the DA's Special Victims Bureau, of those girls I counselled, interviewed and represented. They were tough times, tough cases, and getting information out of those poor victims was very often time-consuming and tortuous. But in the end, I had normally managed it; the trick was – despite my position of authority – getting the girls to trust me.

It had sometimes taken a long time to build that trust though, I remember – sometimes days, more often weeks.

How long do I have now? I ask myself as I approach Lynette across the parking lot. *A single afternoon?*

But it's better than nothing, I know that much; and I am going to do everything I can with what little time I have.

"Do I know you, lady?" Lynette says, and the effect is unnerving. It is the first time I have heard her voice; before, she was a lifeless husk, dead in my arms, photographs on an autopsy table, a corpse on a mortuary slab. Even when she was still breathing, as she'd run across those fields and collapsed, she was little more than a ghost, dead already. But now here she is, alive and vital, and the difference is hard to come to terms with.

I thought I would be delighted to see her alive, not yet the tortured and broken mess that she becomes – *might* become – but instead I am disturbed, as if I am messing with powers and laws that are beyond me. Seeing Lynette walking across this parking lot flies in the face of logic, what my own brain tells me happened; I saw this girl die, I saw what happened to her. How can she still be alive?

But no matter the reason, I tell myself, she *is* alive; and it is up to me to keep her that way.

I almost say *Not yet* in reply to her question, but realize that it is too cryptic, and – although true – would set alarm bells ringing in her head.

"No," I say instead, with a low-key smile. "No, you don't know me." A thousand thoughts fly through my mind, what to say, how to approach her – I can't believe I've not gone through this before in my mind, prepared for how to deal with it – but they suddenly, perfectly consolidate into a single, unified strategy. "I have an offer to make you," I say, just a single vehicle between us now. "If you can prove you *are* Lynette Hyams, daughter of Kim Gaskell and Sydney Baker."

I can't believe I'm using the same ruses as a predator, luring her in with an offer, while making her *want* to prove herself to me.

"Are you a cop?" she says, eyes darting left and right, body tense, ready to run if she has to.

"Do I look like a cop?" I say.

"Yeah," Lynette answers immediately.

"Well," I admit, "I guess I work in a related field. I'm an attorney."

She starts to back up, eyes nervous. "I'm not going home," she says. "I'm never going home, fuck that. Fuck *that*."

"No," I say, moving in for the kill like all good predators do, "you've got me wrong. I'm not here to take you back. I'm here to make a financial settlement with you."

"A . . . what?"

"Money," I say with my low-key smile. "I'm here to offer you money. *If* you want it."

Lynette's eyes move left and right, nervous again, but they settle back on me more quickly this time, and I know I've got her.

The fish is on the hook, and now I just have to reel her in.

"So, what do I have to do?" Lynette asks me, sniffing hard through long-abused nostrils.

We are in the Red Chair Café on East 4th, sitting at a table for two opposite the deli counter. I sip on a latte, while Lynette has already finished three cups of filter coffee. She is nervous, perpetually highly-strung, and the caffeine surely won't help, but I suppose it's not the worst thing she could be taking; on the short drive here

(I didn't want to leave my car outside the shelter forever), she'd already smoked four roll-ups, and I am just waiting for her to visit the bathroom to "powder her nose". Her habits and mannerisms are those of a habitual cocaine user, and I know this is almost certainly how Hobson controls her.

"You don't have to do anything," I tell her. "Not really, anyway." I take another sip of my latte, watching as she looks nervously toward the door. Her movements are fewer now, slower, and I can feel the trust building. Money is always a powerful motivator, and for someone like Lynette – despite her age, a hardened negotiator, a street-savvy business-woman in her own right – it is the *main* motivator, the primary drive, the one thing that she needs above all else.

"Like hell," she says, understandably doubtful. "There's always *somethin'* you need to do." She touches the side of her face reflexively, touching the purple welt left there by her boyfriend, then realizes what she's doing and pulls her hand away.

"Not in this case," I assure her. "Well, nothing that you probably don't want to do anyway."

"What you mean?" she asks, but I pause as lunch arrives – the gargantuan 'Tesla' burger for her, the Turkey Brie sandwich for me.

I watch as she devours the burger with gusto, fries and fixings all going down with it, and I have to reconsider my view of her as an out-of-control addict. Addicts have poor appetites, don't they?

I wait until a natural pause in her onslaught – as she

stops eating long enough to pour more sauce over her fries – and then answer her question.

"Do you like it here?" I ask. "In Anchorage? Do you like what you do?"

"What I do?" she asks, looking up from her sauce-covered fries. "What the hell you think I do, lady?"

"Lynette," I say softly, "I *know* what you do. Remember, you're not in trouble. But are you happy?"

"Well," she says, "you say you know what I do. So why don't you work out if I'm happy or not, yeah? If you're some sort of hot-shit attorney, shouldn't be too hard."

I take a bite of my sandwich, deciding what to say next. It is a balancing act, to try and get her onto my side without alienating her, or making her think I want something. I realize I'm lying, maybe even manipulating her, but what else am I going to say, how else am I going to approach this?

Excuse me, but I know that you are going to be abducted this evening, and then raped and tortured over several days by two or more people, and – even though you escape – the damage you suffer is already too severe, and you die in a snowy field. And how do I know? Well, I've seen it before, you die in my arms. I've come back in time to rescue you. Come with me.

Honest as that story might be, it won't achieve anything except getting her to run.

"Okay," I say as I put the sandwich down, "you're *not* happy, you *don't* like it here, but you probably feel like you don't have any options left."

"Well, give the lawyer a cigar," Lynette says

through a mouthful of burger. I don't blame her for her abrasive attitude; it's actually much better than some of my previous clients'.

"Let me ask you another question," I say. "Do you remember Richard Tyson?"

Lynette stops eating and looks at me across the table. "Of course I remember him," she says. "Why?"

Tyson is Kim Gaskell's second husband, and her longest recorded partner; also, according to the biography I read at Ben's, the most affluent of Gaskell's many spouses, and – I hope – the one Lynette felt most comfortable with. That was a phase of her life with the least problems at school, the least problems *anywhere*. Cause of eventual divorce was infidelity on his part.

"I don't know how to say this," I say uneasily, "but Mr. Tyson is dead. Cancer, nothing anyone could do." I try and read Lynette's expression, but it's hard. Is she upset? Glad? It's impossible to tell, the eyes glassy, unresponsive. "I am the executor of his will," I add, knowing that those words will bring her back to reality. "And you are one of the benefactors."

"What?" she asks, eyes wide, surprised.

"Ms. Lynette Hyams is one of the benefactors of Mr. Tyson's will," I add, continuing to lie through my teeth in a bid to save this girl. "Now, is that you?"

"Y . . . Yes," she stumbles. "But why would he . . .? I've not seen him for . . ."

"He felt bad about leaving you, about the divorce, about what happened," I lie, and these lies are coming easier now, and I can't escape the horrific idea that I am no better than the predator that would have abducted her.

No, another voice tells me, *that's ridiculous. You want to help this girl, not harm her.*

"I can't even remember him," she says, "not really . . . My mom, she married him when she got out of prison. Things had been bad before then, ah . . . just really bad, you know. But he was nice, at least while it lasted, mom was happy, I think *I* was happy . . . but things fucked themselves up I guess, like they always do. He left, and then . . . well," she says, wiping her dripping nose with the cuff of her jacket, "let's just say that mom's next boyfriend wasn't so nice, okay? Shit, maybe he does owe me, after all? If he'd stayed then . . . well, I guess it don't much matter now, anyway." She finishes the burger, looks back up at me. "How much?" she asks.

"First," I say, "the proof. How do I know you really are Lynette Hyams?"

"Here," she says, pulling out a battered purse and rooting around in it until she finds a plastic card, holding it up for me.

"A learner's permit?" I ask, surprised.

"Yeah," she says, "one of the only things I've got Den to thank for, I guess."

I nod my head as I take the card, examining it, taking note of the details. Some pimps don't want their girls having a license, knowing it would make it easier for them to leave; others, however, see it as an advantage, the ability to drive making them more mobile, able to cover a wider territory. Not that she can actually drive yet – you can get your learner's permit in Alaska at fourteen, but still have to wait until you're sixteen for a restricted license.

But whatever the reason she has one, I know it means that she can board a domestic flight, even as a minor. I might have to fill out some paperwork at the airport, but she will be able to travel.

"Okay," I say, handing her the card back, "and now for the conditions."

"I thought you said I didn't have to do anything?"

"It's nothing you don't want to do," I say. "You told me you don't like this place, right? You're not happy?"

"I didn't say that," Lynette answers quickly. "*You* did."

"And you didn't object to my assessment," I remind her.

"Okay," she says slowly, making me work for it. "So, what do you mean, 'conditions'?"

"You need to move," I tell her. "Mr. Tyson, when he found out about his own condition, he hired people to find you, find out what had happened to you."

(*lies, lies, it's all lies, she'll find out, it's* lies . . .)

"And it was his dying wish for you to leave this life, to get out from it while you still can."

(*Emotional manipulation, you're really scraping the bottom of the barrel now* . . .)

"So, his explicit instructions are for you to leave Anchorage. Today."

379

"What the fuck? *Today?*"

I tap the side of my head, as if I have memorized his entire will. "He said that – if you want the money – then you have to leave Anchorage as soon as his attorney makes contact with you, you need to fly to . . ."

(*Shit! Where? Where, where, where, why didn't you think this through before you opened your big mouth?*)

". . . to Gainesville," I say, face flushed.

"Gainesville?" she asks, brow furrowed. "Where the fuck is that?"

"Florida," I say, knowing why I said it, because it is about as far south of Alaska – in the continental United States, at least – that you can possibly get, more than four thousand miles from Anchorage, from Dennis Hobson, from the killers that even now might be waiting to abduct this girl, to rape her, to torture her until she dies. Maybe also because I've been there recently, it's on my mind – it seems safe, it seems like a place she might enjoy living.

"Florida?" she says in disbelief. "How the hell am I going to get *there?*"

"I'm going to buy you a ticket," I tell her, "put you on the plane myself."

Lynette eats some fries, drinks some coffee, then looks at me. "It's warm in Florida," she says, with the hopeful look of the little girl she is, a look that breaks my heart, "isn't it?"

"It is," I say, trying not to cry, trying to stop the bleeding of my heart for this poor girl, abused for so long and – if I don't stop it – with only more agony to look forward to. I asked myself, days before, if I would swap places with Lynette Hyams, if it meant that she wouldn't have to experience what she experienced, go through what she went through. I wasn't sure at the time, but I am sure now – *of course I would.* "I was only there the other day," I continue, gathering myself, "it was so hot I had to stay indoors, scared I'd get a sunburn."

"Wow," she says wistfully, "I've always wanted to go somewhere I might get a sunburn. There's palm trees there too, right?"

I nod. "There sure are," I say. "Palm trees everywhere."

"My mom . . . sometimes used to take me into travel centers, you know, places with holidays, sold holidays, you know . . . well, she'd look like she was going to get us a holiday, she'd talk to the guys there, think about it, make *me* think about it, I'd look at those . . . what do ya call 'em, brochures? Yeah, brochures, I'd look at these great hotels, these warm, warm places, palm trees and beaches, and that's where I wanted to go." She pauses, breathes, drinks more coffee. "We never did go anywhere though." She looks up at me, eyes searching. "Florida, huh?"

I nod my head. "Florida," I confirm.

"So," she says again, "how much?"

"Twenty thousand dollars," I say, knowing that the payment is going to come straight from my own pocket. I want it to be enough to entice her, to convince her, an amount that might actually change her life, enable her to get a foot in the door; but at the same time, I don't want it to seem like an amount that Richard Tyson simply wouldn't have.

As it is, I know that a single phone call might show my story for what it is – total bullshit. But if I keep her occupied, if I don't let her out of my sight until she's on that plane to Florida, then by the time she can speak to anyone who can tell her that Tyson is still alive, she'll be in Gainesville with twenty thousand dollars in her pocket. And then, what will it matter if she discovers I was bullshitting all along? She'll be safe anyway, safe and far away.

I watch her face as I give her the figure, this girl who turns tricks for fifty bucks a shot, most of which will get turned over to her pimp, the rest of which will go on drugs, and I can see the change in her as she starts to understand what this might mean, the opportunity to start again, the chance to reinvent her life. She is young, she *can* start again; but first and foremost, she needs to *survive*.

She needs to get out of Anchorage, out of *Alaska*, for good.

"So what do you say?" I ask her. "Will you go?"

I watch as she looks into the dregs of her coffee cup, her gaze indistinct, unclear.

I suddenly feel like a predator again, watching and waiting, wondering if my prey is going to accept my bait.

The feeling makes me uneasy, but I try and ignore it as I wait for her reply.

In the end, she looks at me and nods her head

firmly, her mind made up. "Yeah," she says, the first beginnings of a smile on her face. "Fuck it. I'll go."

I look at her, taking her in, thinking for the first time that I'm *not* seeing a ghost, that I'm seeing a vibrant, young life that *won't* be taken before it's time.

Good for you, I think as I look at her, unspeakable happiness in my heart, tears in my eyes, though I try and hide them.

Yes, Lynette, I think, *good for you.*

You've just saved yourself.

5

This is taking too long, I think as I nervously take another look through the broken blinds of the apartment window to the parking lot below.

"Lynette?" I shout through to her. "You going to be long?"

We're in the room that Hobson rents for her, where he often stays with her. The façade of the two-story structure looks out on West Benson Boulevard, but parking and the actual entrances are on West 29th Place, the road running parallel to the south. Lynette's unit is on the second floor, up a wooden balcony and along a narrow terrace. The car's left out front in a numbered slot, and I'm starting to worry about it getting stolen; some of the people I saw hanging about outside were not exactly friendly-looking.

The room itself was probably once quite neat and tidy; now it is a pit of desperation however, filled with the fumes of nicotine and weed, sweat and sex. It looks like it hasn't been cleaned in a long time, maybe not even since Hobson started renting it, and I'm not surprised when I see roaches scuttling away into the corner.

Lynette has already shoved what clothes she needs into a relatively new-looking sports bag, and is apparently gathering some other things from the bathroom.

I start to get an idea of what she's really doing though, and suddenly rush across the room and rip open the door – and when I see her poised over the sink, starting to sniff the coke she's poured there, I grab her and pull her away.

"Dammit, what the hell are you doing?" I shout at her.

"What the fuck?" she spits back, wrestling free of my grip. "What the hell you doin', what the fuck you care?"

"I care," I say slowly, trying to regain my composure, "because you're about to go to an airport – the security guys see you're high, you're not getting on a plane anywhere. They've got sniffer dogs too, you want one of those going off at you?"

She pauses as she considers what I say, then shakes her head. "They couldn't give a shit what people do, so long as they pay for their ticket."

"Maybe you're right," I say, "but maybe you're wrong. You want to risk it? Which would you rather be, twenty grand richer in the Florida sunshine, or broke in an Anchorage jail cell?"

She looks as if she's going to argue with me again,

then thinks better of it. If anything's going to get her to kick the habit, it's the promise of money. "Okay," she says, "shit, okay. Maybe you're right. Maybe you're right."

And yet I know that she might try something again, her desire for a hit so strong that she might be powerless to oppose it. I start to look through her bag, looking for anything else that might set the dogs off.

"Hey!" she yells, sniffing helplessly. "Get your freakin' hands off my shit!"

I hand the bag to her, only half-convinced it's clean. "If you have any of that shit in there, get rid of it."

"There isn't any," she says angrily.

"Okay," I say, then notice the white powder that has spilled onto her top, traces of it in her hair. *Aw, shit.* "You need to get changed," I tell her, "or you're going to get picked up. Have a shower, wash your hair, and get changed."

"You're shitting me, right?"

"No," I say, "I'm not. You need to get out of here today, I need you on a flight to Florida."

"Why the big rush?" she says, although I can see she's already starting to take the jacket off.

"I don't know," I say. "Mr. Tyson didn't specify. He just wanted you gone from here the same day I made contact."

"Shit," she says, looking around the room, "is it really that bad?" She must see the look on my face, because a smile breaks out for the first time that day, and she nods her head. "Yeah," she says, "I guess it is, right?"

I smile back and shrug my shoulders. What can I say?

The girl is smiling now, but I can still see the need in those tired eyes of hers, I understand how much she still needs that hit. Maybe I was wrong? Maybe money isn't the most important motivating factor in her life, after all.

She strips unselfconsciously, and although I don't stare, I still see that her pale, young body – except for the absence of the more obvious damage – is not so much different from the corpse that lay on the autopsy table.

I follow her into the bathroom, watch as she gets into the shower. How can I leave her alone now? Who knows what other shit she has hidden in here.

She looks at me and shakes her head sadly, understanding why I'm keeping guard but obviously disappointed in me doing it; but she's not exactly won my trust yet, so what else can I do?

"Make it as quick as you can," I tell her.

I desperately want her out of here, out of the apartment, out of the country; every minute she remains is another minute that she could still be abducted, still be hurt, still be killed.

And today, Anchorage seems to be a maelstrom of dangers, a melting pot of potential suspects – Artie Jenkins is working at the shelter, and I've also seen the

Latimer twins *and* Paul in very close proximity. And then there is –

"Who the *fuck* are *you?*" the angry voice growls from the apartment doorway, and my heart sinks.

Oh, shit.

Dennis Hobson.

6

I turn slowly, aware that Lynette doesn't know he's here, the sound of the water drowning out his voice.

He is similar enough to the photo I've seen that I don't need further proof – the hard, stubbled jaw; the acne scars on the pockmarked cheeks; the deep-set, sullen eyes; the scar that goes through an eyebrow onto the bridge of his nose; the greasy hair swept back into a short ponytail, ears filled with gold studs.

Yes, I think as I struggle to breathe, it's him, alright.

"I asked you a question, bitch", he says again, his voice like rough gravel, grating and harsh.

"I'm . . . a friend of Lynette's," I say at last.

"Yeah?" he asks, eyeing me up and down like a vulture about to pick up some roadkill. "You a working girl? I don't recognize you."

"I'm not from around here."

"I know that," he says, edging closer, and my heart rate is racing as I remember that this is a man who carries a straight razor and is happy to use it as a matter of routine. "So where you from?"

"Seattle," I say, improvising again. "I've been hired to track down Lynette by her mother."

He smiles with no warmth or humor, horribly reptilian. "Her mother?" he says with a raised eyebrow. "I seriously doubt *that*, from what she's told me about her."

I shrug. "I don't know what you've heard, but that woman is worried sick about her daughter. Believe me." In the background, I can still hear the shower, and I don't know if it would be better for Lynette to be here or not. From the look on Hobson's face, I'm thinking *not*.

"So, are you a private eye?" he asks with a smirk.

"In a way," I say. "I work for an investigative firm."

"So, you're not licensed then," he deduced, "which means you got fuck-all right to be doin' anythin', am I right?" He gestures to the bathroom. "So, what's she said? She wants to go with you, go running off back to Mommy?"

"No," I say, knowing what his reaction would be to *that*. "I think she wants to stay here. Her mother wants her home, but not if she's not willing. She just wants to know that her daughter is okay."

Hobson keeps edging toward me, toward the bathroom, his presence menacing, threatening.

"And what are you gonna tell her?" he whispers.

"Well," I say, trying to keep my voice cool, "she

has a place to live, she can obviously support herself through . . . *work* . . . and she seems to have also met a nice young man who I am sure has only her best intentions in mind."

He grins, and I see blackened teeth and receding gums. "Yeah?" he says. "Hah, I like that. Yeah, I like that. Best interests, huh?" He looks toward the shower. "Well," he says, "I guess it looks like she's getting ready for *work*, so maybe it's time that you left? Wouldn't want to get in the way of her making money and supporting herself, would you?"

I wonder what I am going to do, how I am going to handle the situation. I need to get her out of here, need to get past Hobson. But how? I don't have anything to hit him with, and I'm not sure if I'm even capable of knocking him out, even if I *did* have a weapon. The horrific image of the dead body of Douglas Menders flashes through my mind then, his head smashed open with the brass lamp.

You are *capable*, the voice tells me. *You* are.

But still, I see no weapon.

I know I could leave, observe her, follow her, and pick her up later, when Hobson's eye is not on her and we have a chance . . . but what if Hobson is the person that abducts her? Witnesses have him in Anchorage pretty much continually over the next few days, but maybe he just abducts her, hands her over to someone else? Maybe he's been offered money for one of his girls?

Anything is possible, and I know I can't take the

chance of leaving her alone with him. The shower is still running – didn't I tell her to hurry up? – but I know it can't last forever, soon she will be out and . . . then what?

I see Hobson's gaze shift then, see his expression change from one of unverified suspicion to one of pure rage as he sees the sports bag, packed and ready to go, lying on the filthy sheets of the double bed.

His eyes snap back to me, and he is already reaching for something – the razor? – from his coat pocket, when I hear the words, "Get down!" coming from right behind me.

I duck in immediate response, and I hear the spray of an aerosol above me, the *click* of a lighter, the roar of a flame, and I look up and see a stream of fire passing over me and hitting Hobson in the face; look behind me, see Lynette, still naked and soaking wet, holding a can of hairspray in one hand, a cigarette lighter in the other, combining them into a flamethrower that burns the flesh off Hobson's face; I hear his screams as the flame hits, hear Lynette's screams as she sees what she's done, what she's still doing . . .

And then the flames stop, the pimp drops to floor, writhing helplessly as he screams, hands covering his burned face; at the same time, Lynette drops her makeshift weapons, a look of shock, of horror, on her young face, and I stand and embrace her, turning her away from the sight of Hobson.

"It's okay," I whisper to her, "it's okay, get changed. Go on, hurry, we need to get out of here."

Lynette's eyes are wide, wild, and I know she is starting to go into shock from what she's done; I need to keep her mind off it, keep her moving, keep her thinking of what lies ahead.

"Hurry," I repeat, "you'll be out of all this soon, you'll be out of it for good. Go on."

She goes, and I turn to Hobson, feeling sorry as he claws at his savaged features; he might be a monster himself, but it is a horrible thing to happen to a human being, and my stomach turns at the sight of him.

I think about approaching, but I know he might still be dangerous; he still has the straight razor somewhere, and if he becomes lucid again, he might still use it.

Hurry up, Lynette, I think. *Hurry up.*

I ease past Hobson's body, hoping the screams don't get the police here too quickly, and grab the sports bag from the bed; a hand reaches out and grabs my ankle but I kick out with my other foot, hard, into the man's gut and there is a puff of air from his lungs, a deep groan, and he lets go. I can hear him trying to form words, hurl insults, but his lips don't move, charred and burned, the flesh peeling off them, and I feel guilty for kicking him.

"I'm ready," Lynette says, by my side, and I turn and nod my head at her, and lead her quickly from the apartment, keeping her eyes away from the gruesome sight of her boyfriend as we reach the door and emerge into daylight at last.

There are people nosing around, neighbors from

other rooms emerging to see what is going on, teenagers on the other side of the street watching us as we race down the steps to the line of cars waiting outside.

Maybe they'll report us, maybe they won't; but we've got bigger things to worry about right now.

As we get to my car and rip the doors open, I can't help but think about the bravery of Lynette's actions back in the house; Hobson must have been a man who terrified her, she had been living under the threat of his violence for a long time already. Where did she find the strength to turn on him like that?

But I suppose there must be so much built-up anger in the girl, so much hate; maybe she had been waiting months for an opportunity like this one. But up until today, she had no way out, no way to leave him, no chance of escape.

And now she does.

I pull out of the parking space before Lynette has even closed her door, and we shoot off down West 29th, the sounds of Dennis Hobson's screams chasing us all the way.

7

Well, here I am again, I think as we look at the departures board.

Ted Stevens Anchorage International Airport.

And there it is, the same flight to Minneapolis, 17:10.

I look at my watch, see that it is just after three o'clock. Not long to go now, I think; if nothing else goes wrong, Lynette should be home free.

But did someone see my car on West 29th? Did they take the registration? Call the police? Is there a patrol car on its way here now, to bring us in over the attempted murder of Dennis Hobson?

It is possible, I know; it is definitely possible.

But there is no use worrying over every little detail; we need to move, and we need to move now.

I approach the Delta desk, pay for a ticket, sign a form to say that Lynette is okay to travel as an unaccompanied minor.

I think again about Hobson. Is it possible that he

has recovered sufficiently to come here, to chase after us? Does he even know where we are? He saw the bag, but he might not immediately have thought "airport". We may have been driving, or various other options. Could he send some of his friends to check out the airport anyway?

Again, I think, it's possible, and the faster we can get Lynette through security, the better.

I don't think Hobson will have told anyone, anyway. How can he? His lips were blistered and burned through, hanging loosely from his face like bloody pieces of chopped liver; he was unable to speak at all, at least when we'd left him. His eyes, too, were surely useless to him now, the flame burning them in their sockets. I think of the sight of Hobson's dripping, bleeding eyeballs and feel sick again.

Did Hobson deserve it? It is a hard thing to consider. Yes, he is a terrible man, one who has done terrible things. He seduces young girls with tales of money and fast living, gets them hooked on drugs, then pimps them out, beats and cuts them if they get out of line.

But did he deserve to have his face burned off?

Lynette was only acting out of fear though, not revenge; to hear her tell it, anyway. On the drive in, she'd explained how she'd heard him talking, how she'd become terrified, known that he would kill her if he discovered she was leaving for good. She'd left the shower running to cover the sound of her movements, had got out and looked around the bathroom desperately for a weapon of some kind, of *any* kind.

Then she'd seen the can of hair spray, remembered a scene from a James Bond film that one of her stepfathers had liked, grabbed the lighter and waited for her chance.

I hope she wouldn't remember it for too long.

But then again, I know the flight is going to be hard enough anyway; five hours to Minneapolis without a hit of any kind, whether nicotine or hard drugs. But she's already proved herself to be a survivor, and I know she's going to be okay.

We approach security, and I know that our short time together will soon be at an end.

Will she be okay? Will she avoid the fate that I've already seen? If she does, will her new life be any better than her last?

If she lives, will my own life go back to normal? When I wake up tomorrow, will it finally *be* tomorrow?

I don't know the answers to any of it. All I know is that Lynette Hyams has *already* saved my life – Hobson was reaching for his razor, and his girlfriend saved me.

I just hope that I am doing the same for her.

We reach security, and we turn to one another. "So, I guess this is it," she says.

"I guess so," I say. "Except for this." I reach into my purse, pull out a check book. Old-fashioned perhaps, but I can't send her to Florida with twenty thousand dollars in cash on her.

I write the check in front of her, watch her eyes as the zeros go down in black ink. "Lynette Hyams?" I ask, and she nods.

"Yeah," she says. "Lynette Hyams."

"You have a bank account?" I ask, and she shakes her head.

"Get one," I say.

"Yeah," she says, taking the check, eyes still wide. "Yeah, okay."

"When you get to Gainesville," I say, a thought suddenly occurring to me, "if you need help – with the check, a bank account, getting somewhere to live, anything – look up a guy called Dr. Glen Kelly. Lives at Pine Hills Retirement Village. Tell him that Jessica Hudson sent you. Tell him the Red Moon is back."

"Tell him what?" she asks, brow furrowed. "What the hell does *that* mean?"

"He'll understand," I tell her, knowing it to be true. He'll know that she's a girl I've saved; he won't know what from, but he will do his best to help her.

Suddenly, Lynette's adrenaline from the fight, from fleeing the apartment is gone, along with the excitement of the twenty-thousand-dollar check. "Did I kill him?" she asks softly. "Do you think I killed him?"

My heart breaks as I see the hurt on her face, the guilt; despite what he's done to her, she can't come to terms with what she has now done to *him*.

"No," I say, hugging her to me, holding her close, just like that day in the past, in the future, maybe never, when I held her close and she died in my arms. Only this time her heart is strong, vital, she is very much alive, alive and strong. I hope she stays that way. "No," I repeat, "you didn't kill him. He's alive. Not very happy perhaps, but he's alive." Lynette laughs gently through her tears, and I hold her tighter, all of a sudden not wanting to stop, not wanting to let her go.

I've come so far, done so much, can I now release her to a fate I can't predict, that I can't control?

But I must . . . I must . . .

And finally, I *do* let go, and we look at each other for a few moments, almost as if seeing each other properly for the first time.

And then she puts up a hand, gives a small wave.

Turns.

And is gone.

It is only nine o'clock in the evening, but I am exhausted. After everything that has happened, in fact, "exhausted" might not even cover it.

I stayed at the airport until the flight left, watching as the airplane took off into the darkening night; I even checked with the desk that everyone had been on board, that nobody had failed to turn up. But the flight was full; Lynette Hyams *is* on board, and will now be just an hour or so away from Minneapolis. A couple more stops, a few more hours, and she will be ready to start her new life in Florida.

I am back home now, was even able to help Amy sort the horses out for the evening before having a chat and sending her on her way with my genuine and heartfelt thanks.

I fed the dogs, fed myself, and finally dragged

myself upstairs and collapsed into bed.

I am exhausted, but will sleep come? I can't wait to sleep, can't wait to wake up and find out if it has worked, if I've saved the girl, if I've changed reality once more.

Will time return to normal?

Will I break out of this mind-bending, mind-shredding cycle?

But I know that the more I want to sleep, the harder it will be, despite my exhaustion.

I want to call Ben, to talk to him, to hear his voice; my hand even goes to my phone, until I realize that he has shared none of my recent experiences. As far as he's concerned, we barely know each other; our only meeting has been when he came here after I moved to introduce himself and offer his help if I ever needed it.

I don't know him at all.

I sigh, try to sleep again, but every time I close my eyes, I see the burned, ruined face of Dennis Hobson. I see the faces of the Latimer twins, of Paul; I see the twisted, dead body of Douglas Menders.

Eventually, I get up, go back downstairs and get a bottle of gin. I wonder, idly, if this is the exact same bottle that I drank that first night, the night I first discovered Lynette on those fields outside my house.

I pour myself a tall glass – the same glass? – and drink the whole thing down as I stare out of the kitchen window at those fields.

The whole experience has been beyond words, beyond comprehension, really.

I pour myself another glass, drink it, and feel the warm liquid turn even warmer as it hits my stomach.

I turn, say goodnight one more time to my three dogs, giving them each a kiss on the head, and start back upstairs, bottle in one hand, glass in the other.

The bottle is empty, and my drowsy, bloodshot eyes see that the glass is, too; sleep is so near now, so near.

Beauty gallops before me, I see Jack falling.

Dennis Hobson, Paul, Mike and Victoria Latimer, Artie and Pat Jenkins, faces swirling before me, in and out, around and around . . .

The Red Moon . . .

The Red Moon . . .

And, finally, I sleep.

DAY SEVEN

1

When I wake, it is the darkness I notice first.

Has it worked? What day is it? What –

And then the pain hits me, hot and scorching, as if my entire body is on fire.

Aaaarrrggghh!!!

I try and scream but all that comes out is a muffled cry, and I realize there is a cloth in my mouth, bound tight.

And then I realize that the reason I can't see is because my eyes are covered with a blindfold, I can feel the rough material now, grazing my eyelids.

What the hell has happened?

Where the hell am I?

I try and use my senses, try and ignore the pain as I attempt to locate myself in time and space.

It is then I feel my arms, hoisted above my head, wrists bound together; I sense my bare feet scraping the floor, feel the pressure through my arms, shoulders and chest, and understand that I am being hung by my bound wrists, my chin resting slackly on my chest.

There is no sensation of clothing, and I can feel a cool, chill breeze on my body; recognizing my nakedness, I instinctively try and cover myself, but this only pulls my bonds tighter, makes the pain worse.

The fear hits me hard, coursing through my veins, turning them to ice, and the effect is even worse than the pain, it is a fireball in the pit of my stomach and I begin to wretch violently, then choke on the soiled gag in my mouth. Fluids run from my nose and eyes, and the feeling makes me tense my body again – and again, I am hit by searing pain through my arms and shoulders.

I am a fish on a hook, and I have nowhere to go.

I can't even hear properly, it feels as if there is water inside my ears, as if I am underwater; my head is swimming with pain and disorientation. It is as if I have been drugged. Am I awake? Asleep? Hallucinating?

Or am I already dead?

The tears start in earnest now, my body wracking uncontrollably with the sobs.

"That's . . . it," I hear a muffled voice say, again as if it's coming from underwater, my blocked ears barely able to discern it at all. "Fucking . . . cry . . . you little . . . bitch."

Old or young, man or woman, friend or stranger, I have no idea, the words are so indistinct, like they are coming from miles away instead of right next to me.

Why am I here? Where is here? What's going on?

Please, please, what is going on?

I feel a sharp pain as a hand slaps me hard in the

face; my head turns violently with the unexpected blow, my neck wrenched with the whiplash. I gasp, but it is muffled through the cloth in my mouth, causing me to choke again.

"Bitch," I hear the sinister, underwater voice say again, and then I feel a piercing agony on my naked breast, a searing pain that can only come from being burned. A cigarette? my mind wonders, before going blank, the pain the only thing I can focus on, the terrible, searing, burning pain.

Then it is removed, and I sigh in relief, mixed with terror or what might be coming next, the dichotomy of emotion causing an anxiety that is almost as bad as the pain itself.

Then the pain is back, worse than ever, as the red-hot end of

(the cigarette?)

is placed against my nipple, held there until I can smell the burning flesh, know for sure that my nipple is being slowly burned off my breast.

I cry, I moan, I scream, but no sound can penetrate the cloth in my mouth, and my violently twisting body just causes even more pain, and then – just when I feel I am going to pass out – the burning stops.

Everything stops.

And there is nothing but silence, and in its own way, this is even worse; I know someone is there, maybe more than one person, and I know they are going to hurt me again – torture me, rape me, kill me, like they did to Lynette,

(where is she? where is Lynette?)

maybe like they've done to many more girls besides. I do not know when the next pain will come, what it will be like, and the anticipation is horrendous, the fear like nothing I have felt before, it is like a hideous entity living inside me, fighting with me, killing me from the inside.

"Why . . . did you . . . send the girl . . . away?" the disembodied voice asks, and I suddenly realize why I'm here, I'm here because Lynette's abductor was watching her, waiting to take her, then must have seen me helping her and decided to take *me* instead.

Oh no.

No, no, no, no, no.

I've seen Lynette's broken body, I've read the crime reports, the autopsy, the medical examiner's notes.

I know exactly what happened to her . . . what's going to happen to me.

The words come back to me, flashing before my blindfolded eyes, taunting me, threatening me.

Three ribs fractured . . . twenty-two incisions on the victim's lower trunk . . . deepest cut pierced the lower intestine, causing internal bleeding . . . subjected to forced sexual intercourse . . . foreign object insertion . . . violently sodomized . . . labia minora sewn closed with black thread . . . prepuce mutilated . . . glans clitoris crudely removed . . . severe head trauma . . . repeated heavy impact of a blunt instrument such as a ball hammer . . .

No, no, no, no, no . . .

This can't be happening to me, it can't, it can't, it

can't, I won't let it happen, no, no, no, no, no . . .

I feel hands go to my gag, rip it painfully away, pull the cloth out of my mouth.

I choke and gag and I want to vomit, but instead I breathe in deeply, trying to fill my lungs with sweet, sweet air, to –

Another slap sends the air right out of me again, and the voice is back, menacing in its lack of identity, its absence of humanity.

"I . . . asked you . . . why . . ."

I am not sure how to answer, what to answer, and my throat and mouth seem too dry to form words anyway, and I suddenly wonder if there is anyone else nearby, anyone else who might hear me, might come and help me . . .

And so I scream, scream harder and louder than I have ever screamed before, even though my ears still don't register the sound, my own violent screams sounding distant, under the same thick, noiseless water that masks the voice of my tormentor.

And then all the air is driven from me as I feel a sharp, crushing pain in my side, as though my body has been smashed in half with a massive hammer.

(. . . a ball hammer . . .)

I gag again, feel my ribs broken, my insides ruptured, and I feel blood trickling out of my mouth, and I hear the sounds of laughter in the background, sinister, evil laughter . . .

I want to cry, but there is nothing left inside – no tears, no sound, no hope.

"You'll . . . talk . . ." the voice says, and I know it is right, I will talk, I will tell everything I know, anything they want to hear, anything to stop the pain.

"I . . . want to . . . fuck her . . ." a voice says, and the ice hits my veins again, I know there are at least two people here with me for sure now, I know that I have no chance . . . no chance at all . . .

"Go . . . on . . . then . . ." the first voice says. "Fuck . . . the . . . bitch . . ."

There is more laughter, and then I feel hands on my body, all over me, I feel hands roughly parting my legs, pushing them aside, I feel other hands holding me, restraining me; and then I feel a hot pain as something hard, something warm, forces its way violently inside me, I hear laughter, grunting, grunting and laughter as I am raped, and the tears stream down my face, I scream again, louder now, louder, louder, I scream and scream and scream until he finishes inside me and pulls out, slamming his fist into my gut a moment later and leaving me doubled in pain, and I hear the muttered curse of *Whore* as the hands come away and I am left there, swinging helplessly from my rope, a hateful wetness dripping from my thighs, crying, crying and still screaming . . .

. . . screaming . . .

. . . and then I pass out, and – mercifully – can feel no more.

<u>2</u>

Another savage blow to my gut wakes me up, long before I have reached the point where I can be transported away, to a different time, a different day.

I feel cool metal against my flesh then, know that one of my abductors is holding a knife to my skin, know that more pain is coming, know that if I turn away, try and struggle free, then the pain will only be worse, and so I grit my teeth and tense, tense, tense as the sharp blade slices through the skin of my thighs, opening me up, I try and ignore the sharp, stinging agony of the wounds, the feel of blood as it drips down my body, even as the knife traces higher, cuts across my abdomen, up to my arms, stabbing deeper, the blade penetrating the muscle tissue of my biceps, twisting, tearing . . .

And then the pain is too much, and I start to scream again, unable to help myself, and I twist and turn on my hook in a desperate, useless bid for freedom, the movement making the knife dig deeper, cut harder, hurt more . . .

And in the background is the laughter, the deep, sinister laughter of the shadow-killers as they play their games with me, safe in the knowledge that they will never be found, never be caught, never be brought to justice . . .

Through the pain and the agony, I know that if I can only just fall asleep, if I can only be left alone long enough to sleep, I might still be able to get away from here, to get out, to escape to a different time . . .

"Just . . . need more time . . ." I whisper helplessly, the words barely audible.

"More . . . time . . ?" the voice queries, followed by a slap to the face, a punch to the gut. "More . . . time . . ?" A laugh follows, sharp and guttural. "Sure . . . have some . . . time . . . but we . . . will be . . . back . . ."

A slap, then a door opens and closes, and then there is silence, a silence only interrupted by the pitter-patter of my blood as it drips onto the cold floor beneath me.

The door opens again, and my heart reacts badly, my stomach churning hard, but there is no pain, no hitting, only the sound of a loudly ticking clock, placed somewhere close by. "There's . . . your fucking . . . time . . . Whore . . ." one of the voices says, and I hear the door close again.

Have they gone? I wonder, my body still tense as I await further punishment. Have they really gone?

The next few tentative, terrifying moments turn into minutes, and I start to believe they really have left me alone, for now at least, and the space gives me time to reflect on what they have done to me, how they have hurt me, degraded me, defiled me in a way worse than I could have ever imagined.

But you knew they did this to Lynette, don't you?

But that was her! This is me!

You think you're better than her? Because of your rich daddy? Is that it? She deserves this, and you don't?

No, no, that's not what I meant, it's not, I don't think that, I don't!

Bullshit, you believe it, you think Lynette and girls like her ask for this, but not you, not a do-gooder little rich kid daddy's girl like you, right? Right? Right?

No! Shut up!

Why won't even my mind leave me alone?

I have to ignore those voices, I have to sleep, I have to force myself to sleep, to sleep, sleep sleep sleep sleep sleep . . .

I don't know how much time passes, but it is enough for my body to take over from my mind, to begin to relax, and I start to count the ticks of the clock, to take my mind off the horrors I am facing, the horrors I have yet to face.

Sixty ticks . . . a minute . . .

Three hundred . . . five minutes . . .

A thousand . . .

And at last, I feel myself starting to drift off, drift away into the dream-world, a dream-world that might be my only chance of salvation.

I see my dogs, bouncing and happy, the horses in my fields, the sky blue and wonderful overhead, I am in one of the green, green fields stroking Hero's flank, my house a pretty picture in the background, I am –

The shrill, piercing noise of an old-fashioned alarm bell rings then, a deafening din that wakes me instantly, shocks me, frightens me, terrifies me, a noise that goes right through me.

A moment later, I hear the door open, people laughing, and I know that leaving me alone was just one more form of torture, they were allowing me to relax, just so that they could frighten me anew, weaken my defenses, make me even more vulnerable than before.

And then the terror starts again, I feels blows raining down on me, feel my legs pulled roughly apart as I am raped once more, beaten around the head, the legs, the arms, and I feel my will to live leaving me slowly but surely, and I long to be left alone by these animals, I long for death as the torture continues, blood dripping from my skin, from inside me . . .

And then they are gone once more, with wild grunts of *whore* and *bitch* their only form of communication with me, and I wonder if they are right, I *am* a bitch, I *am* a whore, I deserve this . . . I deserve this . . .

I am left again with the ticking clock, asking myself if it is worth it, to be here instead of Lynette Hyams, for the anger of my abductors to be vented on *me* instead of her, and I hate myself for my answer but NO! it is not worth it, not worth it at all, I would swap places with her in a heartbeat if given a choice right now, I would send her here and go back to my quiet life of ignorance

414

and innocence, away from this prison, away from these people . . .

I hate myself, but I would sacrifice her for my own safety, I would, I would, I would . . .

You wouldn't . . .

Yes I would, I fucking would!

Fuck Lynette Hyams, damn her to hell! Damn her to hell!!!

She should be here instead of me!

The clock continues to tick, taunting me, teasing me, terrifying me, until the alarm rings again and brings a fresh batch of HELL upon me, I am raped once more, cut by knives, hit by hammers, my nails pulled from my fingertips, bones cracked, teeth broken, and then they leave me again . . .

And on and on the pattern continues, pain mounting upon pain, insult upon insult, fear upon fear, terror upon terror . . .

The rape, the torture, the beating . . . the ticking of the clock in the cold, dank emptiness of my prison . . . the alarm . . .

I do not know how long I have been here for, I do not know when I last ate or drank, I do not know how many times I have been raped, stabbed, cut, hit, punched, kicked, I do not know what is left of me, if there is any trace of Jessica Hudson left or if I am just an empty shell, a living corpse.

All I know, when the alarm sounds, is that my tormentors are back, but this time I am taken down from the rope and pinned down on the ground, bent over, and before I can react I feel something hard being forced inside me from behind, something hard and wooden forced inside my . . . my . . .

The pain is intense, worse than before, and the pain and humiliation is too much to bear, too much to accept, and I know one of the men will be there soon, in its place, the ultimate defilement, and know there is only one way out, one option left, and I bite down hard on my tongue, as hard as I can, bite through the thick meat with my jagged, broken teeth, and I feel my tongue erupt in a geyser of blood, filling my mouth, and I gag but keep my mouth tightly closed, choking on my own blood, killing myself with my own blood . . .

Anything, anything but this, better death than this I think as I bite deeper, more blood filling my throat, choking me, and my lips keep shut, keeping the blood in, and I can't breathe, I can't see, I can't feel . . .

I do not know if death will transport me, if I will switch days before it is too late, or if everything will soon be over, but as the mist descends and I see the red moon, the huge RED MOON within that mist, brutal, massive and all-knowing, I understand – as I continue to choke on my own blood – that either way, the end is near.

The end, mercifully, is *here*.

DAY EIGHT

1

I wake up screaming.

I am screaming and I cannot stop.

I tell myself to stop, to stop, to stop, but I cannot.

The screams come from a place I cannot access, that I have no power over.

Am I alive? Am I dead?

I do not know, I cannot see anything, can hear nothing except for the screams, *my* screams, the screams that I know might never end, *should* never end, not after what has happened to me, what has been *done* to me.

I hear another sound then, and without conscious thought, my screams die down, become rapid, ragged breaths, helpless and weak.

The other sound, I realize now, is the sound of dogs whining . . . *my* dogs, whining at the door, pawing at it, scared by my screams.

My eyes are adjusting now too, and I start to see again, little by little . . .

I am in my room, the door the dogs are pawing at

is my bedroom door.

I am here. I am home.

I start to sob now – deep, convulsing sobs that wrack my entire body – as images, memories, sensations, flood my mind, things I never want to think of again, things I never want to feel again.

The pain, the terror, the violation of my body, my mind, it is all too much for me to handle and I pull the covers tight around me, ignoring the dogs, I just curl into a protective ball and cry. I cry, and I do not stop, I cannot stop.

I know the horses are outside, I need to go to them, but I can't, I daren't; I'm too afraid, I cannot leave my room, I cannot leave my *bed*.

All I can do is hold myself, and cry.

I don't know how long it lasts – maybe minutes, perhaps hours; but by the time the tears are gone, eyes swollen and painful, the sunlight filtering into my room through the half-closed curtains is stronger than when I'd first woken, the sun high in the sky.

I wonder – did it happen?

Did it really happen?

I let the covers drop slightly, turn my face to the light; the terror is still with me, but – although it takes a few moments – I realize that the pain has gone; the terrible, mind-numbing, soul-crushing pain that consumed me entirely for hours, maybe days, has finally gone.

Did it even happen in the first place?

My hands reluctantly pull the covers down further and I fearfully examine my body – no bruises, no cuts, no scars; no damage whatsoever. I daren't check any further, don't want to look there, don't want to think about it, never want to think about it again – even the thought of checking brings back those images again, those memories, the fear, the pain, the humiliation, the devastation, the . . .

And then the covers are up around me once more, I am curled in ball, and I am not sure if I will ever move again.

By the time I finally summon the courage to check my cellphone, it reads *12:18*. The morning has gone, filled with tears and dread, confusion and horror.

I check the date, re-check it; it's October 7th, the day *before* I drive to Anchorage and rescue Lynette, substitute myself for her into the killer's sick prison.

Nothing has happened at all, none of my experiences, none of it at all – Lynette is still alive, Douglas Menders is still alive, nobody has been arrested or seen the inside of a jail cell, Dennis Hobson hasn't had his face burned off.

My body sags. What was the point? I wonder. What the hell was the point of waking up on the 8th? Of going to Anchorage? Putting Lynette on that plane?

She's still there, being pimped out by her boyfriend. *What the fuck was the point?*

I get the confidence to check the rest of my body, look beneath the covers and check everything, every little part of me, from head to toe.

There are no marks, no bruises, nothing; I am clean, uninjured.

Like nothing ever happened.

Maybe nothing did *happen?*

Maybe it was all a dream, just a dream, none of it was real, none of it at all . . .

And yet the memories are so vivid, so brutal, so *intense*, that it is inconceivable that it was all a dream, just impossible.

Isn't it?

What sort of proof is there, if nothing has happened yet?

I grab the phone again, call Palmer PD. "Is Chief Taylor there?" I ask when the call is answered. I don't have Ben's number on my cell anymore, and I didn't memorize it.

The lady at the other end tells me he is, asks who's calling, tells me to wait . . . and then, after an interminably long time, what seems like hours but is probably only seconds, the friendly, familiar voice of Ben Taylor comes on the line.

"Ms. Hudson," he says, "how are you? How can I help you today?"

"Do you like jazz?" I ask, realizing how odd the question sounds but no longer caring. What does any of it matter anymore, anyway?

"What's that?" Ben asks, obviously confused. "Do I like jazz? Why –"

"Please don't ask why I'm asking," I say quickly,

"just know that it's important. To me, anyway. Do you like it? Listening to it? Playing it?"

"Well," he says, his voice unsure, "yeah, I do as a matter of fact, I love it. Listening to it, playing it, both. Do a bit on the piano when I can, you know, when I'm not too busy."

Holy shit, I think. *It's not a dream. None of it.*

"But come on," he says, "I've got to know, why are you asking?"

"Oh," I say, thinking quickly, "someone mentioned you liked it, and I've got some records an old boyfriend left me, I thought I'd bring them to the party on Saturday night, if you're going?"

"What, Artie's party?"

"Yeah," I say. "Artie's party."

"Yeah, I guess I'll be there. And if you've got records, I'd be glad to take them off your hands for you, thank you for thinking of me."

"Oh, it's no problem at all," I say, my mind still whirling. "It's no problem at all."

An hour later and I am dressed and outdoors, tending to the horses; I am tired of calling Dawn at the AER, tired of asking Amy to come and help.

I am nervous still, frightened, and I have the Cane Corsos with me, close by my side as I walk the fields.

There are no physical scars on my body, nothing to remind me of what has happened; but the mental scars run deep, might never be healed. I want to spend the rest of my life back in my house, my room, my bed; but the horses deserve better than that, the dogs deserve better.

And I still have to answer the question that has been buzzing around my mind all day, even while I was cowering beneath my covers, struggling to forget.

What was the point of it all?

Because I know there *is* a reason, I can feel it somewhere deep inside; and the knowledge that there is a purpose helps me to concentrate on something else, something other than my torment at the hands of those rapists, those killers.

There is a reason, and it's teasing at the edge of my consciousness, there but just beyond my reach.

But I know that I *do* understand the reason, I do know why I am back here, why things haven't sorted themselves out, why time didn't go back to normal, why getting Lynette to safety wasn't enough; I just don't want to admit it, to verbalize it out loud.

Because if I admit it, I am going to have to deal with it.

And I am too scared to do what needs to be done.

Because I know, in my heart of hearts, that I made a mistake; all I did when I put Lynette Hyams on that plans was remove a single victim, save a single person.

But the killers were – *are* – still out there, able to do whatever they want, to whoever they want.

Like me.

And I know that the reason I am here, on this day, is because I got the mission wrong.

It was never about saving Lynette, at least not

directly.

No, I think as I look out across my fields, the fields where Lynette still might die in just a few short days, *the mission wasn't about saving the girl.*

It was – it *is* – about finding the killers.

And something I saw, or heard, something that happened during my time with those bastards, I know that it is *this* that holds the key.

But I don't want to think about it, don't want to consider what it might be, because that would mean remembering what happened to me, giving a voice to my worst experiences, my darkest fears.

No, I don't want that.

But at the same time, I know that time is running out.

I am back here, on this particular day, for a reason; and if I don't act on it, I might never get out of this nightmare.

I sigh loudly, put one hand on the head of Luna, the other on Nero, using them for support – physical, mental, and emotional.

I know that there is no getting around it.

There is something in my mind that will help me find those killers, help me put an end to this for good.

All I have to do is face my fears once more.

2

I stare at the house of Arthur Jenkins, terror in my heart.

I know I shouldn't be here, know that it is a mistake; but at the same time, I know there is no other option, no other way out.

But I have the gun this time, have at last remembered to unlock it from the cabinet in the kitchen.

I hope I don't have to use it.

I've been here before, of course; maybe more than once.

The first time was the party, to be held next Saturday; I meet his brother, chat in the bedroom to Larraine, then leave, and find Lynette running across the fields toward me.

The second time – if there *was* a second time – was much, much worse.

I don't have a lot to go on, although I spent long agonizing minutes analyzing my experiences, only able to get through it by imagining that it was somebody else it was happening to.

Details are sparse – I was in a cold, damp room which had the feel of a basement, was almost certainly below-ground; there was more than one person, and although I could not tell from the voices if they were male or female, from my experiences I know that at least one of them was a man. Or a boy – and although I am outside Arthur Jenkins' house, I still cannot rule out Mike Latimer's involvement.

But I feel drawn to this place, feel that it is at the center of it all.

I first saw Lynette running across the fields toward my house, and I understand that this might cross Jenkins' (I can no longer think of it as "Artie's") house off the list. But the position of the homes within the valley means that she could have been running from anywhere; she could have been running from this place, just gone a different route to me.

Of course, it could have been from any of the others too – Larraine's, the Latimer's, Judge Judd's, the Eberle's, the Townsend's. It could even have been from Douglas Mender's, high up in the hills.

But I don't think it was.

I think she was running from here, from right here, the very place where we were all partying, drinking and having fun.

It was the clock that did it, the one piece of "evidence" I have.

I remember it vividly even now, the ticking of the

clock, the countdown to the next period of abuse, of rape, of torture.

The same sound that I heard from the clock in the bedroom in Jenkins' house, when Larraine and I had talked, upstairs at the party.

I knew that there was something, something I was missing, and that was it.

The clock.

I can't get the sound out of my mind, it is imprinted there, scorched into the circuits of my brain for eternity – the ticking, the tocking, the ringing of the alarm bell, the arrival of my tormentors . . . the pain . . .

I use all of my discipline to cut off those thoughts, to concentrate on my plan.

It is simple, really – I am going to break into Jenkins' house and find that clock. I'm going to set the alarm, listen to its ring; it is a sound I will never forget, and will be all the proof I need.

If it is the same clock, if I have found the right place, I will search for that basement, search for the hidden chambers which I know will have to be there; and if I can't find anything, I will call in a tip for the police, naming Arthur Jenkins as a suspect in the disappearance of local teenagers, prostitutes and runaways, link him to the Chugach bodies, tell them he has a torture chamber in his basement, hope that maybe *they* can find something.

I know that all of the houses in the valley were searched by the cops, by the ABI; but I also know that the owners had early warning. If one of them was the killer, they would have had the chance to get rid of any evidence, clear things up.

And if they find nothing?

I shake my head; I'll cross that bridge if I come to it.

I know that Jenkins isn't in; I've already called the shelter, made sure he's at work. I've checked up on the Latimers too, verified that they're in school; the last thing I need is any nasty surprises. I've even checked in Seattle, made sure that Patrick Jenkins isn't up here yet.

Everything seems all-clear, and I know I have to make my move.

And yet my feet remain rooted to the spot, unable to propel me forward.

I am too scared.

I have no marks on my body, but the marks on my mind will never leave me.

Why am I going back into the lion's den, the worst place in the world?

Because you have to, or else the nightmare will never end.

Yes, I decide, I *have* to.

Steeling myself, gun in my pocket, I approach the door.

3

Alaskans, I have learned, are trusting sorts, especially around here. After ringing the doorbell, to make sure that nobody is inside, I try and open the door. I half-expect it to be unlocked, but I'm not that lucky – it is bolted tight. My own door is rarely locked, does that mean he has something to hide?

But I have two guard dogs living inside my house, whereas Jenkins doesn't even have a cat; no alarm system either, I see with relief.

Despite the locked door, there *is* an open window by the kitchen though, and I spend several moments levering myself up, glad that this side of the house can't be seen by anyone, not even by Douglas Menders with his telescope.

The thought of Menders gives me pause, though; what if he was watching me approach the house, watched as I disappeared around the side? What would he think? Who would he call? Or would he do nothing, content to sit back and watch, reluctant voyeur that he is?

I shake the thoughts out of my head, determined to concentrate only on the mission at hand – gaining access to the house, finding that clock, finding proof – to me, at least – that I am on the right track.

I pull myself in through the narrow window-space, slowly dropping down to the sink unit on the other side. I take a moment, gather myself, and climb down to the kitchen floor.

I wonder how to get to the basement – wonder if I even *want* to go there, know that I don't, but will if I have to – and then ignore the thought. First things first – find the bedroom, find the clock.

I leave the kitchen, pad down the hallway to the stairs. The house looks gigantic now that it is not full of people, and I realize that – despite my interest in this case, my suspicions about Jenkins – I have no real idea about the man's life. Who *is* he? Why does a man who lives alone *need* a house this size? I know his wife died, and he might want to keep her memory alive by living here, but it was a long time ago. It is a hell of a lot of house to take care of, and most people I know would have downsized years ago.

I reach the staircase and move slowly, carefully, upwards, pistol in my hand now; I might have checked the whereabouts of everyone that I can, but what about people I *can't* check up on? I have no idea where Paul is, still don't know if he's a part of this thing. Could he be here, in this house, right now? My grip tightens on the gun as I think about it.

Could he have been one of my attackers, in the basement dungeon?

I grit my teeth, knowing the answer.

He could.

Anybody could.

But Arthur Jenkins knew the girl, she had already been to his shelter, he might have known she was coming back; hell, he might have known her for a while. And his brother might have known her too, from back in Seattle.

Why didn't I ask her, when I had the chance?

But I knew the reason – I thought I no longer had to solve the crime, to find those responsible, if I removed the victim from the equation.

But I'd forgotten about all the other victims, the ones that had been killed before, the ones who would be killed in the future.

I'd forgotten them, but I have been reminded, and now I will never forget.

I shake the thoughts from my mind again, angry with myself for constantly allowing my mind to drift away from the task at hand.

You can't blame yourself, a voice tells me. *Not after what you've been through. Remember how –*

No! Now is not the time, I can't remember, I *won't* remember, damn it!

And then, suddenly, I am in the upstairs hallway, just a short walk down to the room that holds the clock, the room that holds my proof.

I edge nervously down the hall, ready to move the

gun at any moment toward any of the doors, if one of them should suddenly open.

But then I am at the end of the hallway, at the door to the bedroom where Larraine and I had – will have, *might* have – our little chat.

My hand goes tentatively to the handle, touches it, pulls back like it's had an electric shock; the fear is so great, so acute, that it actually makes me go weak at the knees, causes me to stumble.

What is beyond the door? my mind screams, as visions of blood and death flash before me – Doug Menders, head smashed wide open; Paul attacking me in my kitchen, eyes wild, feral; Dennis Hobson, eyeballs on fire in a face of sloughed, mushy flesh; Lynette Hyams, broken body dead in my arms; shadows through a blindfold as I am raped and tortured, as I bite my own tongue off to end my suffering.

And then I wipe the thoughts away, remove them from my mind completely, and reach forward, grab the handle, and rip the door wide open.

It is time to see what is inside.

4

My heart stops as I look at the dresser.

The clock isn't there.

Other than the absence of the clock, the room is exactly as I remember it (and if I remember it, I *must* have been here, I must be right about that, at least).

So where the hell is it?

I pause a moment, listening. The damn thing is so loud, if it's anywhere in this room, I'll hear it.

But there is nothing; just the silence of an empty house.

Am I wrong about this whole thing? Did I imagine the clock? Did I imagine everything?

(*you did, you imagined it all, you're crazy, insane, just like everyone thinks, accept it, accept it . . .*)

No, damn it, I didn't imagine anything!

That clock was here, and it was the same damn clock I heard down in that fucking basement!

Now where the hell is it?

There's dust on the dresser, I notice, and it has

been there a long time; there is no clean space where a clock might have been.

Was it *ever* there?

And then I think, will it ever *be* there? Because I've seen it in the future, not in the past; maybe it's somewhere else in the house right now, and Jenkins only moves it to this room at some stage between now and the party? Maybe he moves it out of the way because he knows the sound will drive his guests crazy.

Yes, I think, grasping hold of the idea like a drowning person who's been thrown a life jacket. *It must be.*

And then I turn into a ball of pure energy, propelled by fear, propelled by anger – I no longer care if there's anyone in the house, couldn't care less if I'm found, if I'm discovered, I am beyond that now, I am beyond worrying about it, the only thing that matters is finding that clock – and I race around the house, tearing the place apart as I look for it.

Every room, every space, every cupboard, every cabinet, every corner, every crevice, I search it all, I search it all until I am dirty with dust, damp with sweat.

It is getting dark now, the sun low in the sky, and I have no idea how long I have been searching.

But still, I have found nothing.

I have found nothing incriminating of any kind, of any kind at all.

But now I am at a doorway by the staircase, the only doorway I still have to go through, the only one I haven't checked; a doorway I know must lead to the basement beneath the house.

I steel myself, jaw clenched tight. The clock is downstairs, surely it is downstairs.

Don't do it! my mind screams.

But I ignore my mind, raise the pistol, and turn the handle.

5

A sound makes me turn suddenly, before I am even on the first step; the sound of a door being unlocked.

A door being . . .

Realization dawns, and I leap back, swing the basement door shut, look left and right for somewhere to hide, can't seem to *think* in time, to *act* in time, can only stand there petrified, rooted to the stop as the door opens and Arthur Jenkins looks at me, an expression of surprise on his face.

I realize I still have the gun in my hand, wonder what to do with it; see that he is not alone, that both Mike *and* Victoria Latimer are by his side, wonder if they are all in on it together, wonder about just pulling the trigger and shooting them all; if that was them down in the dungeon, the things they did to me, the things they were *going* to do to me, they deserve to die, they all deserve to die, die, die . . .

My finger almost presses the trigger, almost sends them all to Hell, but something stays my hand, makes me stop, makes me drop the pistol to my thigh.

What if you're wrong? my mind argues with me. *What if they're not the ones? What if they're innocent?*

But what if they're not? another voice fires straight back, and I do not know which one to listen to, which to believe, which to trust.

"Jess," Jenkins says, brow heavily furrowed, "what's going on?"

Shoot him! Fucking shoot the son of a bitch!

No!

Do it now! Before it's too late! Fucking do it! Do it!

I can't!

You want him to do it again? You want to be down in that basement again?

I . . . I . . .

"I heard some noises," I say, ignoring the voices fighting in my head. "I thought someone was breaking in, I thought . . . I don't know, I grabbed my gun and raced right over here."

The three of them are moving toward me, and I feel penned in, unsafe, and I think again about just shooting them, shooting all of them.

They look through doorways, taking in the sight of the ransacked rooms; it definitely looks as if there *has* been a burglary, anyway. My search for that clock was crazed, frenzied, and left quite a mess.

"Damn," Victoria says to Jenkins, "it looks like you *have* been robbed."

"Shit," Mike says, "did you see anyone? Have you called the police?"

"Yeah," I lie, wanting them to think they police are on their way, to stop them from doing anything to me. "They're on their way."

Jenkins and his two friends – what the hell are they doing here together, anyway? – are looking into each room, and I see my space, my opportunity, and I start moving for the open front door.

"Jess," Jenkins says sharply, and I freeze.

(you still have the gun, you still have the gun)

"Yeah?" I say, turning to him.

"The door was locked," he says. "How come?"

Shit.

What now?

Shoot him, shoot him now!

(shoot that sonofabitch, shoot them all, shoot them all)

No! I can't!

Do it!

"I was scared," I say, not caring if I make sense anymore, only a few feet left until I am out of the door. "I locked myself in."

"But you don't have a key," Jenkins says, eyes suspicious, and I see the other two rounding toward me, attention focusing on me. "How –"

Shoot them!

"I think Larraine is at home," I say, at the doorway now, fresh air filling my lungs, hinting at safety beyond. "Maybe she saw something, I'll go and check. Wait here for the police, they'll be here soon."

And then I am gone, running for the safety of Larraine's house, hoping that they will not chase me.

Hoping that – despite the voices – I will not have to shoot them.

<u>6</u>

"You think *what?*" Larraine Harrigan asks in near-stunned disbelief.

We are in her kitchen, not – as far as I am concerned, at least – for the first time, and she has replaced the pot of tea with a glass of whisky. I'd hidden the gun by the time I arrived at the door, but it was clear that I was distressed, and the alcohol is welcome.

The kids are at home, but when Larraine saw the state of me, she sent them straight upstairs, and I don't blame her; my appearance must be enough to frighten anyone.

I take a deep breath, finish the brandy, and pour myself another from the bottle that Larraine has left on the table, before I respond.

"I think that Arthur Jenkins is involved in something," I tell her again, "something bad. Something to do with the girls that have been going missing."

"Girls from Anchorage?"

"Yeah," I say, "a lot of them were last seen at the

shelter."

"What do you think is happening?" she asks.

"I don't know," I say honestly, "I really don't know, but I think he has somewhere he takes them, I . . . oh, I don't know, why am I even telling you this?"

Why *am* I telling her this? When I came around here, I was convinced I was going to keep the charade going, to ask her if she'd seen anything strange happening at the house, any sign of burglars breaking in; but when she brought me inside and sat me down at the table, all of my well-crafted lies went right out of the window. And instead, I started telling the truth, at least as I understand it.

"It doesn't matter why," Larraine says in her soft, soothing tones, "but if you want to talk, I find it's always best to do so."

I wonder what I'm doing here, why I'm wasting time; right now, Jenkins could be hiding evidence, knowing that I'm onto him. Maybe he's even getting Mike and Victoria to help him, maybe they were involved all along?

I told them that I'd called the police, but of course, I haven't; the police aren't on their way, unless Jenkins has called them himself. And if what I suspect about him is true, then there is no way in hell he would do that.

No, he's going to be undertaking some serious damage control right now, clearing out the basement of anything incriminating.

Isn't he?

"The girls are connected," I say, almost without thinking, almost as if I'm using Larraine as a sounding board, to see if I'm barking up the right tree or if I'm truly going mad.

"Which girls?"

"The girls from around the area," I say, "and the bodies found in Chugach Park back a few years back, maybe even the ones found outside Anchorage a few years before *that*."

"And you think it's *Artie*?" Larraine asks, and I can't tell if the tone is amazement or understanding, or something else altogether.

I shrug, confronted with the question outright. Do I think it's Arthur Jenkins? Obviously, a very large part of me does; otherwise why would I have broken into his house in the first place? It must be Jenkins, maybe in league with others – maybe the Latimer twins, maybe Menders, maybe my own ex-fiancée, here in Alaska unannounced. But the only common denominator in it all is Arthur Jenkins, the man who runs Anchorage Street Shelter, the man who would have known most – if not all – of the missing girls, in one way or another.

But on the other hand, I also realize that I have *not* called the police; and also that, even though I had a gun in my hand and could have shot the man dead, I did not. If I truly believed that he was the one who had burned me, mutilated me, raped me, tortured me, would I have had such self-restraint? If I was really one hundred percent sure?

But of course, I am *not* one hundred percent sure;

and with that realization, I am deflated yet further, and take another long swallow of my newly-poured whisky.

Is Jenkins ringing the police right now? If he's not guilty, then it's a possibility; and what do I do then?

"But I must confess," Larraine says finally, eyes downcast as if she doesn't want to say whatever it is she's going to say, "I've had some . . . *thoughts* about Artie myself."

"What do you mean?" I ask instantly, grasping hold of the lifeline that Larraine has thrown me.

"I mean . . . well, this is sort of hard to say, with Artie being my boss in a way, and of course with him being a friend and neighbor too, but . . . I guess I've always thought his manner with some of the girls was a little bit off, a little bit, I don't know, I guess the word is 'suspect'?"

"But why?" I ask, ignoring the whisky now, my interest fully aroused.

"The way he looks at them sometimes, maybe. The way he talks to them. It's nothing I can really put my finger on, anyway. And like I say, Artie's a friend, I don't want to say anything out of line, you know, but . . ."

"But you have your suspicions," I offer.

"Yes," she says. "You could put it like that, yes. And then, of course, there's his brother."

"His brother?" I ask, interested in this unsolicited piece of information, all of a sudden reminded of our last conversation in this kitchen, over tea and apple pie – a conversation only one of us will remember.

"Yes," she says, "you know the one, Pat, he's coming here this weekend, that party Artie's throwing is for him. Are you going?"

"Good question," I say. "I'm not really sure anymore." I pause, take another – slower – sip of the whisky, before speaking again. "So what about him?" I ask. "His brother?"

Larraine replies like the good gossip girl she is, with the same chapter and verse on his activities in Seattle that she gave me last time – the incident at the school, the job as a dog catcher, the whole thing. Only this time, I think of another question to ask about him.

"Has he been here before?"

"Who, Pat? Oh, I should say so, normally not much is made of it, but he comes over regular."

"How often?"

"Maybe three, four times a year," Larraine answers. "Maybe more."

I stop and think, wondering how this has not been factored in by the ABI. Have they checked this out? Have they cross-referenced dates with reports of missing women?

Damn, this thing just gets more and more complicated.

"So, why the party?" I ask. "Why this time?"

"Well, the conditions of his bail from earlier charges meant that he couldn't really travel out of Washington," Larraine says, "at least that what Artie tells me. So, he's kind of been sneaking over the past few years. But now everything's over with, with that last case, he can travel freely, so this is really the first time he can come over here 'publicly', so to speak."

I don't believe it; Pat Jenkins has been coming here for years – a convicted sex felon – and the police and ABI might not know the first thing about it?

"I see," I say, looking down into my glass, wondering what new spin this puts on things.

"Say," Larraine says, "what the hell happened over there, anyway?"

"I . . ." Hell, what *did* happen over there? It is all getting too much for me – has Jenkins called the police? Are they coming to arrest me? Or else, is he clearing out his basement, removing the evidence? Should I call the police myself?

Damn it all, should I just go over there and shoot the son of a bitch and be done with it?

"I . . . need to use the bathroom," I say at last. I need to splash some cold water on my face, wake myself up. I need a break, a moment to get some perspective on this mess.

"It's just down the hall," Larraine says, "first door on the left. Maybe I'll get a pot of coffee on while you're gone."

She's right again, I think – the whisky has done its work, but I think I'd appreciate the caffeine more than the alcohol right now.

"Thanks," I say as I stand. "I'll be back soon."

"Oh, take your time, dear," she says in her grandmotherly manner. "You just take your time."

7

I walk down the hallway, observing the gold-framed pictures that line the walls, the fine china that fills the cabinets.

It is a nice house – not as big as Jenkins', but much more homely – and again, I find myself taking inspiration. Despite what has happened, despite the reasons that brought me here, I still think about how much I like what she has done with the house, think about how I can apply those lessons to my own home.

I reach for the handle of the first door to my left – as instructed – but then something stops me.

Something familiar.

A ticking sound.

The ticking of a clock.

The terrifying *tick-tock* of *the* clock, coming from a room on the other side of the hall.

I stand stock-still, blood once more turning to ice in my veins.

But then I move – away from the bathroom –

propelled by a curiosity, a morbid search for the truth that I cannot ignore.

I look to the kitchen, see it obscured by the semi-closed door, and creep stealthily across the carpeted floor.

I push open the door to the room opposite, see a neat, old-fashioned sitting room, like something out of a Charles Dickens novel.

And there, above the fireplace, is a clock, ticking loudly.

The same clock that I saw in Jenkins' upstairs room, the Saturday that Lynette Hyams died in my arms.

The clock that – for all I tried – I couldn't find in Jenkins' house today.

What does it mean?

Why is it here?

I approach it slowly, wondering how such a small thing, an inoffensive thing, a simple device used for measuring time, can cause such heart-stopping, nauseating terror. How is that possible?

I see that it is definitely the same clock I saw when Larraine and I were in that room in Jenkins' house, there is no doubt in my mind about *that*.

Damn, that thing's annoying, I remember saying, and Larraine smiled and said, *Yes, it is, isn't it? Do you feel like your life is being counted down?*

It is the same clock as *that*, yes.

But is it the same clock that counted down the hours, the minutes, the seconds, until I was hurt again?

Raped again? Abused again, tortured again, mutilated again?

The tick-tocking fills my ears, my brain, my soul, it is all I can hear, all I can think about, all I can perceive of the world . . .

It is everything, and I stumble, I falter, I am too scared to do what needs to be done, what I *know* should be done . . .

But then something within me grips me, moves me, drives me to the clock despite my fear, my terror . . .

Drives me to pick that damned thing up, to look at the time – eleven minutes past four – and to set the alarm, almost without thinking, to twelve minutes past four.

I can see the large semi-spherical bell sitting astride the curved top of the mantelpiece clock, can imagine how it will sound when struck . . .

But will it?

Will it?

I feel the sweat start to appear at my brow as I wait, feel it start to drip down my face as I listen to the seconds go by.

Tick-tock.

Tick-tock.

Tick-tock.

I want to leave, I want to run, I want to *die* before I hear that alarm again, but I have to know, I have to know, I have to, I have to, I have to –

BBBRRRIINNNNGGGGGGG!!!!

The alarm sounds, and my heart stops dead,

recognizing it for exactly what it is; and in a Pavlovian response, my body freezes up, it tenses, prepares itself for the torture that I know will come, that I know the alarm heralds.

And sure enough – still frozen in place by sheer terror – I hear the sound of a door opening.

I turn, finally, painfully, fearfully, and see Larraine Harrigan standing there in the doorway, eyebrows raised.

"Are you okay, dear?" she asks with what appears to be genuine concern, apparently unaware of my discovery, the significance of the alarm bell.

But why is the clock here? Why is it not at Arthur Jenkins' house?

Lynette escaped on Saturday – kept and tortured for several days.

The clock was there on Saturday.

I was imprisoned, tortured

(*died?*)

before Saturday, and the clock was obviously somewhere else

(*here?*)

at that time.

Where was it?

(*it was here!*)

Why wasn't it at Jenkins' house?

(*it was here!*)

It was here!

It was here!

"It was you . . ." I say before I can stop myself, the

words rolling off my tongue unbidden, "it was you . . ."

And although she cannot possibly understand the specifics, cannot possibly understand the significance the clock holds for me, I can see in her eyes, in her expression, that she understands completely . . .

And in that instant, the Larraine Harrigan that I know and admire is gone in an instant, and the monster, that is surely her *true* self, emerges in all its fury.

8

She races across the room toward me before I can react, murder in her eyes.

I fumble for the gun in my pocket, but she is there before I can pull it clear, there with her hands around my neck, and the force of her body colliding with mine sends us both crashing to the floor.

Larraine lands on top, and the breath is knocked out of me; I feel the hands tighten, fingers strong around my neck, thumbs digging hard into my throat, and I cannot get any air in at all, I cannot breathe, I cannot do anything.

"*Fucking little cunt whore*," I hear her spit in my ear as she strangles the life out of me. "*Fucking slut, you're going to die, you bitch, you're going to fucking die . . .*"

The oxygen to my brain is being cut off, starved, and I start to feel light-headed, as if drunk, I feel everything going . . .

I am floating on clouds, looking down at our happy little hamlet of ranches, and I wonder if Doug Menders is watching us right now, watching with his telescope through Larraine's window; I wonder who she's been doing this with, know it must be Jenkins, maybe his brother too, maybe the Latimers; then I think again that maybe it's everyone in this whole damn valley, this whole damn town; my vision starts to turn red at the edges, and I cannot believe that this woman, this monster, is going to murder someone – murder *me* – with her two children upstairs in the same house.

I see Beauty, in vivid, glorious detail, muscles rippling, coat gleaming, eyes on fire . . .

I see Jack, my loving brother, my only friend, in the open casket at his funeral, all those years ago . . .

I'm coming to see you, Jack, I think; *I'm coming to see you, at last . . .*

But then I see the Red Moon once more, and it obliterates images and ideas of anything else, of *everything* else, it occupies my entire field of vision, it dominates my thoughts, my dreams, my actions . . .

I hear a *BANG!*, a gunshot, and I do not know what has happened; but then I feel the grip on my neck relax, open my eyes to see Larraine's face hovering above mine, disbelief and surprise on it, life dimming from those dark, black, hate-filled eyes; I feel the gun in my hand, do not know how it got there, just feel the grip in my palm, my finger on the trigger; I feel wet, liquid flowing freely down across my body, and I understand that it is Larraine's blood, I have shot her, I have shot her dead . . .

In a panic, I roll her body off mine, throw the gun

away and scramble to my feet, eyes wide in horror at what I've done; I see the body of Larraine Harrigan lying on the floor in an ever-widening pool of dark, crimson blood, the surprise still stark across her monstrous visage, surprise and *hate*, hate and surprise . . .

"What the fuck have you *done*?"

I look up and see Larraine's children looking down at their mother's dead body, feel a terrible shot of guilt race through me. Little Adam is not even twelve years old, Rich just fourteen. What have I –

And then I see that Rich has my gun, is raising the barrel, aiming it at me.

"You're dead, you fucking bitch," he spits at me, more hate in his eyes even than his mothers.

"No," little Adam says then, his eyes the same as his brother's, his mother's, even as he wipes tears from them. "No. I want to fuck her first. Make her pay."

No . . .

It's not possible.

Is it?

But Rich nods his head, gestures at me with the gun. "Come on," he says, voice cold, eyes dead. "You're going down to the fucking basement."

<u>9</u>

"You don't want to do this," I whisper to the boys, but I know they are already doing it; I am halfway down the basement stairs, and I will not be able to reason with them.

"Shut your mouth, you fucking slut," Rich says, poking me in the back with the barrel of my gun.

"You killed our Mom," Adam adds, "you've got to fucking pay for that, right Rich?"

"Yeah," Rich says as we near the bottom, "she's got to fucking pay, all right."

"Hey," Adam says in a high-pitched whine, "I get to go first this time though, okay?"

"Bullshit," Rich says, "I'm the oldest, *I* get to go first."

"Damn it Rich, you always fucking get to go first, I want —"

There is shouting upstairs, crashes and bangs, and we all freeze, there on the cold stone steps. "Shut up," Rich hisses, and then listens. "There's someone up there," he says to his younger brother. "Go and check it out."

"But Rich –"

"Just shut up and go check it out," Rich says, "while I deal with the slut."

Adam sighs, but does as he's told, runs back upstairs to find out what's happening.

Is it Arthur Jenkins? Is it the police?

I feel the metal barrel in my back, know that Rich might kill me if I scream; but I also know that this might be my last chance of getting out of here alive, and I'll be damned if I'm going to let this bastard get me down into that basement again, I'll be damned if I'm going to be raped again, tortured again.

I'll be damned if I'm going to let that happen!

"Help!" I scream at the top of my voice. "Help me, please! I'm down here! Down in the – "

Then I feel the weight of the gun as it crashes into the back of my head, and I am instantly silent, falling down the last few steps into the cold, damp basement below.

Rich stalks down the steps after me, but I am already back on my feet, adrenaline coursing through me, propelled by fear, energized by terror, and I rush toward him, grabbing the wrist of the hand that holds the gun, aiming it downward; he fires off one round, then two, the *crack* of the gunshots almost deafening within the confined walls of the basement, but they hit the floor and ricochet off harmlessly. I hold onto Rich's other arm too, to stop him from slapping me, punching me; I jerk a knee upward, hit him in the balls, and he jerks back, nearly pulling the gun-arm from my grasp, but panic means that my grip is like a vise, nothing is going to make me let go.

The boy-monster in front of me must understand this, because instead of continuing to try and free his arm, instead he flings his head forward, smashing the hard brow of his skull into my unprotected face.

The pain is intense, disorienting, and I feel him stamping down hard on my foot, and I gasp, letting go of the death-grip I had on that arm; I see stars through blurred vision, but I also see him grin and raise the pistol and I brace myself for the impact; I see the flash of a muzzle erupting in the darkened room, flashing off the walls, and know I must die; but in that moment of bright light, I also see the smile break apart as teeth fly from the kid's face, teeth and bone, along with a geyser of black blood that covers me, blinds me, and my hands go to my face to claw away at the blood even as I hear the supersonic *crack* of the round that did it, the sound threatening to burst my ear-drums, the echo reverberating off the walls as Rich's dead body collapses, near-headless, to the floor.

I look behind him, already starting to hyperventilate with the shock, and see a shape there, a shape with a gun of its own, and I collapse to the floor, unable to take it anymore, unable to take any of it . . .

And then the shape is over me, above me, and I can hear the familiar, comforting sounds of Ben Taylor's voice as he tells me, "It's alright now. Just relax.

It's alright now. Nobody can hurt you now."

And I believe him, at last I have found someone I can believe, and then my eyes close and I pass out completely.

EPILOGUE

<u>1</u>

The red moon is low on the horizon as I approach my farm; I am scared by what I will find, but – as I get to the fields – I see that there is nobody there.

No half-dead girl.

Nobody jumping out at me, attacking me.

Nobody at all.

There are just my horses, and I watch as they trot toward me, as they merge into one single body before they get to me, one single animal that is Beauty; for a moment, I am scared, but he is not rearing up anymore, there is no blood dripping from his mouth, there is no violence in him at all.

He is at peace.

I stroke his head as we meet, kiss his nose, then move past him to the house.

I open the door, and see a man waiting for me in my kitchen.

It is my dead brother, Jack; dead no more.

He is no longer the gaunt, drug-addled man who

killed himself by jumping out of an apartment window, but his younger self, fitter and happier.

He comes to greet me, and we embrace, hold one another tight.

It has been a long time.

Eventually, Jack moves me away, looks into my eyes. "You did it, Jess," he says with a smile. "You did it."

"Hey," the soothing voice says, near my ear. "It's okay. It's over. It's over."

But is it?

My eyes flash open, I see Ben Taylor by my bedside – my *hospital* bedside – and I grab my cellphone from the cabinet next to me.

"It's not been ringing," Ben says, but I don't care about that, I only care about what day it is, what's the date, *what's the date?*

And then I see it, and I have been waiting for this for so long that I don't even know how to react to the information anymore.

It is October 8th.

The day after yesterday.

At last, the *real* tomorrow.

The chain has been broken, and I am free at last.

"Her real name was Darlene Williams," Ben Taylor tells me.

I am still in a hospital bed – just precautionary, the doctors say – and it is now October 10th. I still wake every morning in a cold sweat, desperate to know the day, but – so far at least – they have been running like normal, one following the other, just as they should.

I guess I'll never know how that clock ended up at Artie's house. Maybe Larraine brought it around for him, gave it to him as a present? It might have even been a gift for the party, although I don't suppose it really matters anymore.

Ben has been coming in regularly, giving me what updates he can. Most of it is "off the record", but – given what I've been through – he's been pretty good at letting me know the details of the rapidly-expanding case.

I already know that Larraine Harrigan – or Darlene Williams, apparently – is dead, killed by the bullet I fired when she was strangling me.

There are calls for charges to be made in some quarters, but my father has already been here and squared it all away; it was self-defense, and it looks like the possibility of charges being put forward is becoming less and less likely. Knowing what I now know about my past, what Dr. Kelly told me, I even managed to speak to him this time, realizing that perhaps he is not the complete monster that I always thought he was. He was still more concerned over his job than his family, of course, but I now understand that some of his actions were to protect me, he was only doing what he thought was best for me.

Paul has tried to see me too, but I've asked Ben to make sure he stays away; after his attack in my kitchen, I want him as far away from me as possible. He might not be a serial killer, but he is a dangerous man, in his own way. To his credit, Ben put him on a plane home to New York, and warned him not to come back.

Ben also helped me out with another problem too, namely getting Lynette Hyams on that flight to Florida. I explained that Larraine had told me that Lynette was going to be her next victim, and – after learning about the girl – I wanted to help her leave the life she had here. Ben didn't pretend to understand my reasons, but he did what I asked – picked her up, put her on the flight, gave her the money – and he even arrested Dennis Hobson for assault, for good measure.

I'd taken care of sending a bouquet of flowers to Amy at Alaskan Equine Rescue myself, though. It was the least I could do, although I know she will have no idea why I've sent them; the help she gave me was in another time, another reality. But still, I am grateful.

I've learned that Richard Harrigan, the eldest son, died instantly from the bullet to the head fired by Ben. I don't know how he is dealing with the guilt of killing a boy; maybe it's the same way I am dealing with killing the boy's mother – I'm not thinking about it. And because I'm *thinking* nothing, I *feel* nothing.

It won't last, I know; but it will do, for now.

I remember only vaguely the things that happened in that basement now, and I am immensely grateful; now that this whole thing is over, perhaps I do not need the memories anymore, perhaps whatever power caused all of this has taken pity on me, drove those things from my mind that might otherwise cause me too much pain.

I know that things did happen to me there, but no longer recall the details, I only know that I do not wish to remember them, hope that – with time – they will fade away forever.

After all, it didn't happen in *this* reality; maybe I will ultimately forget everything that happened outside of this particular time-frame? The only thing I would miss, I guess, would be the time I'd spent with Ben.

But Ben is here with me now at least, although I know he no longer knows me as I know him; but maybe my memories of him will fade too, like an old photograph exposed to the sun.

Ben tells me that the younger brother, Adam, is still alive, and is being held in custody at Palmer PD; although as of yesterday, he'd not given the cops much to go on. He'd attacked a police officer with a knife back at the house, but he had been easily overpowered and arrested; after all, the boy was not even twelve years old.

"So is he talking now?" I ask Ben, who nods.

"Yes," he says uneasily. "Finally. Although I have to tell you, I kind of wish he wasn't. The things he says . . . well, they're kind of hard to take, if you know what I mean."

I *do* know, more than Ben can ever understand.

But I need to know more.

I need to know the details.

And so I breathe out slowly, readying myself for the tale, hoping that – finally – I will learn the truth.

2

"So, who was Darlene Williams?" I ask.

"A convicted sex offender from Oklahoma," Ben says. "Took the name Larraine Harrigan when she moved here. Now we know, we've pulled her case history from Tulsa PD. Pretty messed up life," he says, shaking his head. "Not that it makes any difference, excuses what she's done, but . . . pretty messed up, all the same."

I listen, learn that she was born into a poor household, her father absconding with another woman when she was only young. Her mother apparently then had a string of boyfriends, many of them abusive, and they moved around the country until she remarried. Darlene's new step-father sexually assaulted her, finally raping her when she was thirteen and making her pregnant. Her mother refused to believe it was her husband's, and allegedly kicked the girl out of the house for being a "slut". She came to live at a home for unwed mothers, where she suffered still more abuse, the baby also being taken from her.

She had a series of odd-jobs – and there is the possibility that she worked for a time as a prostitute herself – but then she became a psychologist, just as she'd claimed when we'd spoken at the party; only the real story was that she'd forged all of her documents, had hardly studied a day in her life. She started to work with children, but was arrested just over a year later, after several accusations of molestation, involving girls ranging in age from twelve to fifteen.

She served a couple of years, and met her future husband not long after she got out; and it was then that her life did seem to get turned around, at least for a short while. She got married, had children, and started – as far as the record shows – to live some semblance of a normal life. Until, that is, she found her husband cheating on her. He moved away with his new girlfriend, leaving her with two young babies and a lot of anger – maybe the same sort of anger that had made her do those terrible things earlier in her life.

"Her husband died in mysterious circumstances soon after," Ben adds with a knowing look, "and even though they were separated, she still got a big payout, as they were still legally married, there'd been no divorce – and it was then she disappeared, moved with the money to Alaska, set up a new identity, a new life."

I wonder if she had anything to do with her husband's death, think that it's more than a little likely, but that we'll probably never know. I think back to her own description of her situation, back in the upstairs bedroom, next to the ticking clock. *So I filed for divorce, got the kids, a big pay-out, and moved out here with them.* Some of it was true, at least.

"And when did she move here?" I ask. "About the same time those first bodies were discovered outside of Anchorage?"

Those early killings were nothing I wouldn't know; everything had been in the papers yesterday, since the press got wind of rumors circulating about a female serial killer. They were having a field-day with it.

Ben nods his head. "We can only speculate about a connection at this stage," he says, "but yeah."

"You know, I also read about some bodies found up in Chugach Park, were they . . ."

Ben nods. "We think Williams killed them, yeah. Sexually assaulted them, then killed them, dumped the bodies in the park."

"How many?" I ask.

"We don't know. Adam – well, *Jared* is the name he was born with actually, Jared Williams – says . . . well, he says that he and his brother – *Dayton* Williams – used to ride around in her car with her, she'd sometimes pull girls over, she'd offer them a lift, that sort of thing, then she'd 'make them sleep', we think it must have been chloroform, something like that, then she'd drive them up into the woods, the mountains, leave the kids in the car and . . . well, if you read about those bodies, then you know."

"Yes," I say, "I know."

"He's vague, but he remembers it being a regular

occurrence anyway, probably once a month, or every six weeks or so. And it turns out that – later, when the boys were a little older – she started getting them more involved in her activities. Forced them to help her." He shakes his head, and I know he can't believe any of it. I know how he feels; it is hard to accept, almost *impossible* to believe. "She got a job at the shelter, used it as a place to identify and pick up victims. Nobody ever suspected her of course, a woman – a nice woman – with two kids by her side. The perfect disguise, I guess."

"Yeah," I say. "She fooled us all."

Ben nods sadly. "Yeah. Anyway, she stopped dumping bodies in Chugach when we started finding them, decided to bring the girls home with her instead. Gave her and the boys more time with them, more time to . . ." Ben's voice trails off, eyes closing in pain as he can't help but think about it. Finally, he looks up again. "There was another room down there," he says, "closed off from the rest of the house, accessed through a secret door hidden behind a section of shelving. All soundproofed in there, the whole works – yesterday, Adam showed us how to get inside."

His voice sounds drained, disturbed and horrified, and I know why the police didn't find anything in that basement when they looked; they didn't really suspect the Harrigans, weren't looking for any hidden rooms.

"We found bodies buried there," Ben says, his voice shaking, no more than a whisper.

I almost don't want to ask. "How many?"

Ben sighs. "Seven so far," he says, "most of them

just skeletons now. The guys are still digging it up, a lot of the graves were concreted over, probably to hide the smell."

A shudder runs through me as I consider how many people met their fates in that horrible dungeon, what happened to them before they died; it is a thought too terrible to consider.

I remember Doug Menders' journal, his numbered codes for the people he saw, and I wonder if Lynette – ab3-9 – would have been the ninth victim, the ninth person to be raped, tortured and buried underneath that evil house?

The thought makes me shiver, especially as I could have been – *was*, in one reality or another – victim nine. Is my dead body, tongue bitten off, lying somewhere, buried under concrete, in a reality that I will never see again?

I turn off the thought as soon as I have it, determined never to think it again.

"What would make anyone do that?" I ask, although I know there is no real answer.

"Best we can figure – from what her son's told us in his first interviews, at least – is that she was just filled with hate, pure *hate*, for those girls. She thought they were promiscuous, loose women, sluts – not even human maybe, not worth bothering with. Why did she think that? Well, her background offers some clues, I guess, but some people go through worse and don't end up doing . . . well, what she did. I can only think that her brain was wired up differently from ours, you know?"

Hate, Larraine had answered when I'd asked her about what motivated such killers, and I remember that the answer had come almost immediately. *What else can it be? This guy, he hates women. Why? Who knows? Maybe his mother beat him as a little kid, maybe his wife cheated on him, maybe the girls laughed at him at school, saw him in the changing room, you know the sort of thing. Hell, maybe all of that and more. But I think anyone who kills women – and from the press reports of those earlier crimes, they all seem to be a part of the same sort of group, teenage girls, young women, on the streets – well, I think anyone who targets that group must hate women, for whatever reason.*

A chill goes through me as I realize she was talking about herself.

I remember how easy she'd been to talk to, how I'd gone to her for advice, how I'd confided in her; that psychology degree might have been fake, but she knew how to talk to people. It is no surprise that she was able to get her victims to go with her; they would all have trusted her, would have gone anywhere she asked.

I guess that – during their talks at the shelter – she was probably able to find out all about them too, including which ones would be missed, and which ones wouldn't be.

She was in a position to select the perfect victims, the poor unfortunates who wouldn't have anyone to ask after them, young women on who she could release her incredible anger, an anger hidden from the world, hidden from everyone except those poor girls.

And, I remind myself, her own children.

"And the kids?" I ask, almost not wanting to hear the answer.

"Forced to do it at first," Ben says with disgust, "at least that's what Adam is saying, and the ABI psychologists are tending to agree with him. First, she just rode with them in the car, used them as decoys, to lure the girls inside. Then they graduated to helping with the abuse – first burning the girls with cigarettes, then using a knife to cut them, basically everything went from there. She gave them beer, vodka, whatever – plenty of alcohol to help numb them, to make them more able to turn themselves off to what they were doing. The older boy was involved sexually from the age of twelve, Adam was invited to 'try' it just a few months ago, not long after he turned eleven. Soon as he was able, really; by that stage, he was so enmeshed in that life, he says he *wanted* to do it. Is it his fault he felt that way?" Ben shrugs, even the thought of it an enormous burden on the soul. "Who knows?"

"But why involve them at all?" I say, still not really able to comprehend what has happened, even though I know the horror of what they have done better than anyone else alive.

"Anger," Ben says, "hate, yet again. Seems to have seen them as an unpleasant reminder of her husband, of everything that's wrong with men, decided to punish them. The doctors examined them; no signs of abuse themselves, but they've both had various STDs already; their mother wouldn't let them use protection when they raped those girls. Adam has herpes and pubic lice,

Richard had gonorrhea, herpes and lice. According to Adam, his mother said that it served them right; she treated them with medications she stole from the shelter, but obviously wouldn't let them be checked out by a proper doctor. Said that this is why those girls needed to be killed – 'punished and destroyed', she called it – because they were spreading disease, and she used her own children as proof that she was doing the right thing. Sick, right?"

"You're not wrong," I say, still not quite able to come to terms with it. At the mention of sexually transmitted diseases, I had felt horrible, a new fear to be confronted, and decided that I would get checked out as soon as possible, before I realized that my attack had never happened, not in this world, at least, not in *this* reality.

"Explains why there was no evidence of rape on the early victims at least," Ben says. "The boys were just too damned young to do it. So Williams did what she could, with whatever she could find."

I think about the stick found near one of the early bodies, the crucifix, and close my eyes.

So, it wasn't Menders at all; it wasn't Paul either, or the Latimer twins, or either of the Jenkins brothers.

I feel bad about some of the thoughts I've had about those people, but I guess that some of those thoughts weren't without reason; Paul has proven himself to be an aggressive date-rapist, and Pat Jenkins is still a very suspect personality, in my opinion. Douglas Menders, too, is clearly an extremely unpleasant man;

but can you arrest a man just for watching?

Ben's cell rings then, and he answers, has a brief conversation and hangs up, turning back to me.

"The crew just found another body," he says, face white. "Brings the total up to eight, not including bodies from the older cases."

He sits down next to me, head in his hands. "Hell, this one is going to be horrible," he says. "All those missing women, all those cold cases, we're going to have to identify them, trace them, let their families know . . ."

Along with the physical evidence from the house, the information in Adam's mind is the key to finding out where it all ends, but even his full confessions – even if entirely truthful – might not reveal everything about the killing career of Darlene Williams and her two young boys.

But maybe, I reflect, it is better if we don't know everything; perhaps the entire truth would simply be too horrific to contemplate.

There is a knock on the door, and a nurse puts her head through into the room.

"Oh, excuse me," she says to Ben, before turning to me. "Your father's waiting outside to see you. Can I send him in?"

I think about it, but not for too long; things have changed, after all. "Yes," I say, "of course you can. It'll be nice to see him."

The things I've been through, the horrors I've seen, the unspeakable things that have happened to me – physical scars or not, I know I will have a hard time forgetting them, I will have a hard time moving on with my life.

But if I can rebuild some parts of that life – maybe with my father, maybe elsewhere, too – then perhaps I can still salvage something from this, after all.

"I'll go," Ben says, standing from my bedside. "I hope you feel better real soon."

Ben turns to leave, and I suddenly think that maybe I shouldn't be thinking about just overcoming the wounds of my past; maybe I should be thinking about building a new future, too.

"Hey, Ben," I say. "When I get out, do you fancy getting a cup of coffee with me sometime?"

Ben smiles, and for the first time today, I feel something that approaches happiness. "Sure," he says. "I'd like that."

And then he is gone, like a ghost that never existed; and while I wait for my father to arrive, I look out of the hospital window, fully awake at last.

There is no moon out there, none at all.

Only the sun remains.

ABOUT THE AUTHOR

J.T. Brannan is the author of the Amazon bestselling political thriller series featuring Mark Cole, as well as the high-concept thrillers ORIGIN (translated into eight languages in over thirty territories) and EXTINCTION (his latest all-action novel from Headline Publishing).

THE THOUSAND DOLLAR MAN – the first novel to feature his new hero, Colt Ryder – was nominated for the 2016 Killer Nashville Silver Falchion Award.

Currently serving in the British Army Reserves, J.T. Brannan is a former national Karate champion and bouncer.

He now writes full-time, and teaches martial arts in Harrogate, in the North of England, where he lives with his wife and two young children.

He is currently working on his next novel.

You can find him at www.jtbrannan.com and www.jtbrannanbooks.blogspot.com, on Twitter @JTBrannan_, and on Facebook at jtbrannanbooks.

Also By The Author

The Colt Ryder series:
THE THOUSAND DOLLAR MAN
THE THOUSAND DOLLAR HUNT
THE THOUSAND DOLLAR ESCAPE
THE THOUSAND DOLLAR CONTRACT
THE THOUSAND DOLLAR BREAKOUT

The Mark Cole series:
STOP AT NOTHING
WHATEVER THE COST
BEYOND ALL LIMITS
NEVER SAY DIE
PLEDGE OF HONOR
THE LONE PATRIOT
SEVEN DAY HERO

Other Novels:
ORIGIN
EXTINCTION
TIME QUEST

Short Story:
DESTRUCTIVE THOUGHTS

Printed in Great Britain
by Amazon